MADDADDAM

BY THE SAME AUTHOR

FICTION

The Edible Woman (1969)

Surfacing (1972)

Lady Oracle (1976)

Dancing Girls (1977)

Life Before Man (1979)

Bodily Harm (1981)

Murder in the Dark (1983)

Bluebeard's Egg (1983)

The Handmaid's Tale (1985)

Cat's Eye (1988)

Wilderness Tips (1991)

Good Bones (1992)

The Robber Bride (1993)

Bones & Murder (1995)

Alias Grace (1996)

The Blind Assassin (2000)

Oryx and Crake (2003)

The Penelopiad (2005)

The Tent (2006)

Moral Disorder (2006)

The Year of the Flood (2009)

MaddAddam (2013)

Stone Mattress (2014)

FOR CHILDREN

Up in the Tree (1978)

Anna's Pet [with Joyce Barkhouse] (1980)

For the Birds (1990)

Princess Prunella and the Purple Peanut (1995)

Rude Ramsay and the Roaring Radishes (2003)

Bashful Bob and Doleful Dorinda (2004)

NON-FICTION

Survival: A Thematic Guide to Canadian Literature (1972)

Days of the Rebels 1815–1840 (1977)

Second Words (1982)

Strange Things: The Malevolent North in Canadian Literature (1996)

Two Solicitudes: Conversations [with Victor-Lévy Beaulieu] (1998)

Negotiating with the Dead: A Writer on Writing (2002)

Curious Pursuits: Occasional Writing (2005)

In Other Worlds: SF and the Human Imagination (2011)

POETRY

Double Persephone (1961)

The Circle Game (1966)

The Animals in That Country (1968)

The Journals of Susanna Moodie (1970)

Procedures for Underground (1970)

Power Politics (1971)

You Are Happy (1974)

Selected Poems (1976)

Two-Headed Poems (1978)

True Stories (1981)

Interlunar (1984)

Selected Poems II: Poems Selected and New 1976–1986 (1986)

Morning in the Burned House (1995)

Eating Fire: Selected Poetry 1965–1995 (1986)

The Door (2007)

Margaret Atwood is the author of more than forty works, including fiction, poetry and critical essays, and her books have been published in over thirty-five countries. Of her novels, *The Blind Assassin* won the 2000 Booker Prize and *Alias Grace* won the Giller Prize in Canada and the Premio Mondello in Italy. In 2005 she was the recipient of the Edinburgh Book Festival Enlightenment Award, for a distinguished contribution to world literature and thought. In 2008, Margaret Atwood was awarded the Prince of Asturias Prize for Literature in Spain. She lives in Toronto.

For more information, visit www.margaretatwood.ca

'Moving, but also very funny ... *MaddAddam* is an extraordinary achievement' *Independent on Sunday*

'A fierce, learned intelligence ... *MaddAddam* is a wild ride ... great fun' *Guardian*

'Atwood has brought the previous two books together in a fitting and joyous conclusion ... Atwood's prose miraculously balances humor, outrage and beauty ... This finale to Atwood's ingenious trilogy lights a fire from the fears of our age, then douses it with hope for the planet's survival' *New York Times*

'There are few writers able to create a world so fiercely engaging, so funny, so teeming – ironically – with life. *MaddAddam* is ultimately a paean to the enduring powers of myth and story, and like the sharpest futuristic visions, it's really about the here and now' *Daily Mail*

000000728916

'This final volume deploys its author's trademark cool, omniscient satire, but adds to that a real sense of engagement with a fallen world. Atwood has created something reminiscent of Shakespeare's late comedies; her wit and dark humour combine with a compassionate tenderness towards struggling human beings ... Since almost everything in the world has been broken or has broken down, the novel's form, whirling as brilliantly as the bits of glass in a kaleidoscope, or the pixels in a complex computer game, seems simply to replicate that chaos. However, behind the apparent disorder Atwood the conjuror remains in firm control, juggling her narrative techniques with postmodern glee' *Independent*

'A haunting, restless triumph ... A writer of virtuoso diversity, with an imagination that responds as keenly to scientific concerns as it does to the literary heritage in which she is steeped ... A dystopia over which Atwood sets swirling a glitterball of different kinds of fiction' *Sunday Times*

'It may have been a decade in the making, but it has been well worth the wait ... Margaret Atwood not only completes one of the most harrowing visions of a near-future dystopia in recent fiction, but lures us even further into new zones of existential terror' *The Times*

MADDADDAM
MARGARET
ATWOOD

virago

VIRAGO

First published in paperback in 2014 by Virago Press
First published in Great Britain in 2013 by Bloomsbury

ISBN 978-1-84408-787-7

Typeset in Bembo by M Rules
Printed and bound in Great Britain by
Clays Ltd, St Ives plc

Virago Press
An imprint of
Little, Brown Book Group
100 Victoria Embankment
London EC4Y 0DY

An Hachette UK Company
www.hachette.co.uk

www.virago.co.uk

For my family
and for Larry Gaynor (1939–2010)

Contents

The MaddAddam Trilogy:
The Story So Far

The first two books in the MaddAddam trilogy are *Oryx* and *Crake* and *The Year of the Flood*. *MaddAddam* is the third book.

1. Oryx and Crake

As the story begins, Snowman is living in a tree by the seashore. He believes he is the last true human being left alive after a lethal pandemic has swept the planet. Nearby live the Children of Crake, a gentle humanoid species bioengineered by the brilliant Crake, Snowman's one-time best friend and rival for his beloved, the beautiful and enigmatic Oryx.

The Crakers are free from sexual jealousy, greed, clothing, and the need for insect repellent and animal protein – all the factors Crake believed had caused not only the misery of the human race but also the degradation of the planet. The Crakers mate seasonally, when parts of them turn blue. Crake tried to rid them of symbolic thinking and music, but they have an eerie singing style all their own and have developed a religion, with Crake as their creator, Oryx as mistress of the animals, and

Snowman as their reluctant prophet. It is he who has led them out of the high-tech Paradice dome where they were made to their present home beside the ocean.

In his pre-plague life, Snowman was Jimmy. His world was divided into the Compounds – fortified Corporations containing the technocrat elite that controlled society through their collective security arm, the CorpSeCorps – and the pleeblands outside Compound walls, where the rest of society lived, shopped, and scammed, in their slums, their suburbs, and their malls.

Jimmy's early childhood was spent at OrganInc Farms, where his father was working on the pigoons – transgenic pigs with human material designed for transplants, including kidneys and brain tissue. Later, his father was transferred to HelthWyzer, a health-and-wellness Corp. It was at the HelthWyzer high school that adolescent Jimmy first met Crake, then known as Glenn. They bonded over internet porn and complex online games. Among these was Extinctathon, run by the cryptic identity MaddAddam: *Adam named the living animals, MaddAddam names the dead ones.* They learned to access MaddAddam via a chatroom accessible only to trusted Grandmasters of the game.

Crake and Jimmy lost touch when Crake was accepted at the well-funded Watson-Crick Institute, while word-guy Jimmy had to make do with the run-down Martha Graham liberal arts academy. Oddly, both Crake's mother and stepfather died of a mysterious illness that caused them to dissolve. Then a bioterrorist group with the codename MaddAddam began using genetically engineered animals and microbes to attack the CorpSeCorps and the ruling infrastructure.

When Jimmy and Crake reconnected years later, Crake was in charge of the Paradice dome, where he was gene-splicing the Crakers. At the same time, he was developing the BlyssPluss pill, which promised sexual ecstasy, birth control, and prolonged youth. Jimmy was surprised to discover that the names of the scientists at Paradice were identical to the user names in the Extinctathon game. In fact, they were the MaddAddamite bioterrorists, traced by Crake via the chatroom, then promised immunity in exchange for their input at Paradice. But the BlyssPluss pill contained a hidden ingredient, and its launch coincided with the onset of the pandemic that erased humanity. In the chaos that resulted, Oryx and Crake both perished, leaving Jimmy alone with the Crakers.

Now, haunted by his memories of dead Oryx and of treacherous Crake, and despairing of his own prospects for survival, an ailing and guilt-ridden Snowman hikes to the Paradice dome in search of the weapons and supplies he knows are there. En route, he's stalked by escaped gen-mod animals, among them the vicious wolvogs and the giant pigoons, made crafty by their human brain tissue.

Oryx and Crake ends with Snowman's discovery of three others who have survived the plague. Should he join them, abandoning the Crakers? Or, knowing the destructive tendencies of his own species, should he kill them? *Oryx and Crake* ends while Snowman is deciding.

2. The Year of the Flood

The Year of the Flood takes place during the same years as *Oryx and Crake,* but is set in the pleeblands outside Compound walls. The story follows the God's Gardeners, a green religion founded by Adam One. Its leaders, the Adams and the Eves, teach the convergence of Nature and Scripture, the love of all creatures, the dangers of technology, the wickedness of the Corps, the avoidance of violence, and the tending of vegetables and bees on pleebland slum rooftops.

The story begins in the present, in Gardener Year Twenty-five – the year of the Waterless Flood, as the Gardeners call the plague. Toby, armed with an archaic rifle, is holed up in the AnooYoo Spa, watching for other survivors – especially Zeb, the streetwise ex-Gardener whom she secretly loves. Violating Gardener codes, she shoots one of the pigoons that have been attacking her kitchen garden. One day she sees a procession of naked people in the distance, headed by a ragged, bearded man. Knowing nothing about Snowman and the Crakers, she believes she is hallucinating.

Meanwhile, young Ren is locked inside the quarantine room of Scales and Tails, the strip club where she's been working. Just before the plague, the club was wrecked by Painballers – dehumanized prisoners of the Corps who have ruthlessly eliminated the other combatants in the Painball arena. Ren knows she will starve to death unless her childhood friend, Amanda, can arrive to unlock the door.

Long before, Toby had been rescued from the abusive Painballer, Blanco, her boss at the unpleasant SecretBurgers stand, by the God's Gardeners. She became an Eve, specializing in mushrooms, bees, and potions. Her teacher, old Pilar – who, like many Gardeners, is a bioscience refugee from the Corps – is secretly still in touch with informants there, including the adolescent Crake.

Ren was one of Toby's Gardener pupils, along with Amanda, a tough but charismatic pleebrat. Ren's mother, Lucerne, had run away from the HelthWyzer Compound with Zeb, but angered by his failure to commit, she fled the Gardeners and returned to HelthWyzer when Ren was thirteen. Teenaged Jimmy seduced Ren but then discarded her. Eventually she chose to earn her living by dancing at Scales and Tails, the best option available to her.

Disagreeing about tactics, Zeb and his supporters split from

Adam One's pacifist Gardeners to engage in active bioterrorist opposition to the Corps, using the MaddAddam chatroom as a rendezvous. The remaining Gardeners, forced into hiding by the CorpSeCorps, continued to prepare for the Waterless Flood.

In the present – Year Twenty-five – Amanda reaches Scales and manages to free Ren. As they celebrate, three of their Gardener friends – Shackleton, Crozier, and Oates – arrive, pursued by Blanco and two other Painballers. The five young people flee, but along the way Ren and Amanda are raped, Amanda is kidnapped, and Oates is murdered.

Ren struggles to the AnooYoo Spa, where Toby nurses her back to health. Then they set out to recover Amanda. After dodging feral pigoons and dealing with vicious Blanco, they find a group of survivors living in a parkette cobb house. Zeb is there, with his group of MaddAddamites; so are a few former Gardeners. They all believe that Adam One must have survived, and are searching for him.

Toby and Ren leave on a risky mission to recover Amanda from her Painballer captors. At the seashore they stumble upon an encampment of strange, partly blue people who have seen two human men and a woman. Guessing these must be Amanda and her Painball kidnappers, Toby and Ren discover them just as Snowman – infected and hallucinating – is about to shoot them with his Paradice spraygun.

The Year of the Flood ends with the Painballers tied to a tree while Ren tends to the battered Amanda and the feverish Snowman. As Toby observes the Gardener forgiveness feast of Saint Julian by serving soup to everyone, the blue-hued Children of Crake approach along the shore, singing their eerie music.

MADDADDAM

Egg

The Story of the Egg, and of Oryx and Crake, and how they made People and Animals, and of the Chaos, and of Snowman-the-Jimmy, and of the Smelly Bone and the coming of the Two Bad Men

In the beginning, you lived inside the Egg. That is where Crake made you.

Yes, good, kind Crake. Please stop singing or I can't go on with the story.

The Egg was big and round and white, like half a bubble, and there were trees inside it with leaves and grass and berries. All the things you like to eat.

Yes, it rained inside the Egg.

No, there was not any thunder.

Because Crake did not want any thunder inside the Egg.

And all around the Egg was the chaos, with many, many people who were not like you.

Because they had an extra skin. That skin is called *clothes.* Yes, like mine.

And many of them were bad people who did cruel and hurtful things to one another, and also to the animals. Such as ... We don't need to talk about those things right now.

And Oryx was very sad about that, because the animals were her Children. And Crake was sad because Oryx was sad.

And the chaos was everywhere outside the Egg. But inside the Egg there was no chaos. It was peaceful there.

And Oryx came every day to teach you. She taught you what to eat, she taught you to make fire, she taught you about the animals, her Children. She taught you to purr if a person is hurt. And Crake watched over you.

Yes, good, kind Crake. Please stop singing. You don't have to sing every time. I'm sure Crake likes it, but he also likes this story and he wants to hear the rest.

Then one day Crake got rid of the chaos and the hurtful people, to make Oryx happy, and to clear a safe place for you to live in.

Yes, that did make things smell very bad for a while.

And then Crake went to his own place, up in the sky, and Oryx went with him.

I don't know why they went. It must have been a good reason. And they left Snowman-the-Jimmy to take care of you, and he brought you to the seashore. And on Fish Days you caught a fish for him, and he ate it.

I know you would never eat a fish, but Snowman-the-Jimmy is different.

Because he has to eat a fish or he would get very sick.

Because that is the way he is made.

Then one day Snowman-the-Jimmy went to see Crake. And

when he came back, there was a hurt on his foot. And you purred on it, but it did not get better.

And then the two bad men came. They were left over from the chaos.

I don't know why Crake didn't clear them away. Maybe they were hiding under a bush, so he didn't see them. But they'd caught Amanda, and they were doing cruel and hurtful things to her.

We don't need to talk about those things right now.

And Snowman-the-Jimmy tried to stop them. And then I came, and Ren, and we caught the two bad men and tied them to a tree with a rope. Then we sat around the fire and ate soup. Snowman-the-Jimmy ate the soup, and Ren, and Amanda. Even the two bad men ate the soup.

Yes, there was a bone in the soup. Yes, it was a smelly bone.

I know you do not eat a smelly bone. But many of the Children of Oryx like to eat such bones. Bobkittens eat them, and rakunks, and pigoons, and liobams. They all eat smelly bones. And bears eat them.

I will tell you what a bear is later.

We don't need to talk any more about smelly bones right now.

And as they were all eating the soup, you came with your torches, because you wanted to help Snowman-the-Jimmy, because of his hurt foot. And because you could tell there were some women who were blue, so you wanted to mate with them.

You didn't understand about the bad men, and about why they had a rope on them. It is not your fault they ran away into the forest. Don't cry.

Yes, Crake must be very angry with the bad men. Perhaps he will send some thunder.

Yes, good, kind Crake.

Please stop singing.

Rope

Rope

About the events of that evening – the events that set human malice loose in the world again – Toby later made two stories. The first story was the one she told out loud, to the Children of Crake; it had a happy outcome, or as happy as she could manage. The second, for herself alone, was not so cheerful. It was partly about her own idiocy, her failure to pay attention, but also it was about speed. Everything had happened so quickly.

She'd been tired, of course; she must have been suffering from an adrenalin plunge. After all, she'd been going strong for two days with a lot of stress and not much to eat.

The day before, she and Ren had left the safety of the MaddAddam cobb-house enclave that sheltered the few survivors from the global pandemic that had wiped out humanity. They'd been tracking Ren's best friend, Amanda, and they'd found her just in time because the two Painballers who'd been using her had almost used her up. Toby was familiar with the ways of such men: she'd been almost killed by one of them before she'd become a God's Gardener. Anyone who'd survived Painball more than once had been reduced to the reptilian brain. Sex until you were worn to a fingernail was their mode; after that, you were dinner. They liked the kidneys.

Toby and Ren had crouched in the shrubbery while the Painballers argued over the rakunk they were eating, and whether to attack the Crakers, and what to do next with Amanda. Ren had been scared silly; Toby hoped she wouldn't faint, but she couldn't worry about that because she was nerving herself to fire. Which to shoot first, the bearded one or the shorthair? Would the other have time to grab their spraygun? Amanda wouldn't be able to help, or even run: they had a rope around her neck, with the other end tied to the leg of the bearded one. A wrong move by Toby, and Amanda would be dead.

Then a strange man had shambled out of the bushes, sunburnt and scabby and naked and clutching a spraygun, and had almost shot everyone in sight, Amanda included. But Ren had screamed and run into the clearing, and that had been enough of a distraction. Toby had stepped out, rifle aimed; Amanda had torn free; and the Painballers had been subdued with the aid of some groin kicks and a rock, and tied up with their own rope and with strips torn from the pink AnooYoo Spa top-to-toe sun coverup that Toby had been wearing.

Ren had then busied herself with Amanda, who was possibly in shock, and also with the scabby naked man, whom she called Jimmy. She'd wrapped him up in the rest of the top-to-toe, talking to him softly; it seemed he was a long-ago boyfriend of hers.

Now that things were tidier, Toby had felt she could relax. She'd steadied herself with a Gardener breathing exercise, timing it to the soothing rhythm of the nearby waves – *wish-wash*, *wish-wash* – until her heart had slowed to normal. Then she'd cooked a soup.

And then the moon had risen.

*

The rising moon signalled the beginning of the God's Gardeners Feast of Saint Julian and All Souls: a celebration of God's tenderness and compassion for all creatures. *The universe is held in the hollow of His hand, as Saint Julian of Norwich taught us in her mystic vision so long ago. Forgiveness must be offered, loving kindness must be practised, circles must be unbroken. All souls means all, no matter what they may have done. At least from moonrise to moonset.*

Once the Gardener Adams and Eves taught you something, you stayed taught. It would have been next to impossible for her to kill the Painballers on that particular night – butcher them in cold blood, since by that time the two of them were firmly roped to a tree.

Amanda and Ren had done the roping. They'd been to Gardener school together where they'd done a lot of crafts with recycled materials, so they were proficient at knotwork. Those guys looked like macramé.

On that blessed Saint Julian's evening, Toby had set the weaponry to one side – her own antiquated rifle and the Painballers' spraygun, and Jimmy's spraygun as well. Then she'd played the kindly godmother, ladling out the soup, dividing up the nutrients for all to share.

She must have been mesmerized by the spectacle of her own nobility and kindness. Getting everyone to sit in a circle around the cozy evening fire and drink soup together – even Amanda, who was so traumatized she was almost catatonic; even Jimmy, who was shivering with fever and talking to a dead woman who was standing in the flames. Even the two Painballers: did she really think they would have a conversion experience and start hugging bunnies? It's a wonder she didn't sermonize as she doled out the bone soup. *Some for you, and some for you, and some for you! Shed the hatred and viciousness! Come into the circle of light!*

But hatred and viciousness are addictive. You can get high on them. Once you've had a little, you start shaking if you don't get more.

As they were eating the soup, they'd heard voices approaching through the shoreline trees. It was the Children of Crake, the Crakers – the strange gene-spliced quasi-humans who lived by the sea. They were filing through the trees, carrying pitch-pine torches and singing their crystalline songs.

Toby had seen these people only briefly, and in daytime. Gleaming in the moonlight and the torchlight, they were even more beautiful. They were all colours – brown, yellow, black, white – and all heights, but each was perfect. The women were smiling serenely; the men were in full courtship mode, holding out bunches of flowers, their naked bodies like a fourteen-year-old's comic-book rendition of how bodies ought to be, each muscle and ripple defined and glistening. Their bright blue and unnaturally large penises were wagging from side to side like the tails of friendly dogs.

Afterwards, Toby could never quite remember the sequence of events, if you could call it a sequence. It had been more like a pleebland street brawl: rapid action, tangled bodies, a cacophony of voices.

Where is the blue? We can smell the blue! Look, there is Snowman! He is thin! He is very sick!

Ren: *Oh shit, it's the Crakers. What if they want . . . Look at their . . . Crap!*

The Craker women, spotting Jimmy: *Let us help Snowman! He needs us to purr!*

The Craker men, sniffing Amanda: *She is the blue one! She*

smells blue! She wants to mate with us! Give her the flowers! She will be happy!

Amanda, scared: *Stay away! I don't . . . Ren, help me!* Four large, beautiful, flower-toting naked men close in on her. *Toby! Get them away from me! Shoot them!*

The Craker women: *She is sick. First we have to purr on her. To make her better. And give her a fish?*

The Craker men: *She is blue! She is blue! We are happy! Sing to her!*

The other one is blue also.

That fish is for Snowman. We must keep that fish.

Ren: *Amanda, maybe just take the flowers, or they might get mad or something . . .*

Toby, her voice thin and ineffectual: *Please, listen, stand back, you're frightening . . .*

What is this? Is this a bone? Several of the women, peering into the soup pot: *Are you eating this bone? It smells bad.*

We do not eat bones. Snowman does not eat bones, he eats a fish. Why do you eat a smelly bone?

It is Snowman's foot that is smelling like a bone. A bone left by vultures. Oh Snowman, we must purr on your foot!

Jimmy, feverish: *Who are you? Oryx? But you're dead. Everyone's dead. Everyone in the whole world, they're all dead . . .* He starts crying.

Do not be sad, Oh Snowman. We have come to help.

Toby: *Maybe you shouldn't touch . . . that's infected . . . he needs . . .*
Jimmy: *Ow! Fuck!*

Oh Snowman, do not kick. It will hurt your foot. Several of them begin to purr, making a noise like a kitchen mixer.

Ren, calling for help: *Toby! Toby! Hey! Let go of her!*

Toby looks over, across the fire: Amanda has disappeared in a flickering thicket of naked male limbs and backs. Ren throws herself into the sprawl and is quickly submerged.

Toby: *Wait! Don't . . . Stop that!* What should she do? This is a major cultural misunderstanding. If only she had a pail of cold water!

Muffled cries. Toby rushes to help, but then:

One of the Painballers: *Hey you! Over here!*

These ones smell very bad. They smell like dirty blood. Where is the blood?

What is this? This is a rope. Why are they tied up with a rope?

Snowman showed us rope *before, when he lived in a tree.* Rope *is for making his house. Oh Snowman, why is the rope tied to these men?*

This rope is hurting these ones. We must take it away.

A Painballer: *Yeah, that's right. We're in fucking agony.* (Groans.)

Toby: *Don't touch them, they'll . . .*

The second Painballer: *Fucking hurry up, Blueballs, before that old bitch . . .*

Toby: *No! Don't untie . . . Those men will . . .*

But it was already too late. Who knew the Crakers could be so quick with knots?

Procession

The two men were gone into the darkness, leaving behind them a snarl of rope and a scattering of embers. Idiot, Toby thought. You should have been merciless. Bashed their heads in with a rock, slit their throats with your knife, not even wasted any bullets on them. You were a dimwit, and your failure to act verges on criminal negligence.

It was hard to see – the fire was fading – but she made a quick inventory: at least her rifle was still there, a small mercy. But the Painballer spraygun was missing. Pinhead, she told herself. So much for your Saint Julian and the loving kindness of the universe.

Amanda and Ren were clinging to each other and crying, with several of the beautiful Craker women stroking them anxiously. Jimmy had toppled over and was talking to a bed of coals. The sooner they could all get back to the MaddAddam cobb house, the better, because they were sitting ducks out here in the dark. The Painballers might come back for the remaining weapons, and if that happened it was already clear to Toby that these Crakers would be no help. *Why did you hit me? Crake will be angry! He will send a thunder!* If she downed a Painballer, the Crakers would throw themselves between her and the finishing shot. *Oh, you have made bang, a man fell down, there is a hole in him, blood is coming out! He is hurt, we must help him!*

But even if the Painballers held off for the moment, there were other predators in the forest. The bobkittens, the wolvogs, the liobams; worse, the enormous feral pigs. And now, with the people gone from the cities and roads, who knew how soon the bears would begin to come down from the north?

'We need to go now,' she told the Crakers. Several heads turned, several sets of green eyes were looking at her. 'Snowman must come with us.'

The Crakers all started talking at once. 'Snowman must stay with us! We must put Snowman back into his tree.' 'That is what he likes, he likes a tree.' 'Yes, only he can talk with Crake.' 'Only he can tell the words of Crake, about the Egg.' 'About the chaos.' 'About Oryx, who made the animals.' 'About how Crake made the chaos go away.' 'Good, kind Crake.' They began singing.

'We need to get medicine,' said Toby desperately. 'Otherwise, Jimmy – otherwise, Snowman might die.' Blank stares. Did they even understand what dying was?

'What is a *Jimmy*?' Puzzled frowns.

She'd made an error: wrong name. 'Jimmy is another name for Snowman.'

'Why?' 'Why is it another name?' 'What does a *Jimmy* mean?' This seemed to interest them much more than death. 'Is it the pink skin on Snowman?' 'I want a Jimmy too!' This last from a small boy.

How to explain? 'Jimmy is a name. Snowman has two names.'

'His name is Snowman-the-Jimmy?'

'Yes,' said Toby, because it was now.

'Snowman-the-Jimmy, Snowman-the-Jimmy,' they repeated to one another.

'Why are there two?' one asked, but the others had switched their attention to the next bewildering word. 'What is *medicine*?'

'Medicine is something to help Snowman-the-Jimmy get better,' she ventured. Smiles: they liked that idea.

'Then we will come too,' said the one who seemed in charge – a tall, brownish-yellow man with a Roman nose. 'We will carry Snowman-the-Jimmy.'

Two of the Craker men lifted Jimmy easily. Toby was alarmed by his eyes: by the thin slits of white shining between his lids. 'Flying,' he said as the Crakers swung him into the air.

Toby found Jimmy's spraygun and gave it to Ren to carry, clicking the safety on first: the girl didn't know how to use the thing – why would she? – but it would be sure to come in handy later on.

She'd assumed that only the two Craker volunteers would come back to the cobb house, but the whole crowd tagged along, children included. They all wished to be close to Snowman. The men took turns carrying him; the rest held their torches high, singing from time to time in their eerie waterglass voices.

Four of the women walked with Ren and Amanda, patting them and touching their arms or hands. 'Oryx will take care of you,' they said to Amanda.

'Don't let any of those blue dicks fucking touch her again,' said Ren to them fiercely.

'What is *blue dicks*?' they asked, bewildered. 'What is *fucking touch*?'

'Just don't, or else,' said Ren. 'Or it's trouble!'

'Oryx will make her happy,' said the women, though they sounded unsure. 'What is *trouble*?'

'I'm okay,' said Amanda faintly to Ren. 'What about you?'

'You are not fucking okay! Let's just get you back to where the MaddAddams are,' said Ren. 'They've got beds, and a water pump, and everything. We can clean you up. Jimmy too.'

'Jimmy?' said Amanda. 'That's Jimmy? I thought he'd be dead, like everyone else.'

'Yeah, so did I. But a lot of people aren't. Well, some people. Zeb's not, and Rebecca, and you and me, and Toby, and . . . '

'Where did those two guys go?' said Amanda. 'The Painballers. I should've brained them when I had the chance.' She laughed a little, blowing off pain in her old pleebrat way. 'How far is it?' she said.

'They can carry you,' said Ren.

'No. I'm fine.'

Moths fluttered around the torches, overhead leaves riffled in the night breeze. How long did they walk? To Toby it seemed like hours, but time is unclear in moonlight. They were heading west, through the Heritage Park; behind them the sound of the waves receded. Though there was a path, she was unsure of the way, but the Crakers appeared to know where they were going.

She listened for sounds, off among the trees – a footfall, a stick cracking, a grunt – keeping herself to the rear of the procession, her rifle at the ready. There was a croaking, a chirp or two: some amphibian, a night bird stirring. She was conscious of the darkness at her back: her shadow stretched huge, blending with the deeper shadows behind.

Poppy

Finally they reached the cobb-house enclave. A single light bulb was burning in the yard; behind the barrier fence, Crozier and Manatee and Tamaraw were standing sentry with their spray-guns, wearing battery-run headlamps gleaned from a bike shop.

Ren ran forward. 'It's us!' she called. 'It's okay! We found Amanda!'

Crozier's headlamp bobbed as he opened the gate. 'Way to go!' he shouted.

'Great! I'll tell the others!' said Tamaraw. She hurried off to the main building.

'Croze! We did it!' Ren said. She threw her arms around him, dropping the spraygun she'd been carrying, and he lifted her, twirled her around, and kissed her. Then he set her down.

'Hey, where'd you get the spraygun?' he said. Ren started crying.

'I thought they'd kill us!' she said. 'Them, the two ... But you should've seen Toby! She was so badass! She had her old gun, and then we hit them with rocks, and then we tied them up, but then ...'

'Wow,' said Manatee, surveying the Crakers who were

crowding in through the gate, talking among themselves. 'It's the Paradice dome circus.'

'So these are them, right?' said Crozier. 'The creepo naked people Crake made? The ones who live down by the shore?'

'I don't think you should call them creepo,' said Ren. 'They can hear you.'

'It wasn't only Crake,' said Manatee. 'All of us worked on them at the Paradice Project. Me, Swift Fox, Ivory Bill . . . '

'Why'd they come with you?' said Crozier. 'What do they want?'

'They're only trying to help,' said Toby. Suddenly she was very tired; all she wanted to do was stumble into her cubicle and conk out. 'Has anyone else been here?' Zeb had left the cobb house at the same time she did, on a search for Adam One and any of the God's Gardeners who might have survived. She wanted to know if he'd returned, but she didn't want to be obvious about it: pining was whining, as the Gardeners used to say, and she'd never worn her heart anywhere near her sleeve.

'Only those pigs again,' said Crozier. 'Trying to dig under the garden fence. We shone the lights on them and they ran off. They know what a spraygun is.'

'Ever since we turned a couple of them into bacon,' said Manatee. 'Frankenbacon, considering they're splices. I still feel kind of weird about eating them. They've got human neocortex tissue.'

'I hope Crake's Frankenpeople aren't moving in with us,' said a blond woman who'd come out of the main cobb building with Tamaraw. Toby recognized her from the brief time she'd spent at the cobb house before her search for Amanda: Swift Fox. She must have been over thirty, but she was wearing what looked like a twelve-year-old's ruffle-edged nightie. Now where had she picked that up? Toby wondered. Some looted Hott-TottsTogs or Hundred-Dollar Store?

'You must be exhausted,' Tamaraw said to Toby.

'I don't know why you brought them with you,' said Swift Fox. 'There's too many of them. We can't feed them.'

'We won't have to,' said Manatee. 'They eat leaves, remember? That's how Crake designed them. So they'd never need agriculture.'

'Right,' said Swift Fox. 'You worked on that module. Me, I did the brains. The frontal lobes, the sensory-input modifications. I tried to make them less boring, but Crake wanted no aggression, no jokes even. They're walking potatoes.'

'They're really nice,' said Ren. 'Anyway, the women are.'

'I suppose the males wanted to mate with you; they'll do that. Just don't make me *talk* to them,' said Swift Fox. 'I'm going back to bed. Night all, have fun with the vegetables.' She yawned and stretched, then sauntered slowly away.

'Why's she so crabby?' said Manatee. 'She's been like that all day.'

'Hormones is my guess,' said Crozier. 'Check out the nightie, though.'

'Too small on her,' said Manatee.

'You noticed,' said Crozier.

'Maybe she has other reasons for being crabby,' said Ren. 'Women sometimes do, you know.'

'Sorry,' said Crozier, putting his arm around her.

Four of the Craker men detached themselves from the group and began to follow Swift Fox, blue penises waving back and forth. Somewhere they'd picked more flowers; they were starting to sing.

'No!' said Toby sharply, as if to dogs. 'Stay here! With Snowman-the-Jimmy!' How to make it clear to them that, even with the aid of floral display and serenading and penis-wagging, they couldn't just pile on to any young non-Craker woman who smelled available to them? But they'd already disappeared around the corner of the main house.

The two Craker carriers lowered Jimmy down. He slumped

limply against their knees. 'Where will Snowman-the-Jimmy be?' they asked. 'Where can we purr for him?'

'He'll need to be in a room by himself,' said Toby. 'We'll find a bed for him, and then I'll get the medicine.'

'We will come with you,' they said. 'We will purr.' They picked Jimmy up again, making a chair for him with their arms. The others crowded around.

'Not all of you,' said Toby. 'He needs to be quiet.'

'He can have Croze's room,' said Ren. 'Can't he, Croze?'

'Who's that?' said Crozier, peering at Jimmy, whose head was lolling to one side, who was drooling into his beard, who was scratching fitfully at himself with one filthy hand through the pink fabric of the top-to-toe, and who noticeably stank. 'Where'd you drag *him* in from? Why's he wearing pink? He looks like a fucking ballerina!'

'It's Jimmy,' said Ren. 'Remember, I told you? My old boy-friend?'

'The one who messed you over? From high school? That child molester?'

'Don't be like that,' said Ren. 'I wasn't really a child. He's got a fever.'

'Don't go, don't go,' said Jimmy. 'Come back to the tree!'

'You're sticking up for him? After how he dumped you?'

'Yeah, right, but he's kind of a hero now,' said Ren. 'He helped save Amanda. He almost, you know, died.'

'Amanda,' said Croze. 'I don't see her. Where is she?'

'She's over here,' said Ren, pointing to the group of Craker women surrounding Amanda, stroking her and purring gently. They moved aside to let Ren into their circle.

'That's Amanda?' said Crozier. 'No shit! She looks like . . . '

'Don't say it,' said Ren, putting her arms around Amanda. 'She'll look a lot better tomorrow. Or next week, anyway.' Amanda started to cry.

'She's gone,' said Jimmy. 'She flew away. Pigoons.'

'Cripes,' said Crozier. 'This is fucking weird.'

'Croze, *everything* is fucking weird,' said Ren.

'Okay, right, I'm sorry. I'm almost off sentry. Let's . . . '

'I think I should help Toby,' said Ren. 'At this moment.'

'Looks like I sleep on the ground, since that fuckwit's tagged my bed,' Croze said to Manatee.

'Please grow up,' said Ren.

That's all we need, thought Toby. Love's young squabbles.

They carried Jimmy into Croze's cubicle and laid him down on the bed. Toby asked two Craker women and Ren to aim the flashlights she'd got from the kitchen. Then she found her medical materials, on the shelf where she'd left them before setting off to find Amanda.

She did all she could for Jimmy: a sponge bath to get off the worst of the dirt; honey applied to the superficial cuts; mushroom elixir for the infection. Then Poppy and Willow, for the pain and for a restful sleep. And the small grey maggots, applied to the foot wound to nibble off the infected flesh. Judging from the smell, the maggots were just in time.

'What are those?' said one of the two Craker women, the tall one. 'Why do you put those little animals on Snowman-the-Jimmy? Are they eating him?'

'It tickles,' said Jimmy. His eyes were half open; the Poppy was taking effect.

'Oryx sent them,' said Toby. That seemed to be a good answer, because they smiled. 'They are called *maggots*,' she continued. 'They are eating the pain.'

'What does the pain taste like, Oh Toby?'

'Should we eat the pain too?'

'If we ate the pain, that would help Snowman-the-Jimmy.'

'The pain smells very bad. Does it taste good?'

She should avoid metaphors. 'The pain tastes good only to the maggots,' she said. 'No. You should not eat the pain.'

'Will he be okay?' Ren said. 'Has he got gangrene?'

'I hope not,' said Toby. The two Craker women placed their hands on him and began to purr.

'Falling,' said Jimmy. 'Butterfly. She's gone.'

Ren bent over him, brushed his hair back from his forehead. 'Go to sleep, Jimmy,' she said. 'We love you.'

Cobb
House

Morning

Toby dreams that she's in her little single bed, at home. Her stuffed lion is on the pillow beside her, and her big shaggy bear that plays a tune. Her antique piggy bank is on her desk, and the tablet she uses for her homework, and her felt-tip crayons, and her daisy-skinned cellphone. From the kitchen comes the sound of her mother's voice, calling; her father, answering; the smell of eggs frying.

Inside this dream, she's dreaming of animals. One is a pig, though six-legged; another is cat-like, with compound eyes like a fly. There's a bear as well, but it has hooves. These animals are neither hostile nor friendly. Now the city outside is on fire, she can smell it; fear fills the air. *Gone, gone*, says a voice, like a bell tolling. One by one the animals come towards her and begin to lick her with their warm, raspy tongues.

At the edge of sleep, she gropes towards the retreating dream: the burning city, the messengers sent to warn her. That the world has been changed utterly; that the familiar is long dead; that everything she used to love has been swept away.

As Adam One used to say, *The fate of Sodom is fast approaching. Suppress regret. Avoid the pillar of salt. Don't look back.*

*

She wakes to find a Mo'Hair licking her leg: a red-head, its long human hair braided into pigtails, each with a string bow: some sentimentalist among the MaddAddamites has been at work. It must have got out of the pen where they're keeping them.

'Move it,' she says to it, shoving it gently with her foot. It gives her a look of addled reproach – they're none too bright, the Mo'Hairs – and clatters out through the doorway. We could use some doors around here, she thinks.

The morning light is filtering in through the piece of cloth that's been hung over the window in a futile attempt to keep out the mosquitoes. If only they could find some screens! But they'd have to install window frames because the cobb house wasn't built to be lived in: it had been a parkette staging pavilion for fairs and parties, and they're squatting in it now because it's safe. It's away from the urban rubble – the deserted streets and random electrical fires and the buried rivers that are welling up now that the pumps have failed. No collapsing building can fall down on it, and as it's only one storey high, it's unlikely to fall down on itself.

She untwists herself from the damp morning sheet and stretches her arms, feeling for sprains and tightness. She's almost too tired to get up. Too tired, too discouraged, too angry with herself over last night's fireside fiasco. What will she tell Zeb when he gets back? Supposing he does get back. Zeb is resourceful, but he's not invulnerable.

She can only hope that he's been more successful with his quest than she has been with hers. There's a chance that some of the God's Gardeners have survived because if anyone would know how to wait out the pandemic that killed almost everyone else, it would be them. During all the years that she spent with them, first as their guest, then as an apprentice, and finally as a high-ranking Eve, they'd planned for catastrophe. They'd built hidden places of refuge and stocked them with supplies: honey, dried soybeans and mushrooms, rose hips, elderberry compote, preserves of various kinds. Seeds to plant in the new, cleansed world they believed would come. Perhaps they'd waited the plague out in one of these refuges – one of their sheltering Ararats, where they hoped they'd be safe while riding out what they termed the Waterless Flood. God had promised after the Noah incident that he'd never use the water method again, but considering the wickedness of the world he was bound to do something: that was their reasoning. But where will Zeb look for them, out there among the ruins of the city? Where to even begin?

Visualize your strongest desire, the Gardeners used to say, *and it will manifest;* which doesn't always work, or not as intended. Her strongest desire is to have Zeb come back safe, but if he does, she'll have to face up once again to the fact that she's neutral territory as far as he's concerned. Nothing emotional, no sexiness there, no frills. A trusted comrade and foot soldier: reliable Toby, so competent. That's about it.

And she'll have to admit her failure to him. *I was a cretin. It was Saint Julian's, I couldn't kill them. They got away. They took a spraygun.* She won't snivel, she won't cry, she won't give excuses. He won't say much, but he'll be disappointed in her.

Don't be too harsh on yourself, Adam One used to say in his patient blue-eyed way. We all make mistakes. True, she replies to him now, but some mistakes are more lethal than others. If Zeb gets killed by one of the Painballers, it will be her fault. *Stupid, stupid, stupid.* She feels like whacking her head against the cobb-house wall.

She can only hope the Painballers were spooked enough to run very far away. But will they stay away? They'll need food. They might scavenge some quasi-food in the deserted houses and shops from whatever hasn't mouldered or been eaten by rats or looted months ago. They may even blast a few animals – a rakunk, a green rabbit, a liobam – but after they use up their cellpack ammunition, they'll need more.

And they know the MaddAddam cobb house will have some. Sooner or later they'll be tempted to attack at the weakest link: they'll grab a Craker child and offer to swap, as they tried to swap Amanda earlier. It will be sprayguns and cellpacks they'll want, with a young woman or two thrown in – Ren or Lotis Blue or White Sedge or Swift Fox – not Amanda, they've already expended her. Or a Craker female in heat, why not? It would be a novelty for them, a woman with a bright blue abdomen; not the best conversationalists, those Crakers, but the Painballers won't care about that. They'll demand Toby's rifle too.

The Crakers would think it was just a matter of sharing. *They want the stick thing? It would make them happy? Why are you not giving it to them, Oh Toby?* How to explain that you can't hand over a murder weapon to a murderer? The Crakers wouldn't understand murder because they're so trusting. They'd never imagine that anyone would rape them – *What is rape?* Or slit their throats – *Oh Toby, why?* Or slash them open and eat their kidneys – *But Oryx would not allow it!*

Suppose the Crakers hadn't untied those knots. What had she intended to do? Would she have marched the Painballers back to the cobb house, then kept them penned up until Zeb got back and took over and did the necessary thing?

He'd have held some sort of perfunctory discussion. Then there would have been a double hanging. Or maybe he'd have skipped the preliminaries and just hit them with a shovel, saying, Why dirty a rope? The end result would be the same as if she'd snuffed the two of them immediately, right then and there at the campfire.

Enough of such dour stocktaking. It's morning. She has to cut out these daydreams in which Zeb performs decisive leadership acts that she ought to have performed herself. She needs to get up, go outside, join the others. Repair what can't be repaired, mend what can't be mended, shoot what needs to be shot. Hold the fort.

Breakfast

She swings her legs off the bed, sets her feet on the floor, stands. Her muscles hurt, her skin feels like sandpaper, but it's not so bad once you're up.

She chooses a bedsheet – lavender with blue dots – from the selection on her shelf. There's a pile of sheets in every cubicle, like towels in a hotel of old. Her pink top-to-toe from the AnooYoo Spa is in rags and may be infected with whatever it is Jimmy might have: she'll need to burn it. When she gets the time she'll sew a few of the sheets together, with arms and a hood, but meanwhile she drapes the lavender sheet around herself toga-style.

There's no shortage of bedsheets. The MaddAddamites have gleaned enough of them from the city's deserted buildings to last a while, and they also have a stash of pants and T-shirts for heavy work. But the sheets are cooler and one-size-fits-all, so they're the MaddAddamite attire of choice. When the bedsheets are used up they'll have to think of something else, but that won't happen for years. Decades. If they live that long.

A mirror is what she needs. Hard to know how much of a wreck she is without one. Maybe she'll be able to get mirrors onto the next gleaning list. Those, and toothbrushes.

She slings her knapsack with her health-care items over one shoulder: the maggots, the honey, the mushroom elixir, the Willow and Poppy. She'll tend to Jimmy first thing, supposing he's still alive. But only after she's had some breakfast: she can't face the day, much less Jimmy's festering foot, on an empty stomach. Then she picks up her rifle and steps out into the full glare of morning.

Although it's still early, the sun's already burning white. She hoists one end of her bedsheet over her head for protection, checks out the cobb-house yard. The red-headed Mo'Hair, still at large, is eyeing the vegetables through the kitchen-garden fence while chewing on some kudzu. Its friends in the Mo'Hair pen are bleating at it: silver Mo'Hairs, blue ones, green ones and pink ones, brunettes and blondes: the full range of colours. *Hair Today, Mo'Hair Tomorrow* went the ad when the creatures had first been launched.

Toby's present-day hair is a Mo'Hair transplant: she didn't use to be so raven-hued. Maybe that was why the Mo'Hair had come into her cubicle to lick her on the leg. It wasn't the salt, it was the faint smell of lanolin. It thought she was a relative.

Just so long as I don't get jumped by one of the rams, she thinks. She'll have to watch herself for signs of sheepishness. Rebecca must be up by now, dealing with breakfast issues over at the cooking shack; maybe she's got some floral-scented shampoo tucked away in her supply room.

Over near the garden, Ren and Lotis Blue are sitting in the shade, deep in conversation. Amanda is sitting with them, staring off into the distance. Fallow state, the Gardeners would say. They used that diagnosis for a wide range of conditions, from depression to post-traumatic stress to being permanently stoned.

The theory was that while in a Fallow state you were gathering and conserving strength, nourishing yourself through meditation, sending invisible rootlets out into the universe. Toby really hopes this is true of Amanda. She'd been such a lively child in Toby's class at the Gardener school, back there on the Edencliff Rooftop Garden. When was that? Ten, fifteen years ago? Amazing how quickly the past becomes idyllic.

Ivory Bill and Manatee and Tamaraw are fortifying the boundary fence. In daylight it looks flimsy, permeable. Onto the skeleton of the old ornamental ironwork paling they've attached an assortment of materials: lengths of wire fencing interwoven with duct tape, a mixture of poles, a row of pointed sticks with their ends set in the ground and the points facing out. Manatee is adding more sticks; Ivory Bill and Tamaraw are on the other side of the fence, with shovels. They appear to be filling in a hole.

'Morning,' says Toby.

'Take a look at this,' says Manatee. 'Something was trying to tunnel under. Last night. Sentries didn't see them, they were chasing those pigs off at the front.'

'Any tracks?' said Toby.

'We think it was maybe more of those pigs,' Tamaraw says. 'Smart – distracting attention, then trying a sneaky dig. Anyway, they didn't get in.'

Beyond the boundary fence there's a semicircle of male Crakers, evenly spaced, facing outward, peeing in unison. A man in a striped bedsheet who looks like Crozier – in fact, it is Crozier – is standing with them, joining in the group pee-in.

What next? Is Crozier going native? Will he shed his clothes, take up a cappella singing, grow a huge penis that turns blue in season? If the first two items were the price of entry for the third, he'd do it in a shot. Soon every single human male among the MaddAddamites will be yearning for one of those. And once that starts, how long before the rivalries and wars break out, with clubs and sticks and stones, and then . . .

Get a grip, Toby, she tells herself. Don't borrow trouble. You really, really, really need some coffee. Any kind of coffee. Dandelion root. Happicuppa. Black mud, if that's all there is.

And if there were any booze, she'd drink that too.

A long dining room table has been set up beside the cooking shack. There's a shade sail deployed above it, gleaned from some deserted backyard. All the patios must be derelict now, the swimming pools cracked and empty or clogged with weeds, the broken kitchen windows invaded by the probing green snoutlets of vines. Inside the houses, nests in the corners made from chewed-up carpets, wriggling and squeaking with hairless baby rats. Termites mining through the rafters. Bats hawking for moths in the stairwells.

'Once the tree roots get in,' Adam One had been fond of saying to the Gardener inner circle, 'once they really take hold, no human-built structure stands a chance. They'll tear a paved road apart in a year. They'll block the drainage culverts, and once the pumping systems fail, the foundations will be eaten away, and no force on earth will be able to stop that kind of water, and then, when the generating stations catch fire or short out, not to mention the nuclear . . . '

'Then you can kiss your morning toast goodbye,' Zeb had once added to this litany. He'd just blown in from one of his mysterious courier missions; he looked battered, and his black pleather jacket was ripped. Urban Bloodshed Limitation was one of the subjects he taught the Gardener kids, but he didn't always practise it. 'Yeah, yeah, we know, we're doomed. Any hope of some elderberry pie around here? I'm starving.' Zeb did not always show a proper reverence towards Adam One.

Speculations about what the world would be like after human control of it ended had been – long ago, briefly – a queasy form of popular entertainment. There had even been online TV shows about it: computer-generated landscape pictures with deer grazing in Times Square, serves-us-right finger-wagging, earnest experts lecturing about all the wrong turns taken by the human race.

There was only so much of that people could stand, judging from the ratings, which spiked and then plummeted as viewers voted with their thumbs, switching from imminent wipeout to real-time contests about hotdog-swallowing if they liked nostalgia, or to sassy-best-girlfriends comedies if they liked stuffed animals, or to Mixed Martial Arts Felony Fights if they liked bitten-off ears, or to Nitee-Nite live-streamed suicides or HottTotts kiddy porn or Hedsoff real-time executions if they were truly jaded. All of it so much more palatable than the truth.

'You know I've always sought the truth,' said Adam One that time, in the aggrieved tone he sometimes adopted with Zeb. He didn't use this tone with anyone else.

'Yeah, right, I do know that,' said Zeb. 'Seek and ye shall find, eventually. And you found. You're right, I don't dispute that. Sorry. Chewing with my mind full. Stuff comes out my mouth.' And that tone said, This is the way I am. You know that. Suck it up.

If only Zeb were here, thinks Toby. She has a quick flash of him disappearing under a cascade of glass shards and chunks of cement as another burnt-out high-rise crashes down, or howling as a chasm opens under his feet and he plummets into an underground torrent no longer controlled by pumps and sewers, or humming carelessly as from behind him appears an arm, a hand, a face, a rock, a knife . . .

But it's too early in the morning to think like that. Also it's no use. So she tries to stop.

Around the table is a collection of random chairs: kitchen, plastic, upholstered, swivel. On the tablecloth – a rosebud-and-bluebird motif – are plates and glasses, some already used, and cups, and cutlery. It's like a surrealist painting from the twentieth century: every object ultra-solid, crisp, hard-edged, except that none of them should be here.

But why not? thinks Toby. Why shouldn't they be here? Nothing in the material world died when the people did. Once, there were too many people and not enough stuff; now it's the other way around. But physical objects have shucked their tethers – Mine, Yours, His, Hers – and have gone wandering off on their own. It's like the aftermath of those riots they used to show in documentaries of the early twenty-first century, when kids would join phone-swarms and then break windows and mob shops and grab stuff, and what you could have was limited only by what you could carry.

And so it is now, she thinks. We have laid claim to these chairs, these cups and glasses, we've lugged them here. Now that history is over, we're living in luxury, as far as goods and chattels go.

The plates look antique, or at least expensive. But now she could break the whole set and it wouldn't cause a ripple anywhere but in her own mind.

Rebecca emerges from the kitchen cooking shack with a platter.

'Sweetheart!' she says. 'You made it back! And they told me you found Amanda too! Five stars!'

'She's not in the best shape,' says Toby. 'Those two Painballers almost killed her, and then, last night . . . I'd say she's in shock. Fallow state.' Rebecca's old Gardener, so she'll understand *Fallow.*

'She's tough,' says Rebecca. 'She'll mend.'

'Maybe,' says Toby. 'Let's hope she's disease-free, and no internal injuries. I guess you heard the Painballers got away. They took a spraygun too. I really messed up on that.'

'Win some, lose some,' says Rebecca. 'I can't tell you how cheered up I am that you're not dead. I thought those two scumbags would kill you for sure, and Ren too. I was worried sick. But here you are, though I have to say you look like shit.'

'Thanks,' says Toby. 'Nice china.'

'Dig in, sweetie. Pig in three forms: bacon, ham, and chops.' It hadn't taken them long to backslide on the Gardener Vegivows, thinks Toby. Even Jelack Rebecca is having no problems with the pork. 'Burdock root. Dandelion greens. Dog ribs on the side. If I keep it up with the animal protein I'm going to get even fatter than I am.'

'You're not fat,' says Toby. Though Rebecca has always been solid, even back when they'd worked together slinging meat at SecretBurgers, before they turned Gardener.

'I love you too,' says Rebecca. 'Okay, I'm not fat. Those glasses are real crystal, I'm enjoying it. Cost a mint, this stuff did once. Remember at the Gardeners? Vanity kills, Adam One used to tell us, so it was earthenware or die. Though I can see the day coming when we're not gonna be bothered with dishes anymore, we'll just eat with our hands.'

'There is a place in even the purest and most dedicated life for simple elegance,' says Toby. 'As Adam One also used to tell us.'

'Yeah, but sometimes that place is the trash can,' says

Rebecca. 'I've got a whole stack of lap-sized linen table napkins, and I can't iron them because there's no iron, and that really bugs me!' She sits down, forks a piece of meat onto her plate.

'I'm glad you're not dead too,' says Toby. 'Any coffee?'

'Yeah, if you can ignore the burnt twigs and roots and crap. There's no caffeine in it, but I'm counting on the placebo effect. I see you brought a whole mob back with you last night. Those – what would you call them, anyway?'

'They're people,' says Toby. Or I think they're people, she adds to herself. 'They're Crakers. That's what the MaddAddam bunch calls them, and I guess they should know.'

'They're definitely not like us,' says Rebecca. 'No way close. That little pisher Crake. Talk about fouling up the sandbox.'

'They want to be near Jimmy,' says Toby. 'They carried him back here.'

'Yeah, I heard that part,' says Rebecca. 'Tamaraw enlightened me. They should go back to – to wherever they live.'

'They say they need to purr on him,' says Toby. 'On Jimmy.'

'Excuse me? Do what on him?' says Rebecca with a small snort of laughter. 'Is that one of their weird sex things?'

Toby sighs. 'It's hard to explain,' she says. 'You have to see it.'

Hammock

After breakfast Toby goes over to take a look at Jimmy. He's suspended between two trees in a makeshift hammock fashioned from duct tape and rope. Over his legs is a child's comforter with a pattern of cats playing fiddles, laughing puppies, dishes with faces on them holding hands with grinning spoons, and cows with bells around their necks jumping over moons that are leering at their udders. Just what you need when you're hallucinating, thinks Toby.

Three Crakers – two women and a man – are sitting beside Jimmy's hammock on chairs that may once have belonged with the dining table: dark wood, with retro lyre backs and yellow-and-brown-striped satiny upholstery. The Crakers look wrong on these chairs, but they also look pleased with themselves, as if they're doing something quietly adventurous. Their bodies gleam like gold-threaded spandex; huge pink kudzu moths are fluttering around their heads in living halos.

They're preternaturally beautiful, thinks Toby. Unlike us. We must seem subhuman to them, with our flapping extra skins, our aging faces, our warped bodies, too thin, too fat, too hairy, too knobbly. Perfection exacts a price, but it's the imperfect who pay it.

Each of the Crakers has one hand on Jimmy. They're purring; the hum gets louder as Toby walks over to them.

'Greetings, Oh Toby,' says the taller of the two women. How do they know her name? They must have listened more carefully than she'd thought last night. And how should she reply? What are their own names, and is it polite to ask?

'Greetings,' she says. 'How is Snowman-the-Jimmy today?'

'He is growing stronger, Oh Toby,' says the shorter woman. The others smile.

Jimmy does look somewhat better. He's pinker, he's cooler, and he's sound asleep. They've fixed him up: tidied his hair, cleaned his beard. On his head is a battered red baseball cap, on his wrist a round watch with a blank face. A pair of sunglasses with one eye missing is perched awkwardly on his nose.

'Maybe he'd be more comfortable without those things on him,' says Toby, indicating the hat and the sunglasses.

'He must have those things,' says the man. 'Those are the things of Snowman-the-Jimmy.'

'He needs them,' says the shorter woman. 'Crake says he must have them. See, here is the thing for listening to Crake.' She lifts the arm with the watch on it.

'And he sees Crake with this,' says the man, pointing to the sunglasses. 'Only he.' Toby wants to ask what the hat is for, but she refrains.

'Why have you moved him outside?' she asks.

'He did not like it in that dark place,' says the man. 'In there.' He nods towards the house.

'Snowman-the-Jimmy can travel better out here,' says the taller woman.

'He's travelling?' says Toby. 'While he's asleep?' Could they be describing some dream they imagine Jimmy is dreaming?

'Yes,' says the man. 'He is travelling to here.'

'He is running, sometimes fast and sometimes slow. Sometimes walking, because he is tired. Sometimes the Pig Ones are chasing him, because they do not understand. Sometimes he is climbing into a tree,' says the shorter woman.

'When he gets to here, he will wake up,' says the man.

'Where was he when he started this travelling?' says Toby cautiously. She doesn't want to convey disbelief.

'He was in the Egg,' says the taller woman. 'Where we were, in the beginning. He was with Crake, and with Oryx. They came out of the sky to meet with him in the Egg, and to tell him more of the stories, so he can tell them to us.'

'That is where the stories come from,' says the man. 'But the Egg is too dark now. Crake and Oryx can be there, but Snowman-the-Jimmy cannot be there any more.' The three of them smile warmly at Toby, as if certain she's understood every word they've said.

'May I look at Snowman-the-Jimmy's hurt foot?' she asks politely. They have no objection, though they keep their hands in place and continue with their purring.

Toby checks the maggots underneath the cloth she wrapped around Jimmy's foot the night before. They're busily at work, cleaning up the dead flesh; the swelling and oozing are diminishing. This batch of maggots is nearing maturity: she'll have to get hold of some rotting meat tomorrow, leave it in the sun, attract flies, create new maggots.

'Snowman-the-Jimmy is coming closer to us,' says the short woman. 'Then he will tell us the stories of Crake, as he always did when he was living in his tree. But today you must tell them to us.'

'Me?' says Toby. 'But I don't know the stories of Crake!'

'You will learn them,' says the man. 'It will happen. Because Snowman-the-Jimmy is the helper of Crake, and you are the helper of Snowman-the-Jimmy. That is why.'

'You must put on this red thing,' says the shorter woman. 'It is called a *hat*.'

'Yes, a *hat*,' says the tall woman. 'In the evening, when it is moth time. You will put this hat of Snowman-the-Jimmy on your head, and listen to this shiny round thing that you put on your arm.'

'Yes,' says the other woman, nodding. 'And then the words of Crake will come out of your mouth. That is how Snowman-the-Jimmy would do it.'

'See?' says the man. He points to the lettering on the hat: *Red Sox*. 'Crake made this. He will help you. Oryx will help too, if the story has an animal in it.'

'We will bring a fish, when it is getting dark. Snowman-the-Jimmy always eats a fish, because Crake says he must eat it. Then you will put on the hat and listen to this Crake thing, and say the stories of Crake.'

'Yes, how Crake made us in the Egg, and cleared away the chaos of bad men. How we left the Egg and walked here with Snowman-the-Jimmy, because there were more leaves for us to eat.'

'You will eat the fish, and then you will say the stories of Crake, as Snowman-the-Jimmy always did,' says the shorter woman. They look at her with their uncanny green eyes and smile reassuringly. They seem entirely confident of her abilities.

What are my choices? thinks Toby. I can't say no. They may get disappointed, and go away by themselves, back to the beach, where the Painballers can grab them. They'd be easy prey, especially the children. How can I let that happen?

'All right,' she says. 'I will come in the evening. I will put on the hat of Jimmy, I mean Snowman-the-Jimmy, and tell you the stories of Crake.'

'And listen to the shiny thing,' says the man. 'And eat the fish.' It seems to be a ritual.

'Yes, all of that,' says Toby.

Shit, she thinks. I hope they cook the fish.

Story

While gathering up the breakfast dishes, Rebecca thought she saw a grim hatchet-face looking at her from under the trees. It seems to have been a false alarm, thinks Toby: no Painballers appeared, and, even better, no spraygun holes opened in Rebecca and no Craker child was yanked screaming into the shrubbery. Still, everyone's tense.

Toby asks the Craker mothers to move closer to the cobb house. When they look puzzled, she tells them it's a message from Oryx.

The day unscrolls without incident. No travellers return: no Shackleton, no Black Rhino or Katuro. No Zeb. Toby spends the rest of the morning in the kitchen garden, digging and weeding: a mindless exercise that calms her and fills the time. There are some chickenpeas beginning to sprout, and spinach leaves thrusting up, and the feathery tops of carrots. Her rifle is propped nearby.

Crozier and Zunzuncito herd the Mo'Hairs out of their paddock so they can graze. Both carry sprayguns: in a Painballer confrontation they'd have the advantage – two weapons against one – unless they were taken by surprise. Toby hopes they'll remember to check above their heads if there are trees nearby:

that must have been how the Painballers caught Amanda and Ren, by dropping down from above.

Why is war so much like a practical joke? she thinks. Hiding behind bushes, leaping out, with not much difference between *Boo!* and *Bang!* except the blood. The loser falls over with a scream, followed with a foolish expression, mouth agape, eyes akimbo. Those old biblical kings, setting their feet on conquered necks, stringing up rival kings on trees, rejoicing in piles of heads – there was an element of childish glee in all of that.

Maybe it's what drove Crake on, thinks Toby. Maybe he wanted to end it. Cut that part out of us: the grinning, elemental malice. Begin us anew.

She eats her lunch early, in solitude, because she's tagged for sentry with her rifle during the regular lunchtime. The food is cold pork and burdock root, with an Oreo cookie from a package gleaned from a pharmacy: a rare treat, carefully rationed. She opens her cookie and licks the white sweet filling before eating the two chocolatey halves: a guilty luxury.

Before the afternoon thunderstorm, five of the Crakers carry Jimmy into the cobb house, along with his Hey-Diddle-Diddle quilt. Toby sits with him while it rains, checks his wound, manages to raise his head so he drinks some of the mushroom elixir, even though he's still unconscious. Her supply is running low, but she doesn't know where to find the right mushrooms for a fresh brew.

A single Craker remains in the room with them, to purr: the others go away. They don't like houses; they'd rather be wet than cooped up. Once the rain stops, four other Crakers appear to carry Jimmy outside again.

The clouds part, the sun comes out. Crozier and Zunzuncito return with the flock of Mo'Hairs. Nothing has happened, they say; or nothing you can put your finger on. The Mo'Hairs were jumpy; it was hard to keep them together. And the crows were making a racket, but what does that tell you? Crows are always making a racket about something.

'Jumpy, how?' says Toby. 'What sort of racket?' But they can't be more specific.

Tamaraw, with a denim shirt over her hunched shoulders and a canvas sunhat, attempts to milk the one Mo'Hair that's producing. The milking doesn't go smoothly: there's kicking and bleating, and the pail tips and spills.

Crozier shows the Crakers how to work the hand pump: a retro decoration once but now the source of their drinking water. God knows what's in it, thinks Toby: it's groundwater, and every toxic spill for miles around may have leaked into it. She'll push for rainwater, at least for drinking; though with faraway fires and maybe nuclear meltdowns sending dirty particulate into the stratosphere, God knows what's in that as well.

The Crakers are delighted with the pump; the children scamper over and clamour to have water pumped onto them. After that, Crozier demonstrates the one piece of solar the MaddAddamites have managed to get running; it's connected to a couple of light bulbs, one in the cooking shack and one in the yard. He tries to explain why the lights go on, but they're puzzled. It's obvious to them that the light bulbs are like lumiroses, or the green rabbits that come out at dusk: they glow because Oryx made them that way.

Supper takes place at the long table. White Sedge in an apron with bluebirds on it and Rebecca with a mauve bath towel tied around her middle with yellow satin ribbon dish out the food from the pots, then sit down. Ren and Lotis Blue are at the far

end, coaxing Amanda to eat. The MaddAddamites not on
sentry duty filter in from their chores.

'Greetings, Inaccessible Rail,' says Ivory Bill. He takes pleasure in calling Toby by her old MaddAddam codename. He has
a tulip-sprinkled bedsheet draped around his sparse form and a
turban-like object made from a matching pillowcase on his
head. His angular nose juts out from his leathery face like a
beak. It was odd, thinks Toby, how the MaddAddamites chose
codenames that mirrored parts of themselves.

'How's he doing?' says Manatee. He's wearing a broad-
brimmed straw hat that makes him look like a chubby
plantation owner. 'Our star patient.'

'He's not dead,' says Toby. 'But he's not what you'd call conscious.'

'If he ever was,' says Ivory Bill. 'We used to call him
Thickney. That was his MaddAddam name, back in the early
days.'

'He was Crake's jackal at the Paradice Project,' says Tamaraw.
'Once he wakes up, there's a lot he needs to tell us. Before I
trample him to death.' She snorts to indicate that she's joking.

'Thickney by name, Thickney by nature,' says Manatee. 'I
don't think he had the least freaking idea. He was just a dupe.'

'Naturally we wouldn't have had a high opinion of him, to
be fair,' says Ivory Bill. 'He was at the Project by choice. Unlike
ourselves.' He sticks his fork into a chunk of meat. 'Dear lady,'
he says to White Sedge, 'could you possibly identify this sub-
stance for me?'

'Ahc-tually,' says White Sedge with her British accent, 'actually, not.'

'We were the brain slaves,' says Manatee, spearing another
chop. 'The captive science brainiacs, working the evolution
machines for Crake. What a power-tripper, thought he could
perfect humanity. Not that he wasn't brilliant.'

'He wasn't alone there,' says slender Zunzuncito. 'It was big business, the BioCorps were backing it. People were paying through the ceiling for those gene-splices. They were customizing their kids, ordering up the DNA like pizza toppings.' He's wearing bifocals. Once we run out of optical products, Toby thinks, it really will be back to the Stone Age.

'Just, Crake was better at it,' says Manatee. 'He put some accessories into these guys nobody else even thought of. The built-in insect repellent: genius.'

'And the women who can't say no. That colour-coded hormonal thing, you have to admire it,' says Zunzuncito.

'As a meat-computer set of problems to be solved, it was an intriguing challenge,' says Ivory Bill, turning his attention to Toby. 'Let me elucidate.' He's talking as if they're all at a graduate seminar, while cutting his greens into small, even squares. 'For instance, the rabbit gizzard, and the baboon platform for certain chromatic features of the reproductive system –'

'The part where they turn blue,' says Zunzuncito helpfully to Toby.

'I was doing the chemical composition of the urine,' says Tamaraw. 'The carnivore-deterrent element. Hard to test at the Paradice Project – we didn't have any carnivores.'

'I was working on the voice box: now that was complex,' says Manatee.

'Too bad you didn't code in a Cancel button for the singing,' says Ivory Bill. 'It gets on the nerves.'

'The singing was not my idea,' says Manatee sulkily. 'We couldn't erase it without turning them into zucchinis.'

'I have a question,' says Toby. They turn and look at her, as if surprised that she's spoken.

'Yes, dear lady?' says Ivory Bill.

'They want me to tell them a story,' says Toby. 'About being made by Crake. But who do they think Crake was, and how do they think he made them? What were they told about that, back in the Paradice dome?'

'They think Crake is some sort of a god,' says Crozier. 'But they don't know what he looks like.'

'How do you know that?' says Ivory Bill. 'You weren't in Paradice with us.'

'Because they fucking told me,' says Crozier. 'I'm their pal now. I even get to piss with them. It's, like, an honour.'

'Good thing they can't ever meet Crake,' says Tamaraw.

'No shit,' says Swift Fox, who has now joined them. 'They'd take one look at their lunatic of a creator and jump off a sky-scraper. If there were still any skyscrapers to jump off,' she adds morosely. She makes a show of yawning, stretching her arms up and behind her head, thrusting her breasts up and out. Her straw-coloured hair is pulled into a high ponytail, held in place by a powder-blue crocheted scrunchie. Her bedsheet has a dainty border of daisies and butterflies, cinched at the waist with a wide red belt. It's a startling touch: angel cloud meets butcher's cleaver.

'No point in repining, fair lady,' says Ivory Bill, switching his gaze from Toby to Swift Fox. He'll be even more pompous, thinks Toby, once the beard he's working on grows in. 'Carpe diem. Take every moment as it comes. Gather ye rosebuds.' He smiles, a demi-leer; his eyes move down to the red belt. Swift Fox stares at him blankly.

'Tell them a happy story,' says Manatee. 'Vague on the details. Crake's girlfriend, Oryx, used to do that sort of thing in Paradice, it kept them placid. I just hope that fucker Crake doesn't start performing miracles from beyond the grave.'

'Like turning everything to diarrhea,' says Swift Fox. 'Oh, excuse me, he's already done that. Is there any coffee?'

'Alas,' says Ivory Bill, 'we are bereft of coffee, dear lady.'

'Rebecca says she has to roast some kind of root,' says Manatee.

'And there won't be any real cream for it when we do get it,' says Swift Fox. 'Only sheep goo. It's enough to make you ice-pick your own temples.'

The light is fading now, the moths are flying, dusky pink, dusky grey, dusky blue. The Crakers have gathered around Jimmy's hammock. This is where they want Toby to tell the story about Crake and how they came out of the Egg.

Snowman-the-Jimmy wants to listen to the story too, they say. Never mind that he's unconscious: they're convinced he can hear it.

They already know the story, but the important thing seems to be that Toby must tell it. She must make a show of eating the fish they've brought, charred on the outside and wrapped in leaves. She must put on Jimmy's ratty red baseball cap and his faceless watch and raise the watch to her ear. She must begin at the beginning, she must preside over the creation, she must make it rain. She must clear away the chaos, she must lead them out of the Egg and shepherd them down to the seashore.

At the end, they want to hear about the two bad men, and the campfire in the forest, and the soup with a smelly bone in it: they're obsessed by that bone. Then she must tell about how they themselves untied the men, and how the two bad men ran away into the forest, and how they may come back at any time and do more bad things. That part makes them sad, but they insist on hearing it anyway.

Once Toby has made her way through the story, they urge her to tell it again, then again. They prompt, they interrupt, they fill in the parts she's missed. What they want from her is a seamless performance, as well as more information than she either knows or can invent. She's a poor substitute for Snowman-the-Jimmy, but they're doing what they can to polish her up.

She's just at the part where Crake is clearing away the chaos for the third time when their heads all turn at once. They sniff the air. 'Men are coming, Oh Toby,' they say.

'Men?' she says. 'The two men who ran away? Where?'

'No, not the ones who smell of blood.'

'Other men. More than two. We must greet them.' They all stand up.

Toby looks where they're looking. There are four – four silhouettes, coming nearer along the cluttered street that borders the cobb-house parkette. Their headlamps are on. Four dark outlines, each bringing a shining light.

Toby feels her body unclench, feels air flowing into her in a long, soundless breath. Can a heart leap? Can a person be dizzy with relief?

'Oh Toby, are you crying?'

Homecoming

It's Zeb. Her wish come true. Larger and shaggier than she remembers, and – although it's only been days since Toby last saw him – older. More bowed down. What's happened?

Black Rhino and Shackleton and Katuro are with him. Now that she's closer she can see how tired they are. They're setting down their packs, and the others are crowding around: Rebecca, Ivory Bill, Swift Fox, Beluga; Manatee, Tamaraw, Zunzuncito, White Sedge; Crozier and Ren and Lotis Blue; even Amanda, hanging back from the group.

Everyone's talking; or all the human people are. The Crakers stay on the sidelines, clustered together, eyes big, watching. Ren is crying and hugging Zeb, which is in order: he is, after all, her stepfather. When they were at the Gardeners, Zeb had lived for a time with Ren's luscious mother, Lucerne, who hadn't appreciated him, thinks Toby.

'It's okay,' Zeb tells Ren. 'Look! You got Amanda back!' He extends an arm; Amanda lets herself be touched.

'It was Toby,' says Ren. 'She had her gun.'

Toby waits, then moves forward. 'Good work, sharpshooter,' Zeb says to her, even though she didn't shoot anyone.

'You didn't find them?' Toby asks. 'Adam One and . . .'

Zeb gives her a sombre look. 'Not Adam One,' he says. 'But we found Philo.'

The others lean in to listen. 'Philo?' says Swift Fox.

'Old Gardener,' says Rebecca. 'He smoked a lot of . . . he liked the Vision Quests. He stayed with Adam One, back when the Gardeners split up. Where was he?' They all understand from Zeb's face that Philo was not alive.

'There were a bunch of vultures on top of a parking garage, so we went up to take a look,' says Shackleton. 'Near the old Wellness Clinic.'

'Where we used to go to school?' says Ren.

'Quite fresh,' says Black Rhino. Which means, thinks Toby, that at least some of the missing Gardeners survived the first wave of the plague.

'None of the others?' she says. 'Nobody else? Was it the . . . was he sick?'

'No sign of them,' says Zeb. 'But I'm guessing they're still out there. Adam could be. Food handy? I could eat a bear.' Which means he doesn't want to answer Toby right now.

'He eats a bear!' the Crakers say to one another. 'Yes! It is as Crozier told us!' 'Zeb eats a bear!'

Zeb nods towards the Crakers, who are gazing at him uncertainly. 'I see we've got company.'

'This is Zeb,' Toby tells the Crakers. 'He is our friend.'

'We are pleased, Oh Zeb. Greetings.'

'He is the one, he is the one! Crozier told us.' 'He eats a bear!' 'Yes. We are pleased.' Tentative smiles. 'What is a *bear*, Oh Zeb – this bear you eat?' 'Is it a fish?' 'Does it have a smelly bone?'

'They came with us,' says Toby. 'From the shore. We couldn't stop them, they wanted to be with Jimmy. With Snowman. That's what they call Jimmy.'

'Crake's buddy?' says Zeb. 'From the Paradice Project?'

'Long story,' says Toby. 'You should eat.'

There's some leftover stew; Manatee goes to get it. The Crakers withdraw to a safe distance; they don't like to be too close to the odours of carnivore cookery. Shackleton wolfs down his stew and moves off to sit with Ren and Amanda and Crozier and Lotis Blue. Black Rhino has two helpings, then goes to take a shower. Katuro says he'll help Rebecca sort out the contents of the packs: they've gleaned more soydines and some duct tape, and a few packs of freeze-dried ChickieNobs, and some Joltbars, and another package of Oreo cookies. A miracle, says Rebecca. It's hard to find any packaged cookies unchewed by rodents.

'Let's check out the garden,' Zeb says to Toby. Toby's heart sinks: there must be bad news he wants to break privately.

The fireflies are coming out. The lavender and thyme are in bloom, releasing their airborne flavours. A few self-seeded lumiroses glimmer along the edges of the fence; several of the shimmering green rabbits are nibbling at their bottom leaves. Giant grey moths drift like blown ash.

'It wasn't the plague that killed Philo,' says Zeb. 'Someone cut his throat.'

'Oh,' says Toby. 'I see.'

'Then we saw the Painballers,' says Zeb. 'The same ones that grabbed Amanda. They were gutting one of those giant pigs. We took a few shots, but they ran off. So we stopped looking for Adam and got back here as fast as we could, because they might be anywhere around here.'

'I'm sorry,' says Toby.

'About what?' says Zeb.

'We caught them, night before last,' she says. 'We tied them to a tree. But I didn't kill them. It was Saint Julian's, I just couldn't. They got away, they took their spraygun.'

She's crying now. This is pathetic, like baby mice, blind and pink and whimpering. It's not what she does. But she's doing it.

'Hey,' says Zeb. 'It'll be fine.'

'No,' says Toby. 'It won't be fine.' She turns away to leave: if she's going to snivel, she should do it alone. Alone is how she feels, alone is how she'll always be. You're used to solitude, she tells herself. Be a stoic.

Then she's enfolded.

She'd waited so long, she'd given up waiting. She'd longed for this, and denied it was possible. But now how easy it is, like coming home must have been once, for those who'd had homes. Walking through the doorway into the familiar, the place that knows you, opens to you, allows you in. Tells you the stories you've needed to hear. Stories of the hands as well, and of the mouth.

I've missed you. Who said that?

A shape against the night window, glint of an eye. Dark heartbeat.

Yes. At last. It's you.

Bearlift

The Story of when Zeb was lost in the Mountains, and ate the Bear

And so Crake poured away the chaos, to make a safe place where you could live. And then ...

We know the story of Crake. We know it many times. Now tell us the story of Zeb, Oh Toby.

The story of how Zeb ate a bear!

Yes! Ate a bear! A bear! What is a *bear*?

We want to hear the story of Zeb. And the bear. The bear he ate.

Crake wants us to hear it. If Snowman-the-Jimmy was awake, he would tell us that story.

Well then. Let me listen to the shiny thing of Snowman-the-Jimmy. Then I can hear the words.

I am listening very hard. It doesn't help me to listen when you are singing.

So. This is the story of Zeb and the bear. Only Zeb is in the story at first. He is all alone. The bear comes later. Maybe tomorrow the bear will come. For bears to come, you must be patient.

*

Zeb was lost. He sat down under a tree. The tree was in a big open space, wide and flat, like the beach except there was no sand and no sea, only some chilly pools and a lot of moss. All around but quite far away, there were mountains.

How did he get there? He flew there, in a ... never mind. That part is in a different story. No, he cannot fly like a bird. Not any more.

Mountains? Mountains are very large and high rocks. No, those are not mountains, those are buildings. Buildings fall down, and then they make a crash. Mountains fall down too, but they do it very slowly. No, the mountains did not fall down on Zeb.

So Zeb looked at the mountains that were all around him but quite far away, and he thought, How will I get through these mountains? They are so large and high.

He needed to get through the mountains because the people were on the other side. He wanted to be with the people. He didn't want to be all alone. Nobody wants to be all alone, do they?

No, they were not people like you. They had clothes on. A lot of clothes, because it was cold there. Yes, it was in the time of the chaos, before Crake poured it all away.

So Zeb looked at the mountains and the pools and the moss, and he thought, What will I eat? And then he thought, Those mountains have a lot of bears living in them.

A bear is a very big, fur-covered animal with big claws and many sharp teeth. Bigger than a bobkitten. Bigger than a wolvog. Bigger than a pigoon. This big.

It speaks with a growl. It gets very hungry. It tears things apart.

Yes, bears are the Children of Oryx. I don't know why she made them so big, with very sharp teeth.

Yes, we must be kind to them. The best way of being kind to bears is not to be very close to them.

I don't think there are any bears very close to us right now.

And Zeb thought, Maybe a bear has smelled me, and maybe it is coming right now, because it is hungry, it is starving, and it wants to eat me. And I will have to fight the bear, and all I have is this quite small knife, and this stick that can make holes in things. And I will have to win the fight, and kill the bear, and then I will have to eat it.

The bear will come into the story quite soon.

Yes, Zeb will win the fight. Zeb always wins the fight. Because that's what happens.

Yes, he knew Oryx would be sad. Zeb felt sorry for the bear. He didn't want to hurt it. But he didn't want to be eaten by it. You don't want to be eaten by a bear, do you? Neither do I.

Because bears can't eat only leaves. Because it would make them sick.

Anyway, if Zeb didn't eat the bear he would have died, and then he wouldn't be here with us right now. And that would be a sad thing too, wouldn't it?

If you don't stop crying I can't go on with the story.

The Fur Trade

There's the story, then there's the real story, then there's the story of how the story came to be told. Then there's what you leave out of the story. Which is part of the story too.

In the story of Zeb and the bear, Toby has left out the dead man, whose name was Chuck. He, too, was lost among the pools and moss and mountains and bears. He, too, did not know the way out. It's unfair to deny him a mention, erase him from time, but putting him into the story would cause more knots and tangles than Toby is prepared to deal with. For instance, she doesn't yet know how this dead man wormed his way into the story in the first place.

'Too bad the fucker died,' says Zeb. 'I'd have twisted it out of him.'

'It?'

'Who hired him. What they wanted. Where he would have taken me.'

'*Died* is a euphemism, I take it. He didn't have a heart attack,' says Toby.

'Don't be harsh. You know what I mean.'

*

Zeb was lost. He sat down under a tree.

Or not lost completely. He did have a rough idea of where he was: he was somewhere on the Mackenzie Mountain Barrens, hundreds of miles from anywhere with fast food. And not under a tree, more like beside, and not a tree exactly, more like a shrub; though not bushy, more like spindly. A spindly kind of spruce. He noticed the details of the trunk, the small dead underbranches, the grey lichen on it, frilly and intricate and see-through, like whores' underpants.

'What do you know about whore's underpants?' says Toby.

'More than you want me to,' says Zeb. 'So. When you focus on details like that – close up, really clear, totally useless – you know you're in shock.'

The AOH 'thopter was still smouldering. Lucky he got clear before it burst, or before the blimp component did, and thank shit the digital release on the seatbelts had still been working: otherwise he'd have been dead.

Chuck was lying belly down on the tundra, his head at a sick angle, peering over his own shoulder one-eighty degrees, like an owl. Not looking at Zeb, though. Looking up at the sky. No angels there, or none had showed up yet.

Blood was coming from somewhere on the top of Zeb's head, he could feel the warmth trickling down. Scalp wound. Not dangerous, but they bleed a lot. Your head's the most shallow part of you, his sociopath of a father had been in the habit of saying. Except for your brain. And your soul, supposing you've been blessed with one, which I doubt. The Rev had been a big cheerleader for souls, in addition to which he thought he was the boss of them.

Now Zeb found himself wondering if Chuck had a soul, and if it was still hovering over his body like a feeble smell. 'Chuck, you stupid fuck,' Zeb said out loud. If he'd been given a brief to kidnap himself on behalf of the brainscrapers, he'd have done a way better job of it than Chuck had, the fuckwit.

Too bad Chuck was dead, in a way – he must've had some good sides to him, maybe he liked puppies – but now there was one less asshole in the world, and wasn't that a plus? A checkmark in the column of the forces of light. Or darkness, depending on who was doing the double-entry moral accounting.

Though Chuck hadn't been an ordinary asshole; not grouchy, not aggressive, not like Zeb himself on his asshole setting. Too much the other way. Too friendly, too eager to be on message, man is obsolete, dooming ourselves to extinction, restore the balance of nature and babble babble, he overdid it so much that he sounded preposterous, and in an outfit like Bearlift, with its full quota of preposterous green-hued furfuckers, that took some effort.

They weren't all furfuckers, however: some claimed to be along for the challenge. Adventurous, devil-may-care, no strings on me, tattoo-upholstered, with greasy ponytails like bikers in old movies – boundary-pushing muscle-flexers, boot soles a little too hot for ordinary strolling. That was how Zeb had positioned himself: bulked up on natural steroids, do what had to be done, could take the pace, wings on the ankles, needed the money, liked the shadowy rimlands where nobody official could stick their tentacles into your back pocket, within which the contents of other people's hacked bank accounts might be bashfully lurking.

The card-carrying furfuckers looked down their narrow green true-believer noses at Zeb and his edgy like, but they didn't push that my-shit-don't-stink agenda too hard. They needed the manpower because not everyone on the planet thought it was a great idea to aero/orno/helithopter numerous dumpsterloads of rancid biotrash around the far north so a bunch of mangy Ursidae could gobble it free of charge.

'This was before the oil shortage really kicked in?' says Toby. 'And the carbon garboil business took off. Otherwise, they'd never have let you waste such valuable primary material on bears.'

'It was before a lot of things,' says Zeb. 'Though the oil prices were already getting pretty steep.'

Bearlift had four old-model 'thopters they'd bought on the grey market. The Flying Pufferfish was their nickname. 'Thopters claimed to use biodesign: they had a helium/hydrogen gas-filled blimp with a skin that sucked in or exhaled molecules like a fish's swim bladder that contracted and expanded and allowed them to lift heavy weights. Plus, they had stabilizing ventral fins, a couple of heli-blades for hovering, and four bird-like flapping wings for manoeuvrability at slow speeds. The upside being minimum fuel consumption, ultra-high freight weight, and the ability to fly low and slow; the downside being that a 'thopter flight took forever, the software on the things failed regularly, and few among them knew how to fix the brutes. Questionable digimechanics had to be called in, or rather smuggled in from Brazil, where the digital darkside flourished.

They'd hack you as soon as look at you down there. Roaring business in politicians' medical records and sordid affairs, celebrities' plastic surgeries – that was the small end. At the big end it was one Corp hacking another. Hacking a powerful Corp was the kind of thing that could get you into the real crapola, even if you were firewalled by being on the blackbox payroll of another powerful Corp.

'So I suppose you did it,' says Toby. 'The kind of thing with the real crapola.'

'Yeah, I'd been down there, just making a living,' says Zeb. 'That was one reason I was taking a breather at Bearlift: it was ultra far from Brazil.'

Bearlift was a scam, or partly a scam. It didn't take anyone with half a brain too long to figure that one out. Unlike many scams it was well meaning, but it was a scam nonetheless. It lived off the good intentions of city types with disposable emotions who liked to think they were saving something – some rag from their primordial authentic ancestral past, a tiny shred of their collective soul dressed up in a cute bear suit. The concept was simple: the polar bears are starving because the ice is almost gone and they can't catch seals any more, so let's feed them our leftovers until they learn to adapt, '*adapt* being the buzzword of those days, if you'll recall, though I doubt you're old enough; you must still have been in playskirts. Learning to wiggle your little mantrap.'

'Stop flirting,' said Toby.

'Why? You like it.'

'I remember *adapt*,' says Toby. 'It was another way of saying *tough luck*. To people you weren't going to help out.'

'You got it,' said Zeb. 'Anyway, feeding trash to the bears didn't help them adapt, it just taught them that food falls out of the sky. They'd start slavering every time they heard the sound of a 'thopter, they had their very own cargo cult.

'But here's the scammiest part. Yes, the ice had mostly melted; yes, some polar bears had starved, but the rest of them were drifting southwards, mating up with the grizzlies, from which they'd separated themselves a mere two hundred thousand years ago. So you'd get bears that were white with brown patches or bears that were brown with white patches, or all brown or all white, but whatever was on the outside was no predictor of temperament: the pizzlies would avoid you most of the time, like grizzlies; the grolars would attack you most of the time, like polar bears. You never knew which kind any given bear might be. What you did know was that you didn't want your 'thopter to fall out of the air over bear country.'

As Zeb's had just done.

'You stupid fuck,' he said again to Chuck. 'And whoever hired you is a double stupid fuck,' he added, not that they were listening. Or – he had a sudden nasty thought – maybe they were.

Crash

Everything was going fine at Bearlift until Chuck turned up. Zeb was in some trouble at that time, true enough . . .

'Unlike at any other time,' says Toby.

'You laughing at me? Victim of a confused youth due to parental abuse? Plus, I grew too fast?'

'Would I laugh?'

'Matter of fact, you would,' says Zeb. 'Heart like shale. What you need is a good fracking.'

Zeb was in some trouble at that time, true enough, but nobody at Bearlift Central seemed to know or care: half of them were in trouble themselves, so it was Don't ask, Don't tell.

The chores were straightforward: load up the edible refuse, in Whitehorse or Yellowknife, sometimes maybe Tuk, where the Beaufort Sea offshore oilrig tankers dumped their garbage when they weren't tipping it illegally. The oilrigs still produced a lot of real-animal-protein leftovers in those days because nothing was too good for the tanker crews. Pork – they ate a lot of pork byproducts – and chicken, or something next door to it. When it was labmeat it was top grade, camouflaged in sausages or meatloaf so you really couldn't tell.

You'd pack the postmeal slops into the 'thopter, then grab a beer, then fly the 'thopter to the Bearlift drop locations, hover while dumping off the loads, fly back. Nothing to it except mind-numbing boredom unless there was bad weather or mechanical failure. In that case you'd have to set the 'thopter down while trying to give the mountainsides a miss, then wait out the weather or kick your heels until Repair showed up. Then repeat. Pretty routine. The worst of it was listening to the green-nosed furfucker sermonizing that went on in the Bearlift-town bars when you were trying to get spongefaced on the crapulous booze they hauled in there and dispensed by the vatful.

Apart from that, it was eat, sleep, and on a good day have a tussle with one or another of the girl staff, though Zeb had to be careful about that because some of them were snarly and others were taken, and he tried to stay out of brawls, never having seen any percentage in rolling around under bar stools with some enraged moron who considered he'd staked eternal twat rights because of his pre-eminent cock and his dimples, and who might have a knife. Unlikely a handgun any more because it was around that time that the CorpSeCorps was confiscating those, having raised the spurious banner of civic safety and thus effectively securing a monopoly for themselves on killing at a distance. Some guys hid their Glocks and other name brands, dug them in under stones in case of dire need, but for the same reason they were unlikely to be carrying. Though not every law and declaration was respected up there in the boonies. Things in the north were always a little fuzzy around the edges, law-wise. So you never knew.

Anyway, the girls. If there was a Back Off sign on a little or big or medium-sized set of cheeks, he always backed off. But if someone crept into his dorm room under cover of darkness, who was he to whimper? He'd been told since a child that he had the morals of a sowbug, and he hated to defeat expectations, in addition to which rejecting a girl's overture would be hurtful to her self esteem. Some of those wouldn't have stood up too well under the light, but one of them had an amazing floppy ass, and another one had a set of boobs like two bowling balls in a string bag, and . . .

'Too much information,' says Toby.

'Don't be jealous,' says Zeb. 'They're dead now. You can't be jealous of a bunch of dead women.'

Toby says nothing. The lush corpse of Zeb's one-time lover, Lucerne, floats in the air between them, unseen, unmentioned, and certainly unburied as far as Toby is concerned.

'Alive is better than dead,' says Zeb.

'No contest there,' says Toby. 'But on second thought you never know till you've tried.'

Zeb laughs. 'You have an amazing ass too,' he says. 'Not floppy, though. Compact.'

'Tell about Chuck,' says Toby.

Chuck entered Bearlift Central as though tiptoeing into a forbidden room while pretending he had a right to be there. Furtive but assertive. To Zeb's mind, his clothes were too new. They looked as if Chuck had just come from one of those crispy outfitter shops, zippers and Velcro and flaps all over, like some kind of kinky video puzzle game. Undo this man, find the leprechaun, win a prize. Never trust a man with new clothes.

'But clothes have to be new sometimes,' says Toby. 'Or they did back then. They weren't created old.'

'Real men know how to dirty up their clothes in about one second,' says Zeb. 'They writhe around in mud. Apart from the clothes, his teeth were too big and white. When I see those kinds of teeth, I always want to give them a gentle tap with a bottle. See if they're fake, watch them shatter. My dad, the Rev, had teeth like that. He used whitener on them. The teeth plus his tan made him look like some kind of light-up deep-sea dev-ilfish or else a long-dead horse's head in a desert. It was worse when he smiled than when he didn't.'

'Back off on the childhood,' says Toby. 'You'll get woeful.'

'Woe, your foe? Say no to woe? Don't preach at me, babe.'

'It works for me. Backing off woe.'

'You sure about that?'

'So, Chuck.'

'So. There was something about his eyes. Chuck's eyes. Laminated eyes. Hard and shiny. They had a sort of transparent lid over them.'

The first time Chuck appeared at the canteen table with his tray and said, 'Mind if I join you?' he scanned Zeb, an overall back-and-forth of those laminated eyes. Like scanning a barcode.

Zeb glanced up at him. He didn't say yes, he didn't say no. He gave an all-purpose grunt and continued work on his rub-bery conundrum of a sausage. You'd have expected Chuck to start with personal questions – where you from, how'd you get here, and so forth – but he didn't. His opening ploy was Bearlift. He said what a great org it was, but since that got no nodding and yupping from Zeb, he intimated that he was only there because he'd hit a bad patch in his life and was, you know, keep-ing quiet for a while, until things blew over.

'What'd you do, pick your nose?' said Zeb, and Chuck gave a dead-horse-teeth laugh. He said that he guessed Bearlift was for guys who, you know, sort of like the Foreign Legion, and Zeb said the foreign what, and that was the end of that one.

Not that he could shake the guy by being rude. Chuck backed off, but he still managed to be ever-present. Zeb would be at the bar labouring away at the next morning's hangover and all of a sudden there would be Chuck, buddying up, offering to get the next round. Go to the can, take a leak, and there would be Chuck, materializing like ectoplasm, taking a leak two stalls down; or Zeb would be sliding round the corner in the seedier part of Whitehorse and, guess what, Chuck would be sliding round the next corner over. He most likely went through Zeb's stuff in Zeb's broom closet of a room when Zeb wasn't in it.

'He was welcome to it,' says Zeb. 'Nothing in my dirty laundry but dirty laundry because the real dirty laundry was in my head.'

But what was his game? Because it was obvious he had one. At first Zeb thought Chuck was gay and was about to start some trouser nuzzling, but it wasn't that.

Over the next few weeks Chuck and Zeb had flown a couple of lifts together. There were always two in a Pufferfish; you'd take turns dozing. Zeb tried to avoid partnering with Chuck, who by this time was giving him the nape prickles, but on the first occasion the guy Zeb was supposed to have flown with was called away by an aunt's funeral and Chuck had inserted himself into the slot, and the second time the other guy got food poisoning. Zeb wondered if Chuck had paid the two of them off to go missing. Or strangled the aunt, or put *E. coli* in the pizza, to make it convincing.

He waited for Chuck to pop the question while they were in mid-air. Maybe he knew about some of Zeb's earlier capers and was hiring for a hitherto-unknown bunch of darksiders who wanted Zeb to tackle a bolus of seriously forbidden hackery; or maybe it was an extortion outfit after some plutocrat, or a hireling connected with IP thieves who needed a skein of professional trackwork to further their kidnapping of a Corp brainiac.

Or maybe it was a sting – Chuck would propose some flagrantly illegal jest, record Zeb agreeing to do it, and then the giant lobster claws of what passed for the justice system would descend and clench; or maybe there'd be some goofy blackmail demand, as if you could get shit from a stone.

But nothing abnormal happened on these two runs. They must've been soothers, to set Zeb at ease. Signal that Chuck was harmless. Was his dinkiness a deep cover?

It almost worked. Zeb started thinking he himself was paranoid. Twitching at shadows. Worrying about a slithery nobody like Chuck.

That morning – the morning of the crash – had started out as usual. Breakfast, some anonymous bunwich with mysterious ingredients, couple of mugs of caffeine substitute, slice of toasted sawdust. Bearlift got its supplies on the cheap: It considered its cause to be so noble and worthy you were supposed to be humble, eat food stand-ins, save the good stuff for the bears.

Then loading up the offal, biodegradable sacks of it forklifted into the belly of the Puffer. Zeb's scheduled flying partner had been scratched off that day's list – cut his foot dancing barefoot on broken glass to show how tough he was in one of the local knocking shops while higher than the ionosphere on some cretinous pharmaceutical, it was said – and Zeb was supposed to be doubling with an okay guy called Rodge. But when he went to get in, there was Chuck, all togged up with his crispy zippers and Velcro flaps, smiling with his enormous white horse teeth but not with his laminated eyes.

'Rodge get a phone call?' said Zeb. 'Grandmother died?'

'Father, in fact,' said Chuck. 'Nice day. Hey, I brought you a beer.' He had one for himself too, just to show he was a regular guy.

Zeb grunted, took the beer, twisted off the top. 'Need to take a leak,' he said. In the can he poured the beer down the hole. Top seemed to be sealed on, but you could fake those things, you could fake just about anything. He didn't want to swill or munch any item that had been in Chuck's hands.

The Puffers were always complex while taking off: the helicopter blades and the helium/hydrogen blimp provided lift, but the trick was to get high enough before you started the wings flapping, and to cut the heli-blades at exactly the right time, or the whole thing could tip and spiral.

But there was no problem that day. The flight was standard, threading the valleys through and around the Pelly Mountains, pausing to bombard the landscape a few times with bear yummies; then over to the high-altitude Barrens with the Mackenzies all around, postcard snow on the tops, with a couple more drops; then crossing the remains of the Old Canol Trail, still marked by the occasional World War Two telephone pole.

The 'thopter responded well. It stopped flapping and started hovering right over the dump spots, the hatch opened as it was supposed to, and the biotrash tumbled out. At the last feeding station, two bears – one mostly white, one mostly brown – were already cantering towards their personal garbage dump as the 'thopter approached; Zeb could see their fur rippling like a shag rug being shaken. Being that close was always a bit of a thrill.

Zeb turned the 'thopter and headed southwest, back towards Whitehorse. Then he handed over to Chuck because the clock said it was Zeb's turn to catch some zizz. He lay back and blew up the neck pillow and closed his eyes, but he didn't allow himself to drift off because Chuck had been far too alert during the entire flight. You don't get that geared up over a non-event.

They were about two-thirds of the way to the first narrow mountain valley when Chuck made his move. Through his almost-closed eyes, Zeb saw the one hand moving stealthily over towards his thigh, holding a thread of glitter. He sat up fast and whacked Chuck across the windpipe. Not hard enough, though, because although Chuck gasped – not a gasp, hard to describe it – although he made that sound and dropped whatever he'd been holding, he grabbed at Zeb's neck with both hands and Zeb whacked him again, and of course nobody was flying the controls at that point, and in the thrashing around something must've been hit by a leg or a hand or an elbow, and that's when the 'thopter folded two of its four wings and tipped sideways and went down.

And Zeb found himself sitting under a tree, staring at the tree trunk. Astonishing, how clear the frilly edges were, of the lichen; light grey with a tinge of green, and an edge that was darker, so intricate . . .

Stand up, he ordered himself. You need to get moving. But his body didn't hear.

Supplies

A long time later – it seemed like a long time, he felt as if he was wading through transparent sludge – Zeb rolled to one side, put his hands on the ground, pushed himself to his feet beside the spindly kind of spruce. Then he threw up. He hadn't noticed feeling sick right before: he just suddenly puked.

'A lot of animals will do that,' he says. 'Under stress. Means you don't have to put the energy into digesting. Lightens the load.'

'Were you cold?' says Toby.

Zeb's teeth were chattering, he was shivering. He took Chuck's down vest, added it to his own. It wasn't ripped much. He checked the pockets, found Chuck's cellphone, mashed it with a rock to destroy any GPS and eavesdropping functions. It started ringing just before he did the mashing; it took everything not to answer it and pretend he was Chuck. Maybe he should've answered, though, and said that Zeb was dead. He might've learned something. A couple of minutes later his own phone rang; he waited until it stopped, then mashed it as well.

Chuck had a few more toys, though nothing Zeb didn't have

himself. Pocketknife, bear spray, bug spray, folded-up tinfoil space-age survival blanket, those things. By great good luck the bear gun they always carried with them in case of groundings and attacks had been tossed out along with Chuck. Bear guns were the exception to the new no-guns rules because even the dickwad CorpSeCorps bureaucrats knew you needed a bear gun up there. The Corps didn't like Bearlift, but they didn't try to shut it down either, though they could have done that with one finger. It served a function for them, sounded a note of hope, distracted folks from the real action, which was bulldozing the planet flat and grabbing anything of value. They had no objection to the standard Bearlift ad, with a smiling green furfucker telling everyone what a sterling lot of good Bearlift was doing, and please send more cash or you'll be guilty of bearicide. The Corps even put some of the cash in themselves. 'That was back when they were still massaging their trust-me images,' says Zeb. 'Once they got a hammerlock on power, they didn't have to bother so much.'

Zeb almost stopped shivering when he saw the bear gun. He could've hugged it: at least now he might have half a chance. He didn't find the needle, though, the one Chuck was going to stick into him; too bad about that, he would've liked to have known what was in it. Knockout potion, most likely. Freeze-frame his waking self, then fly him to some seedy rendezvous where the brainscrapers hired by who-knows-who would be waiting to strip-mine his neural data, suck out everything he'd ever hacked and everyone he'd ever hacked for, then leave him a pithed and shrivelled husk, staggering around with induced amnesia in a far-distant ravaged swamp until the local inhabitants stole his trousers and recycled his organs for the transplant biz.

But even if he'd managed to get hold of the needle, what then? Test it out on himself? Stick it in a lemming? 'Still, I could have kept it in reserve, for emergencies,' says Zeb.

'Emergencies?' says Toby, smiling in the dark. 'This wasn't an emergency?'

'No, a real emergency,' says Zeb. 'Like running into some other person out there. That would be an emergency. Stands to reason it would be a madman.'

'Was there any string?' says Toby. 'In the pockets. You never know when string will come in handy. Or some rope.'

'String. Yeah, now that you mention it. And a roll of fishing line, we always carried that, with a few hooks. Fire-lighter. Mini-binocs. Compass. Bearlift gave us all that Boy Scout stuff, survival basics. I didn't take Chuck's compass though, I already had one. You don't need two compasses.'

'Candy bar?' says Toby. 'Energy rations?'

'Yeah, couple of shitty little Joltbars, faux nuts. Package of cough drops. I took those. Plus.' He pauses.

'Plus what?' says Toby. 'Go on.'

'Okay, warning: this is gross. I took some of Chuck. Hacked it off with the pocketknife, kind of sawed it. Chuck had a fold-up waterproof jacket, so I wrapped it in that. Not much to eat up there in the Barrens, we all knew that, we'd had the Bearlift course. Rabbits, ground squirrels, mushrooms, but I wouldn't have time to hunt for any of that. Anyway, you can die of eating nothing but rabbits. Rabbit starvation, they called it. No fat on those things. It's like that whatchamacallit diet – the all-protein one. You start to dissolve your own muscles. Your heart gets very thin.'

'What part of Chuck did you take?' says Toby. She's surprised she doesn't feel squeamish; she might have, once, back when *squeamish* was an option.

'The fattest part,' says Zeb. 'The boneless part. The part you'd have taken. Or any sane person.'

'Did you feel bad about it?' says Toby. 'Stop patting my bum.'

'Why?' says Zeb. 'Nah, I didn't feel too bad. He'd have done the same. Maybe a stroking action, like this?'

'I'm too skinny,' says Toby.

'Yeah, you could use a little more padding. I'll bring you a box of chocolates, if I can find any. Fatten you up.'

'Add some flowers,' says Toby. 'Roll out the full courtship ritual. I bet you never did that in your life.'

'You'd be surprised,' says Zeb. 'I've presented bouquets in my day. Of a kind.'

'Go on,' says Toby, who doesn't want to think about Zeb's bouquets or what kind they were, or who he may have given them to. 'There you are. Mountains in the distance, part of Chuck lying on the ground and the rest in your pocket. What time was it?'

'Maybe three in the afternoon, maybe five, shit, maybe even eight, it would still have been light then,' says Zeb. 'I'd lost track. It was mid-July, did I say that? Sun hardly sets at all then, up there. Just sort of dips below the horizon, makes a pretty red rim. Then in a few hours up it comes again. That place isn't above the Arctic Circle, but it's up so high it's tundra: two-hundred-year-old willows like horizontal vines, and the wildflowers all bloom at once because the summer's only a couple of weeks long. Not that I was noticing any wildflowers right then.'

He thought maybe he should get Chuck out of sight. He put Chuck's pants back on and stuffed him under one of the 'thopter wings. Changed boots with him – Chuck's were better anyway, and they more or less fit – and left a foot sticking out so anyone looking from a distance would think it was Zeb. He figured he might be safer dead, at least in the short-term.

When Bearlift Central saw they'd lost communication, they were bound to send somebody. Most likely it would be Repair. Once they discovered there was nothing left to repair and that nobody was sitting around setting off little flares and waving a white hanky, they'd go away. That was the ethos: don't waste fuel on dead bodies. Let nature recycle them. The bears would take care of it, the wolves, the wolverines, the ravens, and so forth.

But the Bearlifters might not be the only ones who would come to have a look. For his brain-snatch caper, Chuck clearly wasn't working with the Bearlifters: if he had been, he wouldn't have hesitated to try something right at the base, and he would've had help. Zeb would already be a lobotomized shell parked in some zombie town, ex-mining, ex-oil, with a fake passport and no fingerprints. Not that they'd even bother going that far because who would ever miss him?

Chuck's bosses had to be elsewhere, then: they were wherever it was they'd phoned from. But how close was that? Norman Wells, Whitehorse? Anywhere with an airstrip. Zeb needed to move away from the crash as fast as possible, find a place with cover. Which was not so easy on the next-to-bare-naked tundra.

Grolars and pizzlies could do it, though, and they were bigger. But also more experienced.

Bunkie

Zeb started hiking. The 'thopter had come down on a gentle hillside sloping to the west, and west was the direction he took. He had a rough map of the whole area in his head. Too bad he didn't have the paper map, the one they always kept open on their knees when flying up there in case of digital failure.

The tundra was hard walking. Spongy, waterlogged, with hidden pools and slippery moss and treacherous mounds of tussock grass. There were parts of old airplanes sticking out of the peat – a strut here, a blade there, detritus from rash twentieth-century bush pilots caught by fog or sudden winds, long ago. He saw a mushroom, left it alone: he knew little about mushrooms, but some were hallucinogenic. That's all he'd need, an encounter with the 'shroom god while green and purple teddybears skimmed towards him on tiny wings, grinning pinkly. The day had been surreal enough already.

The bear gun was loaded, and he kept the spray ready. If you surprised a bear it would charge. The spray was no good unless you could see the reds of its eyes, so you had a narrow time window – spray and then shoot. If it was a pizzly, that's how things would go. But a grolar would stalk you, and come up from behind.

In a wet patch of sand he found a print, left front paw, and, farther on, some fresh scat. They were most likely watching him right now. They knew he had a packet of blood and muscle, no matter how tidily wrapped: they could smell it. They could smell his fear.

His feet were already drenched, despite Chuck's superior boots. Those boots didn't fit as well as he'd assumed they would. He pictured his feet turning to pallid, blistery dough inside his socks. To take his mind off them – and off the bears, and off dead Chuck, off everything – and to make some noise to warn the pizzlies so neither he nor they would be surprised, he sang a song. It was a habit left over from his so-called youth, when he'd whistle in the dark, whatever dark he'd been locked into. In the dark, in the darkness, in the darkness that was there even when it was light.

> *Dad's a sadist, Mom's a creep,*
> *Close your eyes and go to sleep.*

No, not sleep, even though he was so tired now. He needed to keep going. Forced march.

> *Idiotic, idiotic, idiotic, idiotic,*
> *Maybe I'm a really bad, a really bad, a bad psychotic.*

There was a line of thicker green downhill that signalled a creek. He headed towards it, over the hillocks and the moss and the bare gravelly spots where pebbles had boiled to the surface during the deep frost of the winters. It wasn't particularly cold on that day, it was in fact hot in the sun, but he was still shivering in fits, like a wet dog shaking. He hugged Chuck's vest around himself, on top of his own.

When he was almost to the creek – it was more of a river, it had a swift current – he thought, What if it's bugged? The vest. What if there's a tiny transmitter sewn into it somewhere? They'll think Chuck is alive and moving, though mysteriously not answering his phone. They'll send someone to pick him up.

He took the vest off, waded across the creek to where the flow was the strongest, held the vest underwater. It puffed with trapped air, it wasn't going to sink. He could put stones in the pockets; but better, he let it float away, away from him. He watched it sail downstream like some odd bloated jellyfish, thinking, That was possibly not very fucking bright. I am not focusing.

He scooped cold water into his mouth – Don't drink too much, you'll waterlog – wondering if he'd just swallowed a pisspotful of beaver fever. But surely there were no beavers up here. What could you catch from wolves? Rabies but not from drinking. Dissolved moose poop – would that have tiny worms in it that would suck and tunnel? Some kind of liver fluke?

Why are you standing in the water talking out loud? he asked. In plain view. Go along the creek valley, he ordered. Keep to the shrubbery, out of sight. He was counting in his head: how long would it take from the moment Chuck hadn't answered his phone? Maybe two hours, if you factored in the what-went-wrong panic, the meeting they'd call, by remote or otherwise, the messaging, the wheel-spinning and buck-passing and veiled recriminations. All that crap.

Shoulder-high willows here, sheltered from the wind; grasses, bushes. Flies, blackflies, mosquitoes. Drove the caribou mad sometimes, it was said. You'd see them floating across the muskeg on their wide snowshoe feet, running to nowhere. He used some of the bug spray: not too much, he needed to ration it. Worked his way west, towards where he remembered – he thought he remembered – that he would hit the remnants of the Canol Road. Nothing much left of that road now, but as he recalled from his overhead flights, there were a few buildings along here. An old bunkie, a shed or two.

He aimed for a leaning telegraph pole, an archaic wooden one. There was a tangle of wire beside it, and a caribou skeleton, the antlers snarled; farther on, an oil drum, then two oil drums, then a red truck, in almost pristine condition but no tires. Local hunters most likely took them, carted them away on their four-by-fours, back when they could afford the fuel to come in this far for game. They'd have had some use for tires like those. The truck was that rounded silhouette, streamlined, from the 1940s, which was when the road was built. Some bureauscheme to transport oil inland through a pipeline during World War Two, to keep it from being blown up by coastal submarines. They'd brought a whole bunch of soldiers up from the South to build the system, black guys, a lot of them. They'd never been in sub-zero cold and five-day blizzards and twenty-four-hour darkness; they must've thought they were in hell. Local legend had it a third of them went crazy. He could see going crazy here, even without the blizzards.

One foot sore now, must be a blister, but he couldn't stop to look. He hopped along the crumbled ribbon of the road, shrubs taller and nearby, one eye on the sky, and there was the bunkie. Long low building, wood, no door, but still a roof on it.

Quick, into the shadow. Then he waited. It was so quiet.

Plates of junkyard metal, scraps of wood, rusted wire. Beds

must have been over there. Armchair ripped apart. Radio shell, must have been once; the rounded breadloaf shape of that decade. A knob on it still. Spoon. Remains of a stove. Smell of tar. Sunlight through ceiling crack, sifting through dust. Wisps of long-gone desolation, bleached-out grief.

The waiting was worse than the walking. Parts of him throbbed: feet, heart. His breath was so raucous.

Then he wondered if he himself was bugged; if Chuck had done that, just in case – slipped a mini-transmitter into his back pocket when he wasn't looking. If so, he was barbecue: they could be hearing him breathing right now. They'd even have heard him singing. They'd pinpoint him, shoot a mini-rocket at him, and poof.

Nothing to be done.

After – what? an hour? – he saw the ornodrone coming in low. Yes, from the northeast: Norman Wells. It went straight to the crash and made a couple of passes, transmitting visuals. Whoever was controlling it back at its base made a decision. It fired at the broken wing where Chuck lay concealed, couple of thuds. Then it blew up whatever was left of the 'thopter. It was as if Zeb could hear the voices: *Nobody left alive. You sure? Couldn't be. Both of them? Has to be. Anyway, made sure, scorched earth now.*

He held his breath, but the drone didn't follow the trail of the floating vest, and it ignored the derelict Canol bunkie; it merely turned and headed back to where it came from. They'd have wanted to get there first and mop up, then disappear fast before Bearlift Repair showed up.

Which it did, in its usual leisurely fashion. Get a move on, Zeb thought. I'm hungry. Repair hovered over the wreckage, Oh-my-Godding, no doubt, Poor-bastarding, Never-had-a-chancing. Then it, too, departed, back towards Whitehorse.

As the red twilight settled in and the mist gathered and the temperature fell, Zeb made a small fire on top of a slab of metal so he wouldn't burn the place down, inside the building so the smoke would hit the ceiling and disperse. No telltale column. He got himself a little warmer that way. Then he did some cooking. Then he ate.

'Just like that?' says Toby. 'Wasn't it a little abrupt?'

'What?'

'Well, it was . . . I mean . . . '

'You mean it was meat? You pulling a vegetarian?'

'Don't be wicked.'

'You wanted me to say a prayer? Thank you, God, for making Chuck such a fuckwit and having him provide for me in this unselfish though truly unintentional dumbass manner?'

'You're making fun.'

'Then don't go all old Gardener on me.'

'Hey! You're old Gardener yourself! You were Adam One's right-hand man, you were a pillar of . . . '

'Well, I wasn't then. A fucking pillar. Anyway, that's a whole other story.'

Bigfoot

It wasn't that easy, of course. Zeb cut small chunks and used a rusted-wire skewer, and also gave a lecture to himself – *This is Nutrition, capital N! You think you'll make it out of here without Nutrition?* Nonetheless, there were some swallowing issues. Luckily he'd had a lot of practise in distancing himself from things that went into his mouth, most recently the grub at Bearlift – some of which probably *was* grub, a popular protein-enhancer in dried and ground form.

But his first tests of that nature had come earlier, one of the Rev's instructive punishments being that those with potty-mouths should be forced to eat the contents of said potty. How not to smell, how not to taste, how not to think: it was like the See No Evil, Hear No Evil, Speak No Evil blind, deaf, and mute monkeys who sat on the miniature oil drum on his mother's dressing table with their paws clamped over their upper orifices, providing a role model for her that she was happy to follow. *Have you been sick? What's that on your chin?* He said, You're a dog, eat your own vomit. He pushed my head into the ... *Now, Zebulon, don't make up stories. You know your father wouldn't have done such a thing! He loves you!*

Slam the trapdoor on that one, roll a boulder. More to the

point was how to stay warm. There was some crumbling tar-paper in the corner, not much use but some. He spread it on the floor, hoping it would act as a heat-retaining vapour barrier. Dry socks would have helped; he made a little teepee of sticks, draped the damp socks over it near the dying embers of his fire, hoping they wouldn't scorch. Then he heated several medium-sized stones in the coals. He bundled his cold feet inside the down vest, unfolded the two space-age reflecting survival blankets, his own and Chuck's, scrunched himself up inside them, added the hot stones underneath. Keep the core warm, that was Lesson One. Keep the feet from dropping off, always a good plan going forward. Remember that hands without fingers are not much use for tasks requiring small-muscle skills, such as doing up your bootlaces.

Was there grunting outside the bunkie in the dim hours, was there scratching? No door on the place, anything could walk right in. Wolverine, wolf, bear. Maybe the smoke kept them off. Did he sleep? He must have. It got light soon enough.

He woke up singing.

Roamin' here, roamin' there, roamin' in my underwear,
I got a sweetie covered in hair,
She's all pussy everywhere . . .

Some hoarse, twisted stagtime bellowing event. Energizing, though. Instant man-cave bonding. 'Shut up,' he told himself. 'You want to die frivolously?' 'Don't much matter, nobody's looking,' he riposted.

His socks weren't dry, but they were drier. What a fool, he should've taken Chuck's socks from his gone but not forgotten fishbelly feet. He put the socks on, folded up the survival blankets, and stuffed them into his pockets – damn things would never go back into their little envelopes once you took them out – packed up his Practical Pig tool-guy trinkets and the remains of his picnic, then took a cautious look out the door.

Mist everywhere. Grey as an emphysema cough. Just as well because now the flying visibility would be low, a good deterrent for airborne snoopers. Though not so good for Zeb himself because now he wouldn't know where he was going, as such. But surely it was a case of follow the yellow brick road, minus the bricks and with no Emerald City at the end.

There were only two possible directions: northeast to Norman Wells, rough going on a decaying track jumbled with glacier-dumped boulders; or southwest to Whitehorse, through the chilly, misty mountain valleys. Both of those destinations were far, far away, and if he were making odds he wouldn't have bet on himself. But the Whitehorse route hooked up on the Yukon side with a real road, one that could handle motorized vehicles. More chance of a hitchhike pickup there. Or something. Or other.

He set off through the mist, keeping to the degraded gravel surface. If this were a movie he'd be fading to white, then gone, and the credits would be rolling up over him. But not so fast, not so fast, he was still alive. 'Enjoy the moment,' he urged himself.

I love to go a-wandering, along the bums of sluts,
And as I go I love to sing, although they drive me nuts.
Fuckeree, fuckera, fuckeree, fucker ah hah hah hah hah ha . . .

'You are not taking this seriously,' he scolded. 'Oh shut up,' he replied. 'I've heard that a lot.' Talking to yourself, not so positive. Doing it out loud, even worse. Delirium had not set in, however; though how could he be sure?

*

The mist burnt off at eleven a.m. or so; the sky turned blue; a wind began to blow. Two ravens were shadowing him, high in the air, dipping to eyeball him, passing rude remarks about him back and forth. They were waiting for something to begin eating him so they could pitch in and grab a snack: not so deft at making the first incisions, ravens, they always hunted with hunters. He ate a Joltbar, he came to a stream with a washed-out bridge, he had to choose: wet boots or crippled bare feet? He chose the boots, removing his socks first. The water was cold, with an X for Xtra. 'This freezing sucks,' he said, and it did.

Then he had to choose between putting the socks back on and getting them wet or the dubious delight of hiking in boots only, sure to accentuate the blister he already had. The boots themselves would soon be borderline useless.

'You get the picture,' he says. 'On and on. It was that kind of thing all day, with the wind blowing and the sun shining.'

'How far had you gone?' says Toby.

'How to measure? Out there, miles don't count. Let's just say not far enough,' he says. 'And by then I was running on empty.'

He spent the night hunkered down between two boulders, shivering like a timber despite the two crackly metal survival blankets and the fire he'd made from dead willow and creekside mini-birch.

By the time the next pink sunset had come round he'd run out of food. He'd stopped worrying about bears; in fact, he was longing to meet one, a big fat one he could sink his teeth into. He dreamed of little globules of fat sifting down through the air like snow, the pellet-shaped kind of snow, not the flakes; he dreamed of it settling down on him, into his bodily creases and crannies, plumping him up. The brain was 100 per cent cholesterol, so he needed the boost, he hungered for it. He could visualize the inside of his body, the ribs encasing a hollow, a hollow lined with teeth. If he stuck out his tongue in such a fatfall the air would taste like chicken soup.

In the gloaming there was a caribou. It looked at him, he looked at it. Too far away for him to shoot, too fast for him to chase. Those things could skim over the top of the muskeg as if on skis.

The next day was bright and almost hot; things in the distance were wobbly at the edges, like a mirage. Was he hungry any more? Hard to tell. He could sense words rising from him, burning away in the sun. Soon he'd be wordless, and then would he still be able to think? No and yes, yes and no. He'd be up against it, up against everything that filled the space he was moving through, with no glass pane of language coming between him and not-him. Not-him was seeping into him through his defences, through his edges, eating away at form, sending its rootlets into his head like reverse hairs. Soon he'd be overgrown, one with the moss. He needed to keep moving, preserve his outlines, define himself by his own shockwaves, the wake he left in the air. To keep alert, to stay attuned to the, to the what? To whatever might come at him and stop him dead.

At the next washed-out bridge a bear congealed from the low shrubs flanking the river. It was not there and then it was there, and it reared up, startled, offering itself. Was there growling, a roar, a stench? No doubt, but Zeb can't remember. He must have sprayed its eyes with the bear spray and shot it pointblank, but there's no photo record.

Next thing he knew he was butchering it, hacking away at it with his inadequate knife. Blood up to the wrists, then bonanza: the meat, the fur. The two ravens stood at a distance, making

R noises, waiting their turn: gobbets for him, followed by pick-
ings for them.

'Not too much,' he told himself, chewing, recalling the dangers of stuffing yourself on an empty stomach, especially on
something so rich and supersaturated. 'Little at a time.' His voice
came to him muffled, as if he was telephoning himself from
underground. What did this taste like? Who cared? Having
eaten the heart, could he now speak the language of bears?

Picture him the next day or the next or sometime, halfway
there, wherever there is, though he retains the belief that it is in
fact somewhere. He's got new footgear – wraps of hide, fur side
in, tied with crisscross strips like a fashion item in a cave-man
comic. He's got a fur cape, he's got a fur hat, and all of it dou-
bles as sleeping gear, heavy and stinky. He's porting a meat cargo
and a big wad of fat. If he had the time he'd render the fat into
grease and smear it on himself, but as it is he injects it into his
mouth like bite-sized fuel. And it is fuel, he's burning it; he can
feel the heat of it travelling through his veins.

'Goodbye to care,' he sings. The ravens are sticking with him,
shadowing him. Now there are four of them: he's the Pied Piper
of ravens. *'There's a bluebird on my windowsill,'* he sings to them.
His mother went in for cheerful, upbeat retro crap. That, and
perky hymns.

And now, coming towards him along the relatively smooth
stretch of road ahead, far in the distance, there's a cyclist. Some
rugged mountain bike adventurer out of his mind on endorphins. They pass through Whitehorse from time to time,
augment their kits at the outfitter stores, head for the hills to test
their endurance mettle on the Old Canol Trail. They pedal as
far as the bunkie – that's their usual trajectory. Then they pedal
back, thinner, stringier, madder. Some bring tales of alien

abductions, some of talking foxes, some of human voices on the tundra at night. Or semi-human voices. Trying to lure them.

No, two cyclists. One quite a bit ahead. Lovers' tiff, he speculates. The normal thing would be to stick together.

Useful things, mountain bikes. Also pannier packs and whatever might be in them.

Zeb hides in the creekside shrubbery, waits for the first one to go past. A woman, blond, sporting the thighs of a stainless-steel nutcracker goddess in her shiny skintight cyclewear. Under her streamlined helmet she's squinting into the wind, frowning fit to kill with her skimpy eyebrows over her trendy little wind/sun goggles. Away she goes, bumpity-bump, ass taut as an implanted tit, and now here comes the guy, keeping his distance, morose, mouth down at the corners. He's pissed her off, he's feeling the whip. He's burdened with a misery Zeb can alleviate.

'Arrgh,' Zeb yells, or words to that effect.

'Arrgh?' says Toby, laughing.

'You know what I mean,' says Zeb.

Short form: he leaps out of the bushes and onto the guy, making a growly noise, in his bear-fur coverings. There's a strangled yelp from the target, then a metallic toppling. No need to bash the poor sucker, he's out cold anyway. Just take the cycle with its twin saddle packs and make off.

When he looks behind, the girl has stopped. He can picture her recently clamped mouth an open O, the O of woe. Now she'll be sorry she tongue-lashed the sad bugger. She'll thunder-thigh back, kneel and minister, rock and cradle, dab at scrapes, shed tears. The lad will come to and gaze into her ungoggled eyes, the simp, and all will be forgiven, whatever it was. Then they will use her cellphone to call for aid.

What will they say? He can imagine.

*

When he's out of sight, down a hill, and around a corner, he goes through the saddlebags. What a trove: a poker hand of Joltbars, some sort of quasi-cheese product, an extra wind-cheater, a mini-stove with fuel cylinder, a pair of dry socks, spare boots with thick soles – too small, but he'll cut out the toes. A cellphone. Best of all, an identity: he can use some of that. He mashes the cellphone and hides it under a rock, then makes his way sideways over the tundra, squish squish, bike and all.

Luckily there's a palsa that's been ripped open, no doubt by an enraged grolar in search of evasive ground squirrels. Zeb digs himself and the bike into the moist black earth, leaving a van-tage point between clods. After a long damp wait, here comes the 'thopter. It hovers over where the two young cyclists must be hugging and shivering and thanking their lucky stars, and down goes the ladder, and, after a time, up go the lovers, and then they're carried away in the slow, low 'thopter, flippity-flop, blimpity-blimp. What a story they will have to tell.

And they tell it. Once in Whitehorse, having shed his bearskin wrappings some time back and sunk them in a pond, having changed into the fresh gear provided by Fortune, having grabbed a hitchhike, having freshened up considerably and altered his hairstyle, having hacked certain features of the cyclist's identity and run some cash through a backdoor known to him by memory, and having swiftly topped up his own cash flow thereby, he reads all about it.

Sasquatches are real after all, and they've migrated to the Mackenzie Mountain Barrens. No, it couldn't have been a bear because bears can't ride mountain bikes. Anyway, this thing was seven feet tall with eyes almost like a man's, and it smelled ter-rible, and it showed signs of almost-human intelligence. There's even a picture, taken on the girl's cellphone: a brown blob, with a red circle around it to signal which of the many brown blobs in the picture is the significant one.

Within a week, Bigfoot-believers from around the world have formed a posse and mounted an expedition to the site of the discovery, and are combing the area for footprints and tufts of hair and piles of dung. Soon, says their leader, they will have a batch of definitive DNA, and then the scoffers will be shown up for the corrupt, fossilized, obsolete truth-deniers that they are.

Very soon.

The Story of Zeb and
Thank You and Good Night

Thank you for bringing me this fish.

Thank you means ... *Thank you* means you did something good for me. Or something you thought was good. And that good thing was giving me a fish. So that made me happy, but the part that really made me happy was that you wanted me to be happy. That's what *Thank you* means.

No, you don't need to give me another fish. I am happy enough for now.

Don't you want to hear about Zeb?

Then you must listen.

After Zeb came back from the high and tall mountains with snow on top, and after he had taken off the skin of the bear and put it on himself, he said Thank You to the bear. To the spirit of the bear.

Because the bear didn't eat him, but allowed him to eat it instead, and also because it gave him its fur skin to put on.

A *spirit* is the part of you that doesn't die when your body dies.

Dies is . . . it's what the fish do when they are caught and then cooked.

No, it is not only fish that die. People do it as well.

Yes. Everyone.

Yes, you as well. Sometime. Not yet. Not for a long time.

I don't know why. Crake made it that way.

Because . . .

Because if nothing ever died, but everything had more and more babies, the world would get too full and there wouldn't be any room.

No, you will not be cooked on a fire when you die.

Because you are not a fish.

No, the bear was not a fish either. And it died in a bear way. Not in a fish way. So it was not cooked on a fire.

Yes, maybe Zeb said Thank You to Oryx too. As well as to the bear.

Because Oryx let Zeb eat one of her Children. Oryx knows that some of her Children eat other ones; that is the way they are made. The ones with sharp teeth. So she knew that Zeb could eat one of her Children too, because he was very hungry.

I don't know whether Zeb said Thank You to Crake. Maybe you could ask Zeb that, the next time you see him. Anyway, Crake is not in charge of bears. Oryx is in charge of bears.

Zeb put on the bear's fur to keep warm.

Because he was very cold. Because it was colder there. Because of the mountains all around, with snow on the top.

Snow is water that is frozen into little pieces called snowflakes. *Frozen* is when water becomes hard like rock.

No, snowflakes have nothing to do with Snowman-the-Jimmy. I don't know why part of his name is almost the same as a snowflake.

I am doing this thing with my hands on my forehead because

I have a headache. A headache is when there is a pain in your head.

Thank you. I am sure purring would help. But it would also help if you would stop asking so many questions.

Yes, I think Amanda must have a headache too. Or some sort of ache. Perhaps you could do some purring for her.

I think that's enough of the story of Zeb for tonight. Look, the moon is rising. It's your bedtime.

I know you don't have beds. But I have a bed. So it is my bedtime now. Good night.

Good night means that I hope you will sleep well, and wake up safely in the morning, and that nothing bad will happen to you.

Well, such as . . . I can't think what sort of bad things might happen to you.

Good night.

Scars

Scars

She's tried to be discreet, sneaking off alone every night after she's told the Crakers their story, then joining Zeb once out of eyesight. But she's not fooling anyone, or anyone among the humans.

Naturally, they see it as funny. Or the younger ones do – Swift Fox, Lotis Blue, Croze and Shackie, Zunzuncito. Even Ren, probably. Even Amanda. Romance among the chronologically challenged is giggle fodder. For the youthful, lovelorn and wrinkly don't blend, or not without farce. There's a moment past which the luscious and melting becomes the crusty and wizened, the fertile sea becomes the barren sand, and they must feel she's passed that moment. Brewing herbs, gathering mushrooms, applying maggots, tending bees, removing warts – beldam's roles. Those are her proper vocations.

As for Zeb, he's probably less comic to them than puzzling. From their socio-bio vantage point, he should be doing what alpha males do best: jumping the swooning nubiles that are his by right, knocking them up, passing his genes along via females who can actually parturiate, unlike her. So why is he wasting his precious sperm packet? they must wonder. Instead of, for instance, investing it wisely in the ovarian offerings of Swift Fox.

Which is almost certainly that girl's take on things, judging from the body language: the eyelash play, the tit thrusts, the hair-tuft flinging, the armpit display. She might as well be flashing a blue bottom, like the Crakers. Baboons in spate.

Stop that, Toby, she tells herself. This is how it starts, among the closed circles of the marooned, the shipwrecked, the besieged: jealousy, dissention, a breach in the groupthink walls. Then the entry of the foe, the murderer, the shadow slipping in through the door we forgot to lock because we were distracted by our darker selves: nursing our minor hatreds, indulging our petty resentments, yelling at one another, tossing the crockery.

Beleaguered groups are prone to such festering: such back-biting, such infighting. At the Gardeners, they'd held Deep Mindfulness sessions about this very subject.

Ever since they've been lovers, Toby has been dreaming that Zeb is gone. In real life he is in fact gone while she dreams, as there isn't enough room for both of them on Toby's single-bed-sized slab in her broom closet of a room. So in the middle of each night Zeb sneaks off like someone in an ancient English country-house farce, groping in the darkness back to his own cramped cubicle.

But in the dreams he really is gone – gone far away, nobody knows where – and Toby is standing outside the cobb-house fence, looking down the road, now overgrown with kudzu vines and choked with parts of broken houses and smashed-up vehicles. There's a soft bleating sound, or is it weeping? 'He won't be back,' says a watercolour voice. 'He won't ever be back.'

It's a woman's voice: is it Ren, is it Amanda, is it Toby herself? The scenario is sweetly sentimental, like a pastel greeting card – awake, she'd be annoyed by it, but in dreams there is no irony. She cries so much that her clothes are damp with tears, luminous tears that flicker like blue-green gasfire in what is now becoming the darkness, or is she in a cave? But then a large cat-like animal comes to console her. It rubs up against her, purring like the wind.

She wakes to find a small Craker boy in the room with her. He's lifted the edge of the damp sheet that entwists her and is gently stroking her leg. He smells of oranges, and of something else. Citrus air freshener. They all smell like this, but the young ones more.

'What are you doing?' she asks as calmly as she can. My toe-nails are so dirty, she thinks. Dirty and jagged. Nail scissors: put them on the gleaning list. Her skin is coarse beside the pristine skin on the hand of this child. Is he glowing from within, or is his skin so fine-grained it reflects the light?

'Oh Toby, you have legs underneath,' says the boy. 'Like us.'

'Yes,' she says. 'I do.'

'Do you have breasts, Oh Toby?'

'Yes, I have those as well,' she says, smiling.

'Are there two? Two breasts?'

'Yes,' she says, resisting the urge to add, 'so far.' Is he expecting one breast, or three, or maybe four or six, like a dog? Has he ever seen a dog up close?

'Will a baby come out from between your legs, Oh Toby? After you turn blue?'

What is he asking? Whether non-Craker people like her can have babies, or whether she herself might have one? 'If I were younger, then a baby might come out,' she says. 'But not now.' Though her age isn't the deciding factor. If her whole life had been different. If she hadn't needed the money. If she'd lived in another universe.

'Oh Toby,' says the Craker boy, 'what sickness do you have? Are you hurt?' He puts up his beautiful arms to hug her. Are those tears in his strange green eyes?

'It's all right,' she says. 'I'm not hurt any more.' She'd sold some of her eggs to pay the rent, back in her pleebland days, before the God's Gardeners had taken her in. There'd been infection: all her future children, precluded. Surely she'd buried that particular sadness many years ago. If not, she ought to bury it. In view of the total situation – the situation of what used to be thought of as the human race – such emotions ought to be dismissed as meaningless.

She's about to add, 'I have scars, inside me,' but she stops herself. *What is a scar, Oh Toby?* That would be the next question. Then she'd have to explain what a scar is. *A scar is like writing on your body. It tells about something that once happened to you, such as a cut on your skin where blood came out. What is writing, Oh Toby? Writing is when you make marks on a piece of paper – on a stone – on a flat surface, like the sand on the beach, and each of the marks means a sound, and the sounds joined together mean a word, and the words joined together mean . . . How do you make this writing, Oh Toby? You make it with a keyboard, or no – once you made it with a pen or a pencil, a pencil is a . . . Or you make it with a stick. Oh Toby, I do not understand. You make a mark with a stick on your skin, you cut your skin open and then it is a scar, and that scar turns into a voice? It speaks, it tells us things? Oh Toby, can we hear what the scar says? Show us how to make these scars that talk!*

No, she should stay away from the whole scar business. Otherwise she might inspire the Crakers to start carving themselves up to see if they can let out the voices.

'What's your name?' she says to the little boy.

'My name is Blackbeard,' says the child gravely. Blackbeard, the notorious murdering pirate? This sweet child? A child who will never have a beard when he grows up because Crake did away with body hair in his new species. A lot of the Crakers have odd names. According to Zeb, Crake named them – Crake, with his warped sense of humour. Though why shouldn't their names be odd, to go with their general oddity?

'I am very happy to meet you, Oh Blackbeard,' she says.

'Do you eat your droppings, Oh Toby?' says Blackbeard. 'As we do? To digest our leaves better?'

What droppings? Edible poo? No one warned her about this! 'It is time to go and see your mother, Oh Blackbeard,' says Toby. 'She must be worried about you.'

'No, Oh Toby. She knows I am with you. She says you are good and kind.' He smiles, showing perfect little teeth: enchant-ment. They are all so attractive – like airbrushed cosmetic ads. 'You are good like Crake. You are kind like Oryx. Do you have wings, Oh Toby?' He cranes his neck, trying to see behind her. Maybe the earlier hug was only a stealthy way of feeling her back for the feathered stubs that might be sprouting there.

'No,' says Toby. 'No wings.'

'I will mate with you when I am bigger,' says Blackbeard. He offers this heroically. 'Even if you are . . . even if you are only a little blue. Then you will have a baby! It will grow in your bone cave! You will be happy!'

Only a little blue. It must mean that he recognizes her com-parative age, though *old* is not something the Crakers have a word for. 'Thank you, Oh Blackbeard,' says Toby. 'Now run along. I have to eat my breakfast. And I must go and visit Jimmy – I must visit Snowman-the-Jimmy, to see if his sickness is better.' She sits up and plants her feet squarely on the floor, a sign for the boy to leave.

Though not a sign he understands. 'What is *breakfast*, Oh Toby?' he says. She forgot: these people don't have meals as such. They graze, like herbivores.

He eyes her binoculars, pokes her stack of bedsheets. Now

he's stroking her rifle, where it stands in the corner. It's something a normal human child might do: idle fiddling, curious handling. 'Is this your breakfast?'

'Don't touch that,' she says a little sharply. 'That is not breakfast, that is a special thing for . . . Breakfast is what we eat in the morning – the people like me, with extra skins.'

'Is it a fish?' says the boy. 'This breakfast?'

'Sometimes,' says Toby. 'But for breakfast today, I will eat part of an animal. An animal with fur. Perhaps I will eat its leg. There will be a smelly bone inside. You wouldn't want to see such a smelly bone, would you?' she says. That will surely get rid of him.

'No,' says the child dubiously. He wrinkles his nose. He seems intrigued, however: who wouldn't want to peek from behind the curtain at the trolls' revolting feasts?

'Then you should go away,' says Toby.

Still he lingers. 'Snowman-the-Jimmy says the bad people in the chaos ate the Children of Oryx,' he says. 'They killed them and killed them, and ate them and ate them. They were always eating them.'

'Yes, they were,' says Toby, 'but they were eating them in the wrong way.'

'Were the two bad men eating them in the wrong way too? The ones who ran away?'

'Yes,' says Toby. 'They were.'

'How are you eating them, Oh Toby? The legs of the Children?' His huge eyes are fixed on her as if she's about to sprout fangs and pounce on him.

'The right way,' she says, hoping he won't ask what the right way is.

'I saw a smelly bone. It was behind the kitchen. Is it breakfast? Do the bad men eat such bones?' says Blackbeard.

'Yes,' says Toby. 'But they do other bad things too. Many bad things. Much worse things. We must all be very careful, and not go into the forest by ourselves. If you see those bad men or anyone like them, you must come and tell me right away. Or tell Crozier, or Rebecca, or Ren, or Ivory Bill. Any of us.' She's gone over this point several times with all of the Crakers, the adults too, but she's not sure they've taken it in. They gaze at her and nod, chewing slowly as if thinking, but they don't seem frightened. It's worrying, their lack of fear.

'Not Snowman-the-Jimmy or Amanda,' the boy says. 'We can't tell them. Because they are sick.' At least he's grasped that much. He pauses as if considering. 'But Zeb will make the bad men go away. Then everything will be safe.'

'Yes,' says Toby. 'Then everything will be safe.' Already the Crakers have constructed a formidable set of beliefs about Zeb. Soon he'll be all-potent and able to fix every ill; and that could be troublesome, because of course he can't. Not even for me, thinks Toby.

But the name of Zeb is reassuring to Blackbeard. He smiles again, lifts his hand, gives a little wave, like a president of old, like a queen in a cavalcade, like a movie star. Where has he picked up that gesture? Now he's sidling backwards through the doorway. He doesn't take his eyes off Toby until he's around the corner.

Did I scare him? she thinks. Will he go back to the others and tell them disgusting marvels, as real children – as children do?

Violet Biolet

Outside the main house the day is underway. The others must already have had their breakfasts, though Swift Fox and Ivory Bill are still at the table, engaged no doubt in some kind of arcane flirtation, she for practise, he in pathetic earnest.

Toby looks around for Zeb, but he is nowhere to be seen; maybe he's taking a shower. Crozier is just setting off with the Mo'Hair flock; Zunzuncito is with him, toting a spraygun, covering his back. Jimmy's hammock is under the tree, watched over by a trio of Crakers.

Lotis Blue and Ren are working on an addition to the cobb house. The MaddAddamites have voted to expand the number of sleeping cubicles; they'll make the new ones roomier, more like a real house. The core structure was built as a demonstration of olden-day ways: ersatz antiquity, like a dinosaur made of cement. The Tree of Life Natural Materials Exchange used to be held in this space; Toby remembers coming here with the God's Gardeners to peddle their recycled soap and their vinegar and honey and mushrooms and rooftop vegetables, back when there had still been buying and people to buy things, selling and people to sell them.

I ought to look around for some bees, she thinks. There must be escapees, living in the trees. It would be calming as well as useful to tend a few hives.

The cobb-house construction has to be done in stages. This morning Ren and Lotis Blue are mixing up the mud, straw, and sand in a plastic wading pool decorated with Mickey Mice. The wood frame is in place, the layers of cobb are being added day by day. Drying each layer is a problem in view of the afternoon thunderstorms, but luckily they've been able to glean some plastic sheeting for coverups.

Amanda sits near the two of them, hands in her lap, doing nothing. She does nothing a lot. Maybe it's slow healing, Toby thinks, like slow cooking. Maybe the end result will be better that way. But at least she's gained some weight. She has been making some effort over the past few days: pulling out a weed or two, culling the odd slug or snail. In the old Edencliff Rooftop Garden days, they'd have relocated Our Fellow Vegetable Eaters by throwing them down onto the street – slugs, too, had a right to live, went the mantra, though not in inappropriate locations such as salad bowls, where they might be harmed by chewing. But now their numbers are too overwhelming – every plant seems to generate slugs and snails as if spontaneously – so by common though unspoken agreement they're being dropped into salt water.

Amanda seems to enjoy that slightly, despite the writhing and frothing. But the cobb-house building work is too much for her. She used to be so strong: nothing used to frighten her. She'd been a tough pleebrat, she'd lived by her wits, she could handle anything. Of the two of them, Ren was the weaker, the more timid. Whatever has happened to Amanda – whatever was done to her by the Painballers – must have been extreme.

Several Craker kids are watching the mud mixing. No doubt they're asking questions. *Why are you doing that? Are you making a chaos? What are those, with the round black things on their heads?*

What is a mickeymouse? *But they do not look like mice, we have seen mice, mice do not have big white hands,* and so forth. Every new thing they discover in the territory of the MaddAddamites is a source of wonder for them. Yesterday Crozier managed to glean a package of cigarettes during his shepherding stroll, and the Crakers have not got over it. *He set fire to a white stick! He put it in his mouth! He breathed in the smoke! Why did you do that, Oh Crozier? Smoke is not for breathing, smoke is for cooking a fish,* and so on.

'Just tell them it's a Crake thing,' said Toby, so Crozier did. The Crake gambit was one-size-fits-all.

Some of the Crakers – a number of the women, several of the smaller kids – are over in the erstwhile playground outside the cobb-house boundary fence, munching away at the kudzu vines draping the swing set. Kudzu is one of their favourite plants, which shows foresight on the part of Crake because there won't be a shortage of kudzu any time soon. They've got the red plastic slide almost uncovered, and the children are stroking it as if it's alive. Who remembered the swing set was under there, before they started gnawing?

Toby heads for the violet biolet, not only because she needs to but also because she doesn't want to arrive at the breakfast table before Swift Fox leaves it. She consciously suppresses the word *slut*: a woman should not use that word about another woman, especially with no exact cause.

Really? says her inner slut-uttering voice. You've seen the way she looks at Zeb. Eyelashes like Venus flytraps, and that sideways leer of the irises, like some outdated cut-rate prostibot commercial: Bacteria-Resistant Fibres, 100% Fluid-Flushing, Lifelike Moans, ClenchOMeter for Optimal Satisfaction.

She takes a breath, calls on her Gardener meditation training. She visualizes her anger pushing out through her skin like a snail horn, then lets the small bud of fury wither and fall away. She smiles gently in the direction of Swift Fox, thinking, All you want is a quick jump, you want to snag him just to show you can. Nail him up on your trophy wall. You know nothing about him, you can't truly value him, he isn't yours, you don't know how long I waited . . .

Which counts for nothing. Nobody cares. There's no fairness, there's no ownership. She has no claims. If Zeb tumbles into bed with Swift Fox – even if he tiptoes into that bed, even if he oozes into it – what she is entitled to say about that is exactly nothing. For all she knows he's double-dipping already, leaving her in affectionate sleepy-time mode – though maybe a little too much like best pals, with a little too much camaraderie between them, no? – but all the time secretly still hungry; then ducking outside, then inside through a different doorway to slide himself voraciously into the voracious Swift Fox.

It doesn't bear thinking about, so she won't think about it. *Will not* think. Wills herself *not*.

The violet biolets are part of the original park installation: three stalls for men, three for women. Their solar cells are still operating, running the ultraviolet LEDs and the small aerating-fan motors. As long as the biolets are still functioning, the MaddAddamites won't have to dig outhouse pits. Luckily there's lots of toilet paper to be gleaned in the nearby streets, as it wasn't an item heavily looted during the pillaging phase of the plague. What would you do with a skid of toilet paper? You couldn't get drunk on it.

The walls inside the biolet are still covered with pleebland inscriptions: several generations of them, one layer on top of another. There'd been a time when those still devoted to some norm of propriety had tried to paint the words over, but a few kids bent on self-expressive anarchy could destroy in an hour a white surface it had taken a crew three days to blandify.

To Daryn, Im ur bitch, ur my King,
I <3 you more than anything
Fk the Corps
Loris a stuck up cunt
I hope ur raped by 100000 pit bulls

People who write on washroom walls, Shld roll their shit in little balls, And those who read these words of wit, Shld have to eat those balls of shit

Call me/ Best for ur $/ Ull scream 24/7 & die in a pond of Cum
STAY OUT MY WAY A HAT OR ILL KNIFE U

And shyly, unfinished: *Try love the World needs*

What to eat, where to shit, how to take shelter, who and what to kill: are these the basics? thinks Toby. Is this what we've come to, or come down to; or else come back to?

And who do you love? And who loves you? And who loves you not? And, come to think of it, who seriously hates you.

Blink

Under the trees Jimmy is still slumbering. Toby checks his pulse – calmer; changes his maggots – the wound on his foot has stopped festering; and pours some mushroom elixir into him, mixed with a little Poppy.

An oval of chairs is arranged around the hammock, as if Jimmy is the central offering at a feast: a giant salmon, a boar on a platter. Three Crakers are purring over him, taking turns: two men and a woman, gold, ivory, ebony. It's a different three every few hours. Do they have only so much purring quotient, are they like batteries that have to be recharged? Naturally they need time off to graze and water themselves, but does the purring itself have a sort of electrical frequency?

We'll never know, thinks Toby, holding Jimmy's nose to make him open his mouth: no way of wiring up their brains for scientific studies, not any more. Which is lucky for them. In the olden days they'd have been kidnapped from the Paradice Project dome by some rival Corp, then injected and jolted and probed and sliced apart to see how they were put together. What made them tick, what made them purr, what made them click. What, if anything, made them sick. They'd have ended up as slabs of DNA in a freezer.

Jimmy swallows, sighs; his left hand twitches. 'How has he been today?' Toby asks the three Crakers. 'Has he been awake at all?'

'No, Oh Toby,' says the gold-coloured man. 'He is travelling.' This one has bright red hair, long slender limbs; despite the skin colour, he looks like something from a children's storybook. An Irish folktale.

'But now he has stopped,' says the ebony man. 'He has climbed into a tree.'

'Not his real tree,' says the ivory woman. 'Not the tree he lives in.'

'He has gone to sleep in this tree,' says the ebony man.

'You mean, he's sleeping inside his sleep?' says Toby. This seems wrong: it shouldn't be possible. 'In the tree in his dream?'

'Yes, Oh Toby,' says the ivory woman. All three of them gaze at her with their lambent green eyes, as if she's twirling a piece of string and they are bored cats.

'Perhaps he will sleep for a long time,' says the golden man. 'He is stuck there, in the tree. If he will not wake up and travel to here, he will not wake up at all.'

'But he's getting better!' says Toby.

'He is afraid,' says the ivory woman in a matter-of-fact voice. 'He is afraid of what is in this world. He is afraid of the bad men, he is afraid of the Pig Ones. He doesn't want to be awake.'

'Can you talk to him?' says Toby. 'Can you tell him it's better to be awake?' No harm in trying: maybe they have some form of inaudible communication that might reach Jimmy, wherever he is. A wavelength, a vibration.

But now they aren't looking at her. They're looking at Ren and Lotis Blue, who are walking over with Amanda in tow, sheltering behind them.

The three of them sit down on the empty chairs, Amanda hesitantly. Ren and Lotis Blue are muddy from their building activities, but Amanda is pristine. The other two give her a shower every morning, choose a fresh bedsheet for her, braid her hair.

'We thought we'd take a break from the house,' says Ren. 'See how Jimmy – see how Snowman-the-Jimmy is doing.'

The ivory woman smiles widely at them, the two men smile less widely: the Craker men are nervous around the younger cobb-house women now. Ever since they've learned that rambunctious group copulation is not acceptable, they don't know what's expected of them. They begin conferring together in low voices, leaving the ivory woman as the sole purrer.

Is she blue? One is blue. Two others were blue, we joined our blue to their blue but we did not make them happy. They are not like our women, they are not happy, they are broken. Did Crake make them? Why did he make them that way, so they are not happy? Oryx will take care of them. Will Oryx take care of them, if they are not like our women? When Snowman-the-Jimmy wakes up, we will ask him these things.

I'd like to be a fly on the wall, thinks Toby. Listening to Jimmy justifying the ways of Crake towards men, or semi-men.

'Will Jimmy – will Snowman-the-Jimmy be okay?' asks Lotis Blue.

'I think so,' says Toby. 'It will depend on his . . . ' She doesn't want to say 'immune system' because the Crakers will hear. (*What is an* immune system? *It is something you have inside yourself that helps you and makes you strong. Where can we find an immune system? Is it from Crake, will he send us an immune system?*, and so on.) 'It depends on his dreaming.' No comment from the Crakers: so far, so good. 'But I'm sure he'll wake up soon.'

'He needs to eat,' says Lotis Blue. 'He's so thin! He can't live on nothing.'

'You can go a long time without food,' says Ren. 'They did fasts, at the Gardeners? You can go for days. Weeks.' She leans over and reaches out, smoothing back Jimmy's hair. 'I wish we could give him a shampoo,' she says. 'He's getting rank.'

'I think he just said something,' says Lotis Blue.

'It was only a mumble. We could sponge him off,' says Ren. 'Like, a sponge bath.' She leans closer. 'He looks a bit shrivelled. Poor Jimmy. I hope he doesn't die.'

'I'm hydrating him,' says Toby. 'And there's the honey, I'm feeding him that.' Why is she sounding like a head nurse? 'We do wash him,' she says defensively. 'We do it every day.'

'Well anyway, he's not so feverish,' says Lotis Blue. 'He's cooling down. Don't you think?'

Ren feels Jimmy's forehead. 'I don't know,' she says. 'Jimmy, can you hear me?' They all watch: Jimmy doesn't twitch. 'I'd say he's warm. Amanda? See what you think.' She's trying to involve her, thinks Toby. Get her interested in something. Ren was always a kindly child.

If she is blue, the Lotis one, should we mate with her? No, we should not. Do not sing to them, do not pick flowers for them, do not wag your penis at them. These women scream with fright, they do not choose us even if we give them a flower, they do not like a wagging penis. We do not make them happy, we do not know why they scream. But sometimes they do not scream with fright, sometimes they . . .

'I need to lie down,' says Amanda. She stands up, walks unsteadily away towards the cobb house.

'I'm really worried about her,' says Ren. 'She threw up this morning, she couldn't eat any breakfast. That's extreme Fallow.'

'Maybe it's a bug,' says Lotis Blue. 'Something she ate. We really need a better way of washing the dishes, I don't think the water is . . .'

'Look,' says Ren. 'He blinked.'

'He is hearing you,' says the ivory woman. 'He is hearing your voice, and now he is walking. He is happy, he wants to be with you.'

'With me?' says Ren. 'Really?'

'Yes. Look, he is smiling.' There is indeed a smile, or the trace of a smile, thinks Toby. Though maybe it's only gas, as with babies.

The ivory woman waves away a mosquito that has settled on Jimmy's mouth. 'Soon he will be awake,' she says.

Zeb in the Dark

Zeb in the Dark

It's evening. Toby has dodged her storytime session with the Crakers. Those stories take a lot out of her. Not only does she have to put on the absurd red hat and eat the ritual fish, which isn't always what you'd call cooked, but there's so much she needs to invent. She doesn't like to tell lies, not deliberately, not lies as such, but she skirts the darker and more tangled corners of reality. It's like trying to keep toast from burning while still having it transform into toast.

'I'll come tomorrow,' she told them. 'Tonight I must do an important thing for Zeb.'

'What is the important thing you must do, Oh Toby? We would like to be your helpers.' At least they didn't ask what *important* means. They seem to have put together an idea of it: somewhere between dangerous and delicious.

'Thank you,' she said. 'But it is a thing that only I can do.'

'Is it about the bad men?' asked little Blackbeard.

'No,' Toby said. 'We have not seen the bad men for many days. Maybe they have gone far away. But we must still be careful, and tell others if we see them.'

One of the Mo'Hairs has gone missing, Crozier has told her privately – the red-headed one with the braids – but it may simply have strayed off while grazing. Or else a liobam got it.

Or something worse, thinks Toby: something human.

The day has been stifling. Even the afternoon thunderstorm hasn't cleared away the humidity. Under normal conditions – but what is *normal*? – lust should have been drained of its supercharge by this weather; muffled, as if under a damp mattress. She and Zeb should have been limp, enervated, exhausted. But instead they'd snuck away from the others even earlier than usual, slippery with longing, every pore avid, every capillary suffused, and thrashed around like newts in a puddle.

Now it's deep twilight. Purple darkness wells up from the earth, bats flit past like leathery butterflies, night flowers open, musking the air. They're sitting outside in the kitchen garden for the evening breeze, what there is of it. Their fingers are loosely entwined; Toby can feel, still, a small current of electricity moving between them. Tiny iridescent moths are shimmering around their heads. What do we smell like to them? she wonders. Like mushrooms? Like crushed petals? Like dew?

'Help me out here,' says Toby. 'I need more to go on, for the Crakers. They're insatiable on the subject of you.'

'Like what?'

'You're their hero. They want your life story. Your miraculous origins, your supernatural deeds, your favourite recipes. You're like royalty to them.'

'Why me?' says Zeb. 'I thought Crake did away with all that. They aren't supposed to be interested.'

'Well, they are. They're obsessed with you. You're their rock star.'

'Lord fuck a dog. Can't you just make up some piece of crap?'

'They cross-examine like lawyers,' says Toby. 'At the very least I need the basics. The raw material.' Does she want to know about Zeb for the sake of the Crakers, or for herself? Both. But mostly for herself.

'I'm an open book,' says Zeb.

'Don't be evasive.'

Zeb sighs. 'I hate going back to all that. I had to live it, I don't like reliving it. Who cares?'

'I do,' says Toby. And so do you, she thinks. You still do care. 'I'm listening.'

'Persistent, aren't you?'

'I've got all night. So, you were born . . .'

'Yeah, admitted.' Another sigh. 'Okay. First you need to understand: we got the wrong mothers.'

'Wrong, how?' she says to the face she can barely see. A plane of cheekbone, a shadow, a glint of eye.

The Story of the Birth of Zeb

I have put on the red hat of Snowman. I have eaten the fish. I have listened to the shiny thing. Now I will tell the story of the birth of Zeb.

You don't have to sing.

Zeb did not come from Crake, not like Snowman. And he wasn't made by Oryx, not like rabbits. He was born, the same way you are born. He grew in a bone cave, just like you, and came out through a bone tunnel, just like you.

Because underneath our clothing skins, we are the same as you. Almost the same.

No, we do not turn blue. Though we might smell blue sometimes. But our bone cave is the same.

I don't think we need to discuss blue penises right now.

I know they are bigger. Thank you for pointing that out.

Yes, we do have breasts. The women do.

Yes, two.

Yes, on the front.

No, I will not show them to you right now.

Because this story is not about breasts. This story is about Zeb.

*

A very long time ago, in the days of the chaos – before Crake cleared it all away – Zeb lived in the bone cave of his mother. And Oryx took care of him there, as she takes care of all those who live in the bone caves. And then he travelled into this world through the bone tunnel. And then he was a baby, and then he grew.

And he had an older brother whose name was Adam. But Adam's mother was not the same mother as the mother of Zeb.

Because when Adam was very young, Adam's mother ran away from Adam's father.

Running away means she went very quickly to a different place. Though she may not have done any running as such. Perhaps she walked, or drove in a . . . So Adam never saw her any more.

Yes, I'm sure it was sad for him.

Because she wanted to mate with more than one male, not only with Zeb's father. Or that is what Zeb's father told him.

Yes, it was a good thing to want, and she would have been happy if she could be living with you. She could mate with four males at once, like you. She would be very happy then!

But Zeb's father did not see it that way.

Because he had done a thing with her called *marriage*, and with marriage there was supposed to be one male for each female and one female for each male. Although sometimes there were more. But there were not supposed to be.

Because it was the chaos. It was a thing of the chaos. That is why you can't understand it.

Marriage is gone now. Crake cleared it away because he thought it was stupid.

Stupid means things Crake didn't like. There were a lot of things Crake thought were stupid.

Yes, good, kind Crake. I will stop telling this story if you sing. Because it makes me forget what I am telling.

Thank you.

So then Adam's father found a new woman to have marriage with, and Zeb was born. Now little Adam was not lonely, because he had a brother. And Adam and Zeb helped each other. But Zeb's father was sometimes hurtful to them.

I don't know why. He thought pain was good for children.

No, he was not as bad as the two bad men who were hurtful to Amanda. But he was not a kind person.

I don't know why some people then were not kind. It was a thing of the chaos.

And Zeb's mother was often taking a nap, or doing other things that interested her. She was not very interested in small children. And she said, 'You will be the death of me.'

Death of me is hard to explain. It meant she was displeased with the things they were doing.

No, Zeb did not kill his mother. *Death of me* is just a thing she said. She said it a lot.

Why did she say it if it wasn't true? It was ... those people talked that way. It wasn't true or not true. It was in between. It was a way of telling about a feeling you might have. It was a manner of speaking. A *manner of speaking* means ...

You are right. Zeb's mother was not a kind person either. Sometimes she helped Zeb's father lock Zeb up in a closet.

Lock up means ... *closet* means ... It was a very small room and it was dark in there, and Zeb couldn't get out. Or they thought he couldn't get out. But soon Zeb learned a lot about opening closed doors.

No. His mother couldn't sing. Not like your mothers. And your fathers. And you.

But Zeb could sing. That is one of the things he did when he was locked inside the closet. He sang.

The PetrOleum Brats

Zeb's mother, Trudy, was the goody-goody, and Adam's mother, Fenella, was the shag-anything trashbunny. Or that was the story told by Trudy and the Rev. Since the two of them claimed that Zeb was so freaking useless and they were so righteous, naturally he thought he'd been adopted, since he couldn't possibly have come from two such pristine sources of DNA as them.

He used to daydream that he'd been left behind by Fenella, who must have been his real, worthless mother. She'd been forced to flee in a hurry, and hadn't been able to tote him along when she was running away – she'd dropped him on the doorstep in a cardboard box, to be taken in and trodden under-foot by this Trudy person, who was unrelated to him and lying about it. Fenella – wherever she was – deeply regretted her abandonment of him, and was planning to come back and get him once she could manage it. Then they would go far, far away together, and do absolutely everything on the long list of things that were frowned upon by the Rev. He saw them sitting on a park bench together, eating licorice twists and happily picking their noses. Just for instance.

But that was when he was little. Once he figured out genetics, he decided that Trudy must've secretly had it off with some fix-it guy with a wrench who doubled as a housebreaker and petty thief. Or else a gardener: she used to snaffle illegal Tex-Mex guys with black hair, like Zeb's. She'd pay them not enough to wheelbarrow soil around, dig up shrubs, dump more rocks on her rock garden, which was the only thing that really held her attention in the way of nurturing and tending, as far as Zeb could tell. She was always out there with one of those little fork-tongued weeders or messing up ant nests with hot vinegar.

' 'Course I could have inherited the criminality from the Rev, he had the chromosomes for it,' says Zeb. 'He just tarted up his misdemeanours and made them look respectable, whereas I was the real raw deal. He was furtive and sly, I was right in the face.'

'Don't be too down on yourself,' says Toby.

'You don't get it, babe,' says Zeb. 'I'm bragging.'

The Rev had his very own cult. That was the way to go in those days if you wanted to coin the megabucks and you had a facility for ranting and bullying, plus golden-tongued whip-'em-up preaching, and you lacked some other grey-area but highly marketable skill, such as derivatives trading. Tell people what they want to hear, call yourself a religion, put the squeeze on for contributions, run your own media outlets and use them for robocalls and slick online campaigns, befriend or threaten politicians, evade taxes. You had to give the guy some credit. He was twisted as a pretzel, he was a tinfoil-halo shit-nosed frogstomping king rat asshole, but he wasn't stupid.

As witness his success. By the time Zeb came along, the Rev had a megachurch, all glass slabbery and pretend oak pews and faux granite, out on the rolling plains. The Church of PetrOleum, affiliated with the somewhat more mainstream Petrobaptists. They were riding high for a while, about the time accessible oil became scarce and the price shot up and desperation among the pleebs set in. A lot of top Corps guys would turn up at the church as guest speakers. They'd thank the Almighty for blessing the world with fumes and toxins, cast their eyes upwards as if gasoline came from heaven, look pious as hell.

'Pious as hell,' says Zeb. 'I've always liked that phrase. In my humble view, pious and hell are the flip sides of the same coin.'

'Humble view?' says Toby. 'Since when?'

'Since I met you,' says Zeb. 'Just one glance at your fine ass, one of the miracles of creation, and I realize what a shoddy construction I am by comparison. Next you'll have me scrubbing the floor with my tongue. Give a guy a break or I might get shy.'

'Okay, I'll allow one humble view,' says Toby. 'Tell on.'

'Can I kiss your clavicle?'

'In a minute,' says Toby. 'After you get to the point.' She's new to flirting, but she's enjoying it.

'You want my point? You talking dirty?'

'Rain check. You can't stop now,' says Toby.

'Okay, deal.'

The Rev had nailed together a theology to help him rake in the cash. Naturally he had a scriptural foundation for it. Matthew, Chapter 16, Verse 18: 'Thou art Peter, and upon this rock I will build my church.'

'It didn't take a rocket-science genius, the Rev would say, to figure out that *Peter* is the Latin word for rock, and therefore the real, true meaning of "Peter" refers to petroleum, or oil that comes from rock. "So this verse, dear friends, is not only about Saint Peter: it is a prophecy, a vision of the Age of Oil, and the proof, dear friends, is right before your eyes, because look! What is more valued by us today than oil?" You have to give it to the rancid bugger.'

'He really preached that?' says Toby. Is she supposed to laugh or not? From Zeb's tone she can't tell.

'Don't forget the Oleum part. It was even more important than the Peter half. The Rev could rave on about the Oleum for hours. "My friends, as we all know, *oleum* is the Latin word for oil. And indeed, oil is holy throughout the Bible! What else is used for the anointing of priests and prophets and kings? Oil! It's the sign of special election, the consecrated chrism! What more proof do we need of the holiness of our very own oil, put in the earth by God for the special use of the faithful to multiply His works? His Oleum-extraction devices abound on this planet of our Dominion, and he spreads his Oleum bounty among us! Does it not say in the Bible that you should forbear to hide your light under a bushel? And what else can so reliably make the lights go on as oil? That's right! Oil, my friends! The Holy Oleum must not be hidden under a bushel – in other words, left underneath the rocks – for to do so is to flout the Word! Lift up your voices in song, and let the Oleum gush forth in ever stronger and all-blessed streams!"'

'That's an imitation?' says Toby.

'Fuckin' right. I could do the whole spiel standing on my head, I had to listen to it enough. Me and Adam both.'

'You're good at it,' says Toby.

'Adam was better. In the Rev's church – and around the Rev's dinner table too – we didn't pray for forgiveness or even for rain, though God knows we could have used some of each. We prayed for oil. Oh, and natural gas too – the Rev included that in his list of divine gifts for the chosen. Every time we said grace before meals the Rev would point out that it was oil that put the food on the table because it ran the tractors that plowed the fields and fuelled the trucks that delivered the food to the stores, and also the car our devoted mother, Trudy, drove to the store in to buy the food, and the power that made the heat that cooked the food. We might as well be eating and drinking oil – which was true in a way – so fall on your knees!

'Around this point in the speech Adam and me would start kicking each other under the table. The idea was to kick the other one so hard he would yelp or flinch, but not to give any sign yourself, because whoever made a noise would get whacked or have to drink piss. Or worse. But Adam was never a yelper. I admired him for that.'

'Not literally?' says Toby. 'The piss?'

'Cross my heart,' says Zeb. 'Now where'd I put that stone-cold heart thing of mine?'

'I thought you liked each other,' says Toby. 'You and Adam.'

'We did. Kicking under the table is a guy thing.'

'You were how old?'

'Too old,' says Zeb. 'Though Adam was older. Only a couple of years older, but he was what the Gardeners would call an old soul. He was wise, I was foolish. It was always like that.'

Adam was a skinny little squirt. Though older, he wasn't nearly as strong as Zeb, once Zeb made it past the age of five. Adam was methodical: he contemplated, he thought things through. Zeb was impulsive: he shot from the hip, he let rage take him over. It got him into trouble and got him out of it in about equal measure.

But in combination the two of them were pretty effective. They were joined at the head: Zeb was the bad one who was good at bad things, Adam was the good one who was bad at good things. Or who used good things as a front for his bad things. Adam and Zebulon: bookends, as in the alphabet. That cute A–Z name symmetry was the Rev's idea: he liked to theme-park everything.

Adam was always being held up as an example. Why couldn't Zeb behave well, the way his brother did? Sit up straight, don't squirm, eat properly, your hand is not a fork, don't wipe your face on your shirt, do what your father says, say yes sir and no sir, and so on. That was how Trudy would talk, almost begging; all she wanted was peace and quiet, she didn't really enjoy the consequences of Zeb's pushbacks and sulkiness – the welts and bruises and scars. She wasn't a sadist as such, not like the Rev. But she was the centre of her own universe, big-time. She wanted the perks, and the Rev was the ever-flowing source of the cash that paid for them.

After telling Zeb what a model kid Adam was, she would go on to say that Adam's line-toeing was all the more special, all the more praiseworthy, considering ... then she would trail off because Adam's mother, Fenella, was never mentioned at length if Trudy and the Rev could help it. You'd think they'd have used her and her scandalous douchebag behaviour as a stick to beat Adam with – disparage his genetic inheritance – but they never did. He was too good at innocence, or the show of it, with his big blue eyes and his thin, saintly looking face.

Zeb got hold of some old photos of Fenella – they were on a thumbdrive, at the bottom of a storage box in the closet, the one he was frequently locked into. He'd hidden a mini-light in there so he could see in the dark. He found the drive, then nicked it and plugged it into the Rev's computer to see what would happen. The thing still worked: there were about thirty pics of Fenella, some with tiny Adam, a few with the Rev, none of them smiling much. The thumbdrive must've been an oversight because there were no other pictures of Fenella in the house. She didn't look in any way slutty; she had the same thin, truthful, big-eyed look that Adam had.

Zeb had quite a crush on her: if only he could talk to her and tell her what was going on she would be on his side, she'd despise the whole setup as much as he did. She must have done, because hadn't she run away? Though she didn't look like the running-away type, she didn't look strong enough.

Sometimes he felt jealous of Adam, because he'd once had Fenella for his mother, and all Zeb had was Trudy. Then he'd let resentment of Adam's failsafe punishment evasion system get the better of him, and he'd mess with Adam in private: turd in the bed, dead mouse in the sink, switch the hot and cold taps in their shower – he'd figured out plumbing by then – or just apple-pie his sheets. Boy meanies. The Rev had done well out of his oil stocks, in addition to the gushing wells of his parishioners' savings, and they lived in a big house, with Trudy and the Rev at the opposite end to Adam and Zeb. So if Adam yelped they wouldn't hear him. Though he never did yelp; he just beamed out the reproachful I-forgive-you gaze that was ten times more annoying.

Sometimes Zeb would tease Adam about Fenella. He'd say she must have tattoos all over, tits and all; he'd say she was a cokehead; he'd say she went off with a biker, no, a dozen bikers, did them all, one after the other; he'd say she was peddling it on the street in Vegas to deranged addicts and syphilitic pimps. Why was he saying those gross and repugnant things about the woman he considered his other self, his fairy-dust spirit helper, next door to a marble goddess? Who knows?

The strange thing was, Adam didn't talk back. He'd just smile in an eerie way, as if he knew something Zeb didn't.

Adam never ratted about Zeb's juvenile pranks. Even then he was a secretive little bugger. Anyway, the two of them mostly worked as a team. At school – CapRock Prep, a private school funded by one of the OilCorps, boys only – they were known as the Holy PetrOleum Brats because of their dad's position, but nobody picked on them openly, not once Zeb was big enough. Adam alone would have been a sitting duck, he was so stringy and transparent; but if anyone lifted a finger in his direction, Zeb would beat the crap out of them. He only had to do that twice. Word got around.

Schillizzi's Hands

In face of the brainwashing team of Trudy and the Rev, Adam and Zeb took joint evasive action. What were they evading, apart from punishment? Anything that might lead in the direction of the path of righteousness, the Holy PetrOleum Path, the path the Rev and Trudy were forever urging them to tread.

In Adam's case, this action took the form of blue-eyed lying – he could make just about anyone except Zeb think he was innocent as an egg unlaid – whereas Zeb had the instincts of a sneak thief. Time spent in the punishment closet had its upside, hairpins had their uses, and it was not long before he had the secret run of the house, tiptoeing through the bureau drawers and emails of his elders while they believed him securely imprisoned among the winter coats and outdated consumer electronics. Lockpicking became his hobby, and soon enough, with the aid of clandestine sessions on the school's digital facilities and free time at the public library, hacking became his vocation. In his fantasy world no code could keep him out, no door could shut him in, and fantasy merged into reality the older and more practised he became.

At first he stuck to porno peepsites and pirated acid rock and freakshow music – all forbidden by the Church, needless to say:

it went in for buttoned-up collars and public chastity vows, and its music sucked like a thousand Monster Leeches from Outer Space. So Zeb would earphone the Luminescent Corpses or the Pancreatic Cancers or the Bipolar Albino Hookworms while trolling onscreen for ever-new and cunningly deployed girl body parts. No harm in it really: they'd already made the videos, so what he was doing was just a form of time travel. He wasn't *causing* anything.

Then, once he felt ready, he decided to up the ante and really test his powers.

The Church of PetrOleum was high-tech enabled, with a dozen sophisticated online social media and donation sites skimming the cash from the faithful 24/7. The security on those sites was supposed to be as foolproof as such things got, with two layers of coding knitware any potential klepto would have to penetrate before making off with the debit accounts. And the system did keep out such kleptos; but it had no defence against an insider job, such as the one Zeb managed to pull off so spectacularly when he was barely sixteen.

The Rev's weak point was his belief in his own invulnerability, so he was careless; and as he had no head for number-letter combos, he wrote down passwords. Then he hid them in places so obvious even the Easter Bunny would scoff. The cufflink box? The toes of the Sunday shoes? Retro-cretin, sighed Zeb, extracting the wafers of paper, memorizing their cryptic scribblings, then replacing box or shoe in its exact previous location.

Once possessed of the keys to the kingdom, Zeb diverted the river of donations – not all of it, a mere .09 per cent, margin of error, he wasn't lobotomized – into several accounts of his own devising, making sure that the donors got the standard grovelling thank-you and guilt-inducing pep-talk message from the church, plus a hate slogan or two directed at the Enemies of

God's Holy Oil: 'Solar Panels Are Satan's Work,' 'Eco Equals FreakO,' 'The Devil Wants You to Freeze in the Dark,' 'Serial Killers Believe in Global Warming.'

For his stash-the-cash hideaways he used an identity pieced together from fragments he'd appropriated by stealth attacks on fuzzily fenced targets, such as 3-D avatar gaming destinations, AdoptAFish and similar bioweepy charities, and Feel-iT-enabled porno installations in suburban malls. ('Haptic feedback gives you true, stimulating flesh-on-flesh sensations! Say goodbye to faked screams and groans, this is the real thing! Warning: Do Not Expose Your Electronic Device to Moisture. Do Not Place Terminals in Your Mouth or Other Mucous Membrane Regions. Severe Burns May Result.')

No surprise, really, for Zeb to discover during one of his trolling expeditions that the Rev himself was a frequent visitor to the haptic wanksites, though he indulged himself at home – he couldn't afford to be caught in a mall – and hid the feedback terminals in his golf club bag. He favoured those sites involving whips, penetration with bottles, and nipple-burning. He was also a big fan of the historical re-enactment beheading sites, which were relatively expensive, maybe because of the props and costumes – 'Mary, Queen of Scots: Feel This Hot Red-Head Spurt,' 'Anne Boleyn: Royal Slut! Did It with Her Brother, She'll Do It with You, Then You Get to Slice Her Dirty Little Neck,' 'Katherine Howard: Turn This Stone Cold Fox Stone Cold with One Whack of Your Powerful Blade,' 'Lady Jane Grey: Make This Elite Virgin Pay the Price of Snootiness, Blindfold Optional.' These gave you the sensation, right in your own hands, of what it felt like to decapitate a woman with an axe. ('Fun! Historic! Educational!')

For extra payment you could decapitate them without their clothes on, which was more exciting. Zeb took a few turns at it himself – courtesy of the Rev's account, which he cooked accordingly – so he had grounds for the clothes versus naked comparison. A naked woman on her knees, about to lose her head – why was this riveting? Was he callous or a psychopath or something? No, psychopaths had a brain chip missing, according to Adam, who read up on these things. They couldn't feel empathy; screaming and tears were just annoying noises as far as they were concerned. So they couldn't feel shitty and/or pervy about what they were doing, not like Zeb.

He thought about hacking in and recoding the program so that when the axe came down you got the sensation not in your hands but in your own neck. What would it feel like to have your head chopped off? Would it hurt, or would the shock cancel that out? Or would you get a rush of empathy? But too much empathy could be dangerous. Your heart might stop.

Were those naked, kneeling, and shortly to be headless women real or not? He guessed not because reality online was different from the everyday kind of reality, where things hurt your body. And they wouldn't be allowed to murder real women right onscreen: surely that was illegal. But the effects were so amazing and 3-D that you ducked the gush of blood.

Adam didn't see the attraction of these activities once he found out about them, which he did because Zeb couldn't resist the urge to share his knowledge about the Rev's secret life. Which was now also, to some extent, his own.

'That is depraved,' was Adam's comment.

'Right! That's the *point*! What are you, gay?' Zeb said, but Adam only smiled.

The Rev's frustrated kink urges must have been in need of an outlet: Zeb was now too large and surly to take a chance on as a sado-subject. He might hit back, and the Rev was at heart a coward, so the belting and piss-drinking and imprisonment were now in the past. Nor was Trudy an option for the warped bastard, since – despite her stand-by-your-mealticket subservience – she would never put up with leather halters and nipple piercing and flagellation with a cane, or eating her own excrement. Information is power, so Zeb thanked his lucky stars for the online haptic-feedback sites, and made a record of the number of times the Rev had used them, and took care to store away this Santa's packsack of red velvet information for future use. Though the Rev might manage to electrocute himself via his own dick in the meantime – blow himself up like an overboiled hotdog – and Zeb would sure like to be an eye at the keyhole for that hilarious little fiasco. He briefly considered rewiring the haptic terminals to achieve this very effect, but was unsure of the voltage it would take. A Rev just badly scorched rather than no-refunds dead could mean big trouble: he'd figure out who did it, for sure.

By this time Zeb had magic fingers: he could play code the way Mozart played the piano, he could warble in cuneiform, he could waltz through firewalls like a tiger of old leaping through a flaming circus hoop without singeing a whisker. He could slip into the PetrOleum Church accounting – both sets of books, the official set and the actual one – in a few swift moves, and he did, on a regular basis. This went on for a couple of years, as the .09 per cents piled up, and Zeb grew taller and sprouted more body hair, and worked out in the gym at CapRock Prep, where he took care to keep in the middle of the bell curve gradeswise, especially in IT, so that his extraterrestrial hacking talents would not be suspected.

In six months he would graduate, and what then? He had some notions, but so did his parental overseers. The Rev had made it known that through his connections he could get Zeb a coveted job in the northern oil desert, driving one of the humungous machines that wrangled oil-rich bituminous gravel.

It would make a man of Zeb, he said, leaving the possible definition of *man* floating in the air between them. (Child torturer? Religious fraudster? Online girl decapitator?) Also, the money was good. Then, when he'd done that for a while, Zeb could decide on what calling he wished to pursue.

There were three subtexts to this: 1) The Rev wanted Zeb to go very far away because he was beginning to be afraid of him, and rightly so. 2) With any luck, Zeb would get lung cancer, or a third eye, or scales like an armadillo: the air up there was so toxic you mutated in about a week.

And 3) Zeb was not brilliant. Not like Adam, who – in the hopes that he would carry on in the old man's fraudchurch biz – had been sent to Spindletop U. and had majored in PetrTheology, Homiletics, and PetrBiology; this last, as far as Zeb could see, required you to learn biology in order to disprove it. That took a certain kind of intellectual adroitness, a kind – it was implied – that Zeb lacked. Galley slave would be more his level.

'I think that's a wonderful idea,' said Trudy. 'You should be so grateful to your father for taking all that trouble. Not every boy has a father like yours.'

Smile, Zeb ordered himself. 'I know,' he said. The word *smile* meant 'carving knife' in Greek. He'd found that on the web, when he wasn't decapitating historical figures.

Zeb missed Adam when he wasn't there, and he suspected it was mutual. Who else could they talk to about the improbable sublayers of their lives? Who else could do a hilarious word-for-word imitation of the Rev's Prayer to Saint Lucic-Lucas, to whom God had revealed the Holy Oil?

When they were apart they avoided text messages, phone calls, or anything else with an electronic signal: the internet, as was well known, leaked like a prostate cancer patient, and the Rev was most likely snooping, if not on Adam, at least on Zeb. But when Adam would come back for vacations it was old-home week. Zeb would welcome him with an amphibian in the shoe or an arthropod in the cuff-link box or a burr or two artfully stuck onto the inside of his Y-fronts, though they were getting too old for this kind of japery, so it was more of a nostalgia thing.

Then they'd go out onto the tennis court and pretend to play a game, and murmur together in brief snatches across the net, comparing notes. Zeb would want to know if Adam had got laid yet, a question that was skilfully evaded. Adam would want to know how much money Zeb had skimmed off from the Church and sequestered in his secret stowaway accounts, since it was their firm plan to disappear from the Rev's charmed circle once they had sufficient funds.

It was Adam's last vacation before graduating. Zeb was sitting at the Rev's home office desk monitor with a pair of medical latex gloves on, humming under his breath, while Adam stood watch at the window in case the Rev's gas-guzzling tycoon car or Trudy's Hummerette drove up.

'You've got Schillizzi's hands,' Adam said to him in that neutral way he had. Was it admiration or merely observation?

'Schillizzi?' said Zeb. 'Hot crap, the botulistic old bugger's embezzling again, only this is a lot more! Look at this!'

'I wish you wouldn't swear,' said Adam in his mildest voice.

'Stuff yourself,' said Zeb cheerfully. 'And he's stashing it in a bank account in Grand Cayman!'

'Schillizzi was a well-known white-hat twentieth-century safe-cracker,' said Adam, who was interested in history, unlike Zeb. 'He never used explosives, only his hands. He was legendary.'

'I bet the old fart's planning a jump,' said Zeb. 'Here today, then zap, and the next morning he's sucking up martinis on a tropical beach and renting lick-your-cleft bimbettes, leaving the fuckin' faithful out in the cold with their pants down.'

'Not in Grand Cayman, he won't,' said Adam. 'They're mostly underwater. But those banks have relocated to the Canaries; there are more mountains there. Only they've kept the Grand Cayman corporate names. Preserving a tradition, I suppose.'

'Wonder if he'll take Trusty Fusty Trudy with him?' said Zeb. Adam's knowledge of banking surprised him, but then Adam's knowledge of a lot of things surprised him. It was hard to know what Adam knew.

'He won't take Trudy,' said Adam. 'She's becoming too financially demanding. She suspects what he's up to.'

'You know this how?'

'An educated guess,' said Adam. 'The body language. She's giving him the narrow eyes at breakfast, when he's not looking. She's nagging him about vacations, and when are they going to take one. Also she's feeling held back in her interior decoration ambitions: note her on-show collection of wallpaper samples and paint chips. She's tired of playing the angel wife for the benefit of the congregation. She feels she's helped to create the domestic surplus, and she wants more scope.'

'Like Fenella,' said Zeb. 'She wanted more scope too. At least she got out early.'

'Fenella didn't get out,' said Adam in his neutral voice. 'She's under the rock garden.'

Zeb turned in the Rev's ergonomic swivel chair. 'She's what?'

'Here they come,' said Adam. 'Both at once, it's a convoy. Power down.'

Mute and Theft

'Say that again,' said Zeb once they were on the tennis court and safely out of hearing. Neither of them was much good at tennis, but they pretended to practise. They stood side by side, serving balls over the net or, more often, into it. Their rooms were bugged – Zeb had discovered that years ago, and enjoyed feeding misinformation into his desk lamp and then looping it back to himself via the Rev's computer – but it was best to play dumb by leaving the bugs where they were.

'Under the rock garden,' said Adam. 'That's where Fenella is.'

'You're sure?'

'I watched them burying her,' said Adam. 'From the window. They didn't see me.'

'This wasn't a ... you didn't dream it?' said Zeb. 'You must've been fucking fetal!' Adam gave him the fisheye: not only did he not approve of obscenity, he never seemed to get used to it. 'I mean, really young,' Zeb amended. 'Kids make stuff up.' For once he was shaken: he could barely think straight.

If Adam's story was true – and why would he invent this? – it changed Zeb's whole view of himself. Fenella had shaped his story about his past, and also the one about his future, but suddenly Fenella was a skeleton: she'd been dead all along. So, no secret helper waiting out there: he'd never had one. There was no understanding family member he would someday locate, once he'd found the Exit sign and unlocked the invisible locks and cut his way out of the Rev's chicken-hawk-wired coop. He was flying a wing-damaged solo, all alone except for his joined-at-the-head-wound brother, who could well turn pious on him for real, he had the talent. Then Zeb himself would be drifting in Voidsville, out in the cold and dark, like a torn-loose astronaut in one of those old five-tomato space flics. He slammed a ball into the net.

'I was almost four,' Adam said in his I-have-spoken-and-therefore-it-is-so voice that was too much like the Rev's for comfort. 'I have clear memories of that time.'

'You never told me,' Zeb said. He was offended: Adam had not deemed him trustworthy. That hurt. They were supposed to be a team.

'You would have let it slip,' said Adam. 'Then who knows what they would've done?' He tossed his ball up, tapped it lightly over the net. 'You could've ended up under the rock garden as well. Not to mention me.'

'Wait,' said Zeb. 'They? You mean fucking Trudy was in on this too?'

'I already told you,' said Adam. 'There is no need to swear.'

'Sorry, it just fucking slipped out,' said Zeb. No way he was going to let Adam tell him how to talk. 'Trudy the Good?'

'Must've been something in it for her,' said Adam in his I-am-loftily-overlooking-your-provocation voice. 'If only blackmail material. Or maybe she wanted Fenella out of the way, to clear her path. My guess is she was already pregnant with you. The Church of PetrOleum doesn't sanction divorce, what with the Holy Oil at the marriage ceremony. As we know.'

So now it was Zeb's fault, the death of Fenella. For having the bad taste to get himself conceived. Shit. 'How did they do it?' he said. 'The two of them? Did they slip arsenic into her tea, or ...' Not a decapitation, he thought, ashamed of himself. They wouldn't have gone that far.

'I don't know. I was only four. I just saw the burial.'

'So all that about her being whore-pill trash, deserting her baby and so forth, that was just ...'

'It's what the congregation wanted to believe,' said Adam. 'And they did believe it. Bad mothers are always a good story, for them.'

'Maybe we should call the CorpSeCorps,' said Zeb. 'Tell them to bring shovels.'

'I wouldn't risk it,' said Adam. 'There's quite a few Petro-baptists on the force, and there are a number of OilCorps heavies on the Church board. There's a lot of overlap because of the benefits to both parties. They're agreed on the need to crush dissent. So the OilCorps would cover up for the Rev over a pure and simple wife murder that didn't per se threaten its holdings, since they'd know there'd be much credibility lost through a scandal. They'd accuse the two of us of mental insta-bility. Shut us away, use the heavy drugs. Or, as I said – dig a couple of new holes in the rock garden.'

'But we're his kids!' said Zeb, sounding about two years old even to himself.

'You think that would stop him?' said Adam. 'Blood is thin-ner than money. He'd hear a convenient voice from God, suggesting a son sacrifice for the greater good. Remember Isaac. He'd slit our throats and set fire to us, because this time God wouldn't send a sheep.'

Which was about as dark as Zeb could remember Adam ever being. 'So,' he said. He was out of breath, although they'd barely been moving. 'Why are you telling me about this now?'

'Because if what you've said about your successful cash-diverting activities is true, we have accumulated enough money,' said Adam. 'Also the Church might catch you doing the diverting. Time to go, while we still can. Before they send you off to die in the tar pits,' he added. 'It would be called an accident. Of course.'

Zeb was touched. Adam was looking out for him. He always thought further ahead than Zeb did.

They waited until the next day, when the Rev had a board meeting and Trudy was heading up the Ladies' Prayer Circle. Then they took a solarcab to the bullet train station, exchanging fake info for the benefit of the driver's flapping ears. Most of those guys were snoops, formal or informal. The script was that Adam was on his way back to Spindletop and Zeb was seeing him off. Nothing unusual in that.

From a net café at the station, Zeb cleaned out the Rev's Grand Cayman hidey-hole account while Adam acted nonchalant and scanned for anyone who looked too interested. Once the Rev's funds were secured and transferred, Zeb sent the infected gonad a couple of messages, using a lilypad pathway to delay potential cyberhounds as long as possible. He hacked into a men's underarm deodorant video ad, clicked on the gleaming, depilatoried stud's belly button – he'd gone through that pixel wormhole before – then skipped to a home and garden site, appropriate under the circumstances, and chose a trowel. From it he launched his messages.

The first message said, 'We know who's under the rocks. Don't follow us.' The second contained the details of the Rev's thefts from the Church of PetrOleum's charity initiative funds, and another warning: 'Don't leave town or this goes public. Stay put and await instructions.' That would give the mildewed old bugger the idea that they'd be back in touch soon for blackmail purposes, which must be their motive, and he could lie in wait for them.

'That should do it,' said Adam, but Zeb couldn't resist adding a third message: a copy of the details of the Rev's Feel-iT haptic site transactions. Lady Jane Grey had been his favourite: he must have decapitated her at least fifteen times.

'Wish I could watch,' said Zeb, once they were on the train. 'When he opens his mail. And even better, when he finds out his Cayman bank stash is gone.'

'Gloating is a character flaw,' said Adam.

'Up yours,' said Zeb.

He spent the trip looking out the window at the passing scenery: gated communities like the one they'd just fled, fields of soybeans, frackware installations, windfarms, piles of gigantic truck tires, heaps of gravel, pyramids of discarded ceramic toilets. Mountains of garbage with dozens of people picking through it; pleebland shanty towns, the shacks made of discarded everything. Kids standing on the shack roofs, on the piles of garbage, on the piles of tires, waving flags made of colourful plastic bags or flying rudimentary kites, or giving Zeb the finger. The odd camera drone drifted overhead, purporting to be scanning traffic, logging the comings and goings of whoknew-who. Those things were bad news if they were hunting for you specifically: he'd gathered that much from web gossip.

But the Rev wouldn't be searching for them yet. He'd still be at the board lunch, gobbling down the labmeat hors d'oeuvres and the farmed tilapia.

Hackety-hack, railroad track,
Momma's in the garden, so don't look back,

Zeb hummed. He hoped Fenella's death had been sudden, with none of the Rev's more puke-making obsessions involved.

Beside him Adam was asleep, looking even whiter and thinner than he did when awake, and more like an idealistic statue of some annoying allegorical figure: Prudence. Sincerity. Faith.

Zeb was too high for sleep. Also jittery, despite himself: they'd crossed a big thick barbed-wire line, they'd robbed the ogre, they'd made off with his treasure. There would be fury. So he kept watch.

Who killed Fenella?
A really evil fella.
Hit her on the head,
Gave her quite a whack,
Everything went black,
Now she's fuckin' dead.

Something was running down his face. He used his sleeve to wipe. No snivelling, he told himself. Don't give him the satisfaction.

Once in San Francisco, Adam and Zeb decided to separate. 'He won't sit still for this,' Adam said. 'He's got a lot of contacts. He'll put out a red alert, use his OilCorps networks. We're overly noticeable together.'

True enough: they were too disparate. Dark and light, hefty and frail; anomalies like that were memorable. And the Rev's description would be of the two of them, not one at a time.

Mutt and Jeff, Zeb hummed to himself. Mute and Theft. Cute and Deft.

'Don't make that pseudo-musical noise,' said Adam. 'It draws attention to us. Anyway you're flat.' He did have a point. Two points.

In a pleebland grey-market hourly-rental morph-your-back-story kitshop, Zeb crafted identities for them – cardboard, wouldn't stand up to scrutiny, time-sensitive, but good for the next stage of the trip. Adam went north, Zeb went south, each heading for camouflage.

He and Adam had agreed on a dropbox in space. It was the topmost rose being strewn by the zephyrs in a print of Botticelli's *The Birth of Venus,* posted on a much-visited Italian tourism site. Zeb opted for the left tit nipple of Venus, but Adam overruled him: too obvious, he said. It would also be too obvious for them to attempt to contact each other for at least six months, he added: the Rev was vindictive, and by now he'd also be frightened.

Zeb pondered the likely consequences of this vindictiveness and fright. What would he himself do if two young wiseass descendants of his that he'd never liked anyway had made off with his foul secrets? The rage. The betrayal. After all he'd done for Adam. And for Zeb, because weren't his physical chastisements in the best interests of the lad's spiritual development? He was probably still deceiving himself with righteous barf like that.

Among other things, he'd hire some DORCS: digital online rapid capture specialists. They charged a lot but were said to produce results. They'd set up a search algorithm geared to detect likely profile matches online. So it was necessary to stay away from digital as much as possible. No surfing. No purchasing. No socializing. No wisecracking. No porn.

'Just don't act like yourself,' was Adam's parting advice.

Deeper into the Pleeblands

Zeb cut his hair in San Fran. He was growing a moustache, and he'd bought some coolish contact lenses on the dark-grey market that not only changed your eye colour but also gave you astigmatism and spurious iris features. But though these might get him through a casual scan, he didn't want to risk closer scrutiny, and the Fickle Fingers of Fake fingerprint distorters he'd also bought were laughable in any professional sense, so it was better not to chance the bullet train again. Also, most of those riding it still believed in the legality of law and the orderliness of order, and might report anything suspicious, as they were constantly being nagged to do.

So he chanced the highways. He hitched south as far as San Jose, working the Truck-A-Pillar convoy stops for rides and trying to look older than he was. Some of the drivers hinted at blowjob payment, but he was too big for them to force it.

The other hazard was the quick-trick pros working the road-side bars. But the only sex he'd had so far had been online, via the haptic-feedback sites; he wasn't ready for actual flesh on flesh. Plus, he was wary of making connections with other people, however brief: who knew how many of them might be trading information on the side? Some of those hustlers were suspiciously well dressed and did not look hungry.

Then there were the diseases. The last thing he needed was to be stuck in a hospital – supposing his ID passed inspection – or enduring a working over from some HospitalCorps security thug, supposing it didn't pass, which was likely. Once the truth of who he was had been vise-gripped out of him, there would be a call to the Rev. Then disposal orders would be issued, or he'd be shipped back in plasticuffs to face the self-righteous music. *I'll teach you to respect me, I have been set in authority over you, God hates you, you are morally worthless, repent on your knees, drink what's in the bucket, flat on the floor, hand me the two-by-four, you want it harder, I'll make you howl*, and so forth and so on, the familiar religio-sado heavy-metal perv litany. Pre-bedtime amusements.

When the Rev had finished with Zeb's neurologically trashed, defenceless, quivering body, it would be into the rock garden with it, eventually; but not before he'd been scorched and zapped into betraying the digital pathway leading to Adam, and had been forced to plant some online lures and instructions for him, including the necessity of not going public with the Rev's fiscal and sexual misdoings and the urgent need for a physical meetup at which all would be explained. Zeb had no illusions about his ability to withstand the kind of implementation the Rev and his helpers would be more than willing to inflict.

So that was the hospital option, supposing he caught pube rot. The alternative to the hospital route didn't appeal either. Dick fester, stiffie shrivel, penis putrefaction: the internet scare sites on that subject were the greeny-yellowy stuff of nightmares. More than enough reason to avoid the beckoning sirens of the Truck-A-Pillar stops, no matter how plump and firm the thighs extending from their red leatherette hot pants, how high their fake-lizard platform shoes, how boldly engraved their dragon and skull tattoos, or how bimplanted the half-melons emerging from their black satin halter tops like rising dough. Not that he'd ever seen rising dough, up close. But he'd seen videos of it. Once-upon-a-time mommy retros that, to tell the truth, made him feel kind of weepy. Had dead Fenella ever done any dough-baking? Because Trudy sure as hell hadn't.

So when the smudgy-mouthed, crack-eyed, jelly-bummed beauties said, 'Hey, big boy, how about a quickie, out behind the doughnut stand?' he did not say, *Coming* and he did not say, *Meet you in heaven when I'm dead* and he did not say, *Are you out of your fuckin' mind?* He said nothing.

In addition to the disease factor, he did not yet know how to navigate the dark and darker pathways of the pleeblands: he didn't want to hook up with a total stranger and then wander blind-eyed into some alley or sleazy motel or dubious knocking-shop washroom and come out on a stretcher or in a body bag, if that. More likely was, they'd toss him into a vacant lot and let the rats and vultures take care of him. Now that more and more of the once-public security services were privatized, there was no margin in the proper burial of a drifter like him, or in the apprehension – they liked to use that word, *apprehension* – of whatever scoundrels might have knifed him for pocket change.

His height and his budding 'stache were scant protection. He was green wood, an easy target; they'd get that at one glance, they'd beeline for him. The pleeblands were far from the school playgrounds of his youth, in which size really did matter. 'The bigger they are, the harder they fall,' the scrappy little bantams – more than one of them – had said to him then. 'Yeah,' he'd replied. 'But the smaller they are, the more often they fall.' Then a swift whack, not even a punch, and down they'd go.

But in the darkest pleeblands, there wouldn't be any verbal foreplay. No rattlesnake-warning quips and banter, just a rapid stab or slice or even a bullet from some obsolete, illegal firearm. The Linthead gang was especially vicious, according to the net. And the Blackened Redfish. And the Asian Fusions. And the Tex-Mexes with their drug-war tricks – the stacks of heads, the legless bodies strung up from old movieland marquees. He figured there must be a lot of Tex-Mexers controlling the Truck-A-Pillar highway heading south, it was close to their territory.

Despite these reservations, or, to be more honest, despite these cowardly fears, he knew that his best hope of cover in the short-term was in the worst part of town. Spending too much money would attract jackals; he was streetwise enough to know that. So once in San Jose he kept a low profile, stayed out of bars, and blended himself into the underclass that swirled around in the lowest pleebs like rats in a dump bin, scrabbling for whatever they could pick up.

For a while he slung quasi-meat products at SecretBurgers. It was ten hours and less than minimum, he had to wear the company T-shirt and a dorkwit cap, but SecretBurgers wasn't fussy about identities. And they had protection against the street gangs for their booth workers, and bought off both official nosies and non-official ones, so nobody hassled him. He felt sorry for the female workers: they were paid less than the guys, and they had to wear tight Ts and fend off customers and management alike. They should have been issued hard plastic visors for their tits.

But his sorrow didn't stop him from finally acquiring in-the-flesh carnal knowledge with one of the SecretBurgers meatbunnies called Wynette, a brownette with big, dark-ringed, starved-looking eyes. In addition to her alluring personality – a euphemism, he now has to admit, for her somewhat meagre snatch, which was the part that fascinated him, and he apologizes for that, but such is the case with hormone-sodden adolescent males, and it's nature's plan, and he thought he was in love, so fuckit – she offered the advantage of a tiny room.

Most of the SecretBurgers meatgirls couldn't even manage that: they shared overcrowded walkups, or squatted in repossessed and decaying houses, or hooked on the side to support some child or addicted relative or tinselly pimp. But Wynette was cautious and frugal, and hadn't squandered, and could afford some privacy. Her place was located above a corner store that sold alcohol tasting of troll piss and paint remover, but Zeb wasn't too choosy at that time, so he used to grab a bottle of it to ply Wynette with before sex because she said it helped her relax.

'Was it as good?' asks Toby.

'Was what as good? As good as what?'

'Sex with Wynette. As good as the decapitated Lady Jane Greys.'

'Apples and oranges,' says Zeb. 'No point comparing them.'

'Oh, give it a try,' says Toby.

'Okay. The Lady Jane Greys were repeatable. Reality's not. And since you're wondering, they're both good sometimes. But it can be disappointing either way.'

Snowman's Progress

Floral Bedsheet

Sunlight wakes her, coming in through her cubicle window. Birdsong, the voices of Craker children, the bleating of Mo'Hairs. Nothing unhappy.

She pushes herself upright, tries to remember what day it is. The Feast of Cyanophyta? *Thank you, Oh Lord, for creating the Cyanophyta, those lowly blue-green Algae so overlooked by many, for it is through them, so many millions of years ago – which timespan however is merely an eyeblink in Thy sight – that our oxygen-rich atmosphere came to be, without which we could not breathe, nor indeed could the other land-dwelling Zooforms, so various, so beautiful, so new each time we are able to see them, and intuit Your Grace through them . . .*

But on the other hand it may be Saint Jane Goodall's Day. *Thank you, Oh Lord, for blessing the life of Saint Jane Goodall, fearless Friend of God's Junglefolk, who braved many a risky situation and also biting Insect to reach out across the Species gap, and through her love for and labour with our close cousins the Chimpanzees, led us to understand the value of opposable thumbs and big toes, and also our own deep . . .*

Our own deep what? Toby rummages for the next phrase. She's slipping: she ought to write such things down. Keep a daily journal, as she did when she was alone at the AnooYoo

Spa. She could go further, and record the ways and sayings of the now-vanished God's Gardeners for the future; for generations yet unborn, as politicians used to say when they were fishing for extra votes. If there is anyone in the future, that is; and if they'll be able to read; which, come to think of it, are two big *ifs*. And even if reading persists, will anyone in the future be interested in the doings of an obscure and then outlawed and then disbanded green religious cult?

Maybe acting as if she believes in such a future will help to create it, which is the kind of thing the Gardeners used to say. She doesn't have any paper, but she could ask Zeb to bring some back on his next gleaning expedition; if he can find any that isn't damp, or nibbled for mouse nests, or eaten by ants. Oh, and pencils too, she'll add. Or pens. Or crayons. Then she could make a start.

Though it's hard to concentrate on the idea of a future. She's too immersed in the present: the present contains Zeb, and the future may not.

She longs for tonight, she longs to skip the day that's just begun and plunge headlong into the night as if into a pool; a pool with the moon reflected in it. She longs to swim in liquid moonlight.

But it's dangerous to live for the night. Daytime becomes irrelevant. You can get careless, you can overlook details, you can lose track. These days she'll find herself upright, in the middle of the room, one sandal in her hand, wondering how she got there; or outside under a tree, watching the leaves riffle, then prodding herself: *Move. Move now. Get moving. You need to . . .* But what exactly is it that she needs to do?

It isn't only her, and it isn't only her nightlife that's causing it. She's noticed others slacking off as well. Standing still for no reason, listening though no one's talking. Then jerking themselves back to the tangible, visibly making an effort. Busying themselves with the garden, the fence, the solar, the extension to the cobb house ... It's tempting to drift, as the Crakers seem to. They have no festivals, no calendars, no deadlines. No long-term goals.

She remembers this floating mood so well from the months that she spent holed up in the AnooYoo Spa, waiting out the plague virus that was killing everyone else. Then – after there was no more crying, no more pleading and pounding at the door, no more bodies collapsing on the lawn – just waiting. Waiting for a sign that there was someone else left alive. Waiting for meaningful time to resume.

She'd stuck to her daily routine: keeping herself fed and watered, filling up the hours with small activities, writing in her daily journal. Pushing back the voices that tried to get into her head, as such voices do when you're solitary. Fending off the temptation to wander away, wander off into the woods, open the door to whatever was going to happen to her or, more honestly, to put an end to her. An ending.

It was like a trance, or sleepwalking. *Give yourself up. Give up. Blend with the universe. You might as well.* It was as if something or someone was whispering, enticing her into the darkness: *Come in, come over here. Finish. It will be a relief. It will be completeness. It won't hurt much.*

She wonders if that sort of whispering is beginning in the ears of some of the others. Hermits in the desert heard those voices, and prisoners in dungeons. But maybe no one's hearing them now: it's not like the AnooYoo Spa here, it's not an isolation cell; everyone has other people. Still, she's conscious of counting heads each morning, making sure all the Madd-Addamites and former Gardeners are still in place: that none among them has strayed away during the night, into the labyrinth of leaves and branches, of birdsong and windsong and silence.

There's a tapping on the wall beside her door. 'Are you inside, Oh Toby?' It's little Blackbeard, come to check up on her. Perhaps on some level he shares her fears and doesn't want her to vanish.

'Yes,' she says. 'I'm here. You wait out there.' She hurries to put on her bedsheet of the day. Something less austere and geometrical than usual: more floral, more sensuous. Roses, full-blown. Vines, entwining. Is she being vain? No, it's a celebration of renewed life, hers: that's her excuse. Does she look ridiculous, mutton dressed as lamb? Hard to tell without a mirror. The main thing is to keep the shoulders back, stride forth with confidence. She pushes her hair behind her ears, twists it into a knot. There, no waving tendrils. Best to show some restraint.

'I will take you to Snowman-the-Jimmy,' Blackbeard says importantly, once she's ready. 'So you can help him. With the maggots.' He's proud of having learned this word, so he says it again: 'The maggots!' He smiles radiantly. 'The maggots are good. Oryx made them. They will not hurt us.' A glance up at her, scanning her face to make sure he's got it right, then another smile. 'And soon Snowman-the-Jimmy will not be sick.' He takes her by the hand, tugs her forward. He knows the drill, he's her little shadow, he's absorbing everything.

If I'd had a child, thinks Toby, would he have been like this? No. He would not have been like this. Don't repine.

Jimmy's still asleep, but his colour is better and his high temperature is gone. She spoons some honey-and-water into him, along with the mushroom elixir. His foot is healing rapidly; soon he won't need the maggots any more.

'Snowman-the-Jimmy is walking,' the Crakers tell her. Four of them are on duty this morning, three men and a woman. 'He is walking very quickly, inside his head. Soon he will be here.'

'Today?' she asks them.

'Today, tomorrow,' they say. 'Soon.' They smile at her. 'Do not be worried, Oh Toby,' the woman says. 'Snowman-the-Jimmy is safe now. Crake is sending him back to us.'

'And Oryx too,' says the tallest man: Abraham Lincoln, possibly. She really must try to sort out their names. 'She, too, is sending him.'

'She told her Children not to harm him,' says the woman. Empress Josephine?

'Even though his piss is weak, and they did not understand at first that they could not eat him.'

'Our piss is strong. The piss of our men. The Children of Oryx understand such piss.'

'The Children with sharp teeth eat those with weak piss.'

'The Children with tusks eat them, sometimes.'

'The Children who are like a bear, big, with claws. We have not seen a bear. Zeb ate one, he knows what is a bear.'

'But Oryx told them not to.'

'Not to eat Snowman-the-Jimmy.'

'Crake sent Snowman-the-Jimmy to take care of us. And Oryx sent him too.'

'Yes, Oryx too,' the others agree. One of them begins to sing.

Girl Stuff

The breakfast table is lively this morning.

Ivory Bill, Manatee, Tamaraw, and Zunzuncito have cleared their plates and are deep into a discussion of epigenetics. How much of Craker behaviour is inherited, how much is cultural? Do they even have what you could call a culture, separate from the expression of their genes? Or are they more like ants? What about the singing? Granted, it must be some form of communication, but is it territorial, like the singing of birds, or might it be termed art? Surely not the latter, says Ivory Bill. Crake couldn't account for it and didn't like it, says Tamaraw, but the team hadn't been able to eliminate it without producing affectless individuals who never went into heat and didn't last long.

The mating cycle is genetic, obviously, says Zunzuncito, as are the changes in female abdominal and genital pigmentation that accompany estrus, and the male equivalent, leading to the polysexual acts. Which in a deer or a sheep you'd have to call rutting, says Ivory Bill, but in the Crakers, would these phenomena vary with circumstances? There'd been no chance to test it, back there in the Paradice dome, which was a pity, they all agree. They could have made some variations, run studies on them, says Manatee. But Crake ruled with an iron hand, says

Tamaraw, and he was so dogmatic: he didn't want to hear about any possible improvements apart from those he thought up himself. And he sure as hell didn't want his prize experiment ruined via the introduction of possibly inferior segments, says Zunzuncito, because the Crakers were going to be a mega-money-spinner. Or that was his story, says Tamaraw.

'Of course he was bullshitting us all along,' said Zunzuncito.

'True, but he got results,' says Ivory Bill.

'For what they're worth,' says Manatee. 'The fucker.'

'The question is more *why* than how,' says Ivory Bill, gazing up at the sky as if Crake really is up there and could send down a thunderous answer. 'Why did he do it? The lethal wipeout virus in the BlyssPluss pills? Why did he want the human race to go extinct?'

'Maybe he was just very, very messed up,' says Manatee.

'For the sake of argument, and to do him justice, he might have thought that everything else was,' says Tamaraw. 'What with the biosphere being depleted and the temperature sky-rocketing.'

'And if the Crakers were his solution, he'd have known he'd need to protect them from the likes of us, with our aggressive if not murderous ways,' says Ivory Bill.

'That's what megalomaniac fuckers like him always think,' says Manatee.

'He'd have seen the Crakers as indigenous people, no doubt,' says Ivory Bill. 'And *Homo sapiens sapiens* as the greedy, rapacious Conquistadors. And, in some respects ... '

'Well, we came up with Beethoven,' says Manatee. 'And, you know, the major world religions, and whatnot. Fat chance of anything like that with this bunch.'

White Sedge is beside them, gazing at them attentively but possibly not listening. If anyone's hearing voices, thinks Toby, it might be her. She's a pretty girl, perhaps the prettiest of the

MaddAddamites. Yesterday she proposed that they start a morning yoga and meditation group, but there weren't any takers. She's wearing a grey bedsheet with white lilies on it; her black hair's knotted into a chignon.

Amanda's at the end of the table. She's still pallid and listless; Lotis Blue and Ren are fussing over her, urging her to eat.

Rebecca's having a cup of what they've all agreed to call coffee. She turns as Toby sits down.

'It's ham again,' she says to Toby. 'And kudzu pancakes. Oh, and if you want, there's some Choco-Nutrino.'

'Choco-Nutrino?' says Toby. 'Where'd you get that?' Choco-Nutrino had been a desperate stab at a palatable breakfast cereal for children after the world chocolate crop had failed. It was said to contain burnt soy.

'Zeb and Rhino and them gleaned it somewhere,' says Rebecca. 'And Shackie. It's not what you'd call fresh, don't even ask about the sell-by date, so I figure we better eat it now.'

'You think so?' says Toby. The Choco-Nutrinos are in a bowl. They're like tiny pebbles, brown and alien-looking, granules from Mars. People used to eat this kind of stuff all the time, she thinks. They took it for granted.

'Last-chance café,' says Rebecca. 'Kind of a nostalgia trip. Yeah, I used to think it was disgusting too, but it's not bad with Mo'Hair milk. Anyway it's fortified with vitamins and minerals. Says so on the box. So we won't have to eat mud for a while.'

'Mud?' says Toby.

'You know, for the trace elements,' says Rebecca. Sometimes Toby can't tell if she's joking.

Toby sticks with the ham and the kudzu pancakes. 'Where are the others?' she asks, keeping her voice neutral. Rebecca counts them off: Crozier has already eaten and is taking the Mo'Hairs out to pasture. Beluga and Shackleton are with him, one spraygun between them, covering his back. Black Rhino and Katuro did sentry last night, so they are sleeping in.

'Swift Fox?' says Toby.

'Taking her time,' says Rebecca. 'Having a doze. I heard her thrashing around in the bushes last night. With a gentleman caller or two.' Her smile says, *Like you.*

No Zeb yet. Toby tries not to peer around too obviously. Is he, too, having a doze?

As she's finishing her bitter coffee, Swift Fox joins them. Today she's wearing a pale gauzy shift, shorts, and a floppy hat, pastel green and pink. She's done her hair in pigtails, with plastic Hello Kitty clips. It's the schoolgirl look, and if it were former times she'd never get away with it, thinks Toby. She'd been a highly qualified gene artist, so she'd have feared ridicule and loss of status, and dressed like a grown-up to advertise her rank. But that kind of rank and status have peeled away, so what exactly is she advertising now?

Don't be so hard on her, Toby tells herself. After all, she took a big risk: she was an undercover MaddAddamite informant before Crake hijacked her and made her a whitecoat brainiac serf inside the Paradice dome, along with the rest of the kidnapped MaddAddamites. He'd scooped most of them.

But not Zeb: Crake never managed to corner him. He'd covered his tracks too well.

'Hi, everyone,' Swift Fox says, stretching her arms up, lifting her breasts, aiming them at Ivory Bill. 'Ooh, I could go right back to bed! Hope you slept well. I fucking didn't! We need to do something about the bugs.'

'There's spray,' says Rebecca. 'We've still got some of that citrus stuff.'

'It wears off,' says Swift Fox. 'Then they bite and you wake up, and then you can hear people talking and etcetera, like in one of those not-your-real-name motels with cardboard walls.' She smiles at Ivory Bill again, ignoring Manatee, who's staring at her, his mouth tight. Is it disapproval or extreme lust? Toby wonders. With some men it's hard to tell the difference.

'I think we should have a curfew on vocal cords,' Swift Fox continues, with a sideways glance at Toby. *I heard you*, that look says. *If you must indulge in dusty, ridiculous middle-aged sex, at least put a sock in it.* Toby feels herself blushing.

'Dear lady,' says Ivory Bill. 'I trust our sometimes heated nocturnal discussions did not awaken you. Manatee and Tamaraw and I—'

'Oh, it wasn't you, and it wasn't a discussion,' says Swift Fox. 'Are those Choco-Nutrinos? I threw up a whole bowlful of those once, back when I still got hangovers.'

Amanda stands up from the table, clamps her hand over her mouth, hurries away. Ren follows her.

'There's something wrong with that girl,' says Swift Fox. 'It's like she's pithed or something. Was she always such a dimwit?'

'You know what she went through,' says Rebecca, frowning a little.

'Yeah, sure, but it's time for her to snap out of it. Do some work like the rest of us.'

Toby feels a rush of anger. Swift Fox is never the first to volunteer for chores, nor has she been within spitting distance of a Painballer: used like a prostibot, leashed like a dog, practically disembowelled. Amanda's worth ten of her. But apart from that, Toby knows she's resenting the snide innuendoes Swift Fox aimed at her earlier, not to mention the gauzy shift and the cute shorts. And the breast weaponry, and the girly-girl pigtails. They don't go with your budding wrinkles, she feels like saying. Tanning takes a toll.

Swift Fox smiles again, but not at Toby: right past Toby. It's a full-disclosure teeth display and dimple trigger. 'Hey,' she says in a softer voice. Toby swivels: it's Rhino and Katuro.

And Zeb. Of course, of course.

'Morning, everyone,' Zeb says evenly: nothing special for Swift Fox. Nor for Toby either: the night is the night, the day is the day. 'Anybody want anything?' he says. 'We're doing a quick scan around the area, couple of hours, just checking. We'll pass a few stores.' He doesn't spell out his real object because he doesn't have to: they all know he'll be looking for signs of the Painballers. It's a patrol.

'Baking soda,' says Rebecca. 'Or baking powder, whichever. I don't know what I'll do when it runs out. If you're going to a mini-super ...'

'Did you know that baking soda comes from the trona deposits in Wyoming?' says Ivory Bill. 'Or it used to come from there.'

'Oh, Ivory Bill,' says Swift Fox, favouring him with a smile. 'With you around, who needs Wikipedia?' Ivory Bill gives a semi-grin: he thinks it's a compliment.

'Yeast,' says Zunzuncito. 'Wild yeast, if you still have the flour. You can make sourdough that way.'

'I guess,' says Rebecca.

'I'll come too,' says Swift Fox to Zeb. 'I need a drugstore.'

There's a pause. Everyone looks at her.

'Just tell us your list,' says Black Rhino. He's scowling at her bare legs. 'We'll get it for you.'

'Girl stuff,' she says. 'You wouldn't know where to look.' She glances in the direction of Ren and Lotis Blue, who are over by the pump, sponging off Amanda. 'I'm gleaning for all of us.'

Another pause. Menstrual wadding, thinks Toby. She has a point: the stash in the storeroom is dwindling. No one wants to fall back on torn-up bedsheets. Or moss. Though we'll come to that sooner or later.

'Bad plan,' says Zeb. 'Those two guys are still out there. They've got a spraygun. They're third-time Painballers, there's nothing left of their empathy circuits. You wouldn't want them to grab you, they won't bother with the formalities. You saw what happened with Amanda. She was lucky to escape with her kidneys.'

'I totally agree. It is in fact a very bad plan for you to leave the confines of our cozy little enclave here. I will go,' says Ivory Bill gallantly, 'if you will trust me with your shopping list, and—'

'But you'll be there with me,' says Swift Fox to Zeb. 'As protection.' She lowers her eyelashes. 'I'll be so safe!'

Zeb says to Rebecca: 'Got any coffee? Or whatever you call that crap?'

'It's okay, I'll change my outfit,' Swift Fox says, switching her tone to brisk. 'I can keep up, I won't be a drag. I know how to handle, you know, a spraygun,' she adds with a little drawl, letting her eyes drift downward. Then she resumes pertness. 'Hey, we can pack a lunch! Have a picnic somewhere!'

'Get it together then,' says Zeb, 'because we're leaving right after we eat.'

Rhino starts to say something, stops. Katuro is gazing upwards. 'I think it will not rain,' he says.

Rebecca looks over at Toby, lifts her eyebrows. Toby keeps her own face as flat as possible. Swift Fox is eyeing her sideways.

Fox by name, fox by nature, she thinks. Handle a spraygun, indeed.

Snowman's Progress

'Oh Toby, come and see! Come now!' It's little Blackbeard, tugging at her bedsheet.

'What is it?' says Toby, trying not to sound irritated. She wants to stay here, say goodbye to Zeb, even though he's not going very far, or for long. Just a few hours. She wants to put some sort of mark on him, is that it? In front of Swift Fox. A kiss, a squeeze. *Mine. Stay away.*

Not that it would be any use. She would make a fool of herself.

'Oh Toby, Snowman-the-Jimmy is waking up! He is waking up now,' says Blackbeard. He sounds both anxious and supercharged, the way kids used to sound if it was a parade or a fireworks display – something brief and miraculous. She doesn't want to disappoint him, so she allows herself to be piloted. She looks behind once: Zeb and Rhino and Katuro are sitting at the table, forking up their breakfasts. Swift Fox is hurrying away, to shed that stupid hat and the lookit-my-legs shorts and don some bottom-hugging camouflage.

Toby. Take charge of yourself. This is not high school, she tells herself. But in some ways, it more or less is.

*

Over at Jimmy's hammock there's a crowd. Most of the Crakers are gathered around, adults and children both, looking happy and as excited as they ever look. Some of them are already beginning to sing.

'He is with us! Snowman-the-Jimmy is with us once more!'

'He has come back!'

'He will bring the words of Crake!'

Toby makes her way to the hammock. Two of the Craker women are propping Jimmy up. His eyes are open; he looks dazed.

'Greet him, Oh Toby,' says the tall man called Abraham Lincoln. They're all watching, they're listening intently. 'He has been with Crake. He will bring us words. He will bring a story.'

'Jimmy,' she says. 'Snowman.' She puts her hand on his arm. 'It's me. Toby. I was there at the campfire, down near the beach. Remember? With Amanda, and the two men.'

Jimmy looks up at her. His eyes are surprisingly clear, the whites white, the pupils a little dilated. He blinks. There's no recognition. 'Crap,' he says.

'What is this word, Oh Toby?' says Abraham Lincoln. 'Is it a word of Crake?'

'He's tired,' says Toby. 'No. Not this word.'

'Shit,' says Jimmy. 'Where's Oryx? She was here. She was in the fire.'

'You've been sick,' says Toby.

'Did I kill anyone? One of those ... I think I had a nightmare.'

'No,' she says. 'You didn't kill anyone.'

'I think I killed Crake,' he says. 'He had hold of Oryx, he had a knife, he cut ... Oh God. There was blood all over the pink butterflies. And then I, then ... I shot him.'

Toby's alarmed. What does he mean? More importantly, what will the Crakers make of such a tale? Nothing, she hopes. It will make no sense to them, it will sound like gibberish, because Crake lives in the sky and cannot possibly be dead. 'You've had a nightmare,' she says gently.

'No. I didn't. Not about that. Oh fuck.' Jimmy lies back, closes his eyes. 'Oh fuck.'

'Who is this *Fuck*?' says Abraham Lincoln. 'Why is he talking to this Fuck? That is not the name of anyone here.'

It takes Toby a moment to figure it out. Because Jimmy said 'Oh fuck' rather than plain 'fuck,' they think it's a term of address, like 'Oh Toby.' How to explain to them what 'Oh fuck' means? They would never believe that the word for copulation could mean something bad: an expression of disgust, an insult, a failure. To them, as far as she can tell, the act is pure joy.

'You can't see him,' says Toby a little desperately. 'Only Jimmy, only Snowman-the-Jimmy can see him. He's—'

'Fuck is a friend of Crake's?' asks Abraham Lincoln.

'Yes,' says Toby. 'And a friend of Snowman-the-Jimmy.'

'This Fuck is helping him?' says one of the women.

'Yes,' says Toby. 'When something goes wrong, Snowman-the-Jimmy calls on him for help.' Which is true, in a way.

'Fuck is in the sky!' says Blackbeard triumphantly. 'With Crake!'

'We would like to hear the story of Fuck,' says Abraham Lincoln politely. 'And of how he has helped Snowman-the-Jimmy.'

Jimmy opens his eyes again, squints. Now he's looking at the quilt covering him, with its Hey-Diddle-Diddle motifs. He strokes the cat and the fiddle, the smiling moon. 'What's this? Fucking cow. Brain spaghetti.' He raises his hand to blot out the light.

'He would like you to move back a little,' says Toby. She leans in close, hoping she'll block out whatever Jimmy says next.

'I fucked it up, didn't I,' he says. Luckily he's almost whispering. 'Where's Oryx? She was right here.'

'You need to sleep,' says Toby.

'Fucking pigoons almost ate me.'

'You're safe now,' says Toby. It's not uncommon for someone waking from a coma to hallucinate. But how to describe 'hallucinate' to the Crakers? *It's when you see something that isn't there. But if it isn't there, Oh Toby, how can you see it?*

'What almost ate you?' she says patiently.

'Pigoons,' says Jimmy. 'The giant pigs. I think they did; sorry. It's all spaghetti. Inside of my head. Who were those guys? The ones I didn't shoot.'

'You don't need to worry about anything right now,' says Toby. 'Are you hungry?' They'll have to start with small quantities, it's best after a fast. If only there were some bananas.

'Fucking Crake. I let him fuck me over. I fucking fucked up. Shit.'

'It's okay,' says Toby. 'You did fine.'

'Fucking not,' says Jimmy. 'Can I have a drink?'

The Crakers have been standing respectfully at a distance, but now they move forward. 'We must purr, Oh Toby,' says Abraham Lincoln. 'To make him strong. In his head there is something tangled.'

'You are right,' says Toby. 'There is something tangled.'

'It is because of the dreaming. And the walking here,' says Abraham Lincoln. 'We will purr now.'

'After that he will tell us the words of Crake,' says the ebony woman.

'And the words of Fuck,' says the ivory woman.

'We will sing to this Fuck.'

'And to Oryx.'

'And to Crake. Good, kind . . . '

'I'll get him some fresh water,' says Toby. 'And some honey.'

'Got any booze?' says Jimmy. 'Crap. I feel like shit.'

Ren and Lotis Blue and Amanda are sitting on the low stone wall near the outdoor pump.

'How's Jimmy?' says Ren.

'He's awake,' says Toby. 'But he's not very lucid. That's normal when you've been out so long.'

'What did he say?' says Ren. 'Is he asking for me?'

'Do you think we could see him?' says Lotis Blue.

'He said the inside of his head feels like spaghetti,' says Toby.

'It was always like spaghetti anyway,' says Lotis Blue. She laughs.

'You knew him?' says Toby. She's aware that there was a connection between Jimmy and Ren in the early days, and then between Jimmy and Amanda. But Lotis Blue?

'Yeah,' says Ren, 'we figured it out. She did.'

'I was his lab partner at HelthWyzer High,' says Lotis Blue. 'In Bio. Intro to Gene Splicing. Before I took the bullet train out west with my family, that time.'

'Wakulla Price. He told me,' says Ren, 'that he had such a crush on you! He says you broke his heart. But you never came across for him, did you?'

'He was so full of bullshit,' says Lotis Blue. Her tone is fond, as if Jimmy is a naughty but adorable child.

'And then he broke my heart,' says Ren. 'And God knows what he told Amanda, after he dumped me. Most likely he said that I broke *his* heart.'

'I'd say he had a commitment problem,' says Lotis Blue. 'I knew guys like that.'

'He used to like spaghetti,' says Amanda: more words than Toby's heard her speak since the night of the Painballers.

'At high school it was fish fingers,' says Ren.

'Twenty per cent real fish, remember?' says Lotis Blue. 'Who knows what was really in them.' They both laugh.

'They weren't all that bad, though,' says Ren.

'Labmeat goo,' says Lotis Blue. 'But what did we know? Hey. We ate them.'

'I wouldn't mind one of those right now,' says Ren. 'And a Twinkie.' She sighs. 'They were so retro-nouveau revival!'

'You felt like you were eating upholstery,' says Lotis Blue.

'I'm going over there,' says Amanda. She stands up, straightens her bedsheet, pushes back her hair. 'We should say hello, see if he needs anything. He's been through a lot.'

Finally, thinks Toby, a sign of the former Amanda, the girl she'd known at the Gardeners. Some of that energy, that resourcefulness: backbone, it used to be called. It was Amanda who'd been the initiator, the transgressor of boundaries. Even the larger boys had given her space, back then.

'We'll come too,' says Lotis Blue.

'We'll say, *Surprise!*' says Ren. The two of them giggle.

So much for broken hearts, thinks Toby: Ren's doesn't appear to have anything fractured about it any more, or not in connection with Jimmy. 'Maybe you should wait a little,' she says. What will it do to Jimmy's state of mind if he opens his eyes and sees three of his former beloveds bending over him like the three Fates? Demanding his everlasting love, his apologies, his blood in a cat food saucer? Or worse: the chance to baby him, play nursie, smother him with kindness? Though maybe he'd like that.

But she needn't have worried, because when they get there Jimmy's eyes are closed. Lulled by the purring, he's gone back to sleep.

*

The gleaner team has moved off along the street, or what used to be a street. Zeb first, then Black Rhino, then Swift Fox, with Katuro bringing up the rear. They're moving slowly, carefully, in and around the rubble. They'll be scoping out possible ambushes, taking no chances. Toby wants to run after them, like a left-behind kid – *Wait! Wait! Let me come with you! I have a rifle!* – but no point in that.

Zeb hadn't asked if there was anything he could bring for her. If he had, what would she have said? A mirror? A floral bouquet? She should have requested at least the paper and the pencils. But somehow she couldn't.

Now they're out of sight.

The day moves on. The sun travels up and across the sky, the shadows flatten, food appears and is eaten, words are spoken; dining table objects are gathered together and washed. Sentries take turns. The cobb-house wall rises a little higher, the fence around it gains a coil of wire, weeds are removed from the garden, laundry is deployed. The shadows begin to stretch again, the afternoon clouds gather. Jimmy is carried inside, and the rain rains, with impressive thunder. Then the skies clear, the birds resume their contests, the clouds begin to redden in the west.

No Zeb.

The Mo'Hairs and their shepherds return, Crozier and Beluga and Shackleton, adding three hormonally charged males to the in-camp population mix. Crozier is dangling around Ren, Shackleton edging up to Amanda, Zunzuncito and Beluga are both eyeing Lotis Blue: the intrigues of love are unfolding as they do among the young, and as they do as well among the snails on the lettuce and the shiny green beetles that plague the kale. Murmurings, the shrug of a shoulder, the step forward, the step back.

Toby proceeds through her tasks as if in a monastery, steadily, dutifully, counting the hours.

Still no Zeb.

What could have happened to him? She blots out the pictures. Or she tries to blot them out. Animal, with teeth and claws involved. Vegetable, a falling tree. Mineral, cement, steel, broken glass. Or human.

Suppose he were suddenly not there. A vortex opens: she closes it. Never mind her own loss. What about the others? The other humans. Zeb has valuable skills, he has knowledge that can't be replaced.

They're so few in number, so necessary to one another. Sometimes this encampment feels like a vacation of sorts, but it isn't. They aren't escaping from daily life. This is where they live now.

She tells the Crakers there will be no story tonight, because Zeb has left the story of Zeb inside her head, but some of that story is hard to understand and she needs to put it in order before she can tell it to them. They ask her if a fish would help, but she says not now. Then she goes to sit by herself in the garden.

You've lost, she tells herself. You've lost Zeb. By now Swift Fox must already have him, firmly clamped in her arms and legs and whatever orifices appeal. He's tossed Toby herself aside like an empty paper bag. Why not? No promises were given.

The breeze dies, damp heat rises from the earth, the shadows blend together. Mosquitoes whine. Here's the moon, not so full any more. The hour of the moth comes round again.

No moving lights approach, no voices. Nothing and no one.

She spends the midnight watch with Jimmy in his cubicle, listening to him breathe. There's a single candle. In its light the nursery-rhyme pictures on his quilt waver and swell. The cow grins, the dog laughs. The dish runs away with the spoon.

Drugstore Romance

In the morning Toby avoids the group at the breakfast table. She's in no mood for lectures on epigenetics, or for curious glances, or for speculation about how she's taking the defection of Zeb. He could have said a firm no to Swift Fox, but he didn't. The message was clear.

She goes around to the cooking shed, helps herself to some cold pork and burdock root from yesterday that's withering under an upside-down bowl: Rebecca doesn't like to throw out food.

She sits down at the table, checks the neighbourhood. In the background the Mo'Hairs mill around, waiting for Crozier to let them out and lead them off to eat the weeds along the pathways. Here he comes now, in his biblical bedsheet getup, holding a long stick.

Over by the swing set Ren and Lotis Blue are walking Jimmy to and fro in an awkward six-legged assemblage. His muscle tone isn't great, but he'll build up his strength quickly enough: underneath the wear and tear he's still young. Amanda's there too, sitting on one of the swings; and several of the Crakers, nibbling on the ubiquitous kudzu vines and watching, puzzled but not frightened.

From a distance the scene is bucolic, though there are off-notes: the missing or escaped Mo'Hair is still escaped or missing, Amanda is apathetic and gazing down at the ground, and from the set of Crozier's tight shoulders and the way he turns his back on Ren, he's jealous of her Jimmy-pampering. Toby herself is an off-note, though she must appear calm to anyone watching. It's best to look that way, and through long Gardener training she knows how to keep her face flat, her smile gentle.

But where is Zeb? Why isn't he back yet? Has he found Adam One? If Adam's injured, he'll need to be carried. That would slow them down. What's happening out there in the ruined city, where she can't see? If only the cellphones still worked. But the towers are down; even if there were still a power source, no one here would know how to repair the tech. There's a hand-cranked radio, but it ceased to function.

We'll have to learn smoke signals all over again, she thinks. One for he loves me, two for he loves me not. Three for smouldering anger.

She spends the day working in the garden, on the theory that it will be soothing. If only she had some beehives to care for. She could share the daily news with the bees, as she and old Pilar used to do, back on the God's Gardeners' rooftop garden before Pilar died. Ask them for advice. Request that they fly out and explore and then report back to her, as if they were cyber-bees.

Today we honour Saint Jan Swammerdam, first to discover that the Queen Bee is not a King, and that all worker Bees in a hive are sisters; and Saint Zosima, eastern patron of Bees, who lived the self-less monastic life in the desert, as we, too, are doing in our own way; and Saint C. R. Ribbands, for his meticulous observations on Bee communication stratagems. And let us thank the Creator for the Bees themselves, for their gifts of Honey and Pollen, for their priceless work of fertilization among our Fruits and Nuts and our flowering Vegetables, yes, and for the comfort they bring to us in times of stress, with, as Tennyson once wrote, the murmuring of innumerable Bees . . .

Pilar had taught her to rub a little royal jelly into her skin before working with the bees: that way, they wouldn't see her as a threat. They'd walk on her arms and face, their tiny feet touching as gently as eyelashes, as lightly as a cloud passing over. The bees are messengers, Pilar used to say. They carry the news back and forth between the seen world and the unseen one. If a loved one of yours has crossed the shadow threshold, they will tell you.

Suddenly, today, there are dozens of honeybees in the garden, busying themselves among the bean flowers. There must be a new wild swarm nearby. One bee alights on her hand, tastes the salt on it. Is Zeb dead? she asks it silently. Tell me now. But it lifts off again without signalling.

Had she believed all that? Old Pilar's folklore? No, not really; or not exactly. Most likely Pilar hadn't quite believed it either, but it was a reassuring story: that the dead were not entirely dead but were alive in a different way; a paler way admittedly, and somewhere darker. But still able to send messages, if only such messages could be recognized and deciphered. People need such stories, Pilar said once, because however dark, a darkness with voices in it is better than a silent void.

In the late afternoon, once the thunder is over, the gleaner team returns. Toby sees them walking down the street, weaving in and out among the abandoned trucks and solarcars, backlit in the declining sun, and counts their silhouettes even before she can identify them. Yes, there are four. Nobody's missing. But also, no one's been added.

As they approach the fence around the cobb house Ren and Lotis Blue run to meet them, with a posse of Craker children following. Amanda runs too, though not as fast as the others. Toby walks.

'It was intense!' Swift Fox is saying as she comes up. 'But at least we made it to the drugstore.' She's flushed, a little sweaty; smudged, jubilant. She sets down her pack, opening it. 'Wait'll you see what I got!'

Zeb and Black Rhino look wiped; Katuro less so.

'What happened?' Toby says to Zeb. She doesn't say, 'I was worried sick.' Surely he knows that.

'Long story,' Zeb says. 'Tell you later. I need a shower. Any trouble?'

'Jimmy woke up,' she says. 'He's kind of weak. And thin.'

'Good,' says Zeb. 'Let's fatten him up and get him walking. We could use some more help around here.' Then he's moving away from her, over towards the back of the cobb house.

Toby feels a blip of rage travelling through her body. Gone for almost two days and that's all he has to say about it? She's not a wife, she has no nagging rights, but she can't stop the images: Zeb rolling around in the aisles of the deserted drugstore with Swift Fox, tearing off her camouflage outfit among the bottles of conditioner and shampoo-in colour, more than thirty exciting tints; or were they a couple of aisles over, near the condoms and sensation-enhancing gels? Maybe they'd squashed themselves in beside the cash register, or over by the baby products – finished off with a whole box of wet wipes. Something of the sort happened. It must have happened, to bring out that smug look on the face of Swift Fox.

'Nail polish, painkillers, toothbrushes! Look, tweezers!' she's saying now.

'Looks like you cleaned the place out,' says Lotis Blue.

'There wasn't that much left,' says Swift Fox. 'Looters were through, looks like they were interested in the pharmaceuticals. The Oxy, the BlyssPluss pills, anything with codeine.'

'Not much use for the hair products?' says Lotis Blue.

'No. And the girl stuff – they didn't take that,' says Swift Fox. She starts unloading the packages of Heavy Days and tampons and Slimlines. 'I made the guys carry some in their own packs. They scored some beer too. Now that was a minor miracle.'

'Why did it take so long?' Toby asks. Swift Fox smiles at her, not snidely. Instead she's too friendly, too guileless, like a teenager who's broken curfew.

'We got kind of trapped,' she says. 'We poked around and gathered stuff, but then in the afternoon, right before we were going to head back, there was a herd of those huge pigs – the ones that used to try raiding the garden before we shot some of them.

'At first they were just lurking along behind us, but when we'd finished in the drugstore and were coming out, we saw they were heading us off. So we ran back into the drugstore, but the front windows were smashed, so there was nothing to keep them out. We managed to get up onto the roof through a little trapdoor in the storeroom ceiling – they can't climb.'

'Did they look hungry?' says Ren.

'How can you tell with a pig?' says Swift Fox.

They're omnivorous, thinks Toby. They'll eat anything. But hungry or not, they'd kill in spite. Or for revenge. We've been eating them.

'So then?' says Ren.

'We stayed up on the roof for a while,' says Swift Fox, 'and then the pigs came out of the drugstore and saw we were up on the roof. They'd found a carton of potato chips, they dragged it outside and had a party, keeping an eye on us the whole time. They were flaunting those chips: they must've known we were hungry. Zeb said to count them in case they split up into groups, with some of them creating a distraction and the others waiting to ambush us. Then they went off to the west, not walking but trotting, as if they'd decided on a goal. And we looked, and there was something over there. There was smoke.'

Every once in a while something in the city catches fire. An electrical connection, still attached to a solar unit; a pile of damp organics, going up in a fit of spontaneous combustion; a cache of carbon garboil, heated by the sun. So smoke is not unheard of, and Toby says so.

'This was different,' says Swift Fox. 'It was thinner, like a camping fire.'

'Why didn't you shoot the pigs?' says Lotis Blue.

'Zeb said it would be a waste of time because there were too many of them. Also we didn't want to run out of energy packs for the sprayguns. Zeb thought we should go over there and take a look, but it was getting dark. So we stayed at the drugstore for the night.'

'On the roof?' said Toby.

'In the storeroom,' said Swift Fox. 'We barricaded the door with some of the boxes in there. But nothing happened, except rats; there were a lot of those. Then in the morning we went over to where we saw the fire. Zeb and Black Rhino figured it was the Painball guys.'

'Did you see them?' asks Amanda.

'We saw the remains of their fire,' says Swift Fox. 'Burnt out. Pig tracks all over it. Also what was left of our Mo'Hair. The one with the red braids? They'd been eating it.'

'Oh no,' says Lotis Blue.

'The Painballers or the pigs?' says Amanda.

'Both,' says Swift Fox. 'But we didn't see any two guys. Zeb says the pigs must've chased them away. We did find a dead piglet, a little farther along: spraygun kill, Zeb said. A hind leg cut off. He says we should go back for it later because those pigs aren't likely to throw themselves in our way again, not after one of their young has been killed, so we should make the most of any stray pork. But we heard some of those crazy vicious dog splices, so maybe we'll have to fight them for it. It's a zoo out there.'

'If it really was a zoo there'd be fences,' says Lotis Blue. 'That Mo'Hair was stolen, right? It didn't just wander off. Those two guys must've been quite close to us and nobody saw them.'

'That's creepy,' says Ren.

Swift Fox isn't listening. 'Look what else I got,' she says. 'Pregnancy tests, the kind where you pee on sticks. I figure we'll all be needing them. Or some of us will.' She smiles, but she doesn't look at Toby.

'Count me out,' says Ren. 'Who'd bring a baby into this?' She sweeps her arm: the cobb house, the trees, the minimalism. 'Without running water? I mean . . . '

'Not sure you'll have that option,' says Swift Fox. 'In the long run. Anyway, we owe it to the human race. Don't you think?'

'Who'd be the dads?' says Lotis Blue with some interest.

'I'd say take your pick,' says Swift Fox. 'The line forms to the left. Just choose the one with the longest tongue hanging out.'

'Guess you'll be stuck with Ivory Bill then,' says Lotis Blue.

'Did I say longest tongue?' says Swift Fox. She and Lotis Blue giggle, Ren and Amanda do not.

'Let's see those pee sticks,' says Ren.

Toby stares into the darkness. Should she follow Zeb? He

must have finished his shower by now: the cobb-house showers are never long, unless it's Swift Fox, using up all the
sun-warmed water. But Zeb is not in evidence.

She stays awake in her cubicle, just in case. Moonlight sil-
vering her eyes. Owls calling, in love with each other's feathers.
Nothing she wants.

Weeding

No Zeb all morning. No one mentions him. She doesn't ask.

Lunch is soup, with meat of some kind – smoked dog? – and kudzu with garlic. Polyberries that could be riper. A salad of mixed greens. 'We need to figure out how to get some vinegar,' says Rebecca. 'Then I can do a proper dressing.'

'First we'd need to make the wine,' says Zunzuncito.

'I'm all for that,' says Rebecca. She's put some arugula seeds into the salad, for a peppery effect. She has a plan for making a saltworks – an evaporating pan, down by the shore. Once the coast is clear, she says. Once the Painballers are accounted for.

After lunch there's indoor time, undercover time. The sun's high and burning, the storm clouds not yet building. The air is sticky with moisture.

Toby stays in her cubicle, trying to nap but sulking instead. No sulking allowed, she tells herself. No wound-licking. She can't even be certain that there's a wound to lick. Though she does feel wounded.

Late afternoon, after the rain. Nobody's around, with the exception of Crozier and Manatee, standing sentinel. Toby's kneeling in the garden, killing slugs. It's an act that would once have made her feel guilty – *For are not Slugs God's creatures too*, Adam One would say, *with as much claim to breathe the air, as long as they do it somewhere else in a place that is more congenial for them than our Edencliff Rooftop Garden?* But right now killing them serves as an outlet for her. An outlet for what? She doesn't wish to ponder that.

Worse, she finds herself editorializing. *Die, evil slug!* She drops each plucked slug into a tin can with wood ash and water in the bottom. They'd used salt earlier, but there's little of that to spare. Perhaps a swift blow with a flat rock would be kinder to the slugs – the wood ash must be painful – but she's not in the mood to weigh the relative kindness of slug execution methods.

She yanks out a weed. *How thoughtlessly we label and dismiss God's Holy Weeds! But* Weed *is simply our name for a plant that annoys us by getting in the way of our Human plans. Consider how useful and indeed edible and delicious so many of them are!*

Right. Not this one. Ragweed, from the look of it. She tosses it onto the pile of discards.

'Hey there, Death Squad,' says a voice. It's Zeb, grinning down at her.

Toby scrambles to her feet. Her hands are dirty; she doesn't know what to do with them. Has he been sleeping in until now, or what? She can't ask what happened with Swift Fox, or if anything did: she refuses to sound like a shrew.

'I'm glad you came back safe,' she says. And she is glad, more glad than she can say, but even to herself her voice sounds fake.

'Me too,' he says. 'Trip was more than I bargained for. Wiped me out, slept like a log, must be getting old.'

Is this a coverup? How suspicious can she get? 'I missed you,' she says. There. Was that so hard?

He grins more. 'Counted on that,' he says. 'Brought you something.' It's a compact, with a small round mirror.

'Thank you,' she says. She manages a smile. Is it a guilt gift, an apology? The roses for the wife after the husband's furtive tumble with the office co-worker? But she's not a wife.

'Got you some paper too. Couple of school notebooks, drug-store still carried them, I guess for pleeb kids who couldn't afford the Wi-Fi tabs. Couple of rollerball pens, pencils. Felt markers.'

'How did you know I wanted those?' she says.

'I worked with a mind reader, once upon a time,' he says. 'Cursive's a Gardener skill, right? Figured you'd want to be keeping track of the days. Hey, what about a hug?'

'I'd get you all muddy,' she says, relenting, smiling.

'I've been dirtier.'

How could she not put her arms around him, despite her slug-slippery fingers?

And the sun is shining, and there are bees, among the yellow squash flowers. 'You know what I really need?' she says to Zeb's smoky beard. 'Some reading glasses. And a hive.'

'Consider them yours.' There's a pause. 'I wanted you to look at this.'

From inside his sleeve he pulls out a shoe: a sandal. It's hand-made, with recycled materials: tire-tread sole, bicycle inner tube straps, silver duct tape accents. Although earth-stained, it's not very worn. 'Gardener,' Toby says. She remembers the fashion well, or rather the lack of it. Then she qualifies: 'Or maybe it is. Not that other people didn't make those, I guess.'

Already she has a picture in her head: Adam One and the surviving Gardeners, hunkered down in one of their Ararat hidey holes – the old mushroom-growing cellars, for instance – cobbling away by candlelight at their handcrafted sandals like a burrowful of elves, nibbling on their stores of honey and soybits while above their heads the cities flamed and collapsed and the human race melted away to nothingness. She wants so much to believe it that it can't possibly be true.

'Where did you find it?' she asks.

'Near the piglet kill,' Zeb says. 'I didn't show the others.'

'You think it's Adam. You think he's still alive. You think he left this for you – or for someone – on purpose.' These aren't questions.

'So do you,' says Zeb. 'You think it too.'

'Don't hope too much,' she says. 'Hope can ruin you.'

'Okay. You're right. But still.'

'If you're right,' she says, 'wouldn't Adam be looking for you?'

Blacklight
Headlamp

The Story of Zeb and Fuck

You don't need to tell them a story every time. Come with me, instead. You can skip a night.

I already skipped one night. I can't disappoint them too much. They might leave here and go back to the beach, and then they'd be easy to attack. Those Painballers would ... I'd never forgive myself if ...

Okay. But make it short?

I'm not sure that's possible. They ask a lot of questions.

Tell them to piss off.

They wouldn't understand that. They think piss is a good thing. Like *fuck* – they think there's an invisible entity called Fuck. A helper of Crake's in time of need. And of Jimmy's, because they heard him saying *Oh fuck*.

I'm with them. Fuck! An invisible entity! A helper in time of need! Dead right!

They want to hear a story about him. About him and you, actually. The two of you, having boyish adventures. You're both stars at the moment. They've been pestering me about it, that story.

Can I listen in?

No. You'd laugh.

See this mouth? Virtual duct tape! If I had some Krazy Glue, I could . . . Hey, I could glue my mouth to your . . .

Don't be so warped.

Life is warped. I'm just in synch.

Thank you for the fish.

See, I am wearing the red hat, and I have listened to the round shiny thing I wear on my arm.

Tonight I will tell you the story of Zeb and Fuck. As you have asked me to do.

Once Zeb had left his home, where his father and his mother were not kind to him, he wandered around in the chaos. He did not know where to go next, and he did not know where his brother, Adam, was, who was his only friend and helper.

Yes, Fuck was his friend and helper too, but he could not be seen.

No, that is not an animal over there in the dark behind the shrub. That is Zeb. He is not laughing, he is coughing.

So, Zeb's brother, Adam, was his only friend and helper that he could see and touch. Was Adam lost? Had he been stolen away? Zeb did not know, and that made him feel sad.

But Fuck kept him company and gave him advice. Fuck lived in the air and flew around like a bird, which was how he could be with Zeb one minute, and then with Crake, and then also with Snowman-the-Jimmy. He could be in many places at once. If you were in trouble and you called to him – *Oh Fuck!* – he would always be there, just when you needed him. And as soon as you said his name, you would feel better.

Yes, Zeb does have a bad cough. But you do not need to purr on him right now.

Yes, it would be good to have a friend and helper like Fuck. I wish I had one too.

No, Fuck is not my helper. I have a different helper, whose name is Pilar. She died, and took the form of a plant, and now she lives with the bees.

Yes, I talk to her even if I can't see her. But she is not quite so ... she is not so abrupt as Fuck. She is less like thunder, and more like a breeze.

I will tell you the story of Pilar some other time.

So Zeb wandered deeper and deeper into dangerous places, where there were a great many bad men doing cruel and hurtful things. And then he came to a place where they cooked and ate the Children of Oryx, which he knew was wrong. And when he called on Fuck for advice, Fuck told him he had to leave that place. And then he lived in some houses with water all around, and he came to know a snake. But it was dangerous there; and he said, Oh Fuck! And Fuck flew through the air, and spoke to Zeb, and said he would help Zeb get away safely.

That's enough of the story for tonight. You already know that Zeb got away safely because he's sitting right over there, isn't he? And he's very happy to be hearing this story. That is why he is laughing now, and not coughing any more.

Thank you for saying good night. I am happy to know that you want me to sleep soundly, without bad dreams.

Good night to you, as well.

Yes, good night.

Good night!

That's enough. You can stop saying good night now.

Thank you.

Floating World

One day Zeb woke up next to Wynette, the SecretBurgers meatslinger, and realized that she smelled like grilled patties and stale cooking oil. As he did himself, granted, but that was different, because it always is, says Zeb, when it's your own smell. But it's not what you want the object of your lust to smell like. This is a primate thing, it's basic, they've done the tests. Ask any of the MaddAddamite biogeeks here.

And the onions, don't forget them, and the gruesome red sauce in squeeze bottles the customers craved so much it most likely had crack in it. When things got energetic and there was a brawl, someone would always go for that red sauce and start squirting it around. Then it would get mixed in with the scalp-wound splatter blood and you couldn't tell whether someone was bleeding to death or had only been doused with red sauce.

The way that combo of smells would seep into their clothing and hair and even the skin pores was unavoidable, working where the two of them did. You couldn't wash off that stink even when there was shower water available, and it didn't blend too well with the cheap glop Wynette would rub on herself to neutralize it: Delilah, it was called, in lotion and cologne forms both, and it was heavy going, like wading through a sea of dying lilies, or a clutch of elderly churchwomen of the kind that populated the Church of PetrOleum. Those two smells – the SecretBurgers, the Delilah – were okay if you were really hungry or really horny, or both. But not so sweet otherwise.

Fuck, Zeb thought, lying there newly awakened that morning and inhaling the dire potpourri. There's no future in this.

Or if there was a future, it was a negative one, because in addition to smelling funny Wynette was getting nosy. In the name of love and getting to know and understand the real, total him, she wanted to explore his deeper depths, figuratively speaking. She wanted his lid off. If she pried too hard – if she unwrapped one after another of his flimsy cover stories, which he hadn't constructed with enough care, he realized, and he vowed to do better next time he conned someone – if she did the unwrapping, there was nothing very convincing immediately underneath. And then if she kept going, she might make some guesses about where he'd come from and who he'd been originally, and then it would only be a matter of time before she weaselled on him so she could collect whatever greyland reward must be on offer, out there in the word-of-mouth rat networks of the pleeblands.

Zeb had no doubt that there was such a reward. There might even be some of his biometrics circulating, such as photos of his ears, and animated silhouettes of his walk, and his schooltime thumbprints. Wynette wasn't connected gangwise so far as he knew, and luckily she was too poor to own a PC or a tab. But there was cheap netstuff available on time-rental in cafés, and she might do some identity surfing if he pissed her off enough.

Already she was beginning to emerge from the initial sex-induced coma created by him through the magic of his first-contact-with-aliens puppy-on-speed gonadal enthusiasm.

Young guys have no taste as such in sexual matters – no discrimination. They're like those penguins that shocked the Victorians, they'll bonk anything with a cavity, and Wynette had been the beneficiary in Zeb's case. Not to brag, but during their nightly tangles her eyes had rolled so far up into her head that she looked like the undead half the time, and the amplified rock-band noises she made had caused thumping and banging both from the alcohol store on the ground floor and from whatever nestful of mournful wage slaves lived above them.

But now she was mistaking Zeb's animal energies for something more profound. She wanted post-hump chat. She wanted them to share their essences, on a spiritual level. She was starting to ask things like, were her breasts big enough, and did this colour of lime green look good on her, and why weren't they doing it twice a night the way they did at first? Questions that mantrapped you any way you answered. These nightly interrogation sessions were becoming wearisome. Maybe, Zeb concluded, his feelings for Wynette hadn't been true love after all.

'Don't look at me like that. I was really young. And don't forget, I'd been improperly socialized,' says Zeb.

'Look at you like what?' says Toby. 'It's darker than the inside of a goat. You can't see me.'

'I can feel the glacial chill of your stone-cold gaze.'

'I just feel sorry for her, that's all,' says Toby.

'No, you don't. If I'd stayed with her, I wouldn't be here with you, right?'

'Okay. True enough. I withdraw the sorrow. But still.'

*

He wasn't a complete shit about it. He left Wynette some cash and a note of undying adoration, with a P.S. saying that his life had been threatened because of a dirty deal – he didn't say what kind – and he couldn't bear the thought of putting her in peril because of him.

'You used that word?' says Toby. 'Peril?'

'She liked romance,' says Zeb. 'Knights and stuff. She had some old paperbacks; they'd been in the room when she rented it. Falling apart.'

'And you didn't want to play the knight?'

'Not for her,' says Zeb. 'For you' – he kisses the tips of her fingers – 'swords at dawn, any time.'

'I can't believe that,' says Toby. 'You've just told me what a liar you are!'

'At least I take the trouble to lie, for you,' says Zeb. 'Lying's more work than the bare-naked truth. Think of it as a courtship display. I'm aging badly, I've got wear and tear, I don't have a giant blue dong like our Craker friends out there, so I need to use my wits. What's left of them.'

Zeb travelled hastily south on the Truck-A-Pillar route, coming to rest in the remnants of Santa Monica. The rising sea had swept away the beaches, and the once-upmarket hotels and condos were semi-flooded. Some of the streets had become canals, and nearby Venice was living up to its name. The district as a whole was known as the Floating World, and it really was floating most of the time, especially when the full moon brought a spring tide.

None of the original owners lived there any more. Unable to collect insurance – for what was the encroaching sea but an Act of God? – they'd fled uphill. Squatters and transients of many kinds had moved in, though there were no municipal services left: the sewage system and the water mains were kaput, and the electricity had been cut off some time ago.

But the district had acquired a raunchy cachet, and middle-aged punters from posher locations on higher ground were willing to venture down to the Floating World for the odd dose of bohemian thrill, navigating the drowned streets in tiny run-about water taxis with solar putt-putt engines on them. They came for the gambling and the illegal-substance dealing and the girls, but also for the real-time carny acts that operated from building to crumbling building, moving shop when the premises got too waterlogged or when a violent storm had swept away yet more of the shoreline and the real estate.

Much was on offer in the Floating World; profitably so, since none of the operators paid rent or taxes. There was a crap game in progress morning and night, with a revolving set of bleary-eyed players left unsatisfied by online gaming and craving the addictive nerve-jangle of potential danger. In addition, they wanted freedom from oversight: they believed that the internet was as full of peepholes as a Truck-A-Pillar motel, and they didn't want to leave any of their virtual DNA on it.

There was a moppet shop, with a mix of real girls and prosti-bots, depending on how much pre-programmed interaction you wanted, not that you could always tell the difference. There was a group of street acrobats who did torch-lit high-wire acts on ropes strung across the flooded streets, and sometimes fell and broke parts of themselves, such as their necks. The possibility of injury or death was a strong attraction: as the online world became more and more pre-edited and slicked up, and as even its so-called reality sites raised questions about authenticity in the minds of the viewers, the rough, unpolished physical world was taking on a mystic allure.

Among the carny acts there was a magician, a sad-eyed guy

of maybe fifty, with a baggy-kneed suit he must have purloined from a thrift store: there wasn't a lot of margin in what he did. He'd set up a makeshift stage on the rapidly mildewing mezzanine floor of a former platinum-grade hotel, where he manipulated cards and coins and handkerchiefs, and sawed women in half and made them disappear from cabinets, and read minds. Those delights had vanished from television and online, since such displays of skill lacked tangibility in the digital realm and were therefore distrusted: how could you tell it wasn't just special effects? But when the Floating World magician put a handful of needles into his mouth you could see they were real needles, and when they emerged threaded you could touch the thread; and when he threw a pack of cards up into the air and the ace of spades stayed there on the ceiling, you'd seen that happen in real time, right in front of your eyes.

The mezzanine was always crowded on Friday and Saturday nights when the Floating World magician put on his shows. He called himself Slaight of Hand, after Allan Slaight, a twentieth-century historian of the hermetic arts. Though few in the audience would know that.

Zeb learned it, however, because it was with Slaight of Hand that he found work. He played Lothar, the muscular assistant, clad in a cornball outfit made of faux-fur leopard skin. He'd heave the cabinet around, turning it upside down to show there was nothing in it, or he'd place the beautiful girl assistant into the box in which she would be sawn in two. Though sometimes he posed as an audience member, gathering information for the mind-reading act, or expressing amazement and thus distracting attention. In the daytimes he was sent on shopping errands outside the Floating World, to where there were mini-supermarkets and people who were awake during the day.

*

'I learned a lot from old Slaight of Hand,' Zeb says.

'How to saw a woman in half?'

'That too, though anyone can saw a woman in half. The trick is to have them smile while you're doing it.'

'I guess that takes mirrors,' Toby says. 'And smoke.'

'I'm sworn to secrecy. Best thing old Slaight taught me was misdirection. Make them look at something else, away from what you're really doing, and you can get away with a lot. Slaight called each one of his beautiful assistants Miss Direction. It was his generic name for them.'

'Maybe he couldn't tell one from another?'

'Maybe not. They didn't interest him in that way. But they had to look good in sequins, not very many sequins. The Miss Direction of the moment was Katrina Wu, a lynx-eyed Asian-Fusion hybrid from Palo Alto. I thought of her as Katrina WooWoo, and tried to get friendly with her – Wynette the SecretBurgers meatslinger had opened up a whole world of possibility, and I was feeling reckless – but Miss Direction WooWoo was having none of it. I held her in my arms every weekend while stuffing her into boxes and cabinets to be sawed and disappeared and laying her out on a table so she could be levitated, and I'd give her the odd squeeze and what I must've thought was a marrow-melting leer, but she'd hiss at me through her smile: *Stop that right now.*'

'You do a good hiss. Maybe getting sawed in half was using up all her vital fluids.'

'Nope. One of the high-wire acrobats was taking care of those. During the week, when she wasn't working for Slaight of Hand, this guy was teaching her trapeze dancing; the two of them were working on a high-wire strip act. She had a couple of outfits for that: a bird one, a snakeskin one. For the snake act she also had a real snake: some sort of lobotomized python. Its name was March because, according to Miss

WooWoo, March was a month of hope, and her python was always hopeful.

'She appeared to like the thing; she'd drape it around her neck during some of her acts, let it do some writhing on her. I got friendly with March, I used to catch mice for it. I figured those terrorized mice could be a way to the WooWoo heart, but no dice.'

'What is it about women and snakes?' says Toby. 'Or women and birds, for that matter.'

'We like to think you're wild animals,' says Zeb. 'Underneath the decorations.'

'You mean stupid? Or subhuman?'

'Cut me some slack here. I mean, ferociously out of control, in a good way. A scaly, feathery woman is a powerful attraction. She's got an edge to her, like a goddess. Risky. Extreme.'

'Okay, we'll split the difference. So then what?'

'*Then what* was that Katrina WooWoo and the high-wire guy took off one day. And March the python – March went with them. That bothered me at the time, not the snake so much, but Miss WooWoo. Infected as I was by Cupid's festering dart. I confess I moped.'

'I can't imagine you moping,' says Toby.

'I did, though. Pain in the butt, I was. Not that anyone noticed, so I was mostly a pain in the butt to myself. Word on the street was that Katrina and the trapeze guy had headed east to make their fortune. Couple of years later I found out that they'd used the snake-and-bird motif and launched an upmarket gents' joint called Scales and Tails. Started small, became a franchise. That was before the sex trades got taken over by the Corps.'

'Like the Scales in the Sinkhole, near the Edencliff Rooftop Garden? Adult entertainment?'

'You got it. Where the Gardener kids used to glean leftover

wine, for making the vinegar. Same franchise. Anyway, saved my ass at a crucial moment, but I'll tell you about that later.'

'Is this going to be about you and that snake woman? You finally scored? I can hardly wait to hear. Was the python in on it too?'

'Ease up. I'm trying to stick with the chronological order here. And hey, not everything's about my sex life.'

Toby wants to say that a lot of it has been so far, but she refrains: it's not fair to demand the whole story and then object to it, she does realize that. 'Okay, fire away,' she says.

'After Katrina WooWoo disappeared from the Floating World, old Slaight of Hand wandered away in search of another Miss Direction, and maybe a more aesthetically attractive performance space that wasn't falling into the water. I was at loose ends, which was most likely good, since – being on the lookout for the next best thing, with eyes open and ears pricked – I noticed a couple of guys hanging around who were making too much of an effort to fit in, riffraff-wise. You can tell when a man is new to his greasy ponytail, his raggedy 'stache, and his garish nose jewellery: too much face fiddling. And their pants were wrong. They hadn't made the mistake of new ones, like Chuck, but their rips and tears and smears were too artful. Or that was my judgment. So I was on the next Truck-A-Pillar I could hitch a ride with.

'This time I went all the way down to Mexico. I figured that whatever tentacles the Rev could stretch out weren't likely to reach that far.'

The Hackery

There was a surplus of paranoid drug peddlers in Mexico who assumed that Zeb was a paranoid drug peddler too, and that their interests clashed with his. After a few too many episodes in which men with arcane tattoos and designs of tulips razored onto their scalps gave him the full frontal scowl, plus a couple of near-misses with knives to make things clear, he moved down the map, shedding spare change all the way. For incidentals he paid cash only: he didn't want to leave a cybertrail, even the cyber-trail of someone named John and then Roberto and then Diaz.

From Cozumel he hopped through the Caribbean Islands, then over to Colombia. But although he further honed the skill of drinking with strangers in bars, and survived those lessons and a few others, nothing in Bogotá held any possibilities for him; in addition to which, he stood out too much.

Rio was another story. Its nickname then was The Hackery; that was before the mini-drone raids and the electrical-grid sabotage events that sent the truly serious operators – those who'd survived – into the Cambodian jungles to set up shop anew. But Rio then was at its zenith. It was said to be the Wild West of the web, filled with youthful bristle-faced blackhat cyberhustlers of every possible nationality. There were hordes of potential customers: businesses were spying on businesses, politicians were setting nets for other politicians, and then there were the military interests: these paid the most of all, though they also did a moderately full security check on prospective employees, and Zeb didn't want that. But all in all, Rio was a seller's market: quick hands for hire, no questions asked, and no matter what you looked like you'd blend in down there as long as you looked odd enough.

He was out of practise keyboard-wise, considering the time he'd spent slinging meat, aiding Slaight of Hand, ogling Miss Direction, and python-wrestling, but it didn't take him long to get his flexibility back. Then he went looking for work. He found an opening suitable to his talents within a week.

His first employer was Ristbones, an outfit that specialized in the hacking of electronic voting machines. That had been easy in the first decade of the century, and also profitable – if you controlled the machines, you could slip in whichever candidate you wanted, as long as the real vote was close to being split – but outrage had been expressed and fusses had been made, and the appearance of democracy was still considered worth preserving back then; so firewalls had been installed and the pickwork was now more complex.

It was also boring – sort of like crocheting, working through the fairly elementary lacework that was more for show than for actual prevention. You could zizz off on the job trying to interest yourself. So when he had an offer from Hacksaw Inc. he took it, a little too rapidly as it turned out. He wasn't drunk at the time, but vodka was involved. That, and a lot of backslapping and loud comradely laughs and compliments. The pickup was made by three suave guys, one with large hands and another with large money. The third was probably the eliminator: he didn't say much.

Hacksaw was located on a joyboat moored off Rio and

posing as an anything-goes sex bazaar. Not just a pose, either, because you could get everything there from chicken soup to nuts, on or off the bone, screams-for-sale extra. He spent a nervous four weeks on that deathstar working for a pod of seedy Russian pussy-smugglers who were tiring of the whininess and bleediness and need-to-feed of their human merchandise and were aiming to supplement their income in ways that required less soft tissue. They put Zeb to work hacking into online PachinkoPoker for skimming purposes, and it was a mite stressful because – said the other code slaves – the Hacksaw folk were known to heave you into the luminous krill if they thought you were taking too long unravelling the digital embroidery.

Or else if you were befriending the software. Misusing it was fine, so long as not much in the way of merchandise was damaged, since damage was a privilege reserved for paying customers. A few weekly free-time coupons for hackstaff were included in the paypacket, along with some complimentary gambling chips and the meals and drinks. But sentimental attachments were strictly off-limits.

The sex bazaar side of the Hacksaw business was beyond tawdry; especially the kids, they were lifting them from the favelas on a limited-time-use basis, turning them over, and fishfooding them at a fast clip. That part was too close to the Rev and his child-rearing practises for Zeb's tastes, and he must've let that show because the cordiality of the jovial comrades was waning rapidly. After working only a month of his contract he'd managed to sneak a go-fast boat by sharing a few vodkas with the Russian guard and then whacking him and pocketing his identity and overboarding him. That was the first time he'd killed anyone, and it was too bad for the guard, a non-too-bright bullet-head who should've known better than to trust a callow though not small and – by definition, considering he was working for Hacksaw – devious youth like Zeb.

He took a few lines of Hacksaw code with him, and a few passwords. Those could come in handy. He also took one of the girls. He'd sweet-talked her into acting as his very own Miss Direction: he used his coupons to book an hour of her time, then got her to walk past the booze-addled guard in what passed for her nightie – some shred of cheeseclothy fabric – looking just seductive enough and just furtive enough – *Where you going?* – to get the coconut-brain to turn his head.

Zeb could have left the girl on the joyboat, but he felt sorry for her. The comrades would figure out that she'd acted the decoy, wittingly or unwittingly they wouldn't care, and they'd mash her like a potato. She was only on the boat because she'd been lured away from her home town in rustbucket Michigan by spurious enticements and a few chunks of third-rate flattery. She'd been told she had talent; she'd been told the job was dancing.

He hadn't been so thick as to take the go-fast boat to a regular marina. The comrades might already have noticed the two absences – three, including the guard – and be on the prowl. He docked at one of the shore hotels and hid the girl behind an ornamental fountain until he could gain entrance to the corridors by booking a room with the guard's identity. Then he worked out the master code, snuck into a well-stocked bedroom, and lifted some clothes for her, and a shirt for himself as well: too small, but he rolled up the sleeves. He left a threatening Miss Direction note scrawled on the bathroom mirror in soap: *I Come Back Later. Revenge.* Chances were that nine-tenths of the guys staying in places like that would have at least one violent and resentful thug in their past, and would thus leave the hotel rapidly without complaining about their missing wardrobe items.

Or their car keys. Or their car.

*

Once they were far enough away, he found a net café where he could lilypad to one of his .09 per cent secret stashes, then transfer a lump of that to a different account and pay it out to himself; after which, he erased all traces. Then he borrowed another car that just happened to be available. People were careless.

So far, so good; but then there was the girl. Her name was Minta, which made him think of organic chewing gum. Fresh, green. She'd held firm during their escape, she hadn't lost her nerve, she'd been silent. Most likely she'd also been in shock, because she hadn't lasted. There was decay from the inside, whether mental or physical he couldn't tell.

She was all right when they were in view, on the street or in a store – she could act normal for short periods – but when they were inside, in this room or that room or even in a car, zigzagging their way north and west, she would spend the time at her two specialties, crying hopelessly and staring vacantly. Television was no distraction for her, nor was sex. Understandably enough she didn't want Zeb to touch her, though out of gratitude and as a form of payment she offered anything he might want in the way of his being touched himself.

'So you took her up on it?' Toby says, keeping her voice light. How can she be jealous of such a wreck, such a wraith?

'No, as a matter of fact,' Zeb says. 'No joy in that. Might as well hire a prostibot wank robot in a mall. It was more fun for me to tell her she didn't have to. After that she did let me hug her a little. I thought it might calm her down, but it only made her shiver.'

Minta started hearing things – stealthy footsteps, heavy breathing, a metallic clanking sound – and she was frightened every time she went out of whatever squalid hotel room they were staying in. Zeb could have afforded classier lodgings, but it was better to keep to the deep pleeblands, in the shadows.

Sad to say, Minta ended by jumping off a balcony in San

Diego. He wasn't in the room at the time, he'd been out getting her a coffee, but he saw the crowd gathering and heard the siren. Which meant he had to leave town in a hurry to avoid the investigation, if any; which in turn meant that his description might be top of the list as a murder suspect, supposing the authorities decided to follow up, which increasingly they didn't. Anyway, where would they start? Minta had no identity. He'd abandoned nothing of his – he made a point of taking everything with him whenever he left a room – but who knows if there were security cameras anywhere near? Not likely in the pleeb shadowlands, but you never knew.

He made it up to Seattle, where he took a quick peek into the *Birth of Venus* zephyr dropbox he shared with Adam. There was a message for him: 'Confirm you're still in the body.' Adam sometimes echoed the Rev's speech patterns in a creepy way.

'In whose body?' Zeb posted in reply.

It was an old joke of his: he always used to make fun of that pious no-longer-in-the-body funeral talk of the Rev's. He made that joke so Adam would know it was really him, not some decoy impersonator. In fact, Adam had most likely planted that in-body query on purpose because he'd know Zeb couldn't resist it; whereas a fake Zeb would just give a straight answer. Adam was usually a few twists ahead of the curve.

His next move was up to Whitehorse. He'd heard about Bearlift in a Rio bar and figured it would be a good place to hide out, since nobody would be expecting him to go there. Not Hacksaw, who had a score to settle: they'd look for him in some other hackers' hotspot, such as Goa. And not the Rev either: Zeb had never shown the least interest in wildlife.

'So that,' says Zeb, 'is how I wound up on the Mackenzie Mountain Barrens wearing a bear skin, and jumping onto a trail biker, and getting mistaken for Bigfoot the Sasquatch.'

'Understandable,' says Toby. 'They might have thought that even without the bear skin.'

'You being snarky?'

'It's a compliment.'

'I'll mull that over. Anyway, I wasn't sad about the way it turned out.'

Fast-forward to Whitehorse again: there he was, washed, dressed, and in his right mind, supposing there was such a thing. He was avoiding the Bearlift headquarters and the usual drinking holes because those people thought he was dead, and why would he want to sacrifice the advantages that non-existence can bring? So he was spending a fair amount of time in the motel room eating faux-peanut objects and sending out for pizza and watching pay-per-view, never mind what, and trying to figure out his next move. Where to go from Whitehorse? How to get out? What was his next incarnation of choice?

Also he was wondering, Who set Chuck up to stick that needle into him? Which of the several parties with an interest in his ill-being would use an inept, A-sombrero dink like Chuck as their choice of poison-dart launcher?

Cold Dish

He existed in two states: his actual camouflaged mode, an any-face with a bogus name; and, in his previous guise, fried to a crisp in a 'thopter crash. Pity about that, some might say, but very convenient for others. And convenient for himself as well.

But he didn't want Adam to think he was dead – there'd been a long communications hiatus during the Bearlift caper – so he needed to make contact before news of that kind leaked out.

He put on all his clothes, including the aviator helmet, the fake goosedown puffy jacket, and the sunglasses, and made a foray to one of the two local net cafés, a tidy operation called Cubs' Corner that served turgid organic soy beverages and under-cooked giant muffins. He ordered both: eating the local foods was a principle of his. Then he paid cash for a half-hour of net time and sent a message to Adam via the zephyr dropbox. 'Some shithead tried to mort me. Everyone thinks I'm f-ing dead.'

He picked up the answer in ten minutes: 'Renouncing pro-fanity will improve your digestion. Stay dead. May have job opportunity. Get to New New York area ASAP, connect with me then.'

'OK, get me jobcheck ID?' he sent back.

'Y. Will be waiting,' Adam replied. Where was he? No clue about that. But he must have landed in a place where he felt safe, or safe enough. That was a relief to Zeb. Losing Adam would be like losing an arm and a leg. And the top part of his head.

He went back to his motel room and thought through the logistics of getting himself to New New York. As a dead person, and with the aid of the temporary patchwork ID he'd put together, he might chance the bullet train once he'd Truck-A-Pillared as far as, say, Calgary.

But the main puzzle was still bothering him. Who'd wanted to nab him via Chuck? He tried to narrow it down. First of all, who could've figured out where he was? Fingered him at Bearlift? By that time his name was Devlon, and before that it was Larry, and before that, Kyle. He didn't look much like a Kyle, but sometimes it was better to go counter-type. And he'd been through at least six earlier names.

He'd bought the better part of the identities on the greyer than grey market, and there was no upside for those guys to sell him out: they had their businesses to run, they had to maintain customer confidence, and anyway they wouldn't have been able to pinpoint a buyer for him. To them he was just one more shirker on the run from bad debts, or rapacious wives, or embezzlement from a Corp, or IP theft, or robbing a convenience store, or a string of psycho murders involving crossdressing and crowbars; they didn't care what. They'd do a preliminary ask, they pretended to have standards and ethics – no baby-fuckers – and he'd serve them up some platters of refried bullshit they both knew was crap. But it was polite to exchange this kind of pewl, just like they'd say, 'Happy to help' and so forth, which meant 'Let's see the cash.'

So for any cybersleuth to pry him out of his layers of

fake shell would've meant the expenditure of considerable resources. He'd covered his trail well enough unless they'd known exactly where to look. Whoever it was would need to be very motivated.

He more or less ruled out Ristbones because what did he have on them that could mess them up if leaked? Voting machine hacking was an open secret, but though there was grumbling in the so-called press, nobody really wanted to go back to the old paper system, and the Corp that owned the machines, picked the winners, and took the kickbacks had done a lunar PR job, so anyone who objected too much was smeared as a twisted Commie bent on spoiling everyone's fun, even the fun of those who weren't having any fun. But spoiling the fun they might have later. Their fun-in-the-sky.

So he was no threat to Ristbones because even if he did try to rouse some sort of mouldy civil-society rabble, anyone who'd listen to him would be credited with a terminal case of brain herpes. If he'd been crazy, he might've tried to double-hack the machines – code in his own virtual senator or something – just as a demo project about how easy it was.

'But you weren't crazy,' says Toby.

'I might have done it for the lulz, if I'd had the time. It would have been one of those ephemeral pranks by which sulky keyboard geniuses like me used to signal their ineffectual objections to the system.'

'So, not Ristbones, then,' says Toby. 'Must have been Hacksaw?'

'They had a case for payback,' says Zeb. 'I'd fishfooded their guard, pilfered their boat, robinhooded one of their maidens in distress; but worse, I'd made them look sloppy. I could see them wanting to stage-manage a public example of me – string me up in chains from a bridge or similar, minus a leg and all my blood; turn me into a gristle display. But in order to capitalize on the publicity they'd have to reveal what I'd done to them, so they'd still lose face.

'Anyway I couldn't see them tracking me as far as Bearlift, way up there in Whitehorse. It was very far from Rio, and most likely they thought it was covered with snow and igloos, if they ever thought about it at all. But more than that, I couldn't see a tightass like Chuck working for those guys. I couldn't even picture them in the same bar together. The Hacksaw types needed to be in a bar with you before they'd take you on, and Chuck didn't compute. He had the wrong wardrobe. None of the Hacksaw guys would be caught dead hiring a guy with such dorky pants.'

The more he thought about Chuck – about the yucky-clean Chuckiness of Chuck – the more he figured that was the key. The smarmy friendliness, the fake white-toothed geniality ... He had to be Church of PetrOleum. But no way the Rev and his buds, even hired professional buds, could've tracked Zeb through all his twists and turns. Just no fucking way.

Then he figured he was looking at the whole thing backwards. The Rev, and the whole Church, and their religious joined-at-the-hippers like the Known Fruits, and their political pals – they were all death on ecofreaks. Their ads featured stuff like a cute little blond girl next to some particularly repellent threatened species, such as the Surinam toad or the great white shark, with a slogan saying: *This? or This?* Implying that all cute little blond girls were in danger of having their throats slit so the Surinam toads might prosper.

By extension, anyone who liked smelling the daisies, and having daisies to smell, and eating mercury-free fish, and who objected to giving birth to three-eyed infants via the toxic sludge in their drinking water was a demon-possessed Satanic minion of darkness, hell-bent on sabotaging the American Way and God's Holy Oil, which were one and the same. And

Bearlift, despite its fuzzy reasoning and its clumsy delivery system, was in a geographical area where more oil might well be discovered, or through which it might well be piped, with the usual malfunctions, spills, and coverups.

So naturally the Rev and his circle would've tried to infiltrate Bearlift. Which was none too choosy about who it let in. Chuck must've been a true PetrOleum believer, sent there to keep an eye on the furfuckers and report on the evils they were concocting. He wouldn't have been looking for Zeb in particular, though when he stumbled across him he would've recognized him. He'd been close to the Rev, then: family picture sharing. *The ungrateful son. But you . . . The son I wish I'd had.* Sigh. Wistful smile. Hand on shoulder. Gruff, manly pat-pat. Like that.

The rest would have followed: the snitch report by Chuck, the instructions from the Rev, the obtaining of the knockout needle, the failed attempt in the 'thopter. The flaming wreckage.

Which made Zeb feel angry all over again.

He put on all his clothes once more and sallied forth to send another batch of messages. This time he used the other net café in town, PrestoThumbs, a seedier place in a mini-mall. It was right next to a haptic-feedback remote-sex emporium called The Real Feel: 'The Real Feel, The Real Deal! Keep It Safe! Thrills, Spills, No Microbes!' But he resisted nostalgia and walked past The Real Feel and logged on at Thumbs.

First he sent a message to the ranking Elder at the Church of PetrOleum, attaching the Rev's embezzlement data and informing him that the actual cash would be found not in the Canary Islands Grand Cayman bank account, where it actually was, but in the form of stocks, in a metal box buried under Trudy's rock garden. He advised the Elder to take not only six men with shovels but also a team of security minions armed with tasers, as the Rev was armed and could be dangerous. He signed the message 'Argus.' The hundred-eyed giant from Greek mythology, that was him: there were pictures of the guy on the same site that hosted *The Birth of Venus*. Not that having a hundred eyes made you attractive from an aesthetic point of view. There was a goddess on there with a hundred tits, yet another illustration of the fact that more is not always better.

Having ruined – he hoped – the Rev's upcoming evening, he cleaned out the Rev's secret Cayman account. He'd peeked at it from time to time during his travels to make sure the Rev had followed instructions and was leaving it alone. Yup, it was all still there. He transferred the whole works to an account he'd set up for Adam under the name of Rick Bartleby, for whom he'd also created a convincing identity: Rick was an undertaker in Christchurch, New Zealand. He left Adam a message saying he'd find an account number and a password and a big surprise via the right nipple of Venus. It did him good to picture Adam clicking – finally – on a nipple.

He felt it was only right to send a message to Bearlift as well: let them know they'd been infiltrated by Chuck, say maybe they should do more of a background check on smarmy rear-lickers who turned up out of the blue, especially in new clothes with too many pockets, and maybe alert them to the fact that not everyone found them and their furfucking ways as charming as they found themselves. He signed that message 'Bigfoot,' which he regretted as soon as he'd hit Send: it was a little too close to a hint.

Then he went back to his crappy motel and sat in the bar where they had a flat-screen, and waited for results from the Rev-O-Rama Show. Sure enough, the discovery of the bones and shreds of Fenella made the evening TV news all over the country. There was the Rev, covering his face while being led away; there was Trudy, sweet as a milkshake, dabbing at her eyes, saying she'd had no idea, and how frightening to have been living all these years with a ruthless killer.

Smart play, points to Trudy: there was no way they could pin anything on her. By that time she must've known about the Rev's secret stash of cash – the Elders would have questioned her about the embezzled funds – and guessed he'd been planning to ditch her. To head out to an offshore safe house, where he could do some basking, and some fondling of underage children, or some flaying of them, whichever appealed to him at the moment. Because of course she'd known, she'd known about his twistiness all along. But she'd chosen not to know.

He got into his winter layers again and hiked to Cubs' Corner, where he sent another message to Adam – a short one, just the URL for where the news item on the arrest was to be found. Adam would surely be pleased: with the Rev out of commission or at least seriously curtailed, both of them could breathe a little easier.

But he needed to leave Whitehorse immediately. The criminal justice folks or equivalent could be trying to trace the message he'd sent to the PetrOleum Elder, and, if they succeeded, they'd start sifting through Whitehorse, which wasn't huge. They wouldn't be looking for Zeb as such – he was dead – but any looking would be bad looking, and it wouldn't take them long to crosshair his position. Maybe they already had: he was getting a bad feeling about that.

So he didn't go back to the motel. Instead he loped out to the nearest highway Truck-A-Pillar stop and hopped a convoy. Once in Calgary, he was able to slide himself onto the sealed bullet train, and after a couple of changes, and before you could say Maybe I Just Did a Really Stupid Thing, he was in New New York.

'A really stupid thing?' says Toby.

'Turning the Rev in and grabbing all his money maybe

wasn't so bright,' says Zeb. 'He must've guessed then that I wasn't really dead. You know what they say about revenge – it's a dish that should be eaten cold, meaning you shouldn't do it out of anger because you'll fuck it up.'

'But you didn't,' says Toby. 'Fuck it up.'

'It was almost a fuckup. But I was lucky,' says Zeb. 'Look, here comes the moon. Some people would call that romantic.'

Sure enough, there it is, rising above the trees to the east, almost full, almost red.

Why is it always such a surprise? thinks Toby. The moon. Even though we know it's coming. Every time we see it, it makes us pause, and hush.

Blacklight Headlamp

New New York was on the Jersey shore, or what was now the shore. Not many people lived in Old New York any more, though it was officially a no-go zone and thus a no-rent zone so a few denizens were still willing to take their chances in the disintegrating, waterlogged, derelict buildings. Not Zeb, though; he didn't have webbed feet and a death wish, and New New York – though no paradise – had more people in it, and therefore more background and cover. More of a crowd to blend into.

Once arrived, he ducked into a shoddy soft-pretzel-infested net café and sent a checking-in message to Adam – *Plan A Yay, What's Plan B?* – then cooled his heels while Adam took his time, wherever the fuck he was, whatever the fuck he was up to. His latest terse communication had read merely *CU soon.*

Zeb had gone to ground in an erstwhile high-life pool-enabled party-roomed condo complex called Starburst – after a firework, perhaps, but at present suggestive of charred inter-stellar debris. Starburst had reached its half-life some time ago: the once-expensive iron scrollwork gate served mainly as a dog-widdle station, and the mouldy, leaking buildings had been turned into divided-space unit rentals. These hosted a coral-reef ecosystem of dealers and addicts and pilotfish and drunks and hookers and pyramid scheme fly-by-nighters and jackals and shell-gamers and rent-gougers, all parasitizing one another.

Meanwhile the Starburst owners dodged the needed repairs and waited for the next spin cycle. First the low-rent artists would move in, full of piss and vinegar and resentment and the delusion that they could change the world. Then the startup designers and graphics companies, hoping a sheen of grubby cool would rub off on them. After that would come the questionable gene-peddler storefronts and the fashion pimps and pseudo galleries and latest-thing restaurant openings, with molecular-mix fusion involving dry ice and labmeat and quorn, and daring little garnishes of dwindling species: starling's tongue pâté had been a fad of late, in such places. The Starburst owners were most likely a bunch of guys who'd cashed in via some superCorp and wanted to fool around in real estate. Once the starling's tongue pâté phase had kicked in, they'd knock down the decaying unit rentals and erect a whole batch of new limited-shelf-life upmarket condos.

But Starburst was nowhere near that sweet spot yet, so Zeb was safe there as long as he minded his own business and shambled enough so anyone looking would think he was just another brain-damaged stoner. He stayed away from everyone and anything because he didn't want to attract any Chuck-like infiltrators.

He knew from his dips into the news that although the Rev was awaiting trial, he was out on bail and issuing statements about his innocence: he was the victim of an anti-religion and anti-Oleum left-wing cabal that had kidnapped and murdered his saintly first wife, Fenella, and then had maliciously spread the rumour that she'd run away to partake of an immoral life; which, since the Rev had believed it, had been an ongoing torture to him. This dastardly cabal had then planted Fenella in the

Rev's yard for the sole purpose of casting dirt upon his name and of sullying the reputation of the Holy Oleum itself.

The Rev on bail would therefore be living in his house, and would thus have access to his Church of PetrOleum network – if not the *true* true believers, who were no doubt shunning him because of the embezzlement charges, then at least the more cynical wing, the ones who were in it for the money. And he'd be filled to the brim with cold, rancorous vengefulness because he would deeply suspect who was to blame for the tipoff about Fenella's pitiful bones turning to plant nutrients in his rock garden.

Meanwhile, main-chance Trudy had sold an autobiographical plaint and was doing numerous online interviews. How deceived she'd been by the Rev, having been convinced when she married him that he was a grieving widower dedicated to the greater good, and she so much wanted to be a partner in his pious works, and a mother to Fenella's son, little Adam. No wonder that young man could not be found, as he was very sensitive, and would hate the glare of publicity as much as she did. How shattering it had been to awaken to the truth of the Rev's murderous nature! Since learning of it, she'd prayed for Fenella's soul and begged her forgiveness, even though she'd had no idea at the time about what had really happened. Because, like everyone else, she, Trudy, had believed the story about Fenella running off with some trashy Tex-Mex or other. She is ashamed of herself for having been so falsely judgmental.

And now some of her very own church members – people she'd thought of as brothers and sisters – were refusing to speak to her, and had even accused her of having been in on the Rev's gory and larcenous activities all along. Only her faith had seen her through this testing and trying ordeal; and she longed for just one glimpse of her beloved lost son, Zebulon, who had strayed from the path, and no wonder, considering what sort of a father he had. But she prayed for him, wherever he was.

That beloved lost son fully intended to stay lost; though the temptation to hack into one of Trudy's online weepies and impersonate a ghostly spirit voice and denounce her was very great. A fine line of DNA he'd inherited: a psychopath of a con artist for a dad, a selfish liar of a mother with an obsessive love of pelf. He could only hope that in addition to her narcissism and greed, Trudy was secretly a skanky cheat who'd pulled a fast one on the Rev and had it off with a dark stranger in the garden tool shed. If so, it was possibly from his real, nameless father – an itinerant spade and sod artist prone to bonking the be-ringed and be-bangled wives of his upper-echelon clients – that Zeb had inherited his more dubious talents: babe-charming, the knack for sneaking in and out of windows both real and virtual, discretion as the better part of valour, and a not always reliable cloak of invisibility.

Maybe that's why the Rev hated Zeb so much: he knew Trudy had saddled him with a cuckoo in the nest, but he couldn't get back at her directly because of their shared digging activities. He had to either kill her or put up with her, her and her sluttish ways. If only Zeb had thought to purloin some of the Rev's DNA – a few hairs or toenail clippings – then he could get the tests done and set his mind at rest. Or not. But at least he'd be sure of his parentage, one way or the other.

No doubt about Adam, though: a definite Rev resemblance there. Though refined by the contribution of Fenella, of course. The poor girl was most likely a pious type – scrubbed hands, no nail polish, pulled-back hairdo, white panties devoid of trim – longing to do good and help people. A sitting duckie. His Warpiness had no doubt sold her on the idea that she would be a precious helpmeet to him and that this was a higher calling, though he'd have told her that one must forgo joy and pleasure as such in the service of him and his mission. Zeb guessed he'd have had no patience with the female orgasm. Crappy sex the two of them must have had, in any normal terms.

This was what Zeb thought about while watching daytime TV in his dank Starburst lair, or tossing on his lumpy, stained mattress while listening to the shouting and screaming going on outside his flimsily locked door. Animal spirits, drug-induced hilarity, hatred, fear, craziness. There were gradations to screams. It was the ones that stopped in the middle that you had to worry about.

Finally Adam came through. A meetup address, a time, and some instructions about what to wear. No red, no orange, a plain brown T-shirt if possible. No green: it was a politically charged colour, what with the vendetta against ecofreaks.

The address was a nondescript Happicuppa in New Astoria, not too near the semi-submerged and dangerously unstable buildings of the waterfront. Zeb sat crammed in behind one of the chi-chi little Happicuppa tables, on one of the teensy chairs that reminded him of kindergarten – he hadn't fitted into those chairs either – nursing his Happicappuccino and fortifying himself with half a Joltbar, and wondering what sort of spitball Adam was about to toss his way. He'd have a job lined up for Zeb – otherwise he wouldn't be calling for a meet – but what sort of job? Worm picker? Nightwatchman at a puppy mill? What order of contacts might Adam have been cultivating, wherever he had been?

Adam had hinted that he'd use an intermediary as the meetup courier, and Zeb worried about safety: the two of them had always been wary about trusting anyone except each other. True, Adam would be cautious. But he was methodical, and methodology could give you away. The only sure camouflage was unpredictability.

From his cramped chair Zeb eyed the entering customers, hoping to spot the courier. Was it this blond hermaphrodite in the halter top and sequined three-horned headdress? He hoped not. This plump, gum-chewing woman with the cream-coloured shorts and the wedgie and the retro cinch belt? She looked too vacuous, though vacuousness was a nearly foolproof disguise, at least for girls. Was it this mild, geeky-looking boy of the type that would some day machine-gun an auditorium full of his pimply fellow classmates? Nope, not him either.

But suddenly, surprise: there was Adam himself. It startled Zeb to see him materialize in the chair opposite, which had been empty just the moment before. Ectoplasmic, you could say.

Adam looked like a passport photo of himself, one that was already fading to light and shadow. It was as if he'd returned from the dead: he had that glowing-eyeball thing about him. His T-shirt was beige, his baseball cap sloganless. He'd bought himself a Happimocha to make it seem as if this was just two oddfellow buddies taking a break from their nerdwork, or else doing a meeting about some startup doomed to implode like a drowning blimp. Happimocha and Adam didn't go together: Zeb was curious to see if he'd actually drink any of the stuff – something so impure.

'Don't raise your voice,' were the first words Adam spoke. Not two seconds back in Zeb's life and already he was giving orders.

'I was thinking of fucking yelling,' said Zeb. He waited to be told not to use profanity, but Adam didn't take the bait. Zeb stared at him: there was something different. His eyes were just as round and blue, but his hair was paler. Could it be turning white? There was a new beard too, also pale. 'Nice to see you too,' he added.

Adam smiled: a flicker of a smile. 'You'll be going into HelthWyzer West near San Francisco,' he said. 'As a data inputter. I've fixed it up. When you leave here, pick up the shopping bag beside your left knee. Everything you'll need is in there. You'll have to get the scans and prints inserted in the ID – I've put the address for that. And you'll need to scrap the old ID: delete anything online. But I don't have to tell you that.'

'Where've you been, anyway?' said Zeb.

Adam smiled in that maddening, saintly way he had. Butter wouldn't melt; it never had melted. 'Classified,' he said. 'Other lives involved.' That was the kind of thing that made Zeb long to put a toad in his bed.

'Right, slap my wrist. Okay, what's this HelthWyzer West, and what'm I supposed to be doing in there?'

'It's a Compound,' said Adam. 'Research and innovation. Drugs, the medical kind; enriched vitamin supplements; materials for transgenic splices and gene enhancement, specifically the hormone blends and simulators. It's a powerful Corp. There are a lot of top brains there.'

'How'd you get me in?' said Zeb.

'I have some new acquaintances,' said Adam, continuing his non-stop I-know-more-than-you smile. 'They'll watch out for you. You'll be safe.' He looked past Zeb's shoulder, then at his watch. Or he appeared to look at his watch. Zeb knew a good piece of misdirection when he saw it: Adam was scanning the room, checking for shadows.

'Cut the bullshit,' said Zeb. 'You want me to do something for you.'

Adam held his smile. 'You'll be a blacklight headlamp,' he said. 'Be extra careful checking in online, once you're there. Oh, and there's a new dropbox, and a new gateway into it. Don't return to that zephyr site, it may have been compromised.'

'What's a blacklight headlamp?' said Zeb. But Adam had

already stood up and straightened his beige tee and was halfway to the door. He hadn't drunk any of his Happimocha, so Zeb obligingly drank it for him. An unconsumed Happimocha might raise eyebrows in a pleeb like this, where only pimps had money to burn.

Zeb took his time getting back to Starburst. The back of his neck prickled all the way there, he was so sure he was being watched. But nobody tried to mug him. Once inside his door he looked up 'blacklight headlamp' on his most recent cheap toss-at-will cellphone. 'Blacklight' was a novelty item from the first decades of the century, he was told: it let you see in the dark, or it let you see some things in the dark. Eyeballs. Teeth. White bedsheets. Glo in the Dark Hair Gel. Fog. As for 'head-lamp,' it was what it said. Bicycle shops sold them, and camping suppliers. Not that anyone really went camping any more except inside derelict buildings.

Thanks a pile, Adam, thought Zeb. That is so fucking instructive.

Then he opened Adam's shopping bag. There was his new skin, all neatly laid out for him. What he had to do now was Truck-A-Pillar over to San Francisco, and then crawl into it.

Intestinal Parasites, the Game

Adam's preparations had been thorough. There was a burn-this to-do list, and a big envelope stuffed with cash because Zeb would need some to pay off the grey marketeer designated to fake his passes. There was plastic as well, so Zeb could get himself the kind of wardrobe Adam thought he should have. He'd supplied descriptions: casual geekwear, with brown cord pants and neutral Ts and plaid shirts – brown and grey – and a pair of round-eyed glasses that didn't magnify anything. As for the footgear, the recommendation was trainers with so much rubber cross-strapping Zeb would look like a gay Morris dancer or some fugitive from a session of Robin Hood cosplay. Hat, a steampunk bowler from the 2010s: those were back in style. Though how would Adam know that? He'd never appeared to take any interest in vestments, but no interest was of course an interest. He must've been noting what other people wore so he could not wear it himself.

Zeb's assigned name was Seth. A little biblical joke of Adam's: Seth meant 'appointed,' as they were both aware, since they'd had the main biblical names and stories drilled into their skulls with a figurative screwdriver. Seth was the third son of Adam and Eve, deputized to take the place of the murdered Abel, who wasn't entirely dead, however, because he still had talking blood that cried out from the ground. So 'Seth' was replacing the departed and presumed dead Zeb. By appointment, courtesy of Adam. Very funny.

Adam requested that Zeb/Seth test the new chatroom before entering HelthWyzer, and then check in once a week to signal he was still walking the planet. So the next day, while making his circuitous way to the grey marketeer to get his prints and iris scans inserted into his fake docs, he chose a net café at random and followed the lilypad trail laid out for him by Adam. (*Memorize, then destroy*, said the note, as if Zeb was a fucking idiot.)

The main gateway was a biogeek challenge game called Extinctathon. Monitored by MaddAddam, it said: *Adam named the living animals, MaddAddam names the dead ones. Do you want to play?* Zeb entered the codename supplied to him by Adam – Spirit Bear – and the password, which was *shoelaces,* and found himself inside the game.

It seemed to be a variant of Animal, Vegetable, Mineral. Using obscure clues provided by your opponent, you had to guess the identities of various extirpated beetles, fish, plants, skinks, and so forth. A roll call of the already erased. It was a certified yawner: even the CorpSeCorps would be put to sleep by this one, plus they'd have no clue as to most of the answers. As – to be fair – Zeb himself did not, despite his time spent with the Bearlifters and their obscure forms of one-upmanship. *You haven't heard of Steller's sea cow? Really?* Tiny, self-satisfied smirk.

Five minutes inside Extinctathon and any self-respecting CorpsMan would run screaming in search of alcoholic beverages. A terminally boring game was almost as effective as a vacuous stare, disguise-wise; plus they'd never think there was anything hidden inside a location that was right out in the open and so obviously ecofreakish. Instead, they'd be combing through bimplant ads and sites where you could shoot exotic animals online without leaving your office chair. Full Points to Adam, thought Zeb.

Could it be that Adam had designed this game himself? A game with his own name embedded as the Monitor? But he'd never shown much interest in animals, as such. Though, come to think of it, he'd been known to view with mild contempt the Rev's interpretation of Genesis, which was that God had made the animals for the sole pleasure and use of man, and you could therefore exterminate them at whim. Was Extinctathon a piece of anti-Rev counterinsurgency on the part of Adam? Had he somehow got mixed up with the ecofreaks? Maybe he'd had a conversion moment while smoking too much of some brain-damaging hallucinogenic and bonded with a plant fairy. Though that was unlikely: it was Zeb who'd been the chemicals risk-taker, not Adam. But Adam was mixed up with someone, for sure, because he'd never be able to pull off something like this on his own.

Zeb continued along the pathway. He chose *Yes* to show readiness and was redirected. *Welcome, Spirit Bear. Do you want to play a general game, or do you want to play a Grandmaster?* The second was the choice to make, said Adam's instructions, so Zeb clicked on it.

Good. Find your playroom. MaddAddam will meet you there.

The path to the playroom was complicated, zigzagging from one coordinate to another through pixels located here and there on innocuous sites: ads, for the most part, though some were lists: top ten SCARY EASTER BUNNY PICS, TEN SCARIEST MOVIES OF ALL TIME, TEN SCARIEST SEA MONSTERS. Zeb found a portal through the buck teeth of a deranged purple plush rabbit with a terrorized infant perched on its knee, from there to a tombstone in a still from *Night of the Living Dead*, the original, and finally to the eye of a coelacanth. Then he was in the chatroom.

Welcome to MaddAddam's playroom, Spirit Bear. You have a message.

Zeb clicked on *Deliver message.*

Hello, said the message. *You see, it works. Here are the coordinates for next week's chatroom. A.*

Minimalist bugger, thought Zeb. He's not going to tell me a thing.

He bought the suggested outfit, or most of it: the round glasses were too much to take, as were the shoes. He broke in the pants and the shirts – spilled food on them, frayed them a little, ran them through the wash a few times. Then he tossed his previous clothes into various dumpsters and wiped his biotraces off his cheesy Starburst room as much as he could.

After paying up at Starburst – no sense in having the skip-tracers on your tail, if avoidable – he made the cross-continent trek to San Francisco. Then he reported at HelthWyzer West as instructed, presented his fraudulent docs, and underwent the welcoming *Hi, Buddy, Happy You're Here, We'll Help You Feel at Home* minuet of the podge-faced greeter.

Nobody said boo. He was expected, he was accepted. Smooth as grease.

Inside HelthWyzer West he was assigned a bachelor condo unit in the residential tower. Nothing rundown about these facilities: nice landscaping around the entranceway, swimming pool on the roof, and the plumbing and electricals all worked, though the interior design was a little Spartan. There was a queen-sized bed, an optimistic signal. Bachelor did not mean celibate in the world of HelthWyzer West, it appeared.

The workspace high-rise had a cafeteria where he was issued

a swipe card that would record his consumption: everyone had a points allowance, which they could use on anything on the menu. The food was real food, not spurious glop like the stuff he'd eaten at Bearlift. The drinks had alcohol in them, which was the least you could expect in a drink.

The HelthWyzer women were brisk, and had jobs to do and not much time for small talk, and – he guessed – no tolerance at all for cheap pickup lines, so he didn't even bother; but though he'd vowed to be careful about personal involvements because of the kinds of questions they could generate, he wasn't made of stone. Already a couple of the younger females had looked at his *Seth* name tag – name tags were a fashion statement at HelthWyzer – and one of them had asked him if he was new because she couldn't recall seeing him before, but of course she was kind of new herself.

Was there a little twist of the shoulders, a giveaway flutter of the eyelids? *Marjorie*, he read, not lingering too long on her name tag, which was perched on a breast of no more than ordinary prominence: obvious bimplants were not common inside the HelthWyzer walls. Marjorie had a blunt-nosed, brown-eyed, acquiescent face, like a spaniel, and in ordinary circumstances he would have proceeded, but as it was he said he hoped he'd see her around. Such a hope was not the top hope on his list of hopes – that spot was reserved for not getting caught – but it was not the bottom hope either.

The job description for Seth was that of a routine low-level IT guy, dime a dozen. Data inputting, using a packet of snoreworthy but serviceable software designed to record and compare the various factoids and buckets o'data the HelthWyzer brainiacs were coming up with. Glorified digital secretary, that's all he was supposed to be.

The duties weren't challenging: he could do the job with two fingers of one hand in much less time than was allotted for it.

The HelthWyzer project managers didn't supervise much, they just wanted him to keep current with the inputting. Meanwhile he could ferret around in the HelthWyzer databank unimpeded. He ran a few IT security tests of his own to see whether any outside pirates were trying to hack in: if they were, it would be useful to know about it.

At first he didn't uncover any telltale signs; but during one of his deep dives he pinpointed something that looked as if it might be a cryptic tunnel. He wiggled through it, found himself outside the HelthWyzer burning ring of firewalls, then lilypadded his way into the Extinctathon chatroom. A message was waiting for him: *Use only when needed. Don't spend long. Wipe all prints. A.* He logged out quickly, then erased his trail. He'd need to build another portal, because whoever was using this tunnel might work out that someone else had been through it.

He decided Seth needed to be known as a guy who did a lot of gaming so that checking into Extinctathon wouldn't stand out should anyone be snooping. That was the operational reason; but also he just wanted to test out the games, and to see how easy it was to fool around during work hours without being reprimanded – staff weren't supposed to waste time in this way, or not too much time – and also how easy it was to cheat. He thought of it as keeping his hand in.

Some of the games on recreational offer were standard – weapons, explosions, and so on – but others were posted by the staff at HelthWyzer West: biogeeks were just as geeky as other geeks, so naturally they designed games of their own. Spandrel was one of the better ones: it let you devise extra, functionally useless features for a bioform, then link them to sexual selection and fast-forward to see what the evolution machine would churn out. Cats with rooster-like wattles on their foreheads, lizards with big red lipstick-kiss lips, men with enormous left eyes – whatever the females chose was favoured, and you could manipulate their bad taste in male attributes, just like real life. Then you played predators against prey. Would the supersexy spandrels impede hunting skills or slow down escape? If your guy wasn't sexy enough, he wouldn't get laid and you'd go extinct; if he was too sexy, he'd get eaten and you'd go extinct. Sex versus dinner: it was a fine balance. Packets of random mutations could be purchased for a small sum.

Weather Monsters wasn't bad either: the game threw extreme weather events at your player – a puny human avatar of either gender – and you tried to see how long your player could survive them. With points won, you could purchase tools for your avatar: boots that allowed it to run faster and jump higher, lightning-proof clothing, floating planks for floods and tsunamis, wet handkerchiefs for covering its nose during brush fires, Joltbars for when it was trapped under a thick wad of snow due to an avalanche. A shovel, some matches, an axe. If your avatar survived the giant mudslide – a killer event – you'd get a whole toolbox and a thousand extra points for your next game.

The one Zeb played the most was called Intestinal Parasites – a nasty gucklunch the biogeeks thought was hilarious. The parasites were truly ugly, with rebarbed hooks all around their mouths and no eyes, and you had to nuke them with toxic pills or deploy an arsenal of nanobots or moteins before they could lay thousands of eggs in you or creep through your brain and out your tear ducts, or split themselves into regenerating segments and turn the inside of your body into a festering patty-melt. Were they real, or had the biogeeks made them up? Worse, were they gene-splicing them right now as part of a bioweaponry project? Impossible to know.

Play Intestinal Parasites too much and you'd get nightmares, guaranteed, said the game's running slogan. So, never one to do as he was told, Zeb did play it too much, and he did get nightmares.

Which didn't stop him from creating an alias of the game, then reworking one of the hideous mouths so that it functioned as a gateway. He stashed his code in a triple-locked thumbdrive for safekeeping, then parked it at the back of his supervisor's desk drawer in a nest of rubber bands, used nosewipes, and orphaned cough drops. No one would ever look there.

Bone Cave

Cursive

Toby is at work on her journal. She doesn't really have the energy for it, but Zeb went to all that trouble to bring her the materials and he's bound to notice if she doesn't use them. She's writing in one of the cheap schooltime drugstore notebooks. The cover has a bright yellow sun, several pink daisies, and a boy and a girl, rudimentary figures of the kind children used to draw. Back when there were human children – how long ago? It seems like centuries since the plague swept through. Though it's less than half a year.

The boy has blue shorts, a blue cap, and a red shirt; the girl has pigtails, a triangular skirt, red, and a blue top. They both have smudgy black blob eyes and thick red upcurved mouths; they're laughing fit to kill.

Fit to die. They are only paper children, but they seem dead now anyway, like all the real children. She can't look at this notebook cover too much because it hurts.

Better to concentrate on the task at hand. Don't brood or mope. Take one day at a time.

*

Saint Bob Hunter and the Feast of Rainbow Warriors, Toby writes. This may not be accurate, time-wise – she's probably out by a day or two – but it will have to do because how can she check? There's no central authority any more for days of the month. But Rebecca might know. There were special recipes for the Festivals and Feasts. Maybe she's memorized them; maybe she's kept track.

Moon: Waxing gibbous. Weather: Nothing unusual. Noteworthy occurrences: Group pig aggression displayed. Painballer evidence sighted by Zeb's expedition: piglet shot and partly butchered. Discovery of a tire tread sandal, possible clue to Adam. No definite sign of Adam One and the Gardeners.

She thinks a minute, then adds: *Jimmy is conscious and improving. Crakers continue friendly.*

'What are you making, Oh Toby?' It's little Blackbeard: she didn't hear him come in. 'What are those lines?'

'Come over here,' she says. 'I won't bite you. Look. I'm doing *writing*: that is what these lines are. I'll show you.'

She runs through the basics. *This is paper, it is made from trees.*

Does it hurt the tree? No, because the tree is dead by the time the paper is made – a tiny lie, but no matter. *And this is a pen. It has a black liquid in it, it is called ink, but you do not need to have a pen to do writing.* Just as well, she thinks: those rollerballs will run out soon.

You can use many things to make writing. You can use the juice of elderberries for the ink, you can use the feather of a bird for the pen, you can use a stick and some wet sand to write on. All of these things can be used to make writing.

'Now,' she says, 'you have to draw the letters. Each letter means a sound. And when you put the letters together they make words. And the words stay where you've put them on the paper, and then other people can see them on the paper and hear the words.'

Blackbeard looks at her, squinting with puzzlement and unbelief. 'Oh Toby, but it can't talk,' he says. 'I see the marks you have put there. But it is not saying anything.'

'You need to be the voice of the writing,' she says. 'When you *read* it. *Reading* is when you turn these marks back into sounds. Look, I will write your name.'

She tears a page carefully from the back of the notebook, prints on it: BLACKBEARD. Then she sounds out each letter for him. 'See?' she says. 'It means you. Your name.' She puts the pen in his hand, curls his fingers around it, guides the hand and the pen: the letter *B*.

'This is how your name begins,' she says. 'B. Like bees. It's the same sound.' Why is she telling him this? What use will he ever have for it?

'That is not me,' says Blackbeard, frowning. 'It is not bees either. It is only some marks.'

'Take this paper to Ren,' says Toby, smiling. 'Ask her to read it, then come back and tell me if she says your name.'

Blackbeard stares at her. He doesn't trust what she's told him, but he takes the piece of paper anyway, holding it gingerly as if it's coated with invisible poison. 'Will you stay here?' he says. 'Until I come back?'

'Yes,' she says. 'I'll be right here.' He backs out the doorway as he always does, keeping his eyes on her until he turns the corner.

She turns back to her journal. What else to write, besides the bare-facts daily chronicle she's begun? What kind of story – what kind of history will be of any use at all, to people she can't know will exist, in the future she can't foresee?

Zeb and the Bear, she writes. *Zeb and MaddAddam. Zeb and Crake.* All of these stories could be set down. But why, but for whom? Only for herself because it gives her a chance to dwell upon Zeb?

Zeb and Toby, she writes. But surely that will be only a footnote.

Don't jump to conclusions, she tells herself. He came to the garden, bringing gifts. You could be misinterpreting, about Swift Fox. And even if not, so what? Take what the moment offers. Don't close doors. Be thankful.

Blackbeard slips into the room again. He's carrying the sheet of paper, holding it in front of him like a hot shield. His face is radiant.

'It did, Oh Toby,' he says. 'It said my name! It told my name to Ren!'

'There,' she says. 'That is *writing.*'

Blackbeard nods: now he's grasping the possibilities. 'I can keep this?' he says.

'Of course,' says Toby.

'Show me again. With the black thing.'

Later – after it's rained, after the rain has stopped – she finds him at the sandbox. He has a stick, and the paper. There's his name in the sand. The other children are watching him. All of them are singing.

Now what have I done? she thinks. What can of worms have I opened? They're so quick, these children: they'll pick this up and transmit it to all the others.

What comes next? Rules, dogmas, laws? The Testament of Crake? How soon before there are ancient texts they feel they have to obey but have forgotten how to interpret? Have I ruined them?

Swarm

Breakfast is kudzu and other assorted forage greens, bacon, a strange flatbread with unidentified seeds in it, steamed burdock. Coffee from a blend of toasted roots: dandelion, chickory, something else. It has an undertaste of ashes.

They're running out of sugar, and there's no honey. But there is Mo'Hair milk. Another of the ewes – a blue-haired one – has given birth to twins, a blonde and a brunette. There have been some jokes about lamb stew, but no one wants to go there: somehow it would be hard to slaughter and eat an animal with human hair; especially human hair that so closely resembles, in its sheen and stylability, the shampoo ads of yore. Every time one of those Mo'Hairs shakes itself it's like watching the back view of a TV hair beauty: the shining mane, the flirtatious ripple and swirl. At any minute, thinks Toby, you expect them to come out with a product spiel. *Every day a bad-hair day? My hair was driving me crazy, but then . . . I died.*

Don't be so dark, Toby, it's only hair. It's not the end of the world.

*

Over the coffee they discuss other food options. Protein variety is lacking, they're all agreed on that. Rebecca says she'd kill for some live chickens because then they could keep them in a henhouse and have eggs; but where are such chickens to be found? There are seabird eggs on top of the derelict towers offshore, down by the beach – there must be, the birds are nesting there – but who is willing to make the perilous trip down to the seashore through the increasingly overgrown Heritage Park that may harbour the Painballers, not to mention a squadron or two of large, malevolent pigs? And they shouldn't even think about climbing up the inner stairs of those towers, which must be very unstable by now.

A debate follows. One side points to the fact that the Crakers wander back and forth at will, singing their polyphonic music. They visit their home base by the shore, a hollow jumble of cement blocks. They keep it protected from animals by peeing in a circle around it, a circle they believe the pigoons and wolvogs and bobkittens won't cross. They spear the ritual fish to present to Toby so she will fulfill the functions of Snowman-the-Jimmy and tell them stories. No animal has molested the Crakers on their woodland walks, or not so far. As for the Painballers, they must be quite far away by now, judging from the location of the last known sign of them, which was the carcass of that recently killed piglet.

The other side argues that the Crakers appear to have ways of keeping the wildlife at bay while in transit, apart from the pissing defence. Maybe it's the singing? If so, and needless to point out, that won't work for normal human beings, whose vocal cords aren't made of organic glass or whatever it is that accounts for those digital-keyboard theremin sounds. As for the Painballers, they could easily have circled back by now, and might be lurking in ambush around the very next kudzu-smothered corner. You can never be too careful, and better safe than sorry, and they cannot afford to sacrifice one or two of their number for the sake of a few gull eggs, which are likely green and taste like fish guts anyway.

An egg is an egg, say the pro-eggers. Why not send a couple of human beings with the Crakers? That way the humans will be protected from wild animals via the Crakers, and the Crakers will be protected from the Painballers via the sprayguns toted by the MaddAddamites. No point in giving sprayguns to the Crakers, since you could never teach them about shooting and killing people. They just aren't capable, not being human as such.

Not so fast: that case has not yet been proven, says Ivory Bill. 'If they can crossbreed with us, then case made. Same species. If not, then not.' He leans forward, peers into his coffee cup. 'Any more?' he asks Rebecca.

'Only half true,' says Manatee. 'A horse plus a donkey gives you a mule, but it's sterile. We wouldn't know for sure until the next generation.'

'I've only got enough for tomorrow,' says Rebecca. 'We need to dig some dandelions. We've used up the ones around here.'

'It would be an interesting experiment,' says Ivory Bill. 'But of course we would need the co-operation of the ladies.' He inclines his head courteously towards Swift Fox, who's wearing a winsome floral print sheet, with bouquets of pink and blue flowers tied with pink and blue bows.

'You've seen those dicks of theirs?' says Swift Fox. 'Too much of a good thing. If I find a dick in my mouth, I want to know it came in at the head end.' Ivory Bill turns away, visibly shocked, silently angry. Laughter from some, frowns from others. Swift Fox likes to potty-mouth the crowd, especially the men; to demonstrate that she isn't just a pretty body, is Toby's guess. She wants to have it both ways.

Zeb is down at the other end of the table. He came late; he hasn't been joining in the debate. He appears to be engrossed in the flatbread. Swift Fox tosses him a glance: is he her intended audience? He pays no attention; but then he wouldn't, would he? That's what those lovelife advisers blogging about office romances used to say: you can tell the guilty parties by the way in which they studiously avoid each other.

'Those guys don't need any co-operation,' says Crozier. 'They jump anything with a c – Sorry, Toby. Anything with a skirt.'

'A skirt!' says Swift Fox, laughing again, showing her white teeth. 'Where've you been? You've seen any of us wearing skirts? Bedsheet wraps don't count.' She twists her shoulders back and forth, as if on a fashion runway. 'You like my skirt? It goes all the way up to my armpits!'

'Leave him alone, he's underage,' says Manatee. Crozier is making a strange face: anger? Embarrassment? Ren's sitting beside him. He gives her a sheepish grin, puts his hand on her arm. She frowns at him like a spouse.

'They're the most fun, the underage ones,' says Swift Fox. 'Frisky. They're packed with endorphins, and their nucleotide sequences are to die for – miles of telomeres left.' Ren stares at her, stone-faced.

'He's not underage,' she says. Swift Fox smiles.

Do the men at the table see it? Toby wonders. The silent mud-wrestle in the air? No, probably not. They're not on the progesterone wavelength.

'They only do that under the right conditions,' says Manatee. 'The group copulation. The woman has to be in heat.'

'That's fine for their own women,' says Beluga. 'They've got clear hormonal signals there, both visual and olfactory. But our women register to them as in heat all the time.'

'Maybe they are,' says Manatee, grinning. 'They just won't admit it.'

'Point being: two different species,' says Beluga.

'Women aren't dogs,' says White Sedge. 'I am finding this

exchange offensive. I don't think you should refer to us like that.' Her voice is calm but her spine's like a ramrod.

'This is merely an objective scientific discussion,' says Zunzuncito.

'Hey,' says Rebecca. 'All I said is, it would be neat to have some eggs.'

Morning worktime, the sun not yet too hot. Bright pink kudzu moths hang in the shade, flocks of butterflies in blue and magenta kite-fight in the air, golden honeybees flock on the polyberry flowers.

Toby's on garden duty again, weeding and deslugging. Her rifle leans against the inside of the fence: she prefers it within reach, wherever she is, because you never know. All around her the plants are growing, weeds and cultivars both. She can almost hear them pushing up through the soil, their rootlets sniffing for nutrients and crowding the rootlets of their neighbours, their leaves releasing clouds of airborne chemicals.

Saint Vandana Shiva of Seeds, she wrote in her notebook this morning. *Saint Nikolai Vavilov, Martyr*. She added the traditional God's Gardener invocation: *May we be mindful of Saint Vandana and Saint Vavilov, fierce preservers of ancient seeds. Saint Vavilov, who collected the seeds and preserved them throughout the siege of Leningrad, only to fall victim to the tyrant Stalin; and Saint Vandana, tireless warrior against biopiracy, who gave of herself for the good of the Living Vegetable World in all its diversity and beauty. Lend us the purity of your Spirits and the strength of your resolve.*

Toby has a flash of memory: herself, back when she was Eve Six among the Gardeners, reciting this prayer along with old Pilar just before they set to work on the bean rows, doing their required stint of slug and snail relocation. Sometimes the homesickness for those days is so strong and also so unexpected that it knocks her down like a rogue wave. If she'd had a camera then, if she'd had a photo album, she'd be poring over the pictures. But the Gardeners didn't believe in cameras, or in paper records; so all she has is the words.

There would be no point in being a Gardener now: the enemies of God's Natural Creation no longer exist, and the animals and birds – those that did not become extinct under the human domination of the planet – are thriving unchecked. Not to mention the plant life.

Though maybe we could do with fewer of some plants, she thinks as she snips off the aggressive kudzu vines already climbing the garden fence. The stuff gets in everywhere. It's tireless, it can grow a foot in twelve hours, it surges up and over anything in its way like a green tsunami. The grazing Mo'Hairs do a little to keep it down, and the Crakers munch away at it, and Rebecca serves it up like spinach, but that hardly makes a dent in it.

She's heard some of the men discussing a plan to make it into wine, but she has mixed feelings about that. She can't imagine the taste – Pinot Grigio crossed with mashed lawn rakings? Pinot Vert with a whiff of compost pile? But apart from that, can their tiny group really afford to indulge in alcohol in any form? It dulls awareness, and they're too vulnerable for that. Their little enclave is poorly defended. One drunken sentry, then infiltration, then carnage.

'Found a swarm for you,' says Zeb's voice. He's come up behind her unseen: so much for her own alertness.

She turns, smiling. Is it a real smile? Not entirely, because she still doesn't know the truth about Swift Fox. Swift Fox and Zeb. Did they or didn't they? And if he simply took the open door, so to speak – if he didn't think twice about it – why should she? 'A swarm?' she says. 'Really? Where?'

'Come into the forest with me,' he says, grinning like a fairy-tale wolf, holding out his paw of a hand. So of course she takes it, and forgives him everything. For the moment. Even though there may not be anything to forgive.

They walk towards the tree edge, away from the cobb-house clearing. It does feel like a clearing now, though the Madd-Addamites didn't clear anything. But now that the vegetation is moving in they're working to keep it clear, so maybe that counts.

It's cooler under the trees. Also more ominous: the green crosshatching of leaves and branches blocks the sight lines. There's a trail, indicated by bent twigs, showing the way Zeb must have come earlier.

'Are you sure this is safe?' Toby says. She's lowered her voice without even thinking about it. In the open you look, because a predator will be seen before it's heard. But among the trees you have to listen, because it will be heard before it's seen.

'I was just back here, I checked it out,' says Zeb, too confidently for Toby.

There's the swarm, a large bee ball the size of a watermelon, hanging in the lower branches of a young sycamore. It's buzzing softly; the surface of the ball is rippling, like golden fur in a breeze.

'Thank you,' says Toby. She ought to go back to the cobb-house enclave, find a container, and scoop the centre of the swarm into it to capture the queen. Then the rest of the swarm will follow. She won't even need to smoke the bees: they won't sting because they aren't defending a nest. She'll explain to them first that she means them well, and that she hopes they will be her messengers to the land of the dead. Pilar, her bee teacher at the Gardeners, told her this speech was necessary when per-suading a swarm of wild bees to come with you.

'Maybe I should get a bag or something,' she says. 'They're already scouting for a good nest site. They'll be flying soon.'

'You want me to babysit them?' asks Zeb.

'It's okay,' she says. She'd like him to come back to the cobb house with her: she doesn't want to walk through the forest alone. 'But could you just not listen to me for a minute? And look the other way?'

'You need to take a leak?' says Zeb. 'Don't mind me.'

'You know how this goes. You were a Gardener yourself,' she says. 'I need to talk to the bees.' It's one of the Gardener practises that, viewed by an outsider, must seem weird; and it still does seem weird to her because part of her remains an outsider.

'Sure,' says Zeb. 'Hey. Do your stuff.' He turns sideways, gazes into the forest.

Toby feels herself blushing. But she pulls the end of her bed-sheet up to cover her head – essential, old Pilar said, or the bees would feel disrespected – and speaks in a whisper to the buzzing furball. 'Oh Bees,' she says. 'I send greetings to your Queen. I wish to be her friend, and to prepare a safe home for her, and for you who are her daughters, and to tell you the news every day. May you carry messages from the land of the living to all souls who dwell in the land of shadows. Please tell me now whether you accept my offer.'

She waits. The buzzing increases. Then several of the scout bees fly down and land on her face. They explore her skin, her nostrils, the corners of her eyes; it's as if a dozen tiny fingers are stroking her. If they sting, the answer is no. If they don't sting, the answer is yes. She breathes in, willing herself to be calm. They don't like fear.

The scout bees lift away from her, spiral back towards the swarm, blend into the moving golden pelt. Toby breathes out.

'You can look now,' she says to Zeb.

*

There's a crackling, a thrashing: something's coming towards them through the undergrowth. Toby feels the blood leave her hands. Oh shit, she thinks. Pig, wolvog? We don't have a spray-gun. And my rifle's back there in the garden. She scans around for a stone to throw. Zeb has picked up a stick.

Saint Dian, Saint Francis, Saint Fateh Singh Rathore: lend me your strength and wisdom. Speak to the animals now. May they turn away from us, and seek their meat from God.

But no, it's not an animal. There's a voice: it's people. There's no Gardener prayer against people. Painballers – they don't know we're here. What should we do? Run? No, they're too close now. Get out of the line of fire. If possible.

Zeb has stepped in front of her, pushed her back with one hand. He freezes. Then he laughs.

Bone Cave

Out of the bushes comes Swift Fox, straightening her pink and blue floral bedsheet. Right behind her is Crozier, similarly straightening, though his bedsheet is an understated black-and-grey stripe.

'Hi, Toby. Hi, Zeb,' he says, overly casual.

'Taking a stroll?' says Swift Fox.

'Bee hunting,' says Zeb. He doesn't seem upset. So maybe I've been wrong, thinks Toby: he's not feeling territorial about her, he doesn't care that she's been flailing among the weeds with Crozier.

As for Crozier, isn't he supposed to be pursuing Ren? Or has Toby been wrong about that as well?

'Bee hunting? Really? Hey, whatever works,' says Swift Fox, laughing. 'Us, we were foraging. For mushrooms. We foraged and foraged. We got down on our hands and knees, we looked everywhere. But we didn't find a single mushroom, did we, Croze?'

Crozier shakes his head, looking down at the ground. It's as if he's been caught with his pants down, but he's not wearing pants, only the striped bedsheet.

'See you,' says Swift Fox. 'Happy bee hunting.' She heads back towards the cobb house, with Crozier following as if pulled on a string.

'C'mon, Bee Queen,' Zeb says to Toby. 'Let's get your supplies. I'll walk you home.'

In a perfect world Toby would already have a Langstroth hive box, complete with supers and moveable frames. She should have prepared one ahead of time, on the off chance of finding a swarm; but, lacking foresight, she did not do this. Barring a proper hive box, what can she use that will appeal to the bees? Any cavity that's protected, with an entrance where they can go in and out; dry enough, cool enough, warm enough.

Rebecca offers a scavenged Styrofoam cooler; Zeb makes an entrance hole in the side, near the top, and several other ventilation holes. Toby and Zeb set it up in a corner of the garden, surround it with rocks for stability and extra shelter, then add a couple of vertical slabs of plywood, raising them above the bottom of the cooler with small stones. It's only a rough approximation of a hive, but it will have to do for now, and perhaps for a long time. The danger is that if the bees get established here they'll be very annoyed if she moves them later.

Toby improvises a catching bag out of a pillowcase, and they trek back into the woods to collect the bees. She uses a long stick, scrapes quickly. The core of the swarm tumbles gently into the bag. The densest part holds the magnet of the queen: like the heart in the body, she's invisible.

They carry the pillowcase to the garden, buzzing loudly; a cloud of loose bees trails behind them. Toby eases the bee ball into the cooler, waits until all strays have found their way out of the pillowcase, then waits some more while the bees explore their new home.

There's always an adrenalin rush for Toby when she's handling bees. It could go badly: she might smell wrong one day and find herself the centre of an angry, stinging horde. Sometimes she feels she could wash herself all over in bees, like a bubble bath; but that's the euphoria of bee handling, like an altitude high or the rapture of the deep. It would be stupid to actually try it.

When the swarm has settled down she closes the lid of the cooler and places a couple of stones on top. Soon the bees are winging in and out of the entrance hole and rummaging for pollen among the garden flowers.

'Thank you,' she says to Zeb; and he says, 'Any time,' as if he's a crossing guard rather than a lover. But it's daytime, she reminds herself: he's always a little brisk in daytime. He lopes off, around the corner of the cobb house, out of sight; mission accomplished.

She covers her head. 'May you be happy here, Oh Bees,' she says to the Styrofoam cooler. 'As your new Eve Six, I promise to visit you every day, if I can, and to tell you the news.'

'Oh Toby, can we do the writing again? With the marks, on the paper?' It's her shadow, little Blackbeard. He's climbed up the garden fence on the outside and is hanging over it, resting his chin on his arms. How long has he been watching her?

'Yes,' she says. 'Maybe tomorrow, if you come early.'

'What is that box? What are the stones? What are you doing, Oh Toby?'

'I'm helping the bees find a home,' says Toby.

'Will they live in the box? Why do you want them to live there?'

Because I want to steal their honey, thinks Toby. 'Because they will be safe there,' she says.

'Were you talking to the bees, Oh Toby? I heard you talking. Or were you talking to Crake, as Snowman-the-Jimmy does?'

'I was talking to the bees,' says Toby. Blackbeard's face lights up with a smile.

'I did not know you could do that,' he says. 'You talk with the Children of Oryx? As we do? But you can't sing!'

'You sing to the animals?' says Toby. 'They like music?'

This question seems merely to puzzle him. 'Music?' he says. 'What is *music*?' The next minute he's dropped down behind the fence and has run off to join the other children.

Smelling of bees when you're not actually with them can attract unwanted insect company: already there are some green flies trying to settle on her, and some interested wasps. Toby goes over to wash her hands at the pump. As she's scrubbing, Ren and Lotis Blue come in search of her.

'We need to talk to you,' says Ren. 'It's about Amanda. We're really worried.'

'Try to keep her busy,' says Toby. 'I'm sure she'll be back to normal in a while. She's had a shock, these things take time. Remember how you were at first, when you were recovering from your own Painballers attack? I'll give her some mushroom elixir, to build up her strength.'

'No, you don't understand,' says Ren. 'She's pregnant.'

Toby dries her hands on the towel hanging beside the pump. She does it slowly, giving herself time to think. 'Are you sure?' she says.

'She peed on the stick,' says Lotis Blue. 'It was positive. The fucking thing showed a happy face.'

'A pink happy face! That stick is so mean! It's horrible!' says Ren. She starts to cry. 'She can't have that baby, not after what they did to her! Not a baby with a Painballer dad!'

'She's walking around like a zombie,' says Lotis Blue. 'She's so depressed. She's just really, really down.'

'I'll talk to her,' says Toby.

Poor Amanda. Who could expect her to give birth to a murderer's child? To the child of her rapists, her torturers? Though there's another possibility, as far as the father goes. Toby recalls the flowers, the singing, the enthusiastic tangle of Craker limbs in the light from the campfire on that chaotic Saint Julian's evening. What if Amanda is harbouring a baby Craker? Is that even possible? Yes, unless they're a different species altogether. But if so, won't it be dangerous? The Craker children are on a different developmental clock, they grow much faster. What if the baby gets too big, too fast, and can't make its way out?

It's not as if there are any hospitals. Or even any doctors. As far as facilities go it will be like giving birth in a cave.

'She's over at the swing set,' says Lotis Blue.

Amanda is sitting on one of the children's swings, moving gently back and forth. She doesn't quite fit the swing; it's close to the ground, and her knees are sticking up awkwardly. Slow tears are rolling down her cheeks.

Standing around her are three of the Craker women, touching her forehead, her hair, her shoulders. They're all purring. Ivory, ebony, gold.

'Amanda,' says Toby. 'It's all right. Everyone will help you.'

'I wish I was dead,' says Amanda. Ren bursts into tears and kneels down, throwing her arms around Amanda's waist.

'Don't say that!' she says. 'We got this far! You can't give up now!'

'I want this thing out of me,' says Amanda. 'Can't I drink some kind of poison? Some of your mushroom stuff?' At least she's showing some energy, thinks Toby. And it's true, there are plants that were once used. She remembers Pilar mentioning various seeds and roots: Queen Anne's lace, evening primrose.

But she's not sure of the quantities: it would be too risky to try such a thing. And if it's a Craker baby, none of that may work on it anyway. They have a different biochemistry, according to the MaddAddamites.

The ivory Craker woman stops purring. 'This woman is not blue any more,' she says. 'Her bone cave is no longer empty. That is good.'

'Why is she sad, Oh Toby?' says the gold woman. 'We are always happy when our bone cave is full.'

Bone cave. That's what they call it; beautiful in a way, and accurate, but right now all Toby herself can visualize is a cave full of gnawed bones. Which is how it must feel to Amanda: death in life. What can Toby do to make this story better? Not much. Remove all knives and ropes, arrange constant companions.

'Toby,' says Ren. 'Can't you . . . '

'Please try,' says Amanda.

'No,' says Toby. 'I don't have that knowledge.' It was Marushka Midwife who did the ob/gyn, at the Gardeners. Toby herself stuck to illnesses and wounds, but maggots and poultices and leeches are no use for this. 'It might not be as bad as you think,' she continues. 'The father might not be a Painballer. Remember that night, around the campfire, on Saint Julian's, when they jumped on . . . where there was a cultural misunderstanding? It might be a Craker baby.'

'Terrific,' says Ren. 'Great choices! An ultracriminal or some kind of gene-spliced weirdo monster. She wasn't the only one, anyway, with the cultural misunderstanding or whatever you want to call it. For all I know, I've got one of those Frankenbabies inside me too. I'm just scared of peeing on the stick.'

Toby tries to think of something to say – something upbeat and soothing. Genes aren't a total destiny? Nature versus nurture, good can come of evil? There are the epigenetic switches to be considered, and maybe the Painballers just had very, very bad nurturing? Or how about: the Crakers may be more human than we think? But none of it sounds very convincing, even to her.

'Oh Toby, do not be sad,' says a child's voice: Blackbeard, nudging up beside her. He takes her hand, pats it. 'Oryx will help, and the baby will come out of the bone cave, and then Amanda will be happy. Everyone is very happy when there is a baby that has just come out.'

Farrow

'Lift up, you're lying on my arm,' says Zeb. 'What's wrong?'

'I'm worried about Amanda,' says Toby, which is accurate, though not the whole story. 'It seems that she's pregnant. She's not overjoyed.'

'Three cheers,' says Zeb. 'First little pioneer born into our brave new world.'

'Anyone ever mention you can be callous at times?'

'Never,' says Zeb. 'I'm all quivering heart. The dad's most likely a Painballer though, judging from what went on, which would triple suck. Then we'd have to drown it like a kitten.'

'Fat chance,' says Toby. 'Those Craker women just love babies. They'd go berserk if you did cruel and hurtful things to it.'

'Women are strange,' says Zeb. 'Not that I couldn't have used a mom like that: protective, cuddly, and so forth.'

'It could be a hybrid. Half a Craker,' says Toby. 'In view of the mob action during the Saint Julian's festivities. But if it is, the baby might kill her. Their fetal growth rates are different, their heads are bigger when they're born, judging from the kids some of those women are toting around, so it could get stuck. I wouldn't even begin to know how to do a C-section. And even before that, what if there's a blood incompatibility?'

'Ivory Bill and those others know anything about that? The genetic blood stuff?'

'I haven't asked them,' says Toby.

'Okay, let's put it on the crisis list. One pregnancy. Call a group meeting. But if the MaddAddams don't know what's likely to happen, I guess it's wait and see?'

'It's wait and see anyway,' says Toby. 'It can't be aborted; no one here has that skill, and it would be way too risky to try it. There's some herbs, but if you don't know what you're doing they can be toxic. Nothing else to be done, unless someone at the group meeting has a brilliant suggestion. But before that, I need to do some consulting.'

'With who? None of our brainiacs are doctors.'

'Don't laugh at me for what I'm about to say.'

'Tongue bitten, mouth stapled. Fire away.'

'Okay, this is going to sound demented: with Pilar. Who, as you know, is dead.'

A pause. 'How you planning to do that?'

'I thought I could pay a visit to her, you know, where we . . . '

'To her shrine? Like a saint?'

'Something like that. Do an Enhanced Meditation. Remember where we buried her, in the park? On the day of her composting? We dressed up as park keepers, we dug a hole in the . . . '

'Yeah, I know the place. You wore those green parkie overalls I stole for you. We planted an elderberry bush on top of her.'

'Yes. That's where I'd like to go. I know it's a bit crazy, as the Exfernal World would have said.'

'First you talk to bees, now you want to talk to dead people? Even the Gardeners never went that far.'

'Some of them did. Think of it as a metaphor. I'll be accessing my inner Pilar, as Adam One would have put it. He'd be right onside with this.'

Another pause. 'Well, you can't do it alone.'

'I know.' Now it's her turn to pause.

A sigh. 'Okay, babe, whatever you want. I volunteer. I'll get Rhino and Shackie to come. We'll keep you covered. One spraygun, plus your rifle. How long you figure it'll take?'

'I'll do the short-form Enhanced Meditation. I don't want to hog too much time.'

'You expect to hear voices? Just so I know.'

'I've got no idea what I'll hear,' says Toby truthfully. 'Most likely nothing. But I need to do it anyway.'

'That's what I like about you. You're game for anything.' Some rustling, some shifting. Another pause. 'Something else eating you?'

'No,' Toby lies. 'I'm good.'

'You're into prevarication?' says Zeb. 'Fine with me.'

'Prevarication. That's a lot of syllables,' says Toby.

'Let me guess. You think I should tell you what happened out in the wilds of the shopping strip with what's-her-name. Little Miss Fox. Whether I groped her or vice versa. Whether sexual congress took place.'

Toby thinks about it. Does she want bad news about what she fears or good news she won't believe? Is she turning into a clinging invertebrate with tentacles and suction cups? 'Tell me something more interesting,' she says.

Zeb laughs. 'Good one,' he says.

So. Stalemate. It's for him to know and for her to try to refrain from finding out. He loves encryption. Even though she can't see him in the dark, she can feel him smiling.

They set out the next morning just at sunrise. The vultures that top the taller, deader trees are spreading their black wings so the dew on them will evaporate; they're waiting for the thermals to help them lift and spiral. Crows are passing the rumours, one rough syllable at a time. The smaller birds are stirring, beginning to cheep and trill; pink cloud filaments float above the eastern horizon, brightening to gold at the lower edges. Some days the sky looks like old paintings of heaven: there should be a few angels floating around, their white robes deployed like the skirts of archaic debutantes, their pink toes daintily pointed, their wings aerodynamically impossible. Instead, there are gulls.

They're walking along what is still a trail, through what is still recognizable as the Heritage Park. The little gravelled paths leading off to the side have vines creeping across them, but the picnic tables and cement barbecues have not yet been obscured. If there are ghosts here, they're the ghosts of children, laughing.

Every one of the drum-shaped trash containers has been tipped over, the lids pried off. That wouldn't have been people. Something has been busy. Not rakunks, though: the trash containers were made to be rakunk-proof. The earth around the picnic tables is rutted and muddy: something's been trampling, and wallowing.

The asphalted main pathway is wide enough for a Heritage Park vehicle, like the one Zeb and Toby used to transport Pilar to the site of her composting. Already there are weed shoots nosing up through. The force they can exert is staggering: they'll have a building cracked like a nut in a few years, they'll reduce it to rubble in a decade. Then the earth swallows the pieces. Everything digests, and is digested. The Gardeners found that a cause for celebration, but Toby has never been reassured by it.

Rhino walks ahead with a spraygun. Shackleton is at the rear. Zeb's in the middle, beside Toby, keeping a close eye on her. He's carrying the rifle for safekeeping, since she's already drunk the short-form Enhanced Meditation mixture. Luckily there were some *Psilocybe* species from the old Gardener mushroom beds among the assortment of dried mushrooms she'd saved over the years and brought with her from the AnooYoo Spa. To the soaked dried mushrooms and the mixed ground-up seeds she'd added a pinch of *muscaria*. Just a pinch: she doesn't want all-out brain fractals, just a low-level shakeup – a crinkling of the window glass that separates the visible world from whatever lies behind it. The effects are beginning: already there's a wavering, a shift.

'Hey, what're you doing here?' says a voice. Shackleton's voice, coming to her along a dark tunnel. She turns: it's Blackbeard.

'I wish to be with Toby,' he says.

'Oh fuck,' says Shackleton. Blackbeard smiles happily. 'And with Fuck too,' he says.

'It's all right,' says Toby. 'Let him come.'

'You can't stop him, anyway,' says Zeb. 'Short of braining him. Though I could tell him to fuck the fuck off.'

'Please,' says Toby. 'Don't confuse him.'

'Where are you going, Oh Toby?' says Blackbeard.

Toby takes the hand he holds up to her. 'To visit a friend,' she says. 'But it's a friend you can't see.' Blackbeard asks no questions; he simply nods.

Zeb looks ahead, looks left, looks right. He's singing to himself, a habit he's had ever since Toby's known him. It usually means he's feeling stressed.

Now we're in the muck,
And that can really suck,
And this is why we're out of luck,
Because we don't know fuck . . .

'But Snowman-the-Jimmy knows him,' says Blackbeard. 'And Crake. He knows him too.' He beams up at Toby and Zeb for verification, pleased with himself.

'You're right there, pal,' says Zeb. 'That's what they know. Both of them.'

Toby can feel the full strength of the Enhanced Meditation formula kicking in. Zeb's head against the sun is circled with a halo of what she realizes must be split ends – he could really use a trim, she must get hold of some scissors – but which nevertheless appears to her as a radiant burst of electric energy shooting out of his hair. A morpho-splice butterfly floats down the path, luminescent. Of course, she remembers, it's luminescent anyway, but now it's blue-hot, like a gasfire. Black Rhino looms up out of his own footsteps, an earth giant. Nettles arc from the sides of the walkway, the stinging hairs on their leaves gauzy with light. All around there are sounds, noises, almost-voices: hums and clicks, tappings, whispered syllables.

And there is the elderberry bush, where they planted it on Pilar's grave so long ago. It's much larger now. White bloom cascades from it, sweetness fills the air. A vibration surrounds it: honeybees, bumblebees, butterflies large and small.

'You stay here, with Zeb,' Toby says to Blackbeard. She lets go of his hand, steps forward, kneels in front of the elderberry.

She gazes at the clustered flowers, thinks, *Pilar*. The wizened old face, the brown hands, the gentle smile. All so real, once. Gone to ground.

I know you're here, in your new body. I need your help.

There's no voice, but there's a space. A waiting.

Amanda. Will she die, will this baby kill her? What should I do?

Nothing. Toby feels abandoned. But really, what did she expect? There is no magic, there are no angels. It was always child's play.

But she can't help asking anyway. *Send me a message. A signal. What would you do in my place?*

'Watch it,' says the voice of Zeb. 'Stay still. Look slowly. To the left.'

Toby turns her head. Crossing the path, within stone-throw, there's one of the giant pigs. A sow, with farrow: five little piglets, all in a row. Soft gruntings from the mother, high screechy pipings from the young. How pink and brightly shining are their ears, how crystalline their hooves, how . . .

'I've got you covered,' Zeb says. He's slowly lifting the rifle.

'Don't shoot,' says Toby. Her own voice in her ears is distant, her mouth feels huge and numbed. Her heart's becalmed.

The sow stops, turns sideways: a perfect target. She looks at Toby out of her eye. The five little ones gather in her shadow, under the nipples, which are all in a row too, like vest buttons. Her mouth upturns in a smile, but that's only the way it's made. Glint of light on a tooth.

Little Blackbeard moves forward. He's golden in the sun, his green eyes lambent, his hands outstretched.

'Get back here,' says Zeb.

'Wait,' Toby says. Such enormous power. A bullet would never stop the sow, a spraygun burst would hardly make a dent. She could run them down like a tank. Life, life, life, life, life. Full to bursting, this minute. Second. Millisecond. Millennium. Eon.

The sow does not move. Her head remains up, her ears pricked forward. Huge ears, calla lilies. She gives no sign of charging. The piglets freeze in place, their eyes red-purple berries. Elderberry eyes.

Now there's a sound. Where is it coming from? It's like the wind in branches, like the sound hawks make when flying, no, like a songbird made of ice, no, like a . . . Shit, thinks Toby. I am so stoned.

It's Blackbeard, singing. His thin boy's voice. His Craker voice, not human.

The next moment, the sow and her young have vanished. Blackbeard turns to smile at Toby. 'She was here,' he says. What does he mean?

'Crap,' says Shackleton. 'There go the spareribs.'

So, thinks Toby. Go home, take a shower, sober up. You've had your vision.

Vector

The Story of how Crake got born

'Still a little buzzed, are you?' says Zeb as they walk towards the trees where Jimmy's hammock was once strung up and where the Crakers are waiting. It's the gloaming: deeper, thicker, more layered than usual, the moths more luminous, the scents of the evening flowers more intoxicating: the short-term Enhanced Meditation formula has that effect. Zeb's hand in hers is rough velvet: like a cat's tongue, warm and soft, delicate and raspy. It sometimes takes half a day for this stuff to wear off.

'I'm not sure *buzzed* is the appropriate word to use of a mystical quasi-religious experience,' says Toby.

'That's what it was?'

'Possibly. Blackbeard's telling people that Pilar appeared in the skin of a pig.'

'No shit! And her a vegetarian. How'd she get in there?'

'He says she put on the skin of the pig just the way you put on the skin of the bear. Except she didn't kill and eat the pig.'

'What a waste.'

'Also she spoke to me, Blackbeard says. He says he heard her do it.'

'That what you think too?'

'Not exactly,' says Toby. 'You know the Gardener way. I was communicating with my inner Pilar, which was externalized in visible form, connected with the help of a brain chemistry facilitator to the wavelengths of the Universe; a universe in which – rightly understood – there are no coincidences. And just because a sensory impression may be said to be "caused" by an ingested mix of psychoactive substances does not mean it is an illusion. Doors are opened with keys, but does that mean that the things revealed when the doors are opened aren't there?'

'Adam One really did a job on you, didn't he? He could spout that crap for hours.'

'I can follow his line of reasoning, so I guess in that sense he did a job, yes. But when it comes to "belief," I'm not so sure. Though as he'd say, what is "belief" but a willingness to suspend the negatives?'

'Yeah, right. I never knew myself how much of it he really believed himself, or believed so much that he'd stick his arm in the fire for it. He was such a slippery bugger.'

'He said that if you acted according to a belief, that was the same thing. As having the belief.'

'Wish I could find him,' says Zeb. 'Even if he's dead. I'd like to know what happened, either way.'

'They used to call that "closure,"' says Toby. 'In some cultures, the spirit couldn't be freed unless the person got a decent burial.'

'Funny old thing, the human race,' says Zeb. 'Wasn't it? So, here we are. Do your stuff, Story Lady.'

'I'm not sure I can. Not tonight. I'm still a little foggy.'

'Give it a try. At least turn up. You don't want to start a riot.'

Thank you for the fish.

I will not eat it right now, because first I have something important to tell you.

Yesterday I listened to Crake on the shiny thing.

Please don't sing.

And Crake said, It is best to cook the fish a little longer. Until it is hot all the way through. Never leave it out in the sun before you cook it. Or keep it overnight. Crake says that is the best way, with a fish, and it is the way Snowman-the-Jimmy always wanted it to be cooked. And Oryx says that if it is the turn of her Fish Children to be eaten, she wants them to be eaten in the best way. Which means cooked all the way through.

Yes, Snowman-the-Jimmy is feeling better, though right now he is sleeping inside, in his own room. His foot does not hurt much any more. It is very good you did so much purring on it. He can't run fast yet, but he is practising his walking every day. And Ren and Lotis Blue are helping him.

Amanda can't help him because she is too sad.

We don't need to talk about why she is sad right now.

Tonight I will not tell a story, because of the fish. And the way it needs to be cooked. Also I am feeling a little . . . I am feeling tired. And that makes it harder for me to hear the story, when I put on the red hat of Snowman-the-Jimmy.

I know you are disappointed. But I will tell you a story tomorrow. What story would you like to hear?

About Zeb? And Crake too?

A story with both of them in it. Yes, I think there is a story like that. Maybe.

Was Crake ever born? Yes, I think he was. What do you think?

Well, I'm not sure. But he must have been born, because he looked like a – he looked like a person, once upon a time. Zeb knew him then. That's how there can be a story with both of them in it. And Pilar is in that story too.

Blackbeard? You have something to say about Crake?

He wasn't really born out of a bone cave, he only got inside the skin of a person? He put it on like clothes? But he was different inside? He was round and hard, like the shiny thing? I see.

Thank you, Blackbeard. Could you put on the red hat of Jimmy-the-Snowman, I mean Snowman-the-Jimmy, and tell us all of that story?

No, the hat won't hurt you. It won't turn you into someone else. No, you won't grow an extra skin; you won't grow clothes like mine. You can keep your very own skin.

It's all right. You don't have to put on the red hat. Please don't cry.

'Well, that was a bit of a fiasco,' says Toby. 'I didn't know they were afraid of it – that old red baseball cap.'

'I was afraid of the Red Sox myself,' says Zeb. 'When I was a kid. I was a gambler at heart even then.'

'It seems to be a sacred object to them. The hat. Sort of taboo. They can carry it around but they can't put it on.'

'Cripes, can you blame them? That thing is filthy! Bet it has lice.'

'I'm trying to have an anthropological discussion here.'

'Have I told you recently you've got a fine ass?'

'Don't be complex,' says Toby.

'*Complex* is another word for pathetic jerkoff?'

'No,' says Toby. 'It's just that . . .' Just that what? Just that she can't believe he means it.

'Okay, it's a compliment. Remember those? Guys give them to women. It's a courtship move – now that's anthropology. So just think of it as a bouquet. Deal?'

'Okay, deal,' says Toby.

'Let's start again. I spotted that fine ass of yours way back when, on that day we composted Pilar. When you took off those baggy Gardener-lady clothes and put on the parkie overalls. Filled me with longing, it did. But you were inaccessible then.'

'I wasn't really. I was . . .'

'Yeah, you kinda were. You were Miss Total God's Gardener Purity, as far as I could tell. Adam One's devoted altar girl. Wondered if he was having it off with you, to tell the truth. I was jealous of that.'

'Absolutely not,' says Toby. 'He never, ever . . .'

'I believe you. Thousands wouldn't. Anyway, I was hooked up with Lucerne at the time.'

'That stopped you? Mister Babe Magnet?'

A sigh. 'I was magnetized to babes, naturally. Back when I was young. It's a hormone thing, it comes with the hairy balls. Wonders of nature. But babes weren't always magnetized to me.' A pause. 'Anyway, I'm loyal. To whoever I'm with, if I'm really with them. A serial monogamist, you could say.'

Does Toby believe this? She isn't sure.

'But then Lucerne left the Gardeners,' she says.

'And you were Eve Six. Talking to the bees, measuring out the head trips. You were like a Mother Superior. Figured you'd slap me down. Inaccessible Rail,' he says, using her old MaddAddam chatroom codename. 'That was you.'

'And you were Spirit Bear,' says Toby. 'Hard to find, but good luck if you happen to see one. That's what the stories said, before those bears went extinct.' She starts to sniffle. The Meditation formula does that too: it melts the fortress walls.

'Hey. What? Did I say something bad?'

'No,' says Toby. 'I'm just sentimental.'

All those years you were my lifeline, she wants to say. But doesn't.

Young Crake

'Now I have to come up with something,' says Toby. 'A story with Crake in it, and you as well. Crake did know Pilar when he was younger, I figured that out. But what am I going to say about you?'

'As it happens, that part's actually true,' says Zeb. 'I knew him before the Gardeners even got started. But he wasn't Crake then, not even close. He was just a fucked-up kid named Glenn.'

Once Zeb was inside HelthWyzer West, he learned its memes and set about mimicking them as fast as he could. Displaying the right memes was the yellow brick road to blending in and thus surviving, so that when the giant Rev monster eye came looking for him via the giant Corps network, as it might at any moment, it would pass right over his head. Protective colouration, that's what he needed.

The officially promoted view of HelthWyzer West was that it was one big happy family, dedicated to the pursuit of truth and the betterment of humankind. To dwell too much on the improvement in value for the shareholders was considered bad taste, but on the other hand there was an employee options package. All staff were expected to be unremittingly cheerful, to meet their assigned goals diligently, and – as in real families – not to ask too much about what was really going on.

Again like real families, there were no-go zones. Some were conceptual, but some were purely physical. The pleebland outside the HelthWyzer Compound was one of these, unless you had a pass and designated protection. The firewalls around IP had become thick and in some cases impenetrable, unless you had an inside track; so if you couldn't hack the system, you grabbed the primary source material. Brainiacs from Corps of all kinds were being kidnapped and smuggled abroad, or – some said – into rival Corps Compounds – and then strip-mined for the gold and jewels their heads were assumed to contain.

This was a cause for serious concern at HelthWyzer West – which meant there was some fairly important stuff going on behind locked doors – and barriers had been put in place. The top biogeeks carried alarm beepers that registered their whereabouts, though these had sometimes been adroitly hacked and then used as a means of targeting their bearers and tracking them down. Here and there on the walls of hallways and meeting rooms, posters reminded the unwary of ever-present perils. FOLLOW THE SAFETY RULES AND KEEP YOUR HEAD! AND ITS CONTENTS! Or: YOUR MEMORY IS OUR IP, SO WE'LL PROTECT IT FOR YOU!

Or: BRAINS ARE LIKE MEADOWS: A CULTIVATED ONE IS WORTH MORE. On this last poster, someone had written with a Sharpie: *Get more cultivated! Eat more shit!* So, thought Zeb, there was at least some hidden dissent among the smiley faces.

As part of the happy family ethos, HelthWyzer West threw a barbecue every Thursday in the central parkette of the

Compound. Adam had told Zeb that these affairs should not be missed, as they were prime territory for eavesdropping and figuring out the invisible power filaments. Those wearing the most casual clothing would most likely be the alphas. Adam also said that Zeb would find some of the recreational pursuits of interest, especially the board games; though he hadn't said why.

So Zeb turned up at the HelthWyzer West barbecue on the first Thursday after his arrival. He sampled the eats: SoYummie ice cream for the kids, pork ribs for the carnivores, SoyOBoy products and quornburgers for the vegans. NevRBled Shish-K-Buddies for those who wanted to eat meat without killing animals – the cubes were lab-cultured from cells ('No Animal Suffered'), and he figured that with enough beer they wouldn't taste too bad. But he intended to limit his drinking because he needed to stay alert, so he stuck with the ribs. You didn't have to be half-cut to appreciate those.

Around the edges of the crowd, various geeky sports were in progress. Croquet and bocci in the sun, ping-pong and foosball under the awnings. Circle games for the under-sixes, variations of tag for the older ones. And for the serious and superintelligent and potentially Aspergerian child brainiacs, a row of umbrella-shaded computers where they could do obsessive-compulsive things online – within HelthWyzer firewalls, of course – and challenge each other to combat without making eye contact.

Zeb scoped out the games: Three-Dimensional Waco, Intestinal Parasites, Weather Challenge, Blood and Roses. Also Barbarian Stomp, a new one on him.

Here came Marjorie with the spaniel's eyes, making a beeline towards him, her beseeching smile at the ready, enhanced by a smear of ketchup on the chin. Time to duck and cover: she had the look of a woman who'd already staked out a claim, and would go through a guy's pants pockets while he was asleep in search of rivals, and would most likely read his email. Though maybe he was being paranoid. But best not to take chances.

'Want to go a round with me?' he said to the nearest youthful brainiac, a thin boy in a dark T-shirt with a stack of gnawed pork ribs on the paper plate beside him. Was that a cup of coffee? Since when was coffee allowable for a kid that age? Where were the parents?

The boy looked up at him with large, green, opaque but possibly mocking eyes. Even the children wore name tags to these barbecues, it seemed: *Glenn,* Zeb read.

'Sure,' said young Glenn. 'Conventional chess?'

'As opposed to?' said Zeb.

'Three-dimensional,' said Glenn indifferently. If Zeb didn't know that, then he couldn't be a very good player. Blatantly obvious.

So that was how Zeb first met Crake.

'But like I said, he wasn't Crake yet,' says Zeb. 'He was just a kid then. Not too much bad stuff had happened to him, though "not too much" is always a matter of taste.'

'Really?' says Toby. 'That long ago?'

'Would I lie to you?' says Zeb.

Toby thinks about it. 'Not about this,' she says.

Zeb generously and also patronizingly let Glenn play White, and Glenn walloped him, though Zeb put up an honourable fight. After that they did a round of Three-Dimensional Waco, and Zeb beat Glenn, who immediately wanted another game. This one ended in a tie. Glenn looked at Zeb with a small increase of respect and asked him where he'd come from.

Zeb then told a couple of lies, but they were entertaining lies:

he put in Miss Direction and the Floating World, and some of the bears from Bearlift, though he changed the name and the location and left out anything about dead Chuck. Glenn had never been outside a Compound, or not that he could remember, so these tales must have had mythic dimensions for him. Though he made a point of not looking impressed.

In any case, Glenn started turning up in Zeb's vicinity at the Thursday barbecue events and hanging around at lunchtimes. It wasn't hero-worship, not exactly; nor did Glenn want Zeb to be his dad. More like an older brother, Zeb decided. There weren't that many kids his age at HelthWyzer West for Glenn to play games with. Or not ones as smart as him. Not that Glenn thought Zeb was up to scratch, smarts-wise, but he was within range. Though there was a slight air of command performance about these proceedings: Glenn as the crown prince and Zeb as the somewhat dim courtier.

How old exactly was Glenn? Eight, nine, ten? It was hard for Zeb to tell because he didn't like to remember what his own life had been like when he'd been eight or nine or ten. He'd spent too much time in the dark back then, one way or another. All of that needed to be forgotten, and he'd worked at forgetting it. Still, when he saw a boy of that age the first thing he wanted to say was, *Run away! Run away very fast!* And the second thing was, *Grow bigger! Grow very big!* If you could grow very big, then whoever they were would cease to have power over you. Or so much power. Though it hadn't worked for whales, he reflected. Or tigers. Or elephants.

There must have been a *they* in the life of young Glenn, or maybe an *it*: something that was haunting him. He had that look about him, a look Zeb used to catch glimpses of when he saw himself unawares in the mirror: a wary, distrustful look, as if he didn't know what bush or parking lot or piece of furniture was going to chasm suddenly to reveal the lurking enemy or the bottomless pit. Though Glenn had no scars, no bruises, and no difficulty eating his meals, or not that Zeb could see; so what was that haunting entity? Nothing definite, perhaps. More like a lack, a vacuum.

After several Thursdays and some close observation, Zeb concluded that neither of Glenn's parents had a lot of time for him. Nor for each other: from the body language, they were well past the stage of irritation or even occasional dislike and were deep into active hatred. When they met in public they resorted to iceman stares and monosyllables, and to walking quickly away. There was a pot of boiling rage on a private stove behind their closed curtains: that bubbling cauldron was taking all their attention, with Glenn relegated to a footnote or else a trading card. Maybe the kid gravitated to Zeb for the same reason children like dinosaurs: when feeling abandoned in a world of forces beyond your control, it's comforting to have a huge, scaly beast who is your friend.

Glenn's mother was on the food admin staff, tracking supplies and devising meal plans. Glenn's dad was a semi-top researcher – an expert in unusual microbes, wonky viruses, odd antigens, and offbeat variants of anaphylaxis biovectors. Ebola and Marburg were among his specialties, but right now he was working on a rare allergic reaction to red meat that was linked to tick bites. An agent in the salivary proteins of ticks caused it, said Glenn.

'So,' said Zeb, 'a tick drools into you and then you can't have steak any more without bursting out in hives and suffocating to death?'

'Bright side,' said Glenn. He was going through a phase: he'd say 'bright side,' then add some gruesome sidebar. 'Bright side, if they could spread it through the population – those tick saliva proteins embedded in, say, the common aspirin – then every-one would be allergic to red meat, which has a huge carbon footprint and causes the depletion of forests, because they're cleared for cattle grazing; and then . . . '

'Not my idea of a bright side,' said Zeb. 'For argument: we're hunter-gatherers, we evolved to eat meat.'

'And to develop lethal allergies to tick saliva,' said Glenn.

'Only in those slated to be eliminated from the gene pool,' said Zeb. 'Which is why it's rare.'

Glenn grinned, not something he did often. 'Point,' he said.

While Zeb and Glenn were playing onscreen games at the Thursday events, Glenn's mother, Rhoda, would sometimes drift over to watch, leaning a little too close to Zeb's shoulder, sometimes even touching it with – what? The business end of her tit? Felt like it: that nubbin shape. Certainly not a finger. Her breath, scented with beer, would riffle the fine hairs near his ear. She never touched Glenn, however. In fact, nobody ever touched Glenn. He somehow arranged it that way: he'd erected an invisible no-fly zone around himself.

'You guys,' Rhoda would say. 'You should get out there and run around. Play some croquet.' Glenn didn't acknowledge these motherly interventions, nor did Zeb: Glenn's mother, although not wizened, was past the optimum freshness date as far as he was concerned, though if he'd been marooned on a liferaft with her. . . . But he wasn't, so he ignored the nipple nudges and the breath-to-ear signals and concentrated on the Blood part of Blood and Roses: eradicating the population of ancient Carthage and sowing the land with salt, enslaving the Belgian Congo, and murdering firstborn Egyptian babies.

Though why stop at firstborns? Some atrocities turned up by the virtual Blood and Roses dictated that the babies be tossed into the air and skewered on swords; others, that they be thrown into furnaces; yet others, that their brains be dashed out against stone walls. 'Trade you a thousand babies for the Palace of Versailles and the Lincoln Memorial,' he said to Glenn.

'No deal,' said Glenn. 'Unless you throw in Hiroshima.'

'That's outrageous! You want these babies to die in agony?'

'They aren't real babies. It's a game. So they die, and the Inca Empire gets preserved. With all that cool gold art.'

'Then kiss the babies goodbye,' said Zeb. 'Heartless little bugger, aren't you? Splat. There. Gone. And by the way, I'm cashing in my Wildcard Joker points to blow up the Lincoln Memorial.'

'Who cares?' said Glenn. 'I've still got the Palace of Versailles, plus the Incas. Anyway, there's too many babies. They make a huge carbon footprint.'

'You guys are awful,' said Rhoda, scratching herself. Zeb could hear the fingernails going behind his back, a sound like cat claws on felt. He wondered which part of herself she was scratching, then made an effort to stop wondering. Glenn had enough troubles without his one reliable friend making the double-backed beast with his unreliable mother.

Before he knew it, Zeb was giving young Glenn some extracurricular lessons in coding, which meant – practically speaking – in hacking as well. The kid was a natural, and he was finally impressed by some of the things Zeb knew and he didn't, and he caught on like magic. How tempting was it to take that talent and hone it and polish it and pass on the keys to the kingdom – the Open Sesames, the back doors, the shortcuts? Very tempting. So that is what Zeb did. It was a lot of fun watching the kid soak it all up, and who was to foresee the consequences? Which is usually the way with fun.

In return for Zeb's coding and hacking secrets, Glenn shared a few secrets of his own. For instance, he'd bugged his mother's room with an audio earlet concealed in her bedside lamp, by which means it became known to Zeb that Rhoda was having it off with an upper-middle-management type called Pete, usually right before lunchtime.

'My dad doesn't know,' said Glenn. He considered for a moment, fixing Zeb with his uncanny green eyes. 'Think I should tell him?'

'Maybe you shouldn't listen in on that shit,' said Zeb.

Glenn gave him a cool stare. 'Why not?'

'Because those things are for grown-ups,' Zeb said, sounding prissy even to himself.

'You would, when you were my age,' Glenn said, and Zeb couldn't deny that it was a thing he'd have done in a millisecond, given the opportunity and the tech. Avidly, gloatingly, without thinking twice.

On the other hand, maybe he wouldn't have done it if it involved his own parents. Even now he can't think about the Rev making umphing sounds while bobbing up and down on top of Trudy – who'd be slippery with perfumed lotion and lubricant, and would resemble an overstuffed pink satin pillow – without feeling queasy.

Grob's Attack

'Here comes the part where I meet Pilar,' says Zeb.

'What on earth was Pilar doing at HelthWyzer West?' says Toby. 'Working for a Corp, inside a Compound?'

But she knew the answer. A lot of the Gardeners had started out inside a Corp Compound, and a lot of the MaddAddamites had as well. Where else was a bioscience-trained person to work? If you wanted a job in research, you had to work for a Corp because that was where the money was. But you'd naturally be focused on projects that interested them, not on ones that interested you. And the ones that interested them had to have a profitable commercial application.

Zeb first met Pilar at one of the Thursday barbecues. He hadn't seen her there before. Some of the more senior people didn't attend the weekly ribfests: they were for younger people who might or might not be angling for a casual pickup or looking to exchange gossip and glean info, and Pilar was beyond that stage. As Zeb learned later, she was well up the seniority ladder.

But she was there that Thursday. All Zeb saw at first was a small, black-and-grey-haired older woman playing chess with

Glenn, over on the sidelines. It was an odd combo – almost-old lady, uppity young kid – and odd combos intrigued him.

He sauntered up casually and loomed over Glenn's shoulder. He watched the game for a while, trying not to kibbitz. Neither side had an obvious advantage. The old dame played relatively quickly, though without fluster, while Glenn pondered. She was making him work.

'Queen to h5,' Zeb said at last. Glenn was playing Black this time. Zeb wondered if he'd chosen it out of bravado or whether they'd flipped for White.

'Don't think so,' said Glenn without looking up while moving his knight to block – Zeb now saw – a possible check. The older woman smiled at Zeb, one of those wrinkly-eyed brown-skinned gnome-in-the-woods smiles that could mean anything from *I like you* to *Watch out*.

'Who is your friend?' she said to Glenn.

Glenn frowned at Zeb, which meant he felt insecure about the game. 'This is Seth,' he said. 'This is Pilar. Your move.'

'Hey,' said Zeb, nodding.

'A pleasure,' said Pilar. 'Good save,' she said to Glenn.

'Catch you later,' Zeb said to Glenn. He wandered off to eat some NevRBled Shish-K-Buddies – he was getting fond of them, despite their ersatz texture – topped off with a SoYummie cone, quasi-raspberry flavour.

He sucked on the cone while looking over the field and ranking all the women he could see. It was a harmless pastime. The scale was one to ten. There were no tens (In a Minute!), a couple of eights (With Mild Reservations), a clutch of fives (If Nothing Else Available), some definite threes (You'd Have to Pay Me), and an unfortunate two (Pay Me a Lot!) – when he felt a touch on his arm.

'Don't act surprised, Seth,' said a low voice. He looked down: it was tiny, walnut-faced Pilar. Was she making a move on him?

Surely not, but if so it could be a delicate moment, politeness-wise: how to say no in an acceptable manner?

'Your shoelaces are untied,' she said.

Zeb stared at her. His shoes didn't have laces. They were slip-ons.

'Welcome to MaddAddam, Zeb,' she said, smiling.

Zeb coughed out a chunk of SoYummie cone. 'Fuck!' he said, but he had the presence of mind to say it softly. Adam and his idiot *shoelaces* password. Who could have remembered?

'It's all right,' said Pilar. 'I know your brother. I helped bring you here. Look bored, as if we're making small talk.' She smiled at him again. 'I'll see you at the next Thursday barbecue. We should arrange to play a game of chess.' Then she wafted serenely away towards the croquet game. She had excellent posture: Zeb sensed a yoga aficionado. Posture like that made him feel personally sloppy.

He longed to go online, zigzag into the Extinctathon MaddAddam chatroom, and ask Adam about this woman, but he knew that wouldn't be prudent. The least said the better online, even if you thought your space was secure. The net had always been just that – a net, full of holes, all the better to trap you with; and it still was, despite the fixes they claimed to be adding constantly, with the impenetrable algorithms and the passwords and thumb scans.

But what else did they expect? With code serfs like him in charge of the security keys, of course the thing was going to leak. The pay was too low, so the temptation to pilfer, snoop, snitch, and sell for high rewards was great. But the penalties were getting more extreme, which was a counterbalance of sorts. Online thieves were increasingly professional, like the outfits he'd worked with in Rio. Few were hacking for the pure lulz of it any more, or even to register protests, as they had in the golden years of legend that middle-aged guys wearing retro

Anonymous masks got all nostalgic about in the dim, cobwebby, irrelevant corners of the web.

What good would registering a protest do you any more? The Corps were moving to set up their own private secret-service outfits and seize control of the artillery; not a month passed without the arrival of some new weapons law pretending to safeguard the public. Old-style demonstration politics were dead. You could get back at individual targets such as the Rev using underhanded means, but any kind of public action involving crowds and sign-waving and then storefront smashing would be shot off at the knees. Increasingly, everyone knew that.

He finished his SoYummie cone, fended off snub-nosed Marjorie, who wanted him to join a game of croquet and acted hurt when he said he was awkward with wooden balls, then meandered over to where Glenn was still sitting, staring at the chessboard. He'd set it up again and was playing against himself. 'Who won?' Zeb asked.

'I almost did,' said Glenn. 'She pulled a Grob's Attack on me. It caught me off-guard.'

'What exactly does she do here?' Zeb asked. 'Is she in charge of something?'

Glenn smiled. He liked knowing things Zeb didn't know. 'Mushrooms. Funguses. Mould. Want to play me?'

'Tomorrow,' said Zeb. 'Ate too much, it's dulling my brain.' Glenn grinned up at him. 'Chickenshit,' he said.

'Maybe just lazy. How come you know her?' said Zeb.

Glenn looked at him a little too long, a little too hard: green cat eyes. 'I already said. She works with my dad. He's on her team. Anyway, she's in the chess club. Been playing her since I was five. She's not too stupid.'

Which, in the high-praise area, was about as far as he went.

Vector

At the next Thursday barbecue, Glenn wasn't there. Nor had he been in evidence for a couple of days. He hadn't been mooching around the cafeteria, or asking Zeb to show him a few more hack moves on the computer. He'd become invisible.

Was he sick? Had he run away? Those were the only two possibilities that Zeb could think of, and he ruled out running away: the kid was surely too young for that, and it was too difficult to get out of HelthWyzer West without a pass. Though with Glenn's newfound robinhooding cryptic skills he could probably fake one.

There was another possibility: the little smartass had been colouring outside the digital lines. He'd broken into some sacrosanct Corps database or other and helped himself, just for the heck of it, because he couldn't possibly be into shady trading with the Chinese grey market, or worse – the Albanians, they were incandescent at the moment – and he'd got himself caught. In which case he'd be in a debriefing room somewhere having his brain pumped out. A person could come out of such affairs with nothing but a year-old dishrag north of the eyes. Would they do such a thing to a mere child? Yes. They would.

He really hoped it wasn't that: if it was, he himself would feel very guilty, because it would mean he'd been a bad teacher. 'Rule Number One,' he'd emphasized. 'Don't get caught.' But that was sometimes easier said than done. Had he been sloppy about the coding fretwork? Had he shown the kid a past-sell-by-date shortcut? Had he missed a few Detour signs, a few spoor marks that meant that he and Glenn were not the only ones on what he'd thought was his very own self-created poacher's jungle trail?

Though he was more than concerned, Zeb didn't want to start asking the teachers or even Glenn's lax and neglectful parents about him. He needed to keep his profile low, not draw attention.

Zeb scanned the barbecue crowd again. Still no Glenn. But Pilar was there, over to the side, under a tree. She was sitting in front of a chessboard, which she appeared to be studying. He assumed his casual saunter and made his way over there, hoping he looked random.

'Up for a game?' he said.

Pilar glanced up. 'Certainly,' she said with a smile. Zeb sat down.

'We'll toss for White,' said Pilar.

'I like to play Black,' said Zeb.

'So I've been told,' said Pilar. 'Very well.'

She opened with a standard queen's pawn, and Zeb decided to opt for a queen's Indian defence. 'Where's Glenn?' he asked.

'Things are not good,' she answered. 'Concentrate on the game. Glenn's father is dead. Glenn is naturally upset. The CorpSeCorps officers told him it was a suicide.'

'No shit,' said Zeb. 'When did that happen?'

'Two days ago,' said Pilar, moving her queen's knight. Zeb moved his bishop, pinning it down. Now she'd have a job developing her centre. 'It's not when, however, it's how. He was pushed off an overpass.'

'By his wife?' Zeb asked, remembering Rhoda's tit pressing against his back, and also the earlet concealed in her bedside lamp. It was a jokey kind of question – he should have been ashamed of himself. Sometimes that kind of thing shot out of his mouth like popcorn. But it was a serious question, as well: Glenn's dad could have found out about Rhoda's lunchtime interludes, they could have gone for a walk to discuss it, outside the walls of HelthWyzer for more privacy, and decided to stroll along the overpass, for the view of the oncoming traffic, and then they could have had a fight, and Glenn's mother could have upended his dad over the railing, a move he'd been unable to defend himself against . . .

Pilar was looking at him. Waiting for him to come to his senses, most likely.

'Okay, I take it back,' he said. 'It wasn't her.'

'He found out something they're doing, inside HelthWyzer,' said Pilar. 'He felt this practice was not only unethical but dangerous to public health, and therefore immoral. He threatened to make this knowledge public; or, well, not public as such, since the press probably wouldn't have touched it. But if he'd gone to a rival Corp, especially one outside the country, they'd have made damaging use of the information.'

'He was on your research team, wasn't he?' said Zeb. He was trying to follow what she was saying, thus losing control of his game.

'Affiliated,' said Pilar, dispatching one of his pawns. 'He confided in me. And now I'm confiding in you.'

'Why?' said Zeb.

'I'm being reassigned,' said Pilar. 'To the HelthWyzer headquarters, out east. Or that's where I hope I'm going, though it may be worse. They may think I'm lacking in enthusiasm, or suspect my loyalty. You'll have to leave here. I can't keep you safe once I've been transferred. Take my bishop with your knight.'

'That's a bad move,' said Zeb. 'It opens the way to . . . '

'Just take it,' she said calmly. 'Then keep it in your hand. I have another one, I'll replace it in the box. No one will know there's a bishop missing.'

Zeb palmed the bishop. He'd learned how to do that from Slaight of Hand, back in his Floating World days. Deftly he slid it up his sleeve.

'What am I supposed to do with it?' he said. With Pilar gone, he'd be isolated.

'Just deliver it,' she said. 'I'll fake you a day pass, with a cover story attached; they'll want to know your business in the plee-blands. Once you're outside the HelthWyzer West Compound, there'll be a new identity waiting. Take the bishop with you. There's a sex club franchise called Scales and Tails, you can look it up on the net. Go to the nearest branch. The password is *oleaginous*. They'll let you in. You'll be leaving the bishop there. It's a container, they'll know how to open it.'

'Deliver it to who?' said Zeb. 'What's in it, anyway? Who's *they*?'

'Vectors,' says Pilar.

'In what sense?' said Zeb. 'Like, math vectors?'

'Let's say biological. Vectors for bioforms. And these vectors are inside some other vectors that look like vitamin pills: three kinds, white, red, and black. And the pills are inside another vector, the bishop. Which will be carried by another vector, you.'

'What's the thing inside the pills?' Zeb asked. 'Brain candy? Code chips?'

'Definitely not. Best not to ask,' said Pilar. 'But whatever you do, don't eat any of them. If you think anyone's following you, shove the bishop down a drain.'

'What about Glenn?' said Zeb.

'Check and mate,' said Pilar, toppling his king. She stood up, smiling. 'Glenn will make his way,' she said. 'He doesn't know they killed his father. He doesn't know yet. Or not directly. But he's very bright.'

'You mean he'll figure it out,' said Zeb.

'Not too soon, I hope,' said Pilar. 'He's too young for that kind of bad news. He might not be able to pretend ignorance, unlike you.'

'Some of mine's real,' said Zeb. 'Like, right now, where do I switch identities? And how do I get the pass?'

'Go into the MaddAddam chatroom, there's a full package waiting for you. Then scramble your present gateway. You can't afford to leave your footprints on these computers.'

'Does any of this involve different facial hair?' Zeb asked, to lighten things up. 'For my new identity? And dorky pants?'

Pilar smiles. 'I've had my beeper switched off all this time,' she says. 'We're allowed to do that on barbecue days, as long as we're in full view. I'm turning it back on now. Don't say anything you don't want overheard. Journey well.'

Scales and Tails

Zeb retrieved his thumbdrive from the desk drawer where he'd hidden it, removed the cough drops that were stuck to it like barnacles, activated Intestinal Parasites on his computer, then slipped through the voracious maw of the blind nightmare worm and thence by lilypad into the chatroom of MaddAddam. Sure enough, there was a how-to pack waiting for him, though no clue as to who had left it. He opened it, assimilated the contents, and scuttled backwards, whisking away his trail as he went. Then he ground the thumbdrive underfoot – or, more accurately, he placed it under one of his bed legs and then jumped on the bed, several times – and flushed the bits down several toilets. They wouldn't have gone down easily by themselves, being metal and plastic, but if you embed . . .

'It's okay,' says Toby. 'I get the picture.'

Zeb's new name was Hector. Hector the Vector, was what he figured. Someone had a reasonably foul sense of humour, but he didn't think it was Pilar: she was not so much the humorous type.

But of course he'd only activate his new Hector identity once he was outside the walls and away from the security cameras of HelthWyzer West. Until then he was still Seth, a minor code-slave chained in the galleyship of data entry, in his geek-wear with the brown corduroy pants. If anything, he was betting his change of identity would score him better pants. There was said to be an outfit waiting for him in the pleeb-lands, stashed in a dumpster he hoped no tramps or crazy people or sacked middle managers would be picking through before he could get to it.

The cover story for his Seth persona was that he was making a service call at a local branch of a beauty-and-mood-enhancing Corp called AnooYoo, which was a dubious affiliate of HelthWyzer. Health and Beauty, the two seductive twins joined at the navel, singing their eternal siren songs. A lot of people would pay through their nose jobs for either one.

HelthWyzer's products – the vitamin supplements, the over-the-counter painkillers, the higher-end disease-specific pharmaceuticals, the erectile dysfunction treatments, and so on – went in for scientific descriptions and Latin names on the labels. AnooYoo, on the other hand, was mining arcane secrets from Wiccan moon-worshippers and from shamans deep in the assassin-bug-rich rainforests of Dontgothere. But Zeb could understand that there was an overlap of interests. If it hurts and you feel sick and it's making you ugly, take this, from Helth-Wyzer; if you're ugly and it hurts and you feel sick about it, take that, from AnooYoo.

Zeb readied himself for his mission by putting on a newly laundered pair of brown cords. He rearranged his face into his marginally shambolic Seth persona and winked at it in the bath-room mirror. 'You're doomed,' he said to it. He wouldn't be sorry to part company with Seth, who'd been foisted on him by Adam in an act of older-brother I-know-better bossiness. He longed to see Adam in person, if only to berate him for that. 'You got any fucking idea of what those pants put me through?' he might say.

Time for Seth to go. He ambled in the direction of the front gate, exit pass in hand, humming to himself:

Hi ho, hi ho,
To jerkoff work I go,
With a hick hack here and a hick hack there,
Hi ho, hi ho, hi ho, hi ho!

Now to remember the cover story of Seth, junior code plumber. He was being sent to investigate the AnooYoo website, and to discover how it had been tampered with. Someone – maybe a jumped-up teenaged hacker like his own younger self – had altered the online images so that when you clicked on any of the mood-enhancing, complexion-improving products, a squad of puce and orange insect animations would nibble into them at hyperspeed and then explode, legs twitching, yellow fumes coming out. It was silly but graphic.

HelthWyzer West didn't want anyone working on the problem from inside their own systems, naturally: the thing, simpleminded though it looked, could be a trap, with its planners hoping for just such an intervention so they could ram in through HelthWyzer's firewalls and filch its valuable IP. Therefore someone had to go to AnooYoo in person: someone minor and – since the gang-riddled pleebs were hazardous – someone expendable. That would be Seth, though at least they were providing a HelthWyzer car, with a driver. Nobody would likely go to the trouble of grabbing Seth for brain excavation: he wasn't inner circle. But still.

AnooYoo didn't want to find out who'd done the hack job, or why: that would be too expensive. They just wanted their firewall repaired. Their own guys hadn't been able to do it, ran the cover story, which wasn't – to Zeb – ultra plausible. But then, AnooYoo was a cheap operation – this was before its plusher days, when it set up the Spa-in-the-Park – so its IT bunch wasn't the A team, and maybe not even the B or C team: ultrabrights got snapped up by richer Corps. They were more like the F team. Obviously, since they'd failed.

But they were going to have a long wait, thought Zeb, because within the hour he would morph into Hector, and Seth would be no more. He had the chess bishop; it was in his baggy corduroy pants pocket, where he was also keeping his left hand just in case, and if anyone was looking they might conclude he was engaged in an act of self-abuse. Which he simulated in a restrained way, in case the car was equipped with spyware, as was likely. Better a wanker than a defector, and a contraband smuggler to boot.

AnooYoo was located in a seedy piece of real estate on the edge of a grey-market pleeb. So it wasn't alien to the streetscape to find an overturned SecretBurgers stand blocking the way, with a full-scale red-sauce fracas going on and a corona of yelling and honking surrounding it, plus flying squadrons of airborne meat patties. Zeb's own driver leaned on the horn, though he knew better than to roll down the window to yell.

But before you could say prestidigitation, the car was mobbed by a dozen Asian Fusions. One of them must've had a digilock popper keyed with the HelthWyzer car's passcode because up shot the lock buttons. In about one second the Fusion thugs had winkled out the thrashing, yelping driver and were going for his shoes and shucking him out of his clothing as if he was a cob of corn. Those pleeb gangs were fast and professional, you had to hand it to them. They'd get hold of the car keys, reverse, and be off like a shot, to sell the vehicle whole or strip it for parts, whichever paid more.

This was Zeb's moment. It had been paid for in advance: the

Asian Fusions were dirty but they were also cheap, and happy to take small jobs. Checking first to make sure the driver's sight-lines were blocked – they had to be, his entire head was now covered in red sauce – Zeb dove out the back door and frog-marched himself down the adjacent alleyway and around the corner, then around another corner, and then a third, where he kept his rendezvous with the designated dumpster.

The brown corduroy pants went into it, good riddance, and some well-aged jeans came out, with accessories to match. Black pleather jacket, black T that read ORGAN DONOR, TRY MINE FREE, reflector shades, baseball cap with a modestly sized red skull on the front. Gold clip-on tooth cap, fake 'stache, newly minted smirk, and Hector the Vector was ready to saunter. He'd taken care to keep the chess bishop safely to hand, and now he zipped it into the inside pocket of the pleather.

Off he went, in a hurry but not in any way looking it: best to seem unemployed. Also best to seem up to no good, in non-specific ways.

The Scales and Tails where he was heading was deeper into the pleeb. If he'd gone there in his geekwear he'd probably have had to defend his personal territory beginning with scalp, nose, and balls, but as it was he attracted not much more than a few narrow-eyed assessments. Worth taking on? Not, was the ver-dict. So his sauntering went unimpeded.

There it was, up ahead: ADULT ENTERTAINMENT in neon, *For Discerning Gentlemen* in subscript. Pics of reptilian lovelies in skintight green scales, most of them with impressive bimplants, some in contorted poses that suggested they had no backbones. A woman who could hook her legs around her own neck had something to offer in the way of novelty, though exactly what was unclear. And there was March the python, looped around the shoulders of a red-hot cobra lady who was swinging from a trapeze, and who greatly resembled Katrina WooWoo, the lovely snake trainer from the Floating World he'd so often helped to saw in half.

Not even very much older. So she was still keeping her hand in. As it were.

It was daytime: no customer traffic inbound. He reminded himself of the ludicrous password he'd been saddled with. *Oleaginous.* How to use it in a plausible sentence? 'You're looking very oleaginous today?' That might get him a slap or a punch, depending on who he said it to. 'Oleaginous weather we're having.' 'Turn off that oleaginous music.' 'Stop being so fucking oleaginous!' None of them sounded right.

He rang the doorbell. The door looked thick as a bank vault, with a lot of metal on it. An eye peered at him through the peephole. Locks clicked, the portal opened, and there was a bouncer as big as himself, only black. Shorn head, dark suit, shades. 'What?' he said.

'Hear you've got some oleaginous girls,' said Zeb. 'Ones that butter you up.'

The guy stared at him from inside his shades. 'Say that again?' he said, so Zeb did. 'Oleaginous girls,' said the guy, rolling the phrase around in his mouth as if it was a doughnut hole. 'Butter you up.' His mouth upended at the corners. 'Good one. Right. Inside.' He checked the street before shutting the door. More locks clicking. 'You want to see *her,*' he said.

Down the hallway, purple-carpeted. Up the stairs: smell of a pleasure factory in the off hours, so sad. That moppet-shop smell that meant false raunchiness, that meant loneliness, that meant you got loved only if you paid.

The guy said something into his earpiece, which must have been very small because Zeb couldn't see it. Maybe it was inside a tooth: some were using those now, though if the tooth got knocked out and you swallowed the thing you might end up talking out your ass. An inner door marked HEAD OFFICE, BODY OFFICE TOO, with a shiny green winking-snake logo and the motto 'We're Flexible.'

'In,' said the big guy once more – not a large vocabulary, him – and in Zeb went.

The room was an office of sorts, equipped with a lot of video screens and some expensive overstuffed furniture that was making a muffled statement, and a mini-bar. Zeb eyed the bar longingly – maybe there was a beer, all this running around and pretense had made him thirsty – but this was not the time.

There were two people in the room, each deep in a chair. One was Katrina WooWoo. She wasn't in her snake outfit: only an oversized sweatshirt that said BITCH #3, tight black jeans, and a pair of silver stilettos that would cripple a stilt dancer. She smiled at Zeb, one of those stage smiles she could always maintain while hissing. 'Long time,' she said.

'Not that long,' said Zeb. 'You still look easy to pick up and hard to put down.'

She smiled. Zeb had to admit he longed to wend his way into her scaly underthings – that boyish yen hadn't faded – but he couldn't concentrate on such goals right then because the other person in the room was Adam. He was wearing a dorky caftan affair that looked as if it was put together by spastic ragpickers for a stage play about leprosy.

'Fuck,' said Zeb. 'Where'd you get that pixie nightshirt?' It was best not to show surprise: it would give Adam an advantage he didn't, at the moment, deserve.

'I note your tasteful T-shirt,' said Adam. 'It suits you. Nice motto, baby brother.'

'Is this place bugged?' said Zeb. One more baby brother quip and he'd deck Adam. No, he wouldn't. He never could bear to hit the guy, not full-out: Adam was too ethereal.

'Of course,' said Katrina WooWoo. 'But we've turned every-thing off, courtesy of the house.'

'I'm supposed to believe that?'

'She actually has turned it off,' said Adam. 'Think about it. She doesn't want any of our footprints on her establishment. She's doing us a big favour. Thanks,' he said to Katrina. 'We won't be long.' She stilt-walked out of the room, teetering a little, casting them a smile over her shoulder: not a hissy smile this time. She was evidently keen on Adam, despite the caftan. 'There's some food later, if you want it,' she said. 'In the girls' caf. I need to get changed, showtime coming up.'

Adam waited until she'd closed the door. 'You made it,' he said. 'Good.'

'No thanks to you,' said Zeb. 'I might've been lynched because of those nerdy brown pants.' He was in fact very pleased to know that Adam was still alive, but he wasn't going to straight-out admit it. 'I looked like a fucking fuckwit in those fucking things,' he added, piling on the profanity.

Adam ignored that part. 'Have you got it?' he said.

'I take it you mean this fucking chess piece,' Zeb said. He handed it over. Adam twisted the head, and off it came. He turned the bishop upside down: out slid the six pills: red, white, black, two of each colour. Adam looked at them, then put them back into the bishop and reattached the head.

'Thank you,' he said. 'We have to think of somewhere very safe for this.'

'What is it?' said Zeb.

'Pure evil,' said Adam. 'If Pilar's right. But valuable pure evil. And very secret. Which is why Glenn's father is dead.'

'What do they do?' said Zeb. 'Supersex pills or what?'

'Cleverer than that,' said Adam. 'They're using their vitamin supplement pills and over-the-counter painkillers as vectors for diseases – ones for which they control the drug treatments.

Whatever's in the white ones is in actual deployment. Random distribution, so no one will suspect a specific location of being ground zero. They make money all ways: on the vitamins, then on the drugs, and finally on the hospitalization when the illness takes firm hold. As it does, because the treatment drugs are loaded too. A very good plan for siphoning the victims' money into Corps pockets.'

'So those are the white ones. What about the reds and the blacks?'

'We don't know,' said Adam. 'They're experimental. Possibly other diseases, possibly a faster-acting formula. We aren't even sure how to find out in any safe way.'

Zeb took this in. 'This is large,' he said. 'I wonder how many brainiacs it took to think that up.'

'It's a small, designated group within HelthWyzer,' said Adam. 'Directed from the top. Glenn's father was being used by them. He thought he was working on a targeted cancer-treatment vector. When he realized the nature of it, the full scope, he couldn't go along with it. He slipped these to Pilar, before . . . '

'Shit,' said Zeb. 'They killed her too?'

'No,' said Adam. 'They don't even know she knows, or so we hope. She's just been transferred to HelthWyzer Central, on the east coast.'

'Mind if I have a beer?' said Zeb. He didn't wait for an answer. 'So now that you have this stuff,' he said after the first refreshing swallow, 'what next? You going to sell these things on the grey market? Foreign Corps would pay a lot.'

'No,' said Adam. 'We couldn't do that. It would be firmly against our principles. All we can do in this world, now, is to learn what to avoid. We'll warn others about the vitamin supplements if we can, but if we were to try going public with this information we wouldn't be believed. We'd only sound paranoid, and after that we would have unfortunate accidents. The press is Corps-controlled, as you know, and any independent regulation is independent in name only. So we will keep the pills hidden until they can be analyzed without danger.'

'Who's this *we?*' said Zeb.

'If you don't know, you can't tell,' said Adam. 'Safer for everyone, including you.'

The Story of Zeb and the Snake Women

'How do I explain all of that to them?' says Toby. 'The Scales and Tails girls, dressed up like snakes?'

'You could just leave it out.'

'I don't think so. It needs to be in. It seems appropriate, a woman who is also a snake. It goes along with the Meditation, and whatever happened with that animal. With that sow. It . . . She really seemed to be communicating with me. And with Blackbeard.'

'You think that thing is part human? A Pig Woman? You really drank the Kool-Aid.' A chuckle.

'No, not exactly, but . . . '

'Too many peyote buttons in that mix of yours. Or whatever you put in.'

'Maybe. No doubt you're right.'

The story tells itself inside Toby's head. She doesn't seem to be thinking about the story, or directing it. She has no control over it; she just listens. Amazing what a few plant molecules will do to your brain, and how long that lasts.

*

This is the story of Zeb and the Snake Women. The Snake Women do not come into the story at first, they come in later. Important things often come into stories later, but also at the beginning. And in the middle as well.

But I have already told the beginning, so right now it's the middle. And Zeb is in the middle of the story about Zeb. He is in the middle of his own story.

I am not in this part of the story; it hasn't come to the part with me. But I'm waiting, far off in the future. I'm waiting for the story of Zeb to join up with mine. The story of Toby. The story I am in right now, with you.

Pilar, who lives in the elderberry bush and talks to us through the bees, was once in the form of an old woman. She gave Zeb a special important thing and told him he had to take care of it – a little thing, like a seed. And the seed would make you sick if you ate it. But some bad people from the chaos were telling all the other people that this seed would make them happy. And only Pilar and Zeb and a small number of other people knew the truth.

Why were the bad people doing that? Because of Money. Money was invisible, like Fuck. They thought that Money was their helper; they thought he was a better helper than Fuck. But they were wrong about that. Money was not their helper. Money goes away just when you need it. But Fuck is very loyal.

So Zeb took the seed, and he went out through the door, because if the bad men knew he had it they would chase him and take it away from him, and then do something very hurtful to him. And he was hurrying without seeming to hurry, and he said, Oh Fuck, and Fuck came flying through the air, very fast, as he always does when you call him; and he showed Zeb how to get to the house of the Snake Women. And the Snake Women opened their door, and took him in.

The Snake Women are ... You have seen a snake, and you have seen women. The Snake Women were both. And they lived with several Bird Women and Flower Women. And they hid Zeb inside a giant ... Inside a great big ... A clam shell. No, a sofa. Or maybe they hid him inside a great big, an enormous ... A flower. A very bright flower with lights on it.

Yes, a light-up flower. No one would look for Zeb inside a flower.

And Zeb's brother, Adam, was inside the flower too. That was nice. They were very happy to see each other, because Adam was the helper of Zeb and Zeb was the helper of Adam.

The Snake Women sometimes bit people, but they didn't bite Zeb. They liked him. They made him a special drink, called a Champagne Cocktail, and then they did a special dance for him. It was a twisty dance, because after all they were snakes.

They were very kind. Because that is how Oryx made them. And they were her Children, because they were part snake. So they had nothing to do with Crake. Or not much.

And the Snake Women let Zeb sleep in a great big bed, a bed that was shiny and green. They said Fuck could sleep in there as well, because there was lots of room.

And Zeb said, Thank you, because the Snake Women were being so kind to him, and also to his invisible helper. And they made him feel much better.

No, they did not purr over him. Snakes can't purr. But they ... they twined. Yes, that is what they did: some twining. And some constriction, they did that too. Snakes have very good muscles for constriction.

And Zeb was really, really tired, so he went to sleep at once.

And the Snake Women and the Bird Women and the Flower Women took care of him, and made sure nothing bad would happen to him while he slept. They said they would protect him and hide him even if the bad men came there.

And the bad men did come. But that is in the next part of the story.

And now I am really, really tired too. And I am going to sleep.

Good night.

That is what she'll say when it's time for the next story.

Piglet

Guru

The morning after her visit to Pilar's elderberry bush, Toby is still feeling the effects of the Enhanced Meditation mixture. The world's a little brighter than it should be, the scrim of its colours and shapes a little more transparent. She puts on a bedsheet in a calming neutral tone – light blue, no pattern – gives her face a quick wash at the pump, and makes it over to the breakfast table.

Everyone else seems to have eaten and gone. White Sedge and Lotis Blue are clearing off the dishes.

'I think there's some left,' says Lotis Blue.

'What was it?' Toby asks.

'Ham and kudzu fritters,' says White Sedge.

Toby has dreamt all night: piglet dreams. Innocent piglets, adorable piglets, plumper and cleaner and less feral than the ones she'd actually seen. Piglets flying, pink ones, with white gauzy dragonfly wings; piglets talking in foreign languages; even piglets singing, prancing in rows like some old animated film or out-of-control musical. Wallpaper piglets, repeated over and over, intertwined with vines. All of them happy, none of them dead.

They did love to depict animals endowed with human

features, back in that erased civilization of which she had once been a part. Huggable, fluffy, pastel bears, clutching Valentine hearts. Cute cuddly lions. Adorable dancing penguins. Older than that: pink, shiny, comical pigs, with slots in their backs for money: you saw those in antique stores.

She can't manage the ham, not after a night full of waltzing piglets. And not after yesterday: what the sow communicated to her is still with her, though she couldn't put it into words. It was more like a current. A current of water, a current of electricity. A long, subsonic wavelength. A brain chemistry mashup. Or, as Philo of the Gardeners once said, Who needs TV? He'd done perhaps too many Vigils and Enhanced Meditations.

'Think I'll skip that,' says Toby. 'It's not so great warmed over. I'll go get some coffee.'

'Are you all right?' says White Sedge.

'I'm fine,' says Toby. She walks carefully along the path to the kitchen area, avoiding the places where the pebbles are rippling and dissolving, and finds Rebecca drinking a cup of coffee substitute. Little Blackbeard is there with her, sprawled on the floor, printing. He's got one of Toby's pencils, and he's swiped her notebook too. But useless to call it 'swiping' – the Crakers appear to have no concept of personal property.

'You didn't wake up,' he says, not reproachfully. 'You were walking very far, in the night.'

'Have you seen this?' Rebecca says. 'The kid's amazing.'

'What are you writing?' Toby says.

'I am writing the names, Oh Toby,' says Blackbeard. And, sure enough, that's what he's been doing. TOBY. ZEB. CRAK. REBECA. ORIX. SNOWMANTHEJIMY.

'He's collecting them,' says Rebecca. 'Names. Who's next?' she says to Blackbeard.

'Next I will write Amanda,' says Blackbeard solemnly. 'And Ren. So they can talk to me.' He scrambles up from the floor and runs off, clutching Toby's notebook and pencil. How am I going to get those back from him? she wonders.

'Honey, you look wiped,' Rebecca says to her. 'Rough night?'

'I overdid something,' says Toby. 'In the Enhanced Meditation mix. A few too many mushrooms.'

'It's a hazard,' says Rebecca. 'Drink a lot of water. I'll make you some clover and pine tea.'

'I saw a giant pig yesterday,' says Toby. 'A sow, with piglets.'

'The more the merrier,' says Rebecca. 'So long as we've got sprayguns. I'm running out of bacon.'

'No, wait,' says Toby. 'It – she gave me a very strange look. I got the feeling that she knew I'd shot her husband. Back at the AnooYoo Spa.'

'Wow, you really went to town on the mushrooms,' Rebecca says. 'I once had a conversation with my bra. So, was she mad about the . . . I'm sorry, I just can't call it a husband! It was a pig, for chrissakes!'

'She wasn't pleased,' says Toby. 'But more sad than mad, I'd say.'

'They're smarter than ordinary pigs, even without the Meditation booster,' says Rebecca. 'That's for sure. By the way, Jimmy came to breakfast today. No more invalid trays for him. He's doing well, but he'd like you to double-check his foot.'

Jimmy has his own cubicle now. It's a new one, in the cobb-house addition they've finished at last. The cobb walls still smell a little damp, a little muddy; but there's a larger window than in the older part of the building, with a screen set into it and a curtain in a vibrant print of cartoon fish, with big curvy mouths and long-lashed eyes on the female ones. The males are playing guitars, with an octopus on the bongos.

This is not the best thing for Toby to be looking at in her present state.

'Where did those come from?' she asks Jimmy, who's sitting up on his bed ledge with his feet on the floor. His legs are still thin, wasted; he'll need to build up the muscles again. 'The curtains?'

'Who knows?' says Jimmy. 'Ren, Wakulla – I mean, Lotis Blue. They felt I needed some cheerful interior decoration. It's like pre-school in here.' He still has his Hey-Diddle-Diddle coverlet.

'You wanted me to look at your foot?' she says.

'Yeah. It's itchy. Driving me crazy. I just hope none of those maggot things got left inside.'

'If they did, they'd have burrowed out by now,' says Toby.

'Thanks a million,' says Jimmy. The scar on his foot is red but sealed over. Toby examines it: no heat, no inflammation.

'That's normal,' she says. 'The itchiness. I'll get you something for it.' A poultice: jewelweed, horsetail, red clover, she thinks. Horsetail might be the easiest to find.

'I heard you saw a pigoon,' says Jimmy. 'And it spoke to you.'

'Who told you that?' says Toby.

'The Crakers, who else?' says Jimmy. 'They're my radio. That kid Blackbeard gave them the whole story, it seems. They think you shouldn't have killed that boar, but they're forgiving you because maybe Oryx said you could. You know those pigs have human prefrontal cortex tissue in their brains? Fact. I should know, I grew up with them.'

'How did the Crakers learn about that?' Toby asks carefully. 'Me shooting the boar?'

'The pigoon gal told Blackbeard. Don't give me that look, I'm just the messenger here. And according to Ren I've been hallucinating for a while, so hey. Maybe I'm not the best judge of reality.' He gives her a lopsided grin.

'Mind if I sit down?' she says.

'Help yourself, thousands do,' says Jimmy. 'Fucking Crakers wander in here whenever the whim takes them. They want to know more shit about Crake. They think I'm his fucking guru. That he talks to me through my wristwatch. 'Course it's my own fucking fault because I made that up myself.'

'And what do you tell them?' Toby asks. 'About Crake?'

'I tell them to go ask you,' says Jimmy.

'Me?' says Toby.

'You're the expert now. I need to take a nap.'

'No, really, they always say you . . . they say you knew Crake, in person. When he was walking the earth.'

'Like that's supposed to be first prize?' Jimmy gives a sour little laugh.

'It gives you a certain authority,' says Toby. 'In their eyes.'

'That's like having a certain authority with a bunch of . . . Crap, I'm so wrecked I can't even think of a smartass comparison. Clams. Oysters. Dodos. What I'm saying is. Because, I'm tired. My guru juice is all used up. They wore me out a while ago, to tell you the truth. I never want to think about Crake again, ever, or listen to any more crapulous poop about how good and kind and all-powerful he is, or how he made them in the Egg and then sweetly wiped everybody else off the face of the planet, just for them. And how Oryx is in charge of the animals, and flies around in the shape of an owl, and even though you can't see her she's there anyway and will always hear them.'

'As I understand it,' says Toby, 'that's consistent with what you've been telling them. It's Gospel as far as they're concerned.'

'I know that's what I fucking told them!' says Jimmy. 'They wanted to know the basic stuff, like where they came from and what all those decaying dead people were. I had to tell them something.'

'So you made up a nice story,' says Toby.

'Well, crap, I could hardly tell them the truth. So yes. And yes, I could've done a smarter job of it, and yes, I'm not a brainiac, and yes, Crake must've thought I had the IQ of an aubergine because he played me like a kazoo. So it makes me puke to hear them grovelling about fucking Crake and singing his fucking praises every time his stupid name comes up.'

'But that's the story we've got,' says Toby. 'So we have to work with it. Not that I've grasped all the finer points.'

'Whatever,' says Jimmy. 'It's over to you. Just keep doing what you're doing. You can add stuff in, go to town, they'll eat it up. I hear they're fanboys for Zeb these days. Stick with that plot-line, it's got legs. Just keep them from finding out what a bogus fraud everything is.'

'That's very manipulative,' says Toby. 'Shoving it all onto me.'

'Yeah, I'm not denying it,' says Jimmy. 'I apologize. Though you're good at it, according to them. Your choice; you can always tell them to piss off.'

'You realize we're under attack, in a manner of speaking,' says Toby.

'The Painballers. Yeah. Ren told me,' he says more soberly.

'So we can't let these people go wandering off on their own too much. They'd most likely be killed.'

Jimmy thinks about that. 'So, then?'

'You need to help me,' says Toby. 'We should get our stories straight. I've been flying in the dark.'

'Nowhere else to fly on the subject of Crake,' says Jimmy gloomily. 'Welcome to my whirlwind. He cut her throat, did you know that? Good, kind Crake. She was so pretty, she was . . . Just thought I'd share that. But I shot the fucker.'

'Whose throat?' Toby asks. 'Who did you shoot?' But Jimmy's face is in his hands now, and his shoulders are shaking.

Piglet

Toby doesn't know what to do. Is a comforting maternal hug in order, supposing she's capable of giving one, or would Jimmy find that intrusive? How about a brisk, nurse-like *Chin up* or a feeble withdrawal, on tiptoe?

Before she can make up her mind, Blackbeard runs into the room. He's unusually excited. 'They're coming! They're coming!' he says. It's almost a shout, which is rare for a Craker: even the kids aren't shouters.

'Who is?' she asks. 'Is it the bad men?' Now where did she leave her rifle? That's the down side of Meditations: you forget how to be properly aggressive.

'They! Come! Come,' he says, tugging at her hand, then at her bedsheet. 'The Pig Ones. Very many!'

Jimmy lifts his head. 'Pigoons. Oh fuck,' he says.

Blackbeard is delighted. 'Yes! Thank you for calling him, Snowman-the-Jimmy! We will need him, to help us,' he says. 'The Pig Ones have a dead.'

'A dead what?' Toby asks him, but he's out the door.

*

The MaddAddamites have dropped their various tasks and are moving in behind the cobb-house fence. Some have armed themselves with axes, and rakes, and shovels.

Crozier, who must have set out to pasture with his flock of Mo'Hairs, is hurrying back along the pathway. Manatee's with him, carrying their spraygun.

'They're coming from the west,' says Crozier. The Mo'Hairs surround him.

'They're ... It's weird. They're marching. It's like a pig parade.'

The Crakers are gathering by the swing set. They don't seem in any way frightened. They talk together in low voices, then the men begin to move west, as if to meet whatever's coming down the path. Several women go with them: Marie Antoinette, Sojourner Truth, two others. The rest stay behind with the children, who clump together and stand silently, though no one has ordered them to do that.

'Make them come back!' says Jimmy, who has joined the MaddAddamite group. 'Those things will rip them open!'

'You can't *make* them do anything,' says Swift Fox, who is holding – somewhat awkwardly – a pitchfork from the garden.

'Rhino,' says Zeb, handing over another spraygun. 'Don't get trigger-happy,' he says to Manatee. 'You could hit a Craker. As long as the pigs don't charge us, don't fire.'

'This is creepy,' says Ren timorously. She's standing beside Jimmy now, holding on to his arm. 'Where's Amanda?'

'Sleeping,' says Lotis Blue, who's on the other side of Jimmy now.

'More than creepy,' says Jimmy. 'They're sly, the pigoons. They've got tactics. They almost cornered me one time.'

'Toby. We'll need your rifle,' says Zeb. 'If they split into two groups, go around to the back. They can root under the fence fast if they've got us distracted out front. Then they'll attack from both sides.'

Toby hurries to her cubicle. When she comes out carrying her old Ruger Deerfield, the herd of giant pigoons is already advancing into the clearing in front of the cobb-house fence.

There are fifty or so in all. Fifty adults, that is: several of the sows have litters of piglets, trotting along beside their mothers. In the centre of the group, two of the boars are moving side by side; there's something lying crossways on their backs. It looks like a mound of flowers – flowers and foliage.

What? thinks Toby. Is it a peace offering? A pig wedding? An altarpiece?

The largest pigs are acting as outriders; they seem nervous, pointing the moist discs of their snouts this way and that, snuffing the air. They're glossy and greyish pink, rounded and plump and streamlined, like enormous nightmare slugs; but slugs with tusks, at least on the males. A sudden charge, an upward slash with those lethal scimitars, and you'd be gutted like a fish. And soon they'll be so close to the Crakers that even a direct hit with a spraygun wouldn't stop their momentum.

A low level of grunting is going on, from pig to pig. If they were people, Toby thinks, you'd say it was the murmuring of a crowd. It must be information exchange; but God knows what sort of information. Are they saying, 'We're scared?' Or 'We hate them?' Or possibly just a simple 'Yum, yum?'

Rhino and Manatee are stationed just inside the fence. They've lowered their sprayguns. Toby has thought it best to conceal her rifle; she's carrying it at her side, a fold of her bedsheet tucked around it. No need to remind them of her boar-murdering exploits, though they probably need no reminders.

'Cripes,' says Jimmy, who's standing behind Toby. 'Would you look at that. They've got to be planning something.'

Blackbeard has left the other Craker children and has clutched himself on to Toby. 'Do not be afraid, Oh Toby,' he says. 'Are you afraid?'

'Yes, I am afraid,' she says. Though not as afraid as Jimmy, she adds to herself, because I have a gun and he doesn't. 'They have attacked our garden more than once,' she says. 'And we have killed some of them, to defend ourselves.' She thinks uneasily of the pork roasts, the bacon, and the chops that have resulted. 'And we have put them into soup,' she says. 'They have turned into a smelly bone. A lot of smelly bones.'

'Yes, a smelly bone,' says Blackbeard thoughtfully. 'A lot of smelly bones. I have seen them near the kitchen.'

'So they are not our friends,' Toby says. 'You are not the friend of those who turn you into a smelly bone.'

Blackbeard thinks about this. Then he looks up at her, smiling gently. 'Do not be afraid, Oh Toby,' he says. 'They are Children of Oryx and Children of Crake, both. They have said they will not harm you today. You will see.' Toby's far from sure about that, but she smiles down at him anyway.

The advance deputation of Crakers has joined the herd of pigoons and is walking back with them. The rest of the Crakers wait silently by the swing set as the pigoons advance.

Now Napoleon Bonaparte and six other men step forward: piss parade, it looks like. Yes, they're peeing in a line. Aiming carefully, peeing respectfully, but peeing. Having finished, they each take a step back. Three curious little piglets scamper forward, snuffle at the ground, then run squealing back to their mothers.

'There,' says Blackbeard. 'See? It is safe.'

The Crakers move into a semicircle behind their demarcation line of urine. They begin to sing. The herd of pigoons divides in two, and the pair of boars moves slowly forward. Then they roll to either side, and the flower-covered burden they've been carrying slips onto the ground. They heave to their feet again and move some of the flowers away, using their trotters and snouts.

It's a dead piglet. A tiny one, with its throat cut. Its front trotters are tied together with rope. The blood is still red, it's oozing from the gaping neck wound. There are no other marks.

Now the whole herd is deploying itself in a semicircle around the – what? The bier? The catafalque? The flowers, the leaves – it's a funeral. Toby remembers the boar she shot at the AnooYoo Spa – how, when she went to collect maggots from the carcass, there were fern fronds and leaves scattered over it. Elephants, she'd thought then. They do that. When someone they love has died.

'Crap,' says Jimmy. 'I hope it wasn't us who nuked that little porker.'

'I don't think so,' says Toby. She would have heard about it, surely. There would have been some culinary chitchat.

The two piglet-bearers have gone forward to the line of piss. Abraham Lincoln and Sojourner Truth are on the other side of it. They kneel so they're at the level of the pigoons: head facing head. The Crakers stop singing. There's silence. Then the Crakers start singing again.

'What's happening?' says Toby.

'They are talking, Oh Toby,' says Blackbeard. 'They are asking for help. They want to stop those ones. Those ones who are killing their pig babies.' He takes a deep breath. 'Two pig babies – one with a stick you point, one with a knife. The Pig Ones want those killing ones to be dead.'

'They want help from . . . ' She can't say *the Crakers*, it isn't what they call themselves. 'They want help from your people?'

If killing is the request, how can the Crakers help? she wonders. According to the MaddAddamites, Crakers are nonviolent by nature. They don't fight, they can't fight. They're incapable of it. That's how they're made.

'No, Oh Toby,' says Blackbeard. 'They want help from you.'

'Me?' says Toby.

'All of you. All those standing behind the fence, those with two skins. They want you to help them with the sticks you have. They know how you kill, by making holes. And then blood comes out. They want you to make such holes in the three bad men. With blood.' He looks a little ill: he isn't finding this easy. Toby wants to hug him, but that would be condescending: he has chosen this duty.

'Did you say three men?' Toby asks. 'Aren't there only two?'

'The Pig Ones say there are three,' says Blackbeard. 'They have smelled three.'

'That's not so good,' says Zeb. 'They've found a recruit.' He and Black Rhino exchange sombre glances.

'Changes the odds,' says Rhino.

'They want you to make blood come out,' says Blackbeard. 'Three with holes in them, and blood.'

'Us,' says Toby. 'They want us to do it.'

'Yes,' says Blackbeard. 'Those with two skins.'

'Then why aren't they talking to us?' says Toby. 'Why are they talking to you?'

Oh, she thinks. Of course. We're too stupid, we don't understand their languages. So there has to be a translator.

'It is easier for them to talk to us,' says Blackbeard simply. 'And in return, if you help them to kill the three bad men, they will never again try to eat your garden. Or any of you,' he adds seriously. 'Even if you are dead, they will not eat you. And they ask that you must no longer make holes in them, with blood, and cook them in a smelly bone soup, or hang them in the smoke, or fry them and then eat them. Not any more.'

'Tell them it's a deal,' says Zeb.

'Throw in the bees and the honey,' says Toby. 'Make those off-limits too.'

'Please, Oh Toby, what is a *deal*?' says Blackbeard.

'A deal means, we accept their offer and will help them,' says Toby. 'We share their wishes.'

'Then they will be happy,' says Blackbeard. 'They want to go hunting for the bad men tomorrow, or else the next day. You must bring your sticks, to make the holes.'

Something appears to have been concluded. The pigoons, who have been standing with ears cocked forward and snouts raised as if sniffing the words, turn away and head west, back from where they came. They've left the dead flower-strewn piglet on the ground.

'Wait,' says Toby to Blackbeard. 'They've forgotten their . . .' She almost said *their child*. 'They've forgotten the little one.'

'The small Pig One is for you, Oh Toby,' says Blackbeard. 'It is a gift. It is dead already. They have already done their sadness.'

'But we have promised not to eat them any more,' says Toby.

'Not kill and then eat, no. But they say you would not be killing it yourselves. Therefore it is permitted. They say you may eat it or not eat it, as you choose. They would eat it themselves, otherwise.'

Curious funeral rites, thinks Toby. You strew the beloved with flowers, you mourn, and then you eat the corpse. No-holds-barred recycling. Even Adam and the Gardeners never went that far.

Palaver

The Crakers have moved apart, over to the swing set, where they are chewing away at the kudzu vines and talking together in low voices. The dead piglet lies on the ground, flies settling on it, encircled by a ring of MaddAddamites, pondering over it as if holding an inquest.

'So, you think those pricks were butchering it?' says Shackleton.

'Maybe,' says Manatee. 'But it wasn't hanging from a tree. That's what you'd do normally, to drain the blood.'

'The pigs told my blue buddies it was just lying on the path,' says Crozier. 'In plain view.'

'You think it's a message to us?' says Zunzuncito.

'Sort of like a challenge,' says Shackleton. 'Like they're calling us out.'

'Maybe that's how come the rope. It was the rope on *them* last time,' says Ren.

'Nah,' says Crozier. 'Why would they use a piglet for that?'

'Maybe like *This will be you next time*. Or *Look how close we can get*. They're triple-time Painball vets, remember. That's Painball style: freak you out,' says Shackleton.

'Right,' says Rhino. 'They really want our stuff now. Must be running out of cellpack power, getting desperate.'

'They'll try to sneak in at night,' says Shackleton. 'We'll have to double up on sentries.'

'Better check the fences,' says Rhino. 'They're still pretty makeshift.'

'They may have tools,' says Zeb. 'From some hardware store. Knives, wire cutters, stuff like that.' He moves off, around the corner of the cobb house, with Rhino following.

'Maybe it's not the Painballers who killed it. Maybe it's persons unknown,' says Ivory Bill.

'Maybe it's the Crakers,' says Jimmy. 'Hey, just joking, I know they'd never do that.'

'Never say never,' says Ivory Bill. 'Their brains are more malleable than Crake intended. They've been doing several things we didn't anticipate during the construction phase.'

'Maybe it's someone in our own group,' says Swift Fox. 'Someone who wanted sausages.'

There's an uneasy, guilty laugh round the circle. Then a silence. 'So. What next?' says Ivory Bill.

'What next is, do we cook it or not?' says Rebecca. 'Suckling pig?'

'Oh, I couldn't,' says Ren. 'It would be like eating a baby.' Amanda starts to cry.

'My dear lady, what's all this about?' says Ivory Bill.

'I'm sorry,' says Ren. 'I shouldn't have said *baby*.'

'Okay, cards on the table,' says Rebecca. 'Hands up, anyone here who didn't know that Amanda's pregnant?'

'I appear to be the only one left in gynecological ignorance,' says Ivory Bill. 'Perhaps such intimate feminine material was considered unfit for my elderly ears.'

'Or maybe you weren't listening,' says Swift Fox.

'Okay, so that's clear,' says Rebecca. 'Now I would like to

open up the circle, as we used to say at the Gardeners ... Ren, you want to do this?'

Ren takes a breath. 'I'm pregnant too,' she says. She begins to sniffle. 'I peed on the stick. It turned pink, it made a smiley face ... Oh God.' Lotis Blue pats her. Crozier makes a move towards her, then stops.

'Three's company,' says Swift Fox. 'Count me in. Bun in the oven, up the spout. Farrow in the barrow.' At least she's cheerful about it, thinks Toby. But whose bun?

There's another silence. 'I don't suppose there is any point,' says Ivory Bill with heavy disapproval, 'in speculating as to the paternity of these ... these various imminent progenies.'

'None whatsoever,' says Swift Fox. 'Or not in my case. I've been doing an experiment in genetic evolution. Reproduction of the fittest. Think of me as a petri dish.'

'I find that irresponsible,' says Ivory Bill.

'I'm not sure it's any of your business,' says Swift Fox.

'Hey!' says Rebecca. 'It is what it is!'

'With Amanda, it may be a Craker,' says Toby. 'From something that happened the night she was ... the night we got her back, from ... That's the best possibility. And that may be what happened with Ren too.'

'It wasn't the Painballers, anyway,' says Ren. 'With me. I know it wasn't.'

'You know that how?' says Crozier.

'I don't want to go into the gory details,' says Ren, 'because you'd think it was oversharing. It's girl stuff. We count the days. That's how.'

'I can definitely rule out the Painballers,' says Swift Fox. 'In my case. And I can rule out a few other guys too.' None of the men look at each other. Crozier suppresses a grin.

'And the Crakers as well?' says Toby, keeping her voice neutral. Who's on her checklist? Crozier, definitely, but who else?

Have there been multitudes? Maybe Zeb was one of them, after all; if so, soon there may be an infant Zeb. Then what will she herself do? Pretend she doesn't notice? Knit babywear? Brood and sulk? The first two options would be preferable, but she's not sure she'll be up to them.

'I did have an interlude or two with the big blues,' says Swift Fox. 'When no one was looking, which didn't give me a huge window of opportunity, since everyone here is so snoopy. It was energetic, and I'm not sure I'd want to make a habit of it. Not much foreplay. But the pink smiley face doesn't lie, and I will soon be heavy with young. The question is, young what?'

'Guess we'll find out,' says Shackleton.

Zeb and Black Rhino return from their inspection of the fences. 'This place is hardly a fortress,' Zeb says. 'Thing is – if we take the weapons with us on the hunt, we leave everyone in the cobb house undefended.'

'Which may be what they want,' says Rhino. 'Lure us out the front, sneak in the back. Make off with the women.'

'We're not just packages,' says Swift Fox. 'We can fight back! You can leave us a couple of sprayguns.'

'Good luck with that plan,' says Rhino.

'We need to move our whole group out of here when we go hunting for those guys,' says Crozier. 'We can't leave anyone behind. Take the Mo'Hairs too. If we're all together, it's harder for them to ambush us.'

'But easier to stampede us,' says Zeb. 'How fast can we all run?'

'I'm not running,' says Rebecca. 'And I need to point out here that there are three pregnant women in this crowd.'

'Three?' says Zeb.

'Ren and Swift Fox,' says Rebecca.

'When did that happen?'

'They told everyone else when you were checking the fences,' says Rebecca.

'They got knocked up by elves overnight,' says Jimmy.

'Not funny, Jimmy,' says Lotis Blue.

'Point is, bad for them to run,' says Rebecca.

'So, we can't keep our end of the deal? We can't go into battle with the pig militia?' says Shackleton. 'They'll have to do it alone?'

'They can't,' says Jimmy. 'They're fucking lethal but they can't climb stairs. If the pigs chase those Painball guys into the city, they'll just move up a floor and shoot down. The pigoons will be decimated.'

'Crozier's right, we should all relocate,' says Toby. 'To a more secure place, with doors that lock.'

'Like where?' says Rebecca.

'We can go back to the AnooYoo Spa,' says Toby. 'I holed up in there for months. There's still some basic food left.' And maybe some seeds, she thinks: I can collect seeds, for the garden. And more bullets, she'd left some there.

'They've got real beds,' says Ren. 'And towels.'

'And solid doors,' says Toby.

'Could be a plan,' says Zeb. 'Vote?'

Nobody votes no.

'Now we must prepare,' says Katuro.

'First we should bury the piglet,' Toby says. 'It would be right. Under the circumstances.'

So they do.

Fallback

It takes them a day to get organized. There are many things they need to take with them: the basic supplies for cooking, a change of daywear bedsheets, duct tape, rope. Flashlights, headlamps: most of the batteries are still good. The sprayguns, of course. Toby's rifle. And any sharp-edged tools, because you wouldn't want such things as knives and picks to fall into the hands of enemies.

'Keep it light,' Zeb tells them. 'If all goes well, we'll be back here in a few days.'

'Or else this place may be burned to the ground,' says Rhino.

'So if you really need it, take it with you,' says Katuro.

Toby worries about her hive of bees. Will they be all right? What could attack them? She hasn't seen any bears, and the Pigoons have made a no-bees deal, or so she must believe. Do wolvogs like honey? No, they're carnivores. Rakunks, perhaps, but they'd be no match for an angry hive.

She covers her head and speaks to the hive, as she's been doing faithfully each morning. 'Greetings, Bees. I bring news to you and your Queen. Tomorrow I must go away for a short time, so I will not be talking with you for several days. Our own hive is threatened. We are in danger, and we must attack those that threaten us, as you would in our place. Be steadfast, gather much pollen, defend your hive if need be. Tell this message to Pilar, and ask for the help of her strong Spirit, on our behalf.'

The bees fly in and out of the hole in the Styrofoam cooler. They seem to like it here in the garden. Several of them come over to investigate her. They test her floral bedsheet, find it wanting, move to her face. Yes, they know her. They touch her lips, gather her words, fly away with the message, disappear into the dark. Pass through the membrane that separates this world from the unseen world that lies just underneath it. There is Pilar, with her calm smile, walking forward along a corridor that glows with hidden light.

Now, Toby, she tells herself. Talking pigs, communicative dead people, and the Underworld in a Styrofoam beer cooler. You're not on drugs, you're not even sick. You really have no excuse.

The Crakers watch the departure preparations with interest. The children hang around the kitchen, staring at Rebecca with their huge green eyes, keeping a distance between themselves and her flitch of bacon and her dried wolvog jerky.

The Crakers don't seem to fully understand why the MaddAddams are moving house, but they've made it clear that they themselves are coming too.

'We will help Snowman-the-Jimmy,' they say. 'We will help Zeb.' 'We will help Crozier, he is our friend, we must help him to piss better.' 'We will help Toby, she will tell us a story.' 'Crake wants us to go there,' and so forth. They themselves have no possessions, so there's nothing they need to carry; but they want to carry other things. 'I will bring this, it is a pot.' 'I will bring this, it is a wind-up radio, what is it for?' 'I will bring this sharp one, it is a knife.' 'This one is a toilet paper, I will carry it.'

'We will carry Snowman-the-Jimmy,' one trio announces, but Jimmy says he can walk.

Blackbeard marches into Toby's cubicle. 'I will bring the writing,' he says importantly. 'And the pen. I will bring those, for us to have there.'

He views Toby's journal as a joint possession of theirs, which is fine, thinks Toby, as it lets her follow his writing progress. Though sometimes it's hard to get the journal away from him so she can write in it herself, and he has to be reminded not to leave it out in the rain.

So far he's concentrated mostly on names, though he's also fond of writing THANK YOU and good night. CRAK GOODNIT GOOD BAD FLOWR ZEB TOBY ORIX THAK YOU is a typical entry. Maybe one of these days she'll gain some new insights into how his mind works, though she can't say she's had any blinding illuminations as yet.

At sunrise the next day they set out from the cobb-house compound in the Tree of Life parkette. It's an exodus, a move away from civilization, such as it is.

Two Pigoons have arrived as escorts; the rest will meet them at the AnooYoo Spa, says Blackbeard. He's got Toby's binoculars, which he's figured out how to use. Every once in a while he steps off to the side, lifts the binocs, focuses. 'Crows,' he announces. 'Vultures.' The Craker women laugh gently. 'Oh Blackbeard, but you knew that without the eye tube things,' they say. Then he laughs too.

Rhino and Katuro walk ahead with the Pigoons, followed by Crozier and the flock of Mo'Hairs. Some of them have bundles tied onto their backs, which is new for them, though they don't seem to mind. With their human hair, curly and straight, and the lumpy packages on top of it, they look like avant-garde hats with legs.

Shackleton stays in the middle of the procession, with Ren,

Amanda, and Swift Fox, who are surrounded in their turn by most of the Craker women, attracted by their pregnant state. The Crakers make cooing noises, they smile and laugh and pat and stroke. Swift Fox appears to find this annoying, but Amanda smiles.

The rest of the MaddAddamite group is behind them, and then the Craker men. Zeb brings up the rear.

Toby walks near the Craker women, rifle at the ready. It seems a long time since she came this way with Ren, searching for Amanda. Ren must be remembering those days as well: she drops behind to join Toby, slipping her arm through Toby's free left arm. 'Thank you for letting me in,' she says. 'At the AnooYoo Spa. And for the maggots. I would have died if you hadn't taken care of me. You saved my life.'

And you saved mine, thinks Toby. If Ren hadn't stumbled along, what would she have done? Waited and waited, shut up inside the AnooYoo by herself, until she went bonkers or dried up of old age.

They stick to the road that leads through the Heritage Park, heading northwest. There's Pilar's elderberry bush, covered with butterflies and bees. One of the Mo'Hairs grabs a mouthful of it on the way past.

Now they've reached the eastern gatehouse – pink, Tex–Mex retro – and the high fence that encloses the AnooYoo grounds. 'We came here,' Ren says. 'That man was inside it. The Pain-baller, the worst one.'

'Yes,' says Toby. It was Blanco, her old enemy. He'd had gangrene, but he was bent on murder despite that.

'You killed him, didn't you?' says Ren. She must have known at the time.

'Let's say I helped him enter a different plane of being,' says

Toby. That was the Gardener way of putting it. 'He would have died soon, but more painfully. Anyway, it was Urban Bloodshed Limitation.' First rule: limit bloodshed by making sure that none of your own gets spilled.

She'd dosed Blanco with Amanita and Poppy: a painless exit, and better than he deserved. Then she'd dragged him onto the ornamental planting ringed with whitewashed stones, as a gift for the wildlife. Was the dose of Amanita strong enough to poison anything that ate him? She hopes not: she wishes the vultures well.

The heavy wrought-iron gate is wide open. Toby had tied it shut when they'd left, but the rope has been chewed apart. The two Pigoons trot through first, snuffle around the walkway to the gatehouse, nose their way in. They come back out, then trot over to Blackbeard. Subdued grunting, eye-to-eye staring.

'They say the three men have been there. But they are not there now,' he says.

'Are they sure?' Toby asks. 'There was a man in there earlier. A bad man. They don't mean that one?'

'Oh no,' says Blackbeard. 'They know about that one. He was dead, on the flowers. At first they wanted to eat him, but he had bad mushrooms in him. So they did not.'

Toby checks out the ornamental flowerbed. It used to say WELCOME TO ANOOYOO in petunias; now it's a lush thicket of meadow weeds. Down among them, is that a boot? She has no desire to probe further.

She'd left Blanco's knife there, with the body. It was a good one: sharp. But the MaddAddamites have other knives. She only hopes the Painballers haven't retrieved it; but they, too, must have other knives.

*

Now they're in the AnooYoo grounds proper. They keep to the main roadway, although there's a forest path: Toby and Ren had taken it earlier, to stay in the shade. That was where they'd come upon Oates, slaughtered by the Painballers and minus his kidneys, strung up in a tree.

He must still be there, thinks Toby. They should find him, cut him down, give him a proper burial. His brothers, Shackleton and Crozier, will welcome that. A true composting, with his own tree planted on top of him. Restore him to the cool peace of rootlets, the calm dissolve of earth. But now is not the time.

Dogs barking, off in the woods. They stop to listen. 'If those things come over wagging their tails, you need to shoot them,' says Jimmy. 'Wolvogs; they're vicious.'

'Ammunition's rationed,' says Rhino. 'Until we find more.'

'They won't attack us now,' says Katuro. 'Too many people. Plus two Pigoons.'

'We must've killed most of them by now,' says Shackleton.

They pass a burnt-out jeep, then an incinerated solarcar. Then a crashed pink mini-van with the AnooYoo logo on it: kissy lips, winky eye.

'Don't look inside,' says Zeb, who has already looked. 'Not pretty.'

And now there's the Spa building up ahead, solid pink, still standing: no one has burned it down.

The main force of the Pigoons is milling around outside, probably finishing off the organic kitchen garden, one-time source of garnishes for the clients' diet salads. Toby remembers the hours she'd spent alone in that garden after the Flood, hoping to raise enough edible plant life so she could keep going. It's all churned earth by now.

At least she left the door unlocked.

Shadow, mildew. Her old self, bodiless, wandering the mirrorless halls. She'd put towels over the glass to blot out her own reflection.

'Come in,' she says to everyone. 'Make yourselves at home.'

Fortress AnooYoo

The Crakers are entranced by the AnooYoo Spa. They walk carefully along the hallways, bending to touch the smooth, polished floor. They lift the pink towels that Toby had hung over the mirrors, glimpse the people in there, look behind the mirrors; then, when they realize the people are themselves, they touch their hair and smile to make their reflections smile too. They sit on the beds in the bedrooms, gingerly, then stand up again. In the gymnasium the children bounce on the trampolines, giggling. They sniff at the pink soap in the washrooms. There is still a lot of pink soap.

'Is this the Egg?' they ask. Or the younger ones do. They have a faint memory of a similar place, with high walls and smooth floors. 'Is this the Egg where we were made?' 'No, the Egg is not the same.' 'The Egg is far. It is more far than this.' 'The Egg has Crake in it, the Egg has Oryx. They are not here.' 'Can we go to the Egg?' 'We do not want to go to the Egg now, it is dark.' 'Does the Egg have the pink things in it, like this? The flower-smelling things we can eat?' 'That is not a plant, that is a soap. We do not eat a soap,' and so on.

At least they aren't singing, thinks Toby. They haven't sung much on the way here either. They've been looking and listening. They seem to know there is danger.

Fortunately there haven't been any leaks in the roof. Toby is happy about that: it means the beds, despite being slightly musty, are still sleepable. As de facto hostess, she assigns rooms. For herself she picks a Couples room. The Spa contained three of those, in the unlikely event that a husband and wife or equivalent would check in together, to undergo joint facials and cleansings and tweaks and polishes. But this offering was not popular, or not among heterosexual couples – usually women liked to have such adjustments done in private so they could emerge like butterflies from a perfumed cocoon and astound the multitudes with their ravishing beauty. Toby used to run this place, so she knows. She knows, also, about the disappointment felt by these women, when, despite the large amounts of money they'd spent, they did not look very much better.

In the closet she stashes her belongings, such as they are. Her well-worn binoculars: she hasn't had much use for them at the cobb house because there were few vistas there, but they'll be essential now. Her rifle, and the ammunition. She left a cache of bullets here at the Spa, so she can top up her supply now. Once that's gone the rifle will be of no use, unless she can learn to make gunpowder.

She places her toothbrush in the ensuite bathroom. She needn't have bothered bringing the one from the cobb house: there are a lot of toothbrushes at the Spa, all pink; and, in the supply room, a whole shelf of AnooYoo's guest mini-toothpastes, two kinds: Cherry Blossom Organic, biodegradable with antiplaque micro-organisms; and Kiss-in-the-Dark Chromatic Sparkle Enhancer.

The second one claims to make your entire mouth glow in the dark. Toby never tried it out, but some women swore by it. She wonders how Zeb would react if he were to be confronted with a disembodied glowing mouth. Tonight will not be the night to find out, however: she'll be on sentry duty, up on the rooftop, and a light-up mouth would make an excellent target for a sniper.

Her old journals; she's gathered them up from where she'd slept on one of the massage tables, out of some nun-like sense of penitence. Here they are, written in AnooYoo appointment books, with the kissy-mouth logo and the winking eye. She'd recorded the Gardener days, the Feasts and Festivals, and the phases of the moon; and the daily happenings, if any. It had helped to keep her sane, that writing. Then, when time had begun again and real people had entered it, she'd abandoned it here. Now it's a whisper from the past.

Is that what writing amounts to? The voice your ghost would have, if it had a voice? If so, why is she teaching this practice to little Blackbeard? Surely the Crakers would be happier without it.

She slides the journals into a dresser drawer. She'd like to read them over sometime, but there's no space for that right now.

The toilets still have water in them, plus a lot of dead flies. She flushes: the collector barrels on the roof must be functional, which is a blessing. And there's a vast supply of pink toilet paper, with flower petals pressed into it. Some of the earlier AnooYoo botanical-items toilet paper experiments had not gone well, as there had been some unexpected allergies.

She needs to post a Boil Water advisory, however. Seeing water actually coming out of a tap, some people might get carried away.

*

After washing her face and putting on a clean pink top-to-toe from the Housekeeping closet, she rejoins the others. There's a heated discussion going on in the main foyer: what to do with the Mo'Hairs overnight? The broad AnooYoo lawn is now thigh-high in meadow growth, so grazing them in the daytime won't pose a problem, but they'll need to be sheltered or guarded once darkness falls: there may be liobams. Crozier is all for herding them into the gym: he's become quite attached to them, and is worried. Manatee points out that the floor is slippery and they may skid and break their legs, not to mention the sheep-shit factor. Toby suggests the kitchen garden: it has a fence, which is still largely intact – the Pigoons have entered by means of the holes they dug, but these can be quickly filled. Then a sentry on the rooftop can keep an eye on the flock and report any unusual bleating.

But where will the Crakers sleep? They don't like sleeping inside buildings. They want to sleep in the meadow, where there are a lot of leaves for them to eat as well. But with the Painballers on the loose and possibly in a hunting mood, that's out of the question.

'On the roof,' says Toby. 'There are some planters up there in case they want a snack.' So that's decided.

The afternoon thunderstorm comes and goes. Once it's over the Pigoons go for a dip in the swimming pool; the fact that it's growing algae and waterweeds and has a lively population of frogs does not deter them. They've solved the problem of how to get in and out of it by shoving a collection of poolside furniture into the shallow end: the deck chairs make a sort of ramp, which provides a foothold. The younger ones enjoy splashing and squealing; the older sows and boars take brief dips, then watch over their piglets and shoats indulgently, lounging at poolside. Toby wonders if pigs get sunburn.

Dinner is somewhat haphazard, though served in grand style on the round tables and pink tablecloths of the main dining room. A foraging posse has scoured the meadow, so there's a hefty salad of wild greens. Rebecca has found a small unopened bottle of olive oil and made a classic French dressing. Steamed purslane, parboiled burdock root, wolvog jerky, Mo'Hair milk. There was a residual jar of sugar in the kitchen, so each of them has a teaspoonful of it for dessert. Toby isn't used to sugar any more: the potent sweetness goes through her head like a blade.

'I've got some news for you,' says Rebecca when they're cleaning up. 'Your pals caught a frog for you. They asked me to cook it.'

'A frog?' says Toby.

'Yeah. They couldn't get a fish.'

'Oh crap,' says Toby. The Crakers will be asking for their nighttime story. With any luck, they've forgotten to bring the red Snowman hat.

It's mellow evening now, the sun subsiding. Crickets trill, birds flock to roost, amphibians ribbet from the swimming pool or twang like rubber bands. Toby looks for something to wrap herself in while standing sentry: the rooftop can be cool.

As she's swaddling up in a pink bedspread, little Blackbeard sidles into her room. He spots himself in the mirror, smiles, waves at himself, does a tiny dance. Once that's over, he delivers his message: 'The Pig Ones are saying that the three bad men are over there.'

'Over where?' says Toby, her heart quickening.

'Across the flowers. Behind the trees. They can smell them.'

'They shouldn't go too close,' says Toby. 'The bad men might have sprayguns. The sticks that make holes. With blood coming out.'

'The Pig Ones know that,' says Blackbeard.

Toby climbs the stairs to the rooftop, binoculars around her neck, rifle slung and ready. A number of the Crakers are already up there, waiting expectantly. Zeb is there too, leaning against the railing.

'You're very pink,' he says. 'The colour suits you. The silhouette too. Michelin Tire Man?'

'Are you being an asshole?'

'Not on purpose,' he says. 'Crows making a racket.' And they are making one. *Caw caw caw* over at the edge of the forest. Toby lifts the binoculars: nothing to be seen.

'It could be an owl,' she says.

'Could be,' says Zeb.

'The Pigoons keep saying there are three men. Not two.'

'I'd be surprised if they're wrong,' says Zeb.

'Do you think it might be Adam?' says Toby.

'Remember what you said about hope?' says Zeb. 'You said it can be bad for you. So I'm trying not to.'

There's a flicker of something light, over among the branches. Is it a face? Gone again.

'The worst thing,' says Toby, 'is the waiting.'

Blackbeard tugs at her bedspread. 'Oh Toby,' he says. 'Come! It is time for us to hear the story that you will tell to us. We have brought the red hat.'

The
Train
to
CryoJeenyus

The Story of the Two Eggs and Thinking

Thank you. I am happy that you remembered to bring the red hat.

And the fish. It is not a fish exactly, it is more like a frog. But you caught it in the water, and we are far from the ocean, so I am sure that Crake will understand, and will know that it was too far for you to go all the way to the ocean in order to catch a fish there.

Thank you for cooking it. For asking Rebecca to cook it. Crake has told me that I do not have to eat all of it. A nibble will be enough.

There.

Yes, the frog . . . the fish has a bone in it. A smelly bone. That is why I spat it out. But we do not need to talk about the smelly bone right now.

Tomorrow is a very important day. Tomorrow, all of us with two skins must finish the work that Crake began – the work of clearing away the chaos. That work was the Great Rearrangement, and it made the Great Emptiness.

But that was only part of the work of Crake. The other part was when he made you. He made your bones out of the coral on the beach, which is white like bones but not smelly. And he made your flesh out of a mango, which is sweet and soft. He did all this inside the giant Egg, and he had some helpers there. And Snowman-the-Jimmy was his friend – he was inside the Egg as well.

And Oryx was there too. Sometimes she was in the form of a woman with green eyes like yours, and sometimes she was in the form of an owl. And she laid two smaller owl eggs, inside the giant Egg. One smaller owl egg was full of animals and birds and fish – all her Children. Yes, and bees. And butterflies too. And ants, yes. And beetles – very many beetles. And snakes. And frogs. And maggots. And rakunks, and bobkittens, and Mo'Hairs, and Pigoons.

Thank you, but I don't think we need to list every one of them.

Because we would be here all night.

Let us just say that Oryx made very many Children. And each one was beautiful in its own special way.

Yes, it was kind of her to make each and every one of them, inside the smaller owl egg that she laid. Except maybe the mosquitoes.

The other egg she laid was full of words. But that egg hatched first, before the one with the animals in it, and you ate up many of the words, because you were hungry; which is why you have words inside you. And Crake thought that you had eaten all the words, so there were none left over for the animals, and that was why they could not speak. But he was wrong about that. Crake was not always right about everything.

Because when he was not looking, some of the words fell out of the egg onto the ground, and some fell into the water, and some blew away in the air. And none of the people saw them.

But the animals and the birds and the fish did see them, and ate them up. They were a different kind of word, so it was sometimes hard for people to understand the animals. They had chewed the words up too small.

And the Pigoons – the Pig Ones – ate up more of the words than any of the other animals did. You know how they love to eat. So the Pig Ones can think very well.

Then Oryx made a new kind of thing, called singing. And she gave it to you because she loved birds and she wanted you to be able to sing that way as well. But Crake did not want you to do the singing. It worried him. He thought that if you could sing like birds you would forget to talk like people, and then you would not remember him or understand his work – all the work that he had done to make you.

And Oryx said, You will just have to suck it up. Because if these people cannot sing, they will be like ... they will be like nothing. They will be like stones.

Suck it up means ... we will talk about that some other time.

Now I will tell a different part of the story, which is about why Crake decided to make the Great Emptiness.

For a long time, Crake thought. He thought and thought. He told no one about all his thoughts, though he told some of them to Snowman-the-Jimmy and some of them to Zeb and some of them to Pilar and some of them to Oryx.

This is what he thought:

The people in the chaos cannot learn. They cannot understand what they are doing to the sea and the sky and the plants and the animals. They cannot understand that they are killing them, and that they will end by killing themselves. And there are so many of them, and each one of them is doing part of the killing, whether they know it or not. And when you tell them to stop, they don't hear you.

So there is only one thing left to do. Either most of them must be cleared away while there is still an earth, with trees and flowers and birds and fish and so on, or all must die when there are none of those things left. Because if there are none of those things left, then there will be nothing at all. Not even any people.

But shouldn't you give those ones a second chance? he asked himself. No, he answered, because they have had a second chance. They have had many second chances. Now is the time.

So Crake made some little seeds that tasted very good; and they made people very happy at first, when they ate them. But then those who ate the seeds would become very sick, and would come to pieces, and would die. And he sprinkled the seeds over all the earth.

And Oryx helped to sprinkle the seeds, because she could fly like an owl. And the Bird Women and the Snake Women and the Flower Women helped too. Though they did not understand about the dying part, only the happy part, because Crake had not told them all of his thoughts.

And then the Great Rearrangement began to happen. And Oryx and Crake left the Egg and flew up into the sky. But Snowman-the-Jimmy stayed behind, to watch over you and to keep bad things away from you, and to help you, and to tell you the stories of Crake. And the stories of Oryx as well.

You can do the singing later.

That is the story of the two eggs.

Now we must all go to sleep, because we must get up very early tomorrow. Some of us will go looking for the three bad men. Zeb will go, and Rhino, and Manatee, and Crozier, and Shackleton. And Snowman-the-Jimmy. Yes, the Pig Ones will go too, many of them. Not the little ones, or their mothers.

But you will stay here, with Rebecca, and Amanda, and Ren. And Swift Fox. And Lotis Blue. And you must keep the door shut, and not let anyone in, no matter what they say. Unless it is ones you already know.

Don't be frightened.

Yes, I will go out looking for the bad men too. And Blackbeard will go, to help us talk with the Pig Ones.

Yes, we will come back. I hope we will come back.

Hope is when you want something very much but you do not know if that thing you want will really happen.

Now I will say good night.

Good night.

Shades

'This is where I waited for you,' says Toby. 'During the Waterless Flood. Up here on the rooftop. I kept expecting you'd stroll out of those woods at any moment.'

The Crakers are all around them, sleeping peacefully. How trusting they are, thinks Toby. They've never learned real fear. Maybe they can't learn it.

'So you didn't think I was dead?' says Zeb.

'I was counting on you,' says Toby. 'I thought, if anyone knew how to stay alive through all of that, it would be you. Some days I did tell myself you were dead, though. I called that "realism." But the rest of the time I was waiting.'

'Worth it?' says Zeb. Invisible grin in the darkness.

'You're having a failure of confidence? You need to ask?'

'Yeah, I kind of do,' says Zeb. 'Used to think I was God's gift, but that gets rubbed off a guy. From the first time I knew you, back at the Gardeners, I could see you were smarter than me, what with the mushrooms and the potions and all of that.'

'But you were craftier,' says Toby.

'Granted. Though I outcraftied myself sometimes. Now where was I?'

'You were living with the Snake Women,' says Toby. 'At Scales and Tails. Keeping yourself to yourself, your eyes open, your hands in your pockets, and your lip zipped.'

'Right.'

They made Zeb a bouncer. It was a fine disguise. He got the shaved head, the black suit, the shades, and the gold tooth that broadcast right into his mouth. Also the tasteful enamelled lapel pin in the shape of a snake eating its own tail: an ancient motif that meant regeneration, said Adam, though you could have fooled Zeb.

He rearranged his face parsley in the deep-pleeb bouncer fuzzdo of the day, which involved a very narrow shaver used to carve a crisscross design into a light layer of stubble, with an effect like a hairy waffle. It was at that time, too, that he got his ears recontoured, at the suggestion of Adam. They were using ears more in identities, said Adam, and it would be as well if Zeb were to rearrange his own so they couldn't be matched with some ear photo of yore, supposing anyone was looking. The actual plasti-cosmi job was courtesy of Katrina WooWoo, who had access to some Grade A flesh-and-fat sculptors. Zeb opted for a more pointy look at the top of the ear and a droopier blob of lobe.

'Don't look now,' he says. 'I got them done a couple of times after that. But for a while there I was sort of a pixie Buddha.'

'It's how I think of you,' says Toby.

Zeb's job was to stand around the bar area, not smiling broadly but not actively threatening: just more or less looming. His partner was a large black guy called – at that moment – Jebediah, though when he joined MaddAddam he became Black Rhino. Zeb and Jeb was how Zeb linked the two of them in his head.

Though he was not Zeb to those at Scales, nor was he Hector the Vector. He had yet another name, which was Smokey. Smokey the Bear, like the old mascot for the so-called Forest Service. It was a fitting name. 'Only YOU can prevent wildfires,' had been the slogan, and that was what he was supposed to do: prevent wildfires.

When there were signs of petulance among the clientele – glowering and scowling, verbal unpleasantness, unseemly grabbing and ripping of the feathery or scaly or petal-shaped fabrics decorating the floorshow, or the chimp-display shaking of beer cans that signalled an exchange of foam-streams followed by can-tossing, bottle-smashing, and punches – Zeb and Jeb would step in. They'd switch their passive looming to active surgical intervention, the goal being to take the aggressors out smoothly and cleanly without triggering an all-in brawl. So prompt action was a must, though of course you didn't want to piss off the clients unnecessarily: a clobbered client was not often a repeat client.

Also – increasingly – a lot of the customers were from the top layers of the Corps layer cake, and those guys liked to go slumming in the pleebs, though not in any life-endangering ways. Just enough so you could feel a little rebellious, a little cool, a little sexually functional. Scales and Tails was gaining a reputation as a sanitary and discreet place in which to get shit-faced and indiscreet, and you could take a prospective business partner there as a complicated form of bribery without fear of exposure.

Thus the light touch was essential when it came to conflict resolution. The best way was to drape a companionable arm around the shoulders of the dickhead in question and to growl warmly into the ear: 'House Special, just for you, sir. Compliments of the management.' Overjoyed to be getting something for free and doubtless already suffering from nano-brain-death due to what he'd already guzzled, the guy would be shepherded down a few hallways and around a few corners with his tongue hanging out a yard. He'd be ushered into a large room with feather decorations and a green satin bedspread, and invisible video surveillance. There he would be lovingly undressed by a couple of the Snake Women, those with the knack of making an actuarial report sound like hot porn, while Zeb or Jeb loomed in the middle distance just out of sight, to keep the guy civil.

Then in would come a lurid mixture in a cocktail glass that might be orange or purple or blue depending on what had been ordered, topped with a green cherry that had a green plastic snake stuck into it. This would be hand-delivered by an orchid or a gardenia or a flamingo or a fluorescent blue skink on stilts, shimmering all over with sequins and tiny LED lights and scales or petals or feathers, with huge tits and a lip-licking smile. *Itchy-kitchy-coo*, this hallucination would say, or words to that effect. *Drinkie-poo!* What red-blooded hominid could say no? Down the hatch would go the mystery liquid, followed quickly by sweet dreams for Mr. Self-Styled Alpha Male, with minimal wear and tear on the hired help.

The chosen one would awaken ten hours later, convinced that he'd just had the time of his life. Which he would have done, said Zeb, because all experience registered by the brain is real, no? Even if it didn't happen in 3-D so-called real time.

This act usually worked fine with Corp exec types, a naive and trusting bunch when it came to the duplicitous mores of the pleeblands. Zeb knew their kind from the Floating World: out for thrills during their night on the town, eager for something they mistook for experience. They led sheltered lives inside their Corp Compounds and the other guarded spaces where they hung out, such as courthouses, statehouses, and religious institutions, and they were gullible about anything outside their walls. It was touching how easily they drank the Kool-Aid on offer, how rapidly they hit the hay or, in fact, the green satin bedspread, how softly they slept, and how cheerily they awoke.

But a different sort of client was establishing a presence at Scales: a less agreeable type, not easily deflected from his own angers. Hate-fuelled, hardened in the fire, bent on carnage and broken glassware. These were rockier cases, and called for an all-points alert.

'I speak of the Painballers, as you must've guessed,' says Zeb. 'Painball had just begun back then.'

Painball Arenas were at that time highly illegal, like cock-fighting and the slaughter and eating of endangered species. But, like them, Painball existed and was expanding, hidden from public view. Spectator positions were reserved for the upper echelons, who liked to watch duels to the death involving skill, cunning, ruthlessness, and cannibalism: it was Corp life in graphic terms. A lot of money was already changing hands at Painball in the form of highroller betting. So the Corps paid indirectly for the infrastructure and the upkeep of the Painball players, and those providing the locations and the services paid directly if caught, and sometimes with their lives when there were turf wars.

This arrangement suited the CorpSeCorps – in its adolescence then – as it provided ample blackmail material through which the CorpSeCorps men could tighten their hold on those considered to be the pillars of what still passed for society.

If you were already locked up in an ordinary prison, you could elect the Painball option: fight your fellow prisoners, eliminate them, and win big prizes, such as getting out of jail free and landing a stint as a pleebland grey-market enforcer.

Perks all round. Of course, once you'd elected to enter Painball, the alternative to winning was death. That was why it was so much fun to watch. Those who survived it did so through guile, the ability to wrongfoot their opponents, and superior murderousness: the eating of gouged-out eyes was a favourite party trick. In a word, you had to be prepared to knife and fillet your best friend.

Once they'd graduated from a stint in Painball, the Painball vets had very high status in the deeper pleebs and also on the higher heights, as Roman gladiators must once have had. Corps wives would pay to have sex with them, Corps husbands would invite them to dinner for the thrill of astounding their friends and watching them smash up the champagne flutes, though security enforcers would always be present in case things looked like they were getting seriously out of hand. A little rampaging was acceptable on these occasions, but uncontrolled mayhem was not.

Fuelled by their greyworld celebrity position, the Painball vets were pumped full of I-won hormones and thought they could tackle anyone, and they welcomed the chance to take a poke at a large, solid-looking bouncer such as Zeb the Smokey Bear. He was warned by Jeb never to turn his back on a Painballer: they'd whack you in the kidneys, blam you on the skull with anything handy, squeeze your neck till your eyes popped out of your ears.

How to recognize them? The facial scars. The blank expressions: some of their human mirror neurons had gone missing, along with big chunks of the empathy module: show a normal person a child in pain and they'd wince, whereas these guys would smirk. According to Jeb you had to get quick at reading the signs because if you were dealing with a psycho you needed to know it. Otherwise they could mangle the female talent before you could say *snapped neck*, and this could be costly: trapeze dancers who could do an artistic strip while hanging from one foot high above the crowd didn't come cheap. Or, for that matter, an orgasm-enhancing near-strangulation with a python. A Painball vet might well feel that biting off a python's head would be an unbeatable slice of alpha chimp display, and even if the bite were to be intercepted, a damaged python would be hard to replace.

Scales kept a regularly updated register of Painballer identities, complete with face pics and ear profiles, which Katrina WooWoo obtained through some obscure back door using God-knows-what as trading cards. She must've been acquainted with someone on the running end of Painball – someone who wanted something she could supply, or else could withhold. Favours and anti-favours were the most respected currency of the deeper pleeblands.

'Hit first and hit dirty, was our rule for those Painball assholes,' says Zeb. 'As soon as they started to get twitchy. Sometimes we'd spike their drinks, but sometimes we took them out permanently, because if we didn't they'd be back for revenge. We had to be careful what we did with the bodies, though. They might have affiliates.'

'What *did* you do with the bodies?' says Toby.

'Let's just say there was always a demand in the deeper pleebs for condensed protein packages, to be utilized for fun, profit, or pet food. But back then, in the early days, before the CorpSeCorps decided to make Painball legal and run it on TV, there weren't very many out-of-control Painballers, so body disposal wasn't a regular thing. More like an improvisation.'

'You make it sound like a leisure-time amusement,' says Toby. 'These were human lives, whatever they'd done.'

'Yeah, yeah, I know, slap my wrist, we were bad. Though you didn't get into Painball unless you were already a multiple killer.

'Point of this whole recital being that it wasn't unknown for us bar guards – me and Jeb – to take a personal interest in what went into the mixed drinks. Sometimes we even mixed them.'

Kicktail

All this time the white chess bishop with the six mystery pills in it had been kept safely hidden pending further instructions. The only people who knew where it was were Zeb himself, Katrina WooWoo, and Adam.

The hiding place was cunning, and right in plain view, a ploy Zeb had learned from old Slaight of Hand: the obvious is invisible. On a glass shelf behind the bar there was an array of novelty corkscrews, nutcrackers, and salt-and-peppers in the shapes of naked women. The arrangement of their parts was ingenious: the legs would open, the corkscrew would be revealed; the legs would open, the nut would be inserted, the legs would close, the nut would be cracked; the legs would open, the head would be screwed around, the salt or pepper would descend. Laughter all round.

The white bishop had been inserted into the salt cavity of one of these iron maidens, a green lady with enamelled scales. Her head still turned, salt still came out from between her thighs, but the bartenders had been told that this one was fragile – no man was too keen to have his salty sex toy's head come off in mid-screw – so they should use the others instead, on the occasions when salt was required. Which were not frequent, though some liked to sprinkle salt in their beer and on their bar snacks.

Zeb kept an eye on the scaly green girl with the inner bishop. He felt he owed it to Pilar. Still, he was jumpy about the chosen location. What if someone got hold of the thing when he wasn't there, fooled around with it, and found the pills? What if they thought the colourful little oblongs were brain candy, and took one or two just to try them? Since Zeb had no idea what the pills might actually do to a person, that possibility made him nervous.

Adam, on the other hand, was remarkably cool about it, taking the view that no one would think to look inside a salt shaker unless it ran out of salt. 'Though I don't know why I'm saying "remarkably,"' says Zeb. 'He was always a cool little bugger.'

'He was living there too?' asks Toby. 'At Scales and Tails?' She can't picture it. What would Adam One have done there all day, among the exotic dancers and their unusual fashion items? When she'd known him – once he'd been Adam One – he'd been quietly disapproving of female vanity, and of colour and ostentation and cleavage and leg in a woman's outfit. But there was no way he could have implemented the Gardener religion at Scales or convinced its workers to follow the simple life. Those women must have had expensive manicures. They wouldn't have put up with being required to dig and delve and relocate slugs and snails, even if there had been any vegetable-plot space available at Scales: ladies of the night do not weed by day.

'Nope, he wasn't living at Scales,' says Zeb. 'Or not living as such. He came and went. It was like a safe house for him.'

'You have any idea what he was doing when he wasn't there?' asks Toby.

'Learning things,' said Zeb. 'Tracking ongoing stories.

Watching for storm clouds. Gathering the disaffected under his wing. Making converts. He'd already had his big insight, or whatever you want to call it – the part where God lightning-bolted a message into the top of his skull. *Save my beloved Species in whom I am well pleased*, and all of that: you know the palaver. I never got one of those messages, personally, but it seems Adam did.

'By that time he was well on the way to assembling the God's Gardeners. He'd even bought the flat-roofed pleeb-slum building for the Edencliff Garden using some of the ill-gotten gains we'd hacked out of the Rev's account. Pilar was sending him secret recruits from inside HelthWyzer; she was already planning to join him at Edencliff. However, I didn't know any of that yet.'

'Pilar?' asks Toby. 'But she can't have been Eve One! She was way too old!' Toby has always wondered about Eve One: Adam had been Adam One, but there had never been any mention of an Eve.

'Nope, it wasn't her,' Zeb says.

One of the ongoing stories Adam was tracking was that of their mutual father, the Rev. After a pleasing flurry of activity sur-rounding his embezzlements from the Church of PetrOleum and the tragic discovery that the Rev's first wife, Fenella, was buried in the rock garden, and then the scandalous publication of the tell-all memoir by his second wife, Trudy, the whole affair had fizzled out.

There was a trial, yes, but the evidence had been inconclu-sive, or so the jury had decided. Trudy had taken the proceeds from her memoir and gone on vacation to a Caribbean island with – some said – a Tex-Mex lawn-maintenance expert, and had been found washing about in the surf after an impetuous naked moonlight swim. Such dangerous things, undertows, said the local police. She must have been dragged down, and hit her head on a rock. Her companion, whoever he was, had vanished. Understandable, since he might have been blamed; though a whisper was going around that he might also have been paid.

So Trudy was not able to give evidence at the trial, and, without that, what could be proven about anything? The skeleton of Fenella had lain so long in the ground: anyone at all might have put it there. Anonymous men, immigrants as a rule, were always walking around with shovels in the more affluent areas of cities, ready to bang trusting, innocent, horticulturally minded ladies on the head, stuff gardening gloves into their mouths, ravish them in the potting shed despite their muffled screams, and plant hens and chicks on top of them, not to mention lamb's ears and snow-in-summer and other drought-resistant succulents. It was a well-known hazard for female homeowners who took an interest in landscaping.

As for his sizable embezzlements, which were beyond a doubt, the Rev had gone the tried and true route: a public confession of temptation, followed by an account of his sinfulness in failing to resist it, then by a further account of the discovery of that sinfulness, which had been a bitter herb, but through his humiliation had saved him from himself. This was topped up with a grovelling, tearful request for forgiveness from both God and man, in particular from the members of the Church of PetrOleum. Bingo, he was absolved, washed clean of stains, and ready for a new start. For who could find it in his heart to withhold forgiveness from a fellow human being who was so obviously contrite?

'He's on the loose,' said Adam. 'Exonerated, reinstated. His OilCorps associates got him off.'

'Fucker,' said Zeb. 'Make that plural.'

'He'll be wanting to hunt us down, and now he'll be able to

access the cash to do it,' said Adam. 'His OilCorps friends will supply it. So be alert.'

'Right,' said Zeb. 'The world needs more lerts.' It was an old joke of his. It used to make Adam laugh, or rather smile, but he didn't smile that time.

One evening, when Zeb was loitering around the Scales bar in his Smokey the Bear shades and black suit and snake lapel pin, wearing his non-smile, non-frown, and listening to the chatter from the faux-gold tooth in his mouth, he heard something from one of the guys at the front door that made him stand up a little straighter.

It wasn't a Painballer warning this time. On the contrary.

'Top of the pyramid, four of them, coming in,' said the voice. 'Three OilCorps, one Church of PetrOleum. That preacher who was on the news.'

Zeb felt the adrenalin shooting through his veins. It had to be the Rev. Would the twisted, kiddie-bashing, wife-murdering sadist recognize him or not? He checked the location of every potential missile within reach, in case there might be a need for one. If there was a cry of 'Seize that man' or any similar melo-drama, he'd hurl a few cut-glass decanters and run like shit. His muscles were so taut they were twanging.

Here they came now, in a festive mood, judging from the japes and laughter and the modified backslaps – more like ten-tative pats – that were the main phrases of the quasi-brotherly body language permitted at the top levels of the Corps. They were on their way to champagne and tidbits, and everything that went with them. Tips would be lavish, supposing they could all get it up. Why be rich if you can't flaunt it by bestowing patron-izing sums of dosh on those who aid you in your quest for self-aggrandizement?

The cool thing for high-status Corps dudes was to pass by the paid security drudges at Scales as if they didn't exist – why make eye contact with a hedge? – which, says Zeb, has probably been the style ever since you could say *Roman emperor*. And that was lucky for Zeb, because the Rev didn't even toss him a glance. Not that he would have spotted Zeb beneath his hairy face waffle and dark shades, with the shaved head, the pointy ears, and all, had he bothered to look. But he didn't bother. Zeb looked at him, though, and the more he looked, the less he liked the view.

The mirror balls were going round and round, sprinkling the clientele and the talent with a dandruff of light. The music was playing, a canned retro tango. Five Scalies in sequins were contorting themselves on the trapezes, tits pointing floorward, bodies curved into a C-shape, one leg on either side of their heads. Their smiles glowed in the blacklight. Zeb backed up to the glass bar shelving, palmed the green lady with the bishop up her snatch, and slid her into his sleeve. 'Taking a leak,' he said to his partner, Jeb. 'Cover for me.'

Once in the can, he unscrewed the bishop and abstracted three of the magic beans: a white, a red, and a black. He licked the salt from his fingers and tucked the pills into a front jacket pocket, then returned to his post and eased the scaly lady back into position on the shelf with not even a clink. No one would notice she'd been gone.

The Rev's foursome was having a high old time. It was a celebration, Zeb figured: most likely in aid of the Rev's return to what they all considered to be his normal life. Slithery lovelies were plying them with drinks, while above them the trapeze dancers did boneless twists and spineless twines. They showed bits of this and that, but never the royal flush: Scales was tonier than that, you had to pay extra if you wanted the full peepshow. Manners demanded a display of appreciative lust: the acrobatic sin charade wasn't really the Rev's thing because nobody was suffering, but he was doing a convincing job of pretending. His smile had that Botox look, as if it was a product of nerve damage.

Katrina WooWoo came over to the bar. Tonight she was dressed as an orchid, in a luscious peach colour with lavender accents. March, her python, was draped around her neck, and also over one bare shoulder.

'They've ordered the House Special for their pal,' she said to the bartender. 'With the Taste of Eden.'

'Heavy on the tequila?' said the barkeep.

'Everything in,' said Katrina. 'I'll tell the girls.'

The House Special involved a private feather room with a green satin bedspread and three reptilian Scalies billed as catering to your every whim, and the Taste of Eden was a headbender kicktail guaranteed to deliver maximum bliss. Once that thing had been swallowed the client would be off in a world of wonders all his own. Zeb had tried some of the stuff on offer at Scales, but he'd never drunk the Taste of Eden kicktail. He was afraid of the visions he might have.

There it was now, standing on the counter. It was dark orange and fizzing slightly, and had a swizzle stick with a plastic snake curled around it, skewering a maraschino cherry. The snake was green and sparkly, with big eyes and a smiling lipstick mouth.

Zeb should have resisted his evil impulses. What he did was reckless, he admits that freely. But you only live once, he told himself, and maybe the Rev had used up his once. Zeb wondered which of the three pills to slip into the drink – the white, the red, or the black. But why be stingy? he admonished himself. Why not all?

'Down the hatch, good buddy.' 'Have a wild trip!' 'Up and at 'em!' 'Knock 'em dead!' Were such archaic chunks of joshery still uttered on occasions like this? It appeared so. The Rev was patted and treated to a bouquet of softly knowing haw-haws, then led away for his treat by three lithe snakelets. All four of them were giggling: eerie to remember that, in retrospect.

Zeb longed to excuse himself from bar duty and slide into the video viewing cubicle where a couple of Scales security personnel monitored the private feather rooms for trouble. He didn't know how those pills would act. Did they make you very sick, and if so, how? Maybe the effect was long-term: maybe those babies didn't kick in for a day, a week, a month. But if it was anything more rapid, he sure as hell wanted to watch.

Doing so, however, would finger him as the perpetrator. So he waited stoically though tensely, ears pricked, humming silently to himself to the tune of 'Yankee Doodle':

My dad loved walloping little kids,
He loved it more than nooky,
I hope he bleeds from every pore,
And chucks up all his cookies.

After a few too many repetitions of that, there was some tooth static: someone else was talking to the gatekeeper guys at the front. After what seemed like a long time but wasn't, Katrina WooWoo came through the doorway that led to the private rooms. She was trying to appear casual, but the clicking of her high heels was urgent.

'I need you to come backstage,' she whispered to him.

'I'm on bar duty,' he said, feigning reluctance.

'I'll call in Mordis from the front. He'll take over. Come right now!'

'Girls okay?' He was stalling: if something bad was happening to the Rev, he wanted it to keep on happening.

'Yes. But they're frightened. It's an emergency!'

'Guy go berserk?' he said. They sometimes did: the effects of the Taste of Eden weren't always predictable.

'Worse than that,' she said. 'Bring Jeb too.'

Raspberry Mousse

The feather room was a cyclone site: a sock here, a shoe there, smears of unidentified substances, bedraggled feathers everywhere. That lump in the corner must've been the Rev, covered by the green satin bedspread. Oozing out from under it was a hand-span of red foam that looked like a badly diseased tongue.

'What happened?' Zeb asked innocently. It was hard to look really innocent with shades on – he'd tried in the mirror – so he took them off.

'I've sent the girls to take showers,' said Katrina WooWoo. 'They were so upset! One minute they were ...'

'Peeling the shrimp,' said Zeb. It was the staff slang for getting a dink out of his clothes, the underpants in particular. There was an art to it, as to everything, said the Scalies. Or a craft. A slow unbuttoning, a long, sensuous unzipping. Hold the moment. Pretend he's a box of candies, lick-a-licious. 'Lick-a-licious,' Zeb said out loud. He's shaken: the effect on the Rev had been far worse than he'd imagined. He hadn't intended actual death.

'Yes, well, good thing they didn't get that far, because he, well, he simply dissolved, according to the monitors in the video room. They've never seen anything like it. Raspberry mousse, is what they said.'

'Crap,' said Jeb, who'd lifted a corner of the bedspread. 'We need a water-vac, it's like a very sick swimming pool under there. What hit him?'

'The girls say he just started to froth,' said Katrina. 'And scream, of course. At first. And tear out feathers – those are ruined, they'll have to be destroyed, what a waste. Then it was no longer screaming, it was gurgling. I'm so worried!' She was understating: scared was more like it.

'He had a meltdown. Must be something he ate,' said Zeb. He meant it for a joke; or he meant it to be mistaken for a joke.

Katrina didn't laugh. 'Oh, I don't think so,' she said. 'Though you're right, it might have been in food. Nothing he ate here though, no way! It has to be a new microbe. Looks like a flesh-eater, only so speeded up! What if it's really contagious?'

'Where could he have caught it?' said Jeb. 'Our girls are clean.'

'Off a doorknob?' said Zeb. Another lame joke. Shut up, pin-head, he told himself.

'Lucky our girls had their Biofilm Bodygloves on,' said Katrina. 'Those will have to be burned. But none of the – none of what came out of – none of whatever it is touched them.'

Zeb was getting an incoming call on his tooth: it was Adam. Since when does he have tooth broadcasting privileges? thought Zeb.

'I understand there's been an incident,' said Adam. He was tinny and far away.

'It's fucking creepy having your voice in my head,' said Zeb. 'You sound like a Martian.'

'No doubt,' said Adam. 'But that is not your number-one problem right now. The man who died was our mutual parent, I'm told.'

'You were told right,' said Zeb, 'but who told you?'

He'd gone into a corner of the room so the conversation would be semi-private, out of consideration for others: it was annoying to have to listen to a person talking to their own tooth. Katrina was in another corner with her intramural cell, calling in the Scales cleanup squad, who were bound to be taken aback. Similar things had been known to occur with older guys during the course of House Specials – the kicktails could be overly powerful for those of diminished bodily abilities and functions – but nothing very similar. Usually it was a stroke or a heart attack. This kind of frothing was unprecedented.

'Katrina called me. Naturally,' said Adam. 'She keeps me informed.'

'She knows he's our . . . ?'

'Not exactly. She knows I have an interest in anything concerning the Corps bookings – especially the OilCorps – so she notified me of the four-party reservation, and of the special surprise arrangements made by three of the clients as a gift to the fourth. Then she sent me the headshots generated automatically by the doorware at the front, and of course I recognized him at once. I was already on the premises, so I came to the front of the house in case I might be needed. I'm out in the bar area now; I'm right beside the glass shelves, where the novelty corkscrews and the salt shakers are displayed.'

'Oh,' said Zeb. 'Good,' he added lamely.

'Which one did you use?'

'Which one of what?' said Zeb.

'Don't play innocent,' said Adam. 'I can count. Six minus three is three. The white, the red, or the black?'

'All of them,' said Zeb. There was a pause.

'Too bad,' said Adam. 'That will make it more difficult for us to determine what exactly was in each one. A more controlled approach would have been preferable.'

'Aren't you going to tell me I'm a fucking stupid fuckwit,' said Zeb, 'for doing such a stupid fucking dickwit thing? Though not in so many words, I guess.'

'It was a little spontaneous of you,' said Adam, 'but worse things could have happened. In the event, it was fortuitous that he didn't recognize you.'

'Wait a minute,' said Zeb. 'You knew he was walking in the door? You didn't warn me?'

'I counted on you to act as the situation would dictate,' said Adam. 'Nor was my confidence misplaced.'

Zeb was outraged: his cunning bastard of a big brother had set him up, the shit! But he'd also trusted Zeb to be competent enough to deal with whatever mayhem might result, so in addition to the outrage he felt all warm and vindicated. *Thank you* didn't really fit the case, so instead he said, 'You fucking smartass!'

'Regrettable,' said Adam. 'And I do regret it. But may I point out that, as a result, that man is permanently off our case. Now, and this is important: get them to collect as much of him – of it – as they can. Put it in a CryoJeenyus Frasket – Katrina always keeps a few on hand for clients with CryoJeenyus contracts. The full-body model would be preferable to the head-only. Many Scales customers who are no longer young have made such arrangements. The protocol is that if they have a – what CryoJeenyus calls "a life-suspending event" – and when speaking of those who have had their lives suspended, please do avoid the word *death*, as CryoJeenyus employees do, since you will shortly be impersonating one of them. If such a life-suspending event occurs, the client is flash-frozen immediately in the Frasket and shipped to CryoJeenyus for re-animation later, once CryoJeenyus has developed the biotech to do that.'

'Which is when pigs can fly,' says Zeb. 'I hope Katrina's got a giant ice-cube tray.'

'Use buckets if necessary,' said Adam. 'We need to get him – we need to get the effluent to Pilar's cryptic team, out on the east coast.'

'Pilar's what?'

'Cryptic team. Our friends,' says Adam. 'They have day jobs in the biotech Corps: OrganInc, HelthWyzer Central, RejoovenEsense, even CryoJeenyus. But they're helping us at night, *cryptic* being a bioterm for camouflage in, say, caterpillars.'

'Since when are you so palsy with caterpillars?' said Zeb. 'Are you warping your brain lurking in that dumb MaddAddam Extinctathon name-the-dead-beetle game site?' Adam overrode him.

'The cryptic team will find out what it was, inside the pills. Or is. Let's hope it can't go airborne; we don't think it can yet, or anyone who was in that room will have been contaminated. It appears to be very rapid-acting, so they'd be showing symptoms. As things stand, we believe it's contact-only. Don't let any of the – of the residue touch you.'

And don't stick my finger in the goo and then shove it up my ass, Zeb thought. 'I'm not a fucking idiot,' he said out loud.

'Live up to that pledge. I know you can,' said Adam. 'I'll see you on the sealed bullet train, with the Frasket.'

'We're going where?' said Zeb. 'You're coming too?' But Adam had rung off, or hung up, or logged out; whatever you did on the other end of a tooth.

While the plastic-film-dressed and face-masked cleanup team was water-vaccing the Rev into enamelled pails and then funnelling him into sealable freezer-friendly metal flasks, Zeb headed off to become a tidier and sweeter version of Smokey the Bear. He disposed of his black outfit, doomed to incineration, and took a quick antimicrobial-enhanced shower – same product the Scalies used – lathering his face, sanctifying his pits, and Q-tipping his pointy ears.

I'm gonna wash that Rev right offa my head,
'Cause he's not only dead, he's red,
He's a red red goo, and a good thing too,
'Cause Daddy I'm through and so are you,
A boobity-doop-de-doop-de-doop-de-doo!

He did a little two-step, a little hip-wiggle. He liked to sing in the shower, especially when danger threatened.

One more river, he sang while putting on a fresh black suit. *And that's the river of boredom! One more molar, There's one more molar to floss.*

Then he resumed his duties, standing sentinel behind Katrina WooWoo – now dressed as a fruit cluster with a fetching set of tooth marks embroidered on one apple-shaped boob – while she and March the python broke the lamentable news to the three OilCorps execs, having first ordered frozen daiquiris on the house, all around, and a platter of mini-fish-fingers, PeaPod Good-as-Real Scallops – No Bottoms Dragged for These, said the label, as Zeb knew from mooching them in the kitchen – some Gourmet's Holiday Poutine, and a plate of deep-fried NeverNetted Shrimps, a new lab-grown splice.

'Your friend has unfortunately had a life-suspending event,' she told the OilCorps execs. 'Total bliss can be taxing on the system. But as you know, he had – excuse me, he *has* a contract with CryoJeenyus – full-body, not head-only – so all is well. I'm so sorry for your temporary loss.'

'I didn't know that,' said one of the execs. 'About the

contract. I thought you wore a CryoJeenyus bracelet or something; I never saw his.'

'Some gentlemen prefer not to advertise the possibility of life suspension,' said Katrina smoothly. 'They choose the tattoo option, which is applied in a concealed and very private location. Of course, at this enterprise we become aware of all such tattoos, as a casual business acquaintance might not.' One more thing to admire about her, thought Zeb, trying not to peer down the front of her apples: she was a tip-top liar. He couldn't have done better himself.

'Makes sense,' said the dominant exec.

'In any case, we did discover this fact in time,' said Katrina, 'and, as you know, the procedure has to be carried out immediately in order to be effective. Luckily we have a fast-track Premium Platinum-level agreement with CryoJeenyus, and their trained operatives are always on call. Your friend is already in a Frasket, and will be on his way to the central CryoJeenyus facility on the east coast almost at once.'

'We can't see him?' said the second exec.

'Once the Frasket is sealed and vacuumized – as it now is – it would defeat the purpose to open it,' Katrina said, smiling. 'I can provide a certificate of authentication from CryoJeenyus. Would you like another frozen daiquiri?'

'Shit,' said the third exec. 'What do we tell that nutbar church of his? *Fell over getting fracked in a moppet shop* won't go down too well.'

'I agree,' said Katrina, a little more coldly. She felt Scales was much more than a moppet shop: it was a *total aesthetic experience*, ran the blurb on the website. 'But Scales and Tails is well known for its discretion in such matters. That is why it is the number-one choice among discerning gentlemen such as yourselves. With us, you do get what you pay for, and more; and that includes a good cover story.'

'Any bright ideas?' said the second exec. He had eaten all the NeverNetted Shrimps and was starting on the scallops. Death made some people hungry.

'Contracted viral pneumonia while working with disadvantaged children in the deeper pleeblands, would be my first suggestion,' said Katrina. 'That would be a popular choice. But we have our own trained PR personnel to assist you.'

'Thank you, ma'am,' said the third exec, watching her through narrowed and slightly reddened eyes. 'You've been very helpful.'

'My pleasure,' said Katrina, smiling graciously and leaning forward to let her hand be shaken and then her fingertips kissed while disclosing enough but not too much of her upper torso real-estate. 'Anytime. We're here for you.'

'What a gal,' says Zeb. 'She could have run any of the top Corps with one thumb, no problem.'

Toby feels the familiar snarly tendrils of jealousy knotting round her heart. 'So did you ever?' she asks.

'Ever what, babe?'

'Ever get into her scaly underthings.'

'It's one of my life-span regrets,' says Zeb, 'but no. I didn't even give it a try. Hands stayed in the pockets, firmly clenched. Jaw clenched likewise. It was an effort to restrain myself, but that's the bare-naked truth: I didn't give it a single grope. Not even a wink.'

'Because?'

'One, she was my boss when I was working at Scales. It's not a smart move to roll around on the floor with a woman boss. It confuses them.'

'Oh please,' says Toby. 'That's so twentieth century!'

'Yeah, yeah, I'm a sexist-wexist pig and so forth, but that

happens to be accurate. Hormone overdrive craps up efficiency. I've watched it in action – women bosses getting all coy and weird about issuing orders to some bullet-headed stud who's just erased their rational faculties and blown off the top of their heads and made them growl like a rakunk in heat and scream like a dying rabbit. It alters the power hierarchy. "Take me, take me, write my speech, get me a coffee, you're fired." So there's that.' He pauses. 'Plus.'

'Plus what?' She's hoping for some revolting feature on the part of Katrina WooWoo, whom, granted, she has never seen, and who is 99.999 per cent likely to be dead; but envy crosses all borders. Maybe she was knock-kneed, or had halitosis or hopeless taste in music. Even a pimple would have been some comfort.

'Plus,' says Zeb, 'Adam loved her. No doubt of it. I'd never poach in his goldfish pond. He was – he's my brother. He's my family. There's limits.'

'You're kidding!' says Toby. 'Adam One? In love? With Katrina WooWoo?'

'She was Eve One,' says Zeb.

The Train to CryoJeenyus

'That's hard to believe,' says Toby. 'How do you know?'

Zeb is silent. Will this be a painful story? It's likely: most stories about the past have an element of pain in them, now that the past has been ruptured so violently, so irreparably.

But not, surely, for the first time in human history. How many others have stood in this place? Left behind, with all gone, all swept away. The dead bodies evaporating like slow smoke; their loved and carefully tended homes crumbling away like deserted anthills. Their bones reverting to calcium; night predators hunting their dispersed flesh, transformed now into grasshoppers and mice.

There's a moon now, almost full. Good luck for owls; bad luck for rabbits, who often choose to cavort riskily but sexily in the moonlight, their brains buzzing with pheromones. There's a couple of them down there now, jumping about in the meadow, glowing with a faint greenish light. Some used to think there was a giant rabbit up there on the moon: they could clearly make out its ears. Others thought there was a smiling face, yet others an old woman with a basket. What will the Crakers decide about that when they get around to astrology, in a hundred years, or ten, or one? As they will, or will not.

But is the moon waxing or waning? Her moontime sense isn't as sharp as it used to be in the days of the Gardeners. How many times had she watched over Vigils when the moon was full? Wondering, from time to time, why there was an Adam One but no Eve One, nor ever any mention of such. Now she'll find out.

'Picture it,' says Zeb. 'Adam and me were on the sealed bullet train together for three days. I'd only seen him twice since we cleared out the Rev's bank account and went our separate ways: in the Happicuppa joint, in the back room at Scales. No time to dig down, So naturally I asked him stuff.'

Zeb had to sacrifice his face waffle, of which he'd become moderately fond despite the meticulous upkeep, what with those stubbly mini-squares to sculpt. He clear-cut the thing with a shaver: all that remained of it was a goatee. He had some new head growth – an unconvincing Mo'Hair glue-on from the early days of that Corp – in a shade of glossy pimp-oil brown.

Luckily he could cover up some of the more fraudulent effects with the dorky hat that was part of the CryoJeenyus outfit for the position that would have once been called 'undertaker's assistant,' though CryoJeenyus used the label Temporary Inertness Caretaker instead. The hat was a modified turban, referencing both magicians and genies. It was reddish in colour and had a flame design on the front.

'Ever-burning flame of life, right?' says Zeb. 'When they showed that third-rate magic-show headrag to me, I said, "You can't be fucking serious! I'm not wearing a boiled tomato on my head!" But then I saw the beauty of it. With it, and with the rest of the ensemble – a purple thing like pyjamas, or maybe a karate concept, with the CryoJeenyus logo plastered across the front – no one could mistake me for anything but an overgrown dim bulb who couldn't get any other job. Frasket-sitting on a train — how pathetic was that? "If you're where no one expects you to be," old Slaight of Hand used to say, "you're invisible."'

Adam had the same uniform, and he looked even stupider in it than Zeb did. So that was some comfort. Anyway, who was going to see them? They were locked into the special CryoJeenyus car with the Frasket plugged into its own separate generator to keep it subzero inside. CryoJeenyus prided itself on being extra secure: DNA theft, not to mention the pilfering of other, larger body parts, was a worry among those who were in love with their own carbon structures: in those circles, the theft of Einstein's brain had not been forgotten.

Thus an armed guard travelled with all Frasket-sitters, riding shotgun near the door. On bona fide CryoJeenyus missions, this individual would have been a member of the consolidated and ever-expanding CorpSeCorps and would have been armed with a spraygun. But since everything about this particular caper was bogus, the role was played by a Scales manager named Mordis. He looked the part: tough, bright eyes like a shiny black beetle, smile impartial as a falling rock.

His weaponry wasn't real, however: the cryptic team could imitate clothing, but they couldn't reproduce that kind of triple-security moving-part tech. So the spraygun was a cunning plastic and painted-foam imitation, which wouldn't matter at all unless someone got close enough to be hit with a fist.

But why would they? As far as anyone else was concerned, this was just a routine dead-run. Or rather, *a ferrying of the subject of a life-suspending event from the shore of life on a round trip back to the shore of life*. It was a mouthful, but CryoJeenyus went in for that kind of evasive crapspeak. They had to, considering the business they were in: their two best sales aids being gullibility and unfounded hope.

'It was the most bizarre trip I ever took,' says Zeb. 'Dressed up like Aladdin, sitting in a locked train compartment with my brother, who was wearing half a squashed pumpkin on his head, and between us a Frasket containing our dad in the form of soup stock. Though we did put the bones and teeth in there, as well. Those didn't dissolve. There was some discussion at Scales about the osseous materials – you could get a good price for human bones in the deeper pleeblands, where carved artisanal human-products jewellery was a fashion: Bone Bling, it was called. But the cooler heads of Adam and Katrina and, I have to say, your humble self overruled the enthusiasts, because even if you boiled those things there was no telling what microbes might remain. As yet, we knew nothing about them.'

A tisket, a tasket, a green and yellow Frasket, Zeb sang.

Adam took out a little notebook and a pencil and wrote: *Watch what you say. We're most likely bugged.*

After showing it to Zeb under cover of his hand, he erased it, and wrote: *And please do not sing. It is very irritating.*

Zeb motioned for the little notebook. After a slight hesitation, Adam handed it over. Zeb wrote: *FU+PO.* Then he wrote, underneath them: *Fuck You and Piss Off.* Then: *You manage to get yourself laid yet?*

Adam read this and blushed. Watching him blush was a novelty: Zeb had never witnessed such a thing before. Adam was so pale you could almost see his capillaries. He wrote: *None of your business.*

Zeb wrote: *Haha, was it K and did you pay?* Since he had long suspected which way the wind of Adam was blowing.

Adam wrote: *I refuse to have that lady spoken about in such a manner. She has been a devoted furtherer of our efforts.*

Zeb should have written: *What efforts?* Then he would have

known more. Instead he wrote, *Haha, hole in one for my score, so to speak :D!! At least you're not gay! :D :D*

Adam wrote: *You are beneath vulgar.*

Zeb wrote: *That would be me! Never mind, I respect true love.* He drew a heart, then a flower. He almost added, *Even if she is running a fancypants blowjob emporium*, but he thought better of it: Adam was getting very huffy, and he might forget himself and take a swipe at Zeb for just about the first time in his life. Then there would be an unseemly scuffle over the remains of their liquefied parent that would not end well for Zeb because he could never bear to deck Adam, not really; so he'd just have to let the pallid little weenie beat him up.

Adam looked mollified – maybe it was the heart and the flower – but still ruffled. He crumpled up all the notebook pages they'd been writing on, then tore them into pieces and went to the can, where – Zeb assumed – he flushed them onto the tracks. Even if some nosy spyster managed to gather them up and stick them together they'd hardly learn anything of interest. Just a bunch of low-calorie dirty talk, of the kind a Frasket-sitter might be expected to employ while killing time out of the hearing of the paying customers.

The rest of the trip passed in silence, Adam with arms folded and a frowny but sanctimonious expression on his face, Zeb humming under his breath while the continent zipped past outside the window.

At the east coast end, the CryoJeenyus dedicated carriage was met by Pilar, posing as a concerned relative of the stiff – or, rather, of the temporarily life-suspended client – and three members from, Zeb assumed, the cryptic team.

'You know two of them,' says Zeb. 'Katuro and Manatee. The third was a gal we lost during Crake's scoop of the

MadAddamites, when he was designing the Crakers and gathering up the brainslaves for his Paradice Project. She tried to run, and I can only assume she went over an overpass and got turned into car tire mush. But none of that had happened yet.'

Pilar shed a few croc tears into a hanky just in case there were any mini-drones or spyware installations around. Then she supervised discreetly as the Frasket was loaded into a long vehicle. CryoJeenyus did not call those vehicles 'hearses': they were 'Life2Life Shuttles.' They were boiled tomato colour and had the perky ever-burning flame of life on the doors: nothing dark to spoil the festive mood.

So into the L2LS went the Rev in his Frasket, headed for an extreme security biosampling unit – not at CryoJeenyus, they weren't equipped for that, but at HelthWyzer Central. Pilar got in as well, and also Zeb. Mordis would change his outfit and head to the local Scales and Tails, where they needed a tougher manager.

Adam would change into his increasingly bizarre streetwear and shuffle off to do whatever it was that Adam did, out there in the deep pleebs. He gave the white bishop to Pilar, having extracted it from the salty cavity of the girl salt shaker: the cryptic team wanted to take a close look at the contents of those pills, and they thought they finally had the equipment to do so without exposing themselves to contagion.

Zeb was slated for yet another identity, which Pilar had already prepared for him: he was to be embedded right inside HelthWyzer Central.

'Do me a favour,' said Zeb to Pilar, once she had assured them that the L2LS had been thoroughly swept for spyware. 'Run a DNA comparison for me. On the Rev. The guy in the Frasket.' He'd never shaken his childhood notion that the Rev was not his real father, and this was surely his last chance to find out.

Pilar said it would be no problem. He handed over a cheek

swab sample of himself, improvised on a piece of tissue, and she tucked it carefully inside a small plastic envelope that contained what looked like a dried-up elf ear, wrinkly in appearance, yellow in colour.

'What's that?' he asked her. He wanted to say, 'What the fuck's that,' but proximity to Pilar did not encourage swearing. 'Gremlin from outer space?'

'It's a chanterelle,' she said. 'A mushroom. An edible variety, not to be confused with the false chanterelle.'

'So, will I come out with the DNA of a fungus?'

Pilar laughed. 'There's not much chance of that,' she said.

'Good,' said Zeb. 'Tell Adam.'

Only problem was, he thought later that night, when drifting off to sleep in his Spartan but acceptable HelthWyzer accommodations – only problem was that if Pilar ran the DNA comparison and the Rev wasn't his dad, then Adam wouldn't be his brother. Adam would be no relation to him at all. No blood relation.

Thus:

Fenella + the Rev = Adam.
Trudy + Unknown Semen Donor = Zeb.
= No shared DNA.

If that was the truth, did he really want to know it?

Lumiroses

Zeb's new title at HelthWyzer Central was that of Disinfector, First Rank. He got a pair of lurid green overalls with the HelthWyzer logo and a big luminous orange *D* on the front; he got a hairnet to keep his own shed follicle-ware from littering the desk spaces of his betters; he got a nose filter cone that made him look like a cartoon pig; he got an endless supply of protective liquid-repelling nanobioform-impermeable gloves and shoes; and, most importantly, he got a passkey.

Only for the bureaucratic offices, however: not for the labs. Those were in another building. But you never could tell what sort of intel a nimble-fingered robinhooder with a few lines of entry code slipped to him by underground cryptics might be able to scoop off an untended computer, late at night, when all good citizens were sound asleep in other people's beds. HelthWyzer was somewhat porous in the spouse department.

Once upon a time Zeb's Disinfector position would have been called 'cleaner,' and before that 'janitor,' and before that 'charwoman'; but this was the twenty-first century and they'd added some nanobioform consciousness to the title. To deserve that title Zeb was supposed to have passed a rigid security check, for what hostile Corp – possibly from a foreign clime –

wouldn't think of disguising one of their keyboard pirates as a minor functionary and ordering him to grab whatever he could find?

To qualify as a Disinfector, Zeb was also supposed to have taken a training course replete with updated modern babble about where germs might lurk and how to render them unconscious. Needless to say, he hadn't taken it; but Pilar had given him the condensed version before he started.

Germs were said to hang out on the usual toilet seats, floors, sinks, and doorknobs, of course. But also on elevator buttons, on telephone receivers, and on computer keyboards. So he had to wipe down all of these with antimicrobial cloths and zap them with death rays, in addition to the floor-washing in hall-ways and such, and the dust-sucking on the carpets in the plushier offices to pick up anything the daily robots might have missed. Those things were always rolling to and fro, backing up to wall outlets to plug themselves in and replenish their battery power, then scuttling away again, emitting beeping sounds so you wouldn't trip over them. It was like navigating a beach lit-tered with giant crabs. When he was alone on a floor he used to kick them into corners or turn them over on their backs, just to see how fast they could recover.

In addition to the outfit he got a new name, which was Horatio.

'Horatio?' says Toby.

'Laughter is uncalled for,' says Zeb. 'It was someone's idea of what a semi-legal Tex-Mex family who snuck under the Wall might have called a son they hoped would make good in the world. They thought I looked kind of Tex-Mex, or maybe like a hybrid that contained some of that DNA. Which I do, as was discovered not long after that.'

'Oh,' says Toby. 'Pilar ran the DNA comparison.'

'You got it,' says Zeb. 'Though it took a while for me to

access the news. She couldn't really be seen with me, because why would she know me? Anyway we'd have to go out of our way to meet, we were on different shifts. So we'd fixed up a fallback code when I gave her my cell sample.

'Before then, when I was on my way in the CryoJeenyus train car and she was putting my Disinfector identity together and getting it slotted into the system, she'd already learned I'd be cleaning the women's washroom down the hall from the lab where she was working. I was night shift – it was all male Disinfectors for that shift, they didn't want any groping or screaming, which might have taken place with a gender mix. So I had the run of the floor after dark. Second cubicle from the left: that was the one I needed to watch.'

'She left a note inside the toilet tank?'

'Nothing so obvious. Those toilet tanks were routinely checked; only an amateur would stash anything important in there. The dropbox was that square container thing they have in those washrooms, for what-have-you. Those items you aren't supposed to flush. But it wouldn't be a note, way too telltale.'

'So, a signal?' Toby wonders what kind. One for joy, two for sorrow? But one and two of what?

'Yeah. Something that wouldn't be out of place, but wouldn't be the usual. Pits, was what she decided.'

'Pits? What do you mean, pits?' Toby tries to visualize pits. Armpits, holes in the ground? 'Like peach pits?' she guesses.

'Correct. Might be from a lunch that got eaten in the washroom. Some of the secretary-type women did that – they sat in the can for some peace and quiet. I did find sandwich remains in those boxes: the odd bacon rind, the odd cheesefood fragment. There was a lot of time pressure in HelthWyzer, and more of it the farther down the status ladder you were, so they liked to sneak breathers.'

'What was the pit selection?' Toby asks. 'For the yes and the no?' The way Pilar thought has always intrigued her: she wouldn't have made the fruit selections haphazardly.

'Peach pit for no: no relationship to the Rev. Date pit for yes: worse luck, the Rev is your dad, hear it and weep because you're at least half psychopath.'

The peach choice makes sense to Toby: peaches were valued among the Gardeners as having been one of the possible candidates for the Fruit of Life in Eden. Not that the Gardeners disparaged dates, or any other fruit that had not been chemically sprayed.

'HelthWyzer must have had access to some pretty expensive fruit. I thought the peach and apple yields plummeted around then, when the big bee die-off was going on. And the plums,' she adds. 'And the citrus varieties.'

'HelthWyzer was making a lot of money,' says Zeb. 'Raking it in, from their vitamin pill business and the medical drugs end. So they could afford the cyber-pollinated imports. It was one of the perks of working at HelthWyzer, the fresh fruit. Only for the higher-ups, naturally.'

'Which did you find?' says Toby. 'Pit-wise.'

'Peach. Two pits. She'd underlined it.'

'How did you feel about that?' Toby asks.

'About the overkill on the expensive fruit?' says Zeb. He's dodging emotion.

'About finding out that your father wasn't your father,' says Toby patiently. 'You must have felt something.'

'Okay. I felt, *I knew it,*' says Zeb. 'I always like to be right, who doesn't? Also less guilty about, you know. Frothing him to death.'

'You felt guilty about that?' says Toby. 'Even if he had been your father, he was such a . . .'

'Yeah, I know. But still. Blood is thicker than blood. It would've bothered me some. The downside was the Adam end of it. I didn't feel so good about that: all of a sudden he was no relation to me. No genetic relation, that is.'

'Did you tell him?' Toby asks.

'Nope. As far as I was concerned, I figured he was my brother. Joined at the head. We shared a lot of stuff.'

'Now I'm coming to a part you won't like much, babe,' says Zeb.

'Because it's about Lucerne?' says Toby. Zeb's not stupid. He must have suspected for a long time how she'd felt about Lucerne, his live-in at the Gardeners. Lucerne the Irritating, dodger of communal weeding duties, shirker of women's sewing groups, sufferer from frequent excuse-making headaches, whiny possessor of Zeb, neglectful mother of Ren. Lucerne the Luscious, one-time denizen of the HelthWyzer Corp, married to a top geek. Lucerne, the romantic fantasist who'd run away with the raggle-taggle Zeb because she'd seen too many movies in which beautiful women did that.

Zeb, in Lucerne's version, had been crazed with irresistible and relentless desire for her. He'd been cross-eyed with lust when he'd spotted her in her pink negligee at the AnooYoo Spa while he was planting lumiroses in his capacity as gardener, and he'd made mad passionate love to her right there and then, on the dew-damp morning grass. Toby had heard that story many times from Lucerne herself, back at the Gardeners, and she'd liked it less every time. If she leaned over the railing and spat, she might be able to hit the very spot where Zeb and Lucerne had first rolled around on the lawn. Or near enough.

'Right,' says Zeb. 'Lucerne. That's what came next in my life. I can skip over it if you like.'

'No,' says Toby. 'I've never heard your side of it. But Lucerne told me about the lumirose petals. How you strewed them over her pulsating body and so forth.' She tries not to sound envious, but it's difficult. Has anyone ever strewn lumirose petals over her own pulsating body, or even thought about it? No. She lacks the temperament for petal-strewing. She would spoil the moment – 'What are you doing with those silly petals?' Or she would laugh, which would be fatal. Right now she needs to shut up and hold back on the commentary or she won't get the story.

'Yeah, well, petal-strewing comes naturally to me, I used to be in the magic biz,' says Zeb. 'It distracts the attention. But some of what she told you was most likely true.'

The first time Zeb and Lucerne set eyes on each other was not at the AnooYoo Spa, however. It was in the women's washroom that Zeb was supposed to be cleaning – was cleaning, in fact – while pawing through the detritus in the metal box for pits, whether peach or date. He hadn't found any yet – it was before Pilar had the results of the Rev mix 'n' match DNA test, or possibly before she could amass the necessary pits – so he was emerging from the second cubicle from the left empty-handed, pit-wise. When who should come into the Women's Room but Lucerne.

'This was the middle of the night?' says Toby.

'Affirmative. What was she doing there? I asked myself. Either she was a robinhooder like me, in which case she was really inept because she'd got caught out of place. Or else she was having it off with some HelthWyzer exec who'd given her an access key to the building so they could flail on his fancy carpet while he was supposed to be working late at the office and she was supposed to be at the gym. Though it was late even for that.'

'Or both,' says Toby. 'The having it off and the robinhood-ing, both.'

'Yeah. They combine well: each can provide an excuse for the other. *Oh no, I wasn't pilfering, I was only cheating on my husband. Oh no, I wasn't cheating, I was only pilfering.* But it was the first one of those, for sure. No mistaking the symptoms.'

Lucerne gave a little scream when she saw Zeb emerging from the cubicle in his impermeable gloves and his alien-from-outer-space nose cone. It wasn't the first time that night she'd given a little scream, in his opinion: she was flushed and breathless, and what you might call dishevelled. Or maybe unbuttoned. Or, if you were being fancy, in disarray. Needless to say, she was very attractive at that moment.

Oh, needless to say, thinks Toby.

'What are you doing in the Ladies?' Lucerne said accusingly. The first rule: when caught wet-handed, accuse first. She did say Ladies, not Women's. That was a clue in itself.

'To what?' says Toby.

'Her character. She had a pedestal complex. She wanted to be on one. Ladies was a step higher than Women.'

Zeb shoved his nose cone up onto his forehead: now he looked like a blunted rhinoceros. 'I'm a Disinfector, First Rank,' he added impressively but pompously. There's something about a gorgeous woman who's obviously been shagging another man that brings out the pompous in a guy: it's a wound to his ego. 'What are *you* doing in this *building*?' he counter-accused. He noted the wedding ring. Aha, he thought. Caged lioness. Needs a holiday from the tedium.

'I had some work to finish up,' Lucerne lied, as convincingly as she could. 'My presence here is entirely legitimate. I have a pass.' Zeb could have called her on it, but he admired a woman who could use the word *legitimate* in such a fraudulent context. So he did not march her off to Security, which would have

triggered a check via the spouse, and set off unpleasant reper-
cussions for the lover, and would almost certainly have
resulted – come to think of it – in Zeb himself being fired. So
he let her get away with it.

'Right, okay, sorry,' he said with acceptable hangdog servility.

'Now, if you don't mind, this is the *Ladies*, and I'd like some
privacy, Horatio,' she said, caressing the name on his tag. She
gazed deep into his eyes. It was a plea – *Don't rat me out* – and
also a promise: *One day I'll be yours*. Not that she intended to
honour that promise.

Well played, thought Zeb as he made his exit.

Thus, when he and Lucerne encountered each other for the
second time, in the first flush of dawn, she barefoot and inad-
equately concealed in a diaphanous pink negligee, he with a
phallic spade and an ardent lumirose bush in hand, right down
there on the freshly sodded lawn of the just-completed
AnooYoo Spa in the middle of Heritage Park, she recognized
him. And she remembered that he'd once been Horatio, but
was now, mysteriously – as his AnooYoo Spa groundskeeper's
name tag had it – Atash.

'You were at HelthWyzer,' she'd said. 'But you weren't . . .'
So, naturally, he'd kissed her, fervently and with unrestrainable
passion. Because she couldn't talk and kiss at the same time.

'Naturally,' says Toby. 'You were supposed to be who? What's
Atash?'

'Iranian,' says Zeb. 'Immigrant grandparents. Why not?
There were a lot of them came over in the late twentieth. It
was safe enough as long as I never bumped into any other
Iranians and they started asking genealogy stuff, and where was
your family from. Though I'd memorized the whole identity,
just in case. I had a good backstory – just enough disappear-

ances and atrocities in it to account for any time/place discrepancies.'

'So Lucerne meets Atash, and suspects he's really Horatio,' says Toby. 'Or vice versa.' She wants to get over the hurtful parts as quickly as possible: with luck, the hot, irresistible sex and the petal-strewing that Lucerne had never tired of describing to Toby won't be mentioned again.

'Right. And that wasn't good, because I'd had to go missing from HelthWyzer very fast. One of the computers had an alarm on it I didn't spot until too late, and it showed that somebody'd been in there. I could tell I'd triggered it right after I did it, and they were going to start tracking who'd been in the building at the time, and that would pinpoint me. I used the MaddAddam chatroom and called for emergency help, and the cryptics got hold of Adam. He had a contact who could stick me into the AnooYoo Spa gardening job, though we both realized it was a stopgap and I'd have to move on soon.'

'So, she knows, and you know she knows, and she knows you know she knows,' says Toby. 'At the lawn encounter.'

'Correct. I had two choices: murder or seduction. I chose the most attractive.'

'Understood,' says Toby. 'I'd have done the same.' He's made it sound like a seduction of convenience, but they both know there was more to it than that. Diaphanous pink negligees are their own excuse for being.

Lucerne was bad luck in some ways, said Zeb. Though she was good luck in others, because you couldn't deny that she –

'You can skip that part,' says Toby.

'Okay, short version: she had me by the nuts, more ways than one. But I hadn't ratted on her that time in the washroom, and she was inclined to return the favour as long as I was attentive enough to her. Then she got hooked on me, and you know the rest: nothing would do but an elopement with a mystery man first spotted when wearing a nose of a pig.

'I moved us around inside the deeper pleeblands, which she found romantic at first. Luckily no one – no one in the CorpSeCorps – was much interested in her disappearance, because she hadn't stolen any IP. Wives did skedaddle from the Compounds out of sheer boredom, it wasn't unheard of. The CorpSeCorps regarded such defections as private, insofar as they regarded anything as private. They didn't bother with them much, especially if the husband wasn't agitating. Which it appears that Lucerne's husband did not.

'Trouble is, Lucerne took Ren with her. Cute little girl, I liked her. But it was way too dangerous for her in the deeper pleeblands. Kids like that could get snatched for the chicken-sex trade just walking along the street, even if they were with adults. There'd be a pleebrat mob scuffle, some SecretBurgers red sauce tossing, an overturned stand or solar-car – in other words, a honking big misdirection – and when you looked again, your child would be gone. I couldn't risk that.'

Zeb got a few more alterations done to his ears and fingerprints and irises – they'd know by now he'd been up to no good on the HelthWyzer computers, they'd be looking for him – and then ...

'And then the three of you turned up at the God's Gardeners,' says Toby. 'I remember that; I wondered from the first what you were doing there. You didn't fit in with the rest of them.'

'You mean I hadn't taken the vow of whatnot and drunk the Elixir of Life? God loves you, and he also loves aphids?'

'More or less.'

'No. I hadn't. But Adam had to put up with me anyway, didn't he? I was his brother.'

Edencliff

'Adam already had his ecofreakshow up and running by that time,' says Zeb. 'At the Edencliff Rooftop Garden. You were there. So were Katuro and Rebecca. Nuala – wonder what happened to her? Marushka Midwife, and the others. And Philo. Too bad about him.'

'Freakshow?' says Toby. 'That's not very kind. Surely the God's Gardeners was more than that.'

'Yeah, it was,' says Zeb. 'Granted. But the pleebland slumfolk tagged it as a freakshow. Just as well: best to be thought of as harmless and addled and poor, in those parts. Adam did nothing to discourage that view; in fact, he encouraged it. Roaming around in the pleebs wearing the simple but eye-catching garb of a lunatic recycler with his choir in tow singing nutbar hymns, then preaching the love of hoofed animals in front of SecretBurger stands – you'd have to be lobotomized to do that, was the street verdict.'

'If he hadn't done those things I wouldn't be here,' says Toby. 'Him and the Gardener kids grabbed me during a street brawl. I was working – I was trapped at SecretBurgers at the time, and the manager had a thing for me.'

'Your pal Blanco,' says Zeb. 'Third-time Painball vet, as I recall.'

'Yes. Girls he had a thing for ended up dead, and I was next on the list. He was already at the violent stage, he was working up to the kill; you could feel it. So I owe a lot to Adam – to Adam One, as I always knew him. Freakshow or not,' she says defensively.

'Don't get it wrong,' says Zeb. 'He's my brother. We had our disagreements, and he had his way of doing things and I had mine, but that's different.'

'You didn't mention Pilar,' says Toby to deflect the conversation from Adam One. It's uncomfortable for her to listen to criticism of him. 'She was there too. At Edencliff.'

'Yeah, HelthWyzer finally got too much for her. She'd been feeding inside stuff to Adam, which was useful to him – he liked to know who might jump ship from a Corp, come over to the side of virtue, which was his side, naturally. But she said she couldn't stay there any longer. With the CorpSeCorps takeover of so-called law-and-order functions, the Corps had the power to bulldoze and squash and erase anything they liked. Their addiction to making a buck was becoming toxic for her: it was poisoning, I quote, her soul.

'The cryptics helped her put together a cover story that allowed her to vanish without inspiring any trackers: she'd had an unfortunate stroke, with instant shipment to CryoJeenyus in a Frasket, and presto, there she was on top of a pleebland tenement building, dressed in a cloth bag and mixing potions.'

'And growing mushrooms, and teaching me about maggots, and keeping bees. She was very good at it,' says Toby a little ruefully. 'Convincing. She had me talking to the bees. I was the one who told them when she died.'

'Yeah. I remember all of that. But she wasn't bullshitting,' said Zeb. 'She believed the whole sackful, in a way. That's why she was willing to run the risks she did at HelthWyzer. Remember what happened to Glenn's dad? She could have gone off an overpass, like him. If they'd caught her; especially if they'd caught her with that white bishop and the three pills.'

'She held on to those?' says Toby. 'I thought she was going to have them analyzed. After Adam gave them to her.'

'She decided it was too dangerous,' says Zeb. 'For anyone to open them up and maybe let out whatever was inside them. They didn't know how to get rid of them. So that bishop stayed right inside HelthWyzer Central as long as she was there. She brought it out with her when she left, and slipped those pills into her own white bishop, in the set she hand-carved. We played with that set of hers, you and me, that time I was recovering. From getting sliced up on one of those pleeb missions I was running for Adam.'

Toby has an image of it: Zeb in the shade, on a hazy afternoon. His arm. Her own hand, moving the white bishop, the death-carrier. Unknown to her then, like so much.

'You always played Black,' she says. 'What happened to that bishop when Pilar died?'

'She willed her set to Glenn, along with a sealed letter. She'd taught him to play chess, back at HelthWyzer West, when he was little. But by the time she died, his mother had married the guy she'd been fooling around with – so-called Uncle Pete – and they'd been upgraded to HelthWyzer Central. Pilar kept in touch with Glenn through the cryptics, and Glenn was the one who arranged the cancer tests for her, found out she was terminal.'

'What was in the letter?'

'It was sealed. How to open the bishop, is my guess. I would have filched it, but Adam had firm control of it.'

'So Adam just handed that stuff over, the chess set with the pills inside? To Glenn – to Crake? He was only a teenager.'

'Pilar said he was mature for his age, and Adam felt Pilar's deathbed wishes should be respected.'

'What about you? It was before I became an Eve, but you were on the council then. They discussed important decisions like that. You must have had an opinion. You were an Adam – Adam Seven.'

'The others agreed with Adam One. I thought it was a bad idea. What if the kid tried those things out on someone without knowing exactly what they'd do, the way I had?'

'He must have, later,' says Toby. 'With some additions of his own. That must've been the core of the BlyssPluss pills: what you got after you'd experienced the bliss.'

'Yeah,' says Zeb. 'I think you're right.'

'Do you think Pilar knew what use he'd make of those microbes or viruses or whatever they were?' she asks. 'Eventually?' She remembers Pilar's wrinkled little face, her kindness, her serenity, her strength. But underneath, there had always been a hard resolve. You wouldn't call it meanness or evil. Fatalism, perhaps.

'Let's put it this way,' says Zeb. 'All the real Gardeners believed the human race was overdue for a population crash. It would happen anyway, and maybe sooner was better.'

'But you weren't a real Gardener.'

'Pilar thought I was, because of my Vigil. Part of the deal with Adam One was that I had to take on a title, that Adam Seven thing: he said it would confer the needed authority, as he put it. Status enhancer. To become one of those, you had to undergo a Vigil. See what was going on with your spirit animal.'

'I did that,' said Toby. 'Talking tomato plants, in-depth stars.'

'Yeah, all of that. I don't know what old Pilar mixed into the enhancer, but it was potent.'

'What did you see?'

A pause. 'The bear. The one I killed and ate, when I was walking out of the Barrens.'

'Did it have a message for you?' says Toby. Her own spirit animal had been enigmatic.

'Not exactly. But it gave me to understand that it was living on in me. It wasn't even pissed with me. It seemed quite friendly. Amazing what happens when you fuck with your own neurons.'

Once he was Adam Seven, Zeb could install himself and Lucerne and little Ren as bona fide members of the God's Gardeners. They didn't meld very well. Ren was homesick for the Compound and her father, and Lucerne had too great an interest in nail polish to make it as a female Gardener. Her investment in vegetable preparation was nil, and she hated the required outfits – the dark, baggy dresses, the bib aprons. Zeb ought to have known she wasn't going to stick with this arrangement, over time.

Zeb himself had no affinity for slug and snail relocation or soap-making or kitchen cleanup, so he and Adam came to an understanding about what his duties would be. He taught the kids survival skills, and Urban Bloodshed Limitation, which was street fighting viewed from a loftier perspective. As the Gardeners gathered members and expanded, and set up branch locations in different cities, he ran courier among the different groups. The Gardeners refused to use cellphones or technology of any kind; apart, that is, from the one secret souped-up computer that Zeb kept at his own disposal, and fitted out with spyware so he could snoop on the CorpSeCorps, and firewalled up the yin-yang.

Running courier for Adam had its advantages – he was away from home, so he didn't have to listen to Lucerne's complaints.

But it also had its disadvantages – he was away from home, which gave Lucerne more to complain about. She liked to nag on about his commitment issues: why, for instance, had he never asked her to go through the God's Gardeners Partnership ceremony with him?

'Where you jumped over a bonfire together and then traded green branches while everyone stood in a circle, and then they had some kind of pious banquet,' says Zeb. 'She really wanted me to do that with her. I said as far as I was concerned it was a meaningless empty symbol. Then she'd accuse me of humiliating her.'

'If it was meaningless, why didn't you do it?' says Toby. 'It might have satisfied her. Made her happier.'

'Fat chance,' says Zeb. 'I just didn't want to. I hated being pushed.'

'She was right, you had commitment issues,' says Toby.

'Guess so. Anyway, she dumped me. Went back to the Compounds, took Ren with her. And then I wanted the Gardeners to get more activist, and everything unravelled.'

'I wasn't there any more, by that time,' says Toby. 'Blanco got out of Painball and went after me. I was a liability to the Gardeners. You helped me change my identity.'

'Years of practice.' He sighs. 'After you left, things got severe. The God's Gardeners was getting too big and successful for the CorpSeCorps. To them, it looked like a resistance movement in the making.

'Adam was using the Garden as a safe house for escapees from the BioCorps, and they were beginning to figure that out; so the CorpSemen were paying the pleebmobs to attack us. Being a pacifist, Adam One couldn't bring himself to weaponize the Garden. I could've helped him turn a toy potato gun into an effective short-range shrapnel thrower, but he wouldn't hear of it. It was too unsaintly for him.'

'You're making fun,' says Toby.

'Just describing. No matter what was at stake, he couldn't go on the offensive, not directly. Remember, he was the firstborn; the Rev got hold of him early, before either of us figured out what a fraud the murderous old bugger actually was. What stuck with Adam was that he had to be good. Gooder than good, so God would love him. Guess he was going to do the Rev thing himself, but do it right – everything the Rev had pretended to be, he would be in reality. It was a tall order.'

'But none of that stuck with you.'

'Not so I noticed. I was the devil-kid, remember? That let me off the goodness hook. Adam depended on that: he never would have turned the Rev into a raspberry soda with his own two hands. He just put me in the way of it. Even so, he had some guilt issues: the Rev was his father, like it or not, and honour your parents, etcetera, even if one of them had buried the other one in the rock garden. He felt he should be forgiving. He beat himself up a lot, Adam did. It was worse after he lost Katrina WooWoo.'

'She went off with someone else?'

'Nothing so pleasant. The Corps decided to take over the sex trade: it was so lucrative. They bought a few politicians, got it legalized, set up SeksMart, forced everyone in the trade to roll in. Katrina played at first, but then they wanted to institute policies she found unacceptable. "Institute policies," that's how they put it. She had scruples, so she became inconvenient. They got rid of the python too.'

'Oh,' says Toby. 'I'm sorry.'

'So was I,' says Zeb. 'Adam was more than sorry. He pined, he dwindled. Something went missing in him. I think he'd had a dream of installing Katrina in the Garden. Not that it would have worked out. Wrong wardrobe preferences.'

'That's very sad,' says Toby.

'Yeah. It was. I should've been more understanding. Instead, I picked a fight.'

'Oh,' says Toby. 'Only you?'

'Maybe both of us. But it was no holds barred. I said he was just like the Rev, really, only inside out, like a sock: neither one of them gave a shit about anyone else. It was always their way or zero. He said I'd always had criminal tendencies, and that was why I couldn't understand pacifism and inner peace. I said that by doing nothing he was colluding with the powers that were fucking the planet, especially the OilCorps and the Church of PetrOleum. He said I had no faith, and that the Creator would sort the earth out in good time, most likely very soon, and that those who were attuned and had a true love for the Creation would not perish. I said that was a selfish view. He said I listened to the whisperings of earthly power and I only wanted attention, the way I always had as a child when I pushed the boundaries.' He sighs again.

'Then what?' says Toby.

'Then I got mad. So I said something I wish I'd never said.' A pause. Toby waits. 'I said he wasn't really my brother, not genetically. He was no relation to me.' Another pause. 'He didn't believe me at first. I backed it up, I told him about the test Pilar had done. He just crumpled.'

'Oh,' says Toby. 'I'm sorry.'

'I felt terrible right away, but I couldn't unsay it. After that we tried to patch it up and paper it over. But things festered. We had to go our own ways.'

'Katuro went with you,' says Toby. She knows this for a fact. 'Rebecca. Black Rhino. Shackleton, Crozier, and Oates.'

'Amanda, at first,' says Zeb. 'She got out, though. Then new ones joined. Ivory Bill, Lotis Blue, White Sedge. All of them.'

'And Swift Fox,' says Toby.

'Yeah. And her. We thought Glenn – we thought Crake was

our inside guy, feeding us stuff from the Corps through the MaddAddam chatroom. But all along, he was setting us up so he could drag us into the Paradice dome to do his people-splicing for him.'

'And his plague-virus-mixing?' says Toby.

'Not from what I hear,' says Zeb. 'He did that on his own.'

'To make his perfect world,' says Toby.

'Not perfect,' says Zeb. 'He wouldn't claim that. More like a reboot. And he succeeded in his own way. Up to now.'

'He didn't anticipate the Painballers,' says Toby.

'He should have. Or something like them,' says Zeb.

It's very quiet, down there in the forest. A Craker child is singing a little in its sleep. Around the swimming pool the Pigoons are dreaming, emitting small grunts like puffs of smoke. Far away something cries: a bobkitten?

There's a faint cool breeze; the leaves go about their business, which is rustling; the moon travels through the sky, moving towards its next phase, marking time.

'You should get some sleep,' says Zeb.

'Both of us should,' says Toby. 'We'll need our energy.'

'I'll spell you – two on, two off. Wish I was twenty years younger,' says Zeb. 'Not that those Painball guys are in great shape, you'd think. God knows what they've been eating.'

'The Pigoons are fit enough,' says Toby.

'They can't pull triggers,' says Zeb. He pauses. 'If we both come out of this tomorrow, maybe we should do the bonfire thing. With the green branches.'

Toby laughs. 'I thought you said it was a meaningless empty symbol.'

'Even a meaningless empty symbol can mean something sometimes,' says Zeb. 'You rejecting me?'

'No,' says Toby. 'How could you even think it?'

'I fear the worst,' says Zeb.

'Would that be the worst? Me rejecting you?'

'Don't push a guy when he's feeling skinless.'

'I just have trouble believing you're serious,' says Toby.

Zeb sighs. 'Get some sleep, babe. We'll work it out later. Tomorrow's on the way.'

Eggshell

Muster

Peach-coloured haze in the east. Day is breaking, so cool and delicate at first, the sun not yet a hot spotlight. The crows are abroad, signalling to one another. *Caw! Cawcaw! Caw!* What are they saying? *Look out! Look out!* Or maybe: *Party time soon!* Where there are wars, there will be crows, the carrion-fanciers. And ravens too, the warbirds, the eyeball gourmands. And vultures, the holy birds of yore, old connoisseurs of rot.

Dump the morbid soliloquies, Toby tells herself. What's needed is a positive outlook. That was what trumpet fanfares were for, and drums, and march music. We are invincible, that music told the soldiers. They had to believe in them, those lying melodies, because who can walk intrepidly towards death without? The bear-shirted berserkers were said to have doped themselves up before battle with northern hallucinogenic fungus: *Amanita muscaria,* perhaps, or so said Pilar, at the Gardeners. *Historical Mushroom Practices, for senior students only.*

Maybe I should spike the water bottles, she thinks. Poison your brain, then stride forth and kill people. Or be killed.

She stands, unwinds herself from the pink bedspread, shivers. There's been a dew: dampness beads her hair, her eyebrows. Her foot's asleep. Her rifle is where she left it, within reach; and the binoculars as well.

Zeb's already up, leaning on the railing. 'I dozed off last night,' she says to him. 'Not much of a watchperson. Sorry.'

'So did I,' he says. 'It's okay, the Pigoons would've sounded the alarm.'

'Sounded?' she says, laughing a little.

'You're such a stickler. Okay, grunted the alarm. Our porky pals have been busy.'

Toby looks where he's looking: over and down. The Pigoons have levelled the meadow, all the way around the spa building, wherever there were tall weeds or shrubs. Five of the larger ones are still at work, trampling and rolling on anything higher than an ankle.

'Nobody's going to be sneaking up on them, that's for sure,' says Zeb. 'Clever buggers, they know about cover.' They've left one tuft of foliage in the middle distance, Toby notes. She peers at it with the binoculars. It must mark the remains of that boar she'd killed, back when there was a turf war between her and the Pigoons over the subject of the AnooYoo garden. Oddly enough they hadn't devoured the carcass, though they'd seemed willing enough to eat their dead piglet. Was there a hierarchy in such matters, among them? Sows eat their farrow, but nobody eats the boars? What next, commemorative statues?

'Too bad about the lumiroses,' she says.

'Yeah, planted them myself. But they'll grow back. Darn things are as hard to kill as kudzu, once they get going.'

'What will the Crakers have for breakfast, though?' says Toby. 'Now that the foliage is gone. We can't have them wandering over there, close to the forest.'

'The Pigoons thought of that too,' says Zeb. 'Look beside the swimming pool.'

Sure enough, there's a heap of fresh fodder. The Pigoons must have gathered it, since there's no one else around.

'That's considerate,' says Toby.

'Crap, they're smart,' says Zeb. 'Speaking of which.' He points.

Toby lifts the binoculars. Three medium-sized Pigoons, two spotted ones and a third that's mostly black, are approaching from the north at a brisk trot. The squad of huge bulldozing Pigoons assiduously levelling the meadow roll themselves upright and lollop out to meet them. There's some grunting, some nuzzling. All ears are forward, all tails are curled and twirling: they're not frightened or angry, anyway.

'I wonder what they're saying?' Toby asks.

'We'll find out,' says Zeb, 'when they're damn ready to tell us. We're just the infantry as far as they're concerned. Dumb as a stump, they must think, though we can work the sprayguns. But they're the generals. I'd bet they've got their strategy all worked out.'

Rebecca must have been ferreting around, discovering odds and ends. For breakfast they have soybits that have been soaked in Mo'Hair milk and sweetened with sugar. On the side, for a treat, a teaspoonful of Avocado Body Butter. The AnooYoo Spa had gone in for cosmetic products that sounded a lot like food: Chocolate Mousse Facial, Lemon Meringue Exfoliating Masque. And the various body butters, so rich in essential lipids.

'There was some of that stuff left?' says Toby. 'I was sure I ate it all.'

'It was in the kitchen, hidden in one of the big soup tureens,' says Rebecca. 'Maybe you put it there yourself, and forgot. You must've been building up an Ararat cache somewhere in this building, all the time you worked here.'

'Yes, but it was in the supply room,' says Toby. 'Here and

there. I disguised it inside the colon cleanser bulk packaging. I wouldn't have left any of my own supplies in the kitchen; someone might have found them. It was most likely one of the staff who hid it. They used to try that – make off with a little of the high-end AnooYoo line, sell it on the pleebland grey market. But I did an inventory every two weeks, so usually I caught them.'

Not that she always reported them: the help was not overpaid. Why wreck a life?

Breakfast concluded, they assemble in the main foyer, where once a welcoming pink fruit-based drink, with or without alcohol, was served to the arriving clients. The MaddAddamites are all present, and the former God's Gardeners. One of the boars is also in attendance, and, staying close to it, little Blackbeard. The rest of the Crakers are still out by the swimming pool munching on their pile of breakfast fodder. So are the rest of the Pigoons, similarly munching.

'So,' says Zeb. 'Here's where we stand. We know the direction the enemy is taking. There are three of them, not two. The pigs – the Pigoons – are sure of that. They haven't seen these guys clearly – the pig scouts kept well out of sight to avoid being shot – but they've tracked them.'

'How far away?' says Rhino.

'Far enough. They've got a head start on us. But, in our favour, the Pigoons say they can't go really fast because one of the three is limping. Dragging a foot. That right?' he says to Blackbeard, who nods.

'A smelly foot,' he says.

'That's the good news. The bad news is that they're heading towards the RejoovenEsense Compound. Which most likely means the Paradice dome.'

'Oh fuck,' says Jimmy. 'The spraygun cellpacks! They'll find them!'

'Think they're going for those?' says Zeb. 'Sorry. Stupid question. We have no way of knowing what they intend.'

'If they aren't just wandering around, we can assume they have a goal,' says Katuro. 'The third one – he might be directing them.'

'We need to head them off,' says Rhino. 'Keep them out of there. Otherwise they'll be well armed, and for a long time.'

'And after a short time we won't be,' says Shackleton. 'We're already running low on the cellpacks.'

'So, only question,' says Zeb. 'Who comes with us, who stays here. Some of that's self-evident. Rhino, Katuro, Shackleton, Crozier, Manatee, Zunzuncito, coming. And Toby, of course. All the pregnant women, staying. Ren, Amanda, Swift Fox. Anyone else with a bun ... anyone else declaring?'

'Gender roles suck,' says Swift Fox.

Then you should stop playing them, thinks Toby.

'Granted,' says Zeb, 'but that's reality now. We can't have anyone doing an unscheduled bleedout in the middle of. ... In the middle. Any more than necessary. White Sedge?'

'She's a pacifist,' says Amanda unexpectedly. 'And Lotis Blue has, you know. Cramps.'

'Staying, then. Anyone else have disabilities, or else qualms?'

'I want to come,' says Rebecca. 'And I am definitely not pregnant.'

'Can you keep up?' says Zeb. 'That's the next question. Be honest. You may pose a danger to self and others. Veteran Painballers don't fool around. There's only three of them, but they'll be lethal. This picnic is not for the squeamish.'

'Okay, scratch that,' says Rebecca. 'Know yourself, out of shape, hand up. Not to mention squeamish. I'll stay here.'

'Me too,' says Beluga.

'And I,' says Tamaraw.

'And I,' says Ivory Bill. 'There comes a time in a man's life when, no matter how agile the spirit, the earthly carapace develops its limitations. Not to mention the knees. And on the subject of the . . . '

'Right. And Blackbeard comes with us. We'll need him: he seems to have a fix on whatever it is the Pigoons want to convey.'

'No,' says Toby. 'He should stay here. He's only a child.' She doesn't think she could live with herself if little Blackbeard got killed, especially in the ways the Painballers would kill him if they got hold of him. 'And he has no fear – or none that's realistic – when it comes to people. He might go running right out into the open, into crossfire. Or get snatched as a hostage. What would happen then?'

'Yeah, but I don't see how we can manage without him,' says Zeb. 'He's our only liaison with the pigs, and they're essential. We'll have to take the risk.'

Blackbeard himself has been following this exchange. 'Do not worry, Oh Toby,' he says. 'I need to come, the Pig Ones have said so. Oryx will be helping me, and Fuck. I have already called Fuck, he is flying to here, right now. You will see.' There's no way Toby can contradict any of this: she herself can't see Oryx or the helpful Fuck, nor can she understand the Pigoons. In the world of Blackbeard she's deaf and blind.

'If they point a stick at you,' she says to him, 'those men, you must fall flat on the ground. Or get behind a tree. If there is a tree. Or else a wall.'

'Yes, thank you, Oh Toby,' he says politely. This is evidently old news to him.

'Right then,' says Zeb. 'Are we clear?'

'I'm coming too,' says Jimmy. Everyone looks at him: they've assumed he'd stay behind. He's still skinny as a twig and pale as a puffball.

'Are you sure?' says Toby. 'What about your foot?'

'It's fine. I can walk. I have to come.'

'Not sure that's wise,' says Zeb.

'Wise,' says Jimmy. He grins a little. 'Never been accused of that. But if we're heading to the Paradice dome, I really have to go.'

'Because?' says Zeb.

'Because Oryx is there.' An embarrassed silence: this is demented. Jimmy looks around the circle, grinning nervously. 'Okay, I'm not crazy, I know she's dead. But you need me,' he says.

'Why?' says Katuro. 'Not meaning to be rude, but . . . '

'Because I've been back there already. Since the Flood,' says Jimmy.

'So?' says Zeb, voice level. 'Nostalgia?' Toby guesses the meaning of that levelness: rid me of this brain-damaged dweeb.

Jimmy stands his ground. 'So, I know where everything is. Such as the cellpacks. And the sprayguns: there's a stash of them too.'

Zeb sighs. 'Okay,' he says. 'But if you lag behind, we'll have to send you back. Under non-hominid escort.'

'You mean those werewolf pigs,' says Jimmy. 'Been there, done that: they think I'm tripe. Forget the escort. I can keep up.'

Sortie

Toby changes into a Spa track suit, with a pillowcase torn open for a sun cover on her head. Too bad about the kissy lips and winky eye on the sweatshirt – not very military – and too bad also about the colour pink, which could make her a target. But there are no khaki textiles at AnooYoo.

She checks her rifle, tucks some of her extra bullets into a pink Spa carrybag. There's some Spa cotton half-socks with fluffy pom-poms at the backs: she puts on a pair of those, takes an extra pair. If Zeb says anything about her getup she'll be tempted to smack him.

In the main foyer she distributes the water bottles, filled with water that's been properly boiled by Rebecca earlier with the aid of Ren and Amanda. The AnooYoo Spa emphasized the need for proper hydration during gym workouts, so there are enough plastic bottles. The MaddAddamites have brought some Joltbars with them from the cobb house, and some cold kudzu fritters. 'Enough energy to run on, not too much or it weighs you down,' says Zeb. 'Keep some for later.' He looks at Toby, her kissy-lipped pink outfit.

'You auditioning for something?' he says.

'It's vivid,' says Jimmy.

'Like a rock star,' says Rhino. 'Kinda.'

'Good camouflage,' says Shackleton.

'They'll think you're a hibiscus,' says Crozier.

'This is a rifle,' says Toby. 'I'm the only one here who knows how to use it. So button up.' They all grin.

Then they set forth.

The three Pigoon scouts are out in front, snuffling along the ground. To either side of them, two more act as outriders, testing the air with the wet disks of their snouts. Odour radar, thinks Toby. What vibrations well beyond our blunted senses are they picking up? As falcons are to sight, these are to scent.

Six younger Pigoons – barely more than shoats – are running messages between the scouts and outriders and the main van of older and heavier Pigoons: the tank battalion, had they been armoured vehicles. Despite their bulk, they can move surprisingly fast. At the moment they're keeping a steady pace, conserving their energy: a marathon gait, not a sprint. There's not much grunting going on, and no squealing: like soldiers on a long march, they're saving their breath. Their tails are curled but inactive, their pink ears are aimed forward. Lit by the morning sun, they look almost like a cartoon version of cute, huggable, smiling pigs, Valentine pigs clutching red heart-shaped candy boxes, the kind with Cupid wings: If This Little Piggie Could Fly He'd Bring You My Love!

But only almost. These pigs aren't smiling.

If we were carrying a flag, thinks Toby, what would be on it?

At first the going is easy. They cross the flattened part of the meadow, which still has a few handbags and boots and bones poking out of the ground from where the plague victims had fallen. If they'd been covered by weeds these objects might have tripped up the marchers, but because they're visible they're easy to avoid.

The Mo'Hairs have been turned loose and are grazing on the far edge of the meadowland that's been left for pasture. Five young Pigoons have been deputized to watch over them. They don't seem to be taking their duties very seriously, which means they smell no danger. Three are rooting around in the plant life, one is rolling in a damp patch of mud, and the fifth is dozing. Would the five of them be a match for a liobam, should one attack? No doubt of it. A pair of liobams? Possibly even that. But before they'd even get close, the youngsters would have the entire Mo'Hair flock rounded up and trotting back to the Spa.

After leaving the meadow the procession takes the roadway to the north, cutting through the forest that borders the AnooYoo grounds and conceals its perimeter fence. The northern gate-house is deserted: no sign of life in or around it, apart from a rakunk that's sunning itself on the walkway. It stands up as they approach but doesn't bother to run away. Overly friendly, those animals: in a harsher world they'd all be hats by now.

The city streets that come next are harder to navigate. Crashed and deserted vehicles clog the pavement, which is littered with shattered glass and twists of metal. Already the kudzu vines are thrusting in, covering the broken shapes with a soft fledging of green. The Pigoons pick their way daintily, avoiding injury to their trotters; the humans have thick foot-gear. Still, they need to proceed carefully and glance down often.

*

Toby has anticipated the problems Blackbeard might have on these streets, with their shards and cutting edges. True, his feet have an extra-thick layer of skin on them, and that's fine for earth and sand and even pebbles; but, as a precaution, Toby has rummaged through the MaddAddamites' stockpile of gleaned footgear and fitted Blackbeard with a pair of Hermes Trismegistus cross-trainers. At first he was very worried about putting such things on his feet – would they hurt, would they stick to him, would he ever be able to get them off? But Toby showed him how to put them on and then take them off again, and said that if his feet got cut by sharp things he wouldn't be able to come any farther, and then who would be able to tell them what the Pigoons were thinking? So after several practice sessions he has agreed to wear them. The shoes have appliquéd green wings on them and lights that flash with every step he takes – the batteries haven't run down yet – and he is now perhaps a little too delighted with them.

He's up at the front of the main body, listening to the intelligence reports of the Pigoon scouts, if you could call it listening: receiving them, in any case, however he does that. Evidently he hasn't learned anything yet that's important enough to pass along. He glances back now and then, keeping track of Zeb, and also of Toby. There's that jaunty little wave of his hand again, which must mean *All is well.* Or maybe just *I see you,* or *Here I am,* or even, just possibly, *Look at my cool shoes!* His high, clear singing comes to her on the air in short bursts: the Morse code of Crakerdom.

The Pigoons alongside tilt their heads to look up at their human allies from time to time, but their thoughts can only be guessed. Compared with them, humans on foot must seem like slowpokes. Are they irritated? Solicitous? Impatient? Glad of the artillery support? All of those, no doubt, since they have human brain tissue and can therefore juggle several contradictions at once.

They appear to have assigned three guards to each of the gunbearers. The guards don't crowd, they don't herd or dictate, but they keep within a two-yard radius of their charges, their ears swivelling watchfully. The MaddAddamites without spray-guns have one Pigoon each. Jimmy, on the other hand, has five. Are they conscious of his fragility? So far he's been keeping up, but he's beginning to sweat.

Toby drops back to check on him. She hands him her water bottle: he seems already to have emptied his own. All eight Pigoons – her three, his five – shift their positions to surround both of them.

'The Great Wall of Pork,' says Jimmy. 'The Bacon Brigade. The Hoplites of Ham.'

'Hoplites?' says Toby.

'It was a Greek thing,' says Jimmy. 'Citizens' army type of arrangement. A wall of interlocked shields. I read it in a book.' He's a little short of breath.

'Maybe it's an honour guard,' says Toby. 'Are you okay?'

'These things make me nervous,' says Jimmy. 'How do we know they aren't leading us astray so they can ambush us and gobble our giblets?'

'We don't know that,' says Toby. 'But I'd say the odds are against it. They've already had the opportunity.'

'Occam's razor,' says Jimmy. He coughs.

'Pardon?' says Toby.

'It was a Crake thing,' says Jimmy sadly. 'Given two possibilities, you take the simplest. Crake would have said "the most elegant." The prick.'

'Who was Occam?' says Toby. Is that a slight limp?

'Some kind of a monk,' says Jimmy. 'Or bishop. Or maybe a smart pig. Occ Ham.' He laughs. 'Sorry. Bad joke.'

They walk on for a block or two in silence. Then Jimmy says, 'Sliding down the razor blade of life.'

'Excuse me?' Toby says. She'd like to feel his forehead. Is he running a temperature?

'It's an old saying,' says Jimmy. 'It means you're on the edge. Plus, you may get your nuts sliced off.' He's limping more visibly now.

'Is your foot all right?' Toby asks. No answer: he stumps doggedly onward. 'Maybe you should go back,' she says.

'No fucking way,' says Jimmy.

The street ahead is blocked by the rubble from a partially fallen condo. There's been a fire in it – most likely caused by an electrical short, says Zeb, who has halted the march while the scouts reconnoitre a detour. The smell of burning is still in the air. The Pigoons don't like it: several of them snort.

Jimmy sits down on the ground.

'What?' says Zeb to Toby.

'His foot again,' says Toby. 'Or something.'

'So, we need to send him back to the Spa.'

'He won't go,' says Toby.

Jimmy's five Pigoons are snuffling at him, but from a respectful distance. One of them moves forward to sniff his foot. Now two of them nudge him, one on either arm.

'Get away!' says Jimmy. 'What do they want?'

'Blackbeard, please,' says Toby, beckoning him over. He huddles with the Pigoons. There's a silent interchange, followed by a few notes of music.

'Snowman-the-Jimmy must ride,' says Blackbeard. 'They say his . . . ' There's a word Toby can't decipher, that sounds like a grunt and a rumble. 'They say that part of him is strong. In the middle he is strong, but his feet are weak. They will carry him.'

One of the Pigoons steps forward, not the fattest. She lowers herself beside Jimmy.

'They want me to do what?' says Jimmy.

'Please, Oh Snowman-the-Jimmy,' says Blackbeard. 'They say you must lie down on the back and hold on to the ears. Two others will go beside you to keep you from falling off.'

'This is dumb,' says Jimmy. 'I'll slide off!'

'That's your only option,' says Zeb. 'Catch a ride, or else you stay here.'

Once Jimmy is in position, Zeb says, 'Got any of that rope? It might help a bit.'

Jimmy is tied onto the Pigoon like a parcel, and they all set off once more. 'So, its name is Dancer, or Prancer, or what?' says Jimmy. 'Think I should pat it?'

'Please, Oh Snowman-the-Jimmy, thank you,' says Blackbeard. 'The Pig Ones are telling me that a scratching behind the ears is a good thing.'

When reciting the story in later years, Toby liked to say that the Pigoon carrying Snowman-the-Jimmy flew like the wind. It was the sort of thing that should be said of a fallen comrade-in-arms, and especially one that performed such an important service – a service that resulted, not incidentally, in the saving of Toby's own life. For if Snowman-the-Jimmy had not been transported by the Pigoon, would Toby be sitting here among them tonight, wearing the red hat and telling them this story? No, she would not. She would be composting under an elderberry bush, and assuming a different form. A very different form indeed, she would think to herself privately.

So, in her story, the Pigoon in question flew like the wind.

The telling was complicated by the fact that Toby could not pronounce the flying Pigoon's name in any way that resembled the grunt-heavy original. But nobody in the Craker audience seemed to mind, though they laughed at her a little. The children made up a game in which one of them played the heroic Pigoon flying like the wind, wearing a determined expression, and a smaller one played Snowman-the-Jimmy, also with a determined expression, clinging to its back.

Her back. The Pigoons were not objects. She had to get that right. It was only respectful.

At the time, things are somewhat different. The progress of the Jimmy-porting Pigoon is lumpy, and its back is rounded and slippery. Jimmy bumps up and down, and is in danger of sliding off, first on one side, then on the other. When this happens the flanking Pigoons give him a sharp upward nudge with their snouts, under the armpits, which causes him to yell maniacally because it tickles.

'For fuck's sake, can't you get him to shut up?' says Zeb. 'We might as well be playing the bagpipes.'

'He can't help it,' says Toby. 'It's a reflex.'

'If I bonk him on the head, that'll be a reflex too,' says Zeb.

'They probably know we're coming,' says Toby. 'They may have seen the scouts.'

They're following the lead of the Pigoons, but it's Jimmy who provides the verbal guidelines. 'We're still in the pleebs,' he says. 'I remember this part.' Then: 'We're coming up to No Man's Land, cleared buffer zone before the Compounds.'

Then: 'Main security perimeter coming up.' After a while: 'Over there, CryoJeenyus. Next up, Genie-Gnomes. Look at that fucking light-up genie sign! The solar must still be working.'

Then: 'Here comes the biggie. The RejoovenEsense Compound.' Crows on the wall: four, no, five. One crow, sorrow, Pilar used to say; more, and they were protectors, or else tricksters, take your choice. Two of the crows lift off, circle overhead, sizing them up.

The Rejoov gates stand open. Inside, dead houses, dead malls, dead labs, dead everything. Tatters of cloth, derelict solar-cars.

'Thank God for the pigs,' says Jimmy. 'Without them, needle in a haystack. The place is a labyrinth.'

But the Pigoons are sure of the trail. They trot steadily forward, not hesitating. A corner turned, another corner.

'There it is,' says Jimmy. 'Up ahead. The gates of Paradice.'

Eggshell

Crake had planned the Paradice Project himself. There was a tight security perimeter around it, in addition to the Rejoov barrier wall. Inside that was a park, a microclimate-modifying planting of mixed tropical splices, tolerant alike to drought and downpour. At the centre of it all was the Paradice dome, climate-controlled, airlocked, an impenetrable eggshell harbouring Crake's treasure trove, his brave new humans. And at the very centre of the dome he'd placed the artificial ecosystem where the Crakers themselves in all their strange perfection had been brought into being and set to live and breathe.

They reach the perimeter gate, stop to reconnoitre. No one in the gatehouses to either side, according to the Pigoons: their inactive tails and ears are semaphoring as much.

Zeb signals a rest stop: they need to gather their energy. The humans resort to their water bottles and eat half a Joltbar each. The Pigoons have found an avomango tree and are gobbling down the windfalls, the orange ovals pulped by their jaws, the fatty seeds crushed. Fermented sweetness fills the air.

I hope they aren't getting drunk, thinks Toby. That wouldn't be good, drunk Pigoons. 'How are you doing?' she asks Jimmy.

'I remember this place,' says Jimmy. 'In every detail. Shit. I wish I didn't.'

Ahead of them is the roadway leading through the forest. Untrimmed branches reach into the corridor of light above it, opportunist weeds push into it from the margins, renegade vines overhang it. Out of the swelling foam of vegetation the curved dome rises like the white half-eye of a sedated patient. It must once have seemed so bright and shining, that dome; so much like a harvest moon, or like a hopeful sunrise, but without the burning rays. Now it looks barren. More than that, it looks like a trap: for who can tell what's hidden in it, and what's hiding?

But that's only because of what we know, thinks Toby. There's nothing in the image itself that would signal death to an innocent observer.

'Oh Toby!' says Blackbeard. 'Look! It is the Egg! The Egg where Crake made us!'

'Do you remember it?' says Toby.

'I don't know,' says Blackbeard. 'Not very much. Trees were growing in it. It rained, but it did not thunder. Oryx came to visit us every day. She taught us many things. We were happy.'

'It might not be the same any more,' says Toby.

'Oryx is not there,' says Blackbeard. 'She flew out because she wanted to help Snowman-the-Jimmy when he was sick, didn't she?'

'Yes, I'm sure she did,' says Toby.

The young Pigoon scouts have been sent ahead to sniff out possible roadside ambushes. They're racing back now, along the leaf-strewn asphalt. Their ears are back, their tails out straight behind them: cause for alarm.

The elders leave their rooting party among the fallen

avomangoes; Blackbeard runs over to them; there's a quick huddle. The MaddAddamites gather around. 'What's up?' Zeb asks.

'They say the bad ones are near the Egg,' says Blackbeard. 'Three. One with ropes tied on. He has white feathers on his face.'

'What's he wearing?' Toby asks. Is it for instance a caftan, like those Adam One always wore? But how to ask that? She revises: 'Does he have a second skin?'

'Shit,' says Jimmy. 'Keep them out of the emergency storeroom! They'll get all the sprayguns, and then we're toast!'

'Yes, he has a second skin, like you,' says Blackbeard. 'Only not pink. It is different colours. It is dirty. He has only one of these, on his foot. A shoe.'

'How'll we do that?' says Rhino. 'We can't move fast enough.'

'We send some of the pigs,' says Zeb. 'The faster ones. They can cut through the woods.'

'Then what?' says Rhino. 'They can't hold the main door. Those guys have a spraygun. We don't know how much of their cellpack is left.'

'We can't just let the Pigoons be shot down like rats in a barrel,' says Toby. 'Jimmy. When you go through the Paradice entranceway, where's the storeroom?'

'There's the two doors, the airlock door, the inner one. They're both open, I left them open. You go down the hall to the left, take a right, another left. The fucking pigs need to get into that room and hold the door shut from the inside.'

'Okay, how do we tell them this?' says Zeb. 'Toby?'

'Right and left could be a problem,' says Toby. 'I don't think the Crakers know about those.'

'Think hard,' says Zeb. 'Clock's ticking.'

'Blackbeard?' says Toby. 'This is a picture of the Egg, if you were up at the top looking down at it.' She draws a round circle in the dirt, with a stick. 'Do you see?'

Blackbeard looks at it and nods, though not with much assurance. We hang by a thread, thinks Toby. 'Good,' she says with false heartiness. 'Can you say this to the Pig Ones? Tell them they need to run very fast. Five of them, through the trees. They need to go past the bad men, right into the Egg. Then they need to go here' – she traces with the stick – 'and in here. That right?' she asks Jimmy.

'Right enough,' says Jimmy.

'They need to shut the door. They need to lean against it, to keep the bad ones from going into that room,' says Toby. 'Can you tell them all of that?'

Blackbeard looks puzzled. 'Why do the men want to go into the Egg?' he asks. 'The Egg is for making. They are already made.'

'They want to find some killing things,' says Toby. 'The sticks that make holes.'

'But the Egg is good. It does not have killing things.'

'It does now,' says Toby. 'We have to hurry. Can you tell them?'

'I will try,' says Blackbeard. He kneels on the ground. Two of the largest Pigoons lower their huge heads, one to either side of his face. There's a white tusk right beside his neck. Toby shivers. He begins to sing while tracing over Toby's marks in the sand with her stick. The Pigoons sniff at the diagram. Oh no, thinks Toby. This isn't going to work. They think it's something to eat.

But then the Pigoons lift their snouts and move to join the others. Low grunting, restless tail movements. Indecision?

Five of the medium-sized ones detach from the group and head off at a canter, two to the left of the road, three to the right. The undergrowth swallows them up.

'Looks like they got it,' says Rhino. Zeb grins.

'Good,' he says to Toby. 'Always knew you had potential.'

'They are going to the Egg,' says Blackbeard. 'They say they will not move too close to those men. They will be careful about the stick things, with blood coming out.'

'Hope they make it,' says Zeb. 'Let's hike.'

'It's not far,' says Jimmy. 'Anyway, they can't shoot us from the windows because there aren't any windows.' He laughs feebly.

'Zeb?' says Toby as they move off down the road. 'The third guy? I'm not sure. But I think it's Adam One.'

'Yeah, I know,' says Zeb. 'I figured that for a while.'

'What can we do to get him back?'

'They'll want to trade him,' says Zeb.

'For what?'

'Sprayguns, supposing the pigs block them out. Other stuff.'

'Like, for instance?'

'Like, for instance, you,' says Zeb. 'In their place, it's what I'd do.'

Right, thinks Toby. They'll want revenge.

The Paradice dome lies in front of them. All is silent. The airlock door is open. Three shoats go through it, then come out again. 'They are inside, the men,' says Blackbeard. 'But far inside. Not near the door.'

'I need to go in first,' says Jimmy. 'Just for a minute.' Toby stays close behind him.

There are two destroyed skeletons on the floor of the airlock. The bones have been gnawed and jumbled, no doubt by animals. Rags of mouldering cloth, a small pink and red sandal.

Jimmy falls to his knees; his hands are over his face. Toby touches his shoulder. 'We need to go now,' she says, but he says, 'Leave me alone!'

There's a dirty pink ribbon tied in the long black hair of one of the skulls: hair decays very slowly, the Gardeners always said.

Jimmy unties the bow, twists the ribbon in his fingers. 'Oryx. Oh God,' he says. 'You fucker, Crake! You didn't have to kill her!'

Zeb is standing beside Toby now. 'Maybe she was already sick,' he says to Jimmy. 'Maybe he couldn't live without her. Come on, we need to get in there.'

'Oh fuck, spare me the fucking clichés!' says Jimmy.

'We can just leave him here for now, he'll be safe; let's go in,' says Toby. 'We need to be sure they didn't get into the storage room.'

The others are right outside the doorway – the Madd-Addamites, the main body of the Pigoons. 'What's up?' says Rhino.

Little Blackbeard is tugging at her hand. 'Please, Oh Toby, what is *clichés*?' he says.

Toby hardly knows what she answers, because now the truth is hitting him: Oryx and Crake are these skeletons. He heard Jimmy say that; it registered. He turns his frightened face up to her: she can see the sudden fall, the crash, the damage.

'Oh Toby, is this Oryx, and is this Crake?' he says. 'Snowman-the-Jimmy said! But they are a smelly bone, they are many smelly bones! Oryx and Crake must be beautiful! Like the stories! They cannot be a smelly bone!' He begins to cry as if his heart will break.

Toby kneels, folds her arms around him, hugs him tight. What to say? How to comfort him? In the face of this terminal sorrow.

The Story of the Battle

Toby cannot tell the story tonight. She is too sad, because of the dead ones. The ones who became dead, in the battle. So now I will try to tell this story to you. I will tell it in the right way, if I can.

First I am putting the red hat on my head, the hat of Snowman-the-Jimmy. These markings on it – look, it is a voice, and it is saying: RED. And it is saying: SOX.

SOX is a special word of Crake. We do not know what it means. Toby does not know either. Maybe we will know later.

But see – the red hat is on my head, and it does not hurt me. I am not growing an extra skin, I have my own skin, the same. I can take the hat off, I can put it back on again. It does not stick to my head.

Now I will eat the fish. We do not eat a fish, or a smelly bone; that is not what we eat. It is a hard thing to do, eating a fish. But I must do it. Crake did many hard things for us, when he was on the earth in the form of a person. He cleared away the chaos for us, and . . .

You do not have to sing.

. . . and he did many other hard things, so I will try to do this hard thing of eating the smelly bone fish. It is cooked. It is very small. Perhaps it will be enough for Crake if I put it into my mouth and take it out again.

There.

I am sorry for making the noises of a sick person.

Please take the fish away and throw it into the forest. The ants will be happy. The maggots will be happy. The vultures will be happy.

Yes, it does taste very bad. It tastes like the smell of a smelly bone, or the smell of a dead one. I will chew many leaves to get rid of that taste. But if I did not do the hard thing with the bad taste, I would not be able to hear the story Crake is telling me, and then tell it to you. That is the way it was with Snowman-the-Jimmy, and that is the way it is with Toby. The hard thing of eating the fish, the smelly bone taste – that is what needs to be done. First the bad things, then the story.

Thank you for the purring. I am not feeling so sick now.

This is the Story of the Battle. It tells how Zeb and Toby and Snowman-the-Jimmy and the other two-skinned ones and the Pig Ones cleared away the bad men, just as Crake cleared away the people in the chaos to make a good and safe place for us to live.

And Toby and Zeb and Snowman-the-Jimmy and the two-skinned ones and the Pig Ones needed to clear away the bad men, because if they did not do it, our place would never be safe. The bad men would kill us as they killed the Pig One baby, with a knife. Or with a stick that makes holes with blood coming out. So that is why.

Toby told this reason to me. It is a good reason.

And the Pig Ones helped them, because they did not want any more of their Pig One babies to be killed with a knife. Or a stick thing. Or in any other way, such as a rope.

The Pig Ones can smell better than any. We can smell better than the ones with two skins, but the Pig Ones can smell better than us. So they helped, by smelling the footprints of the bad men, and showing where they had gone. And by helping to chase after them.

And I was there too, so that I could tell the others what the Pig Ones were saying. I had shoes on my feet. You see those shoes, they are here, see? They have lights on them, and wings. They are a special thing from Crake, and I am grateful for having them, and I say, Thank you. But I do not need to put them on unless there is danger, and other bad men that must be cleared away. So I do not have them on my feet right now. But I have them here beside me, because they are part of the story.

But that time I put those shoes on my feet, and we walked a long way, into the place where the buildings are, where we do not go because they can fall down. But I went there that time, and I saw many things. I saw things left over from the chaos, many. I saw empty buildings, many. I saw empty skins, many. I saw metal and glass things, many. And the Pig Ones carried Snowman-the-Jimmy.

Then the Pig Ones were following the bad men with their noses, and they found where they had gone. And the bad men went into the Egg, even though the Egg should only be for making, not for killing. And some of the Pig Ones went into the Egg also, to the room where the killing things were, so the bad men could not get those things. So the bad men were running, and they were hiding inside the Egg, in the hallways of the Egg. And at first we could not see them.

The Egg was dark, not light, as it used to be. We could see when we were inside the Egg, I do not mean that kind of dark. The Egg had a dark feeling. It had a dark smell.

And Snowman-the-Jimmy went into the first doorway of the Egg, and he found a pile of smelly bones and another pile of smelly bones, all mixed together, and he was very sad, and he fell down onto his knees, and he cried. And Toby wanted to purr on him, but he said, 'Leave me alone!'

And then he took a pink twisty thing from the hair of one of the smelly bone piles, and he held it in his hands, and he said, 'Oryx. Oh God.' And then he said, 'You fucker, Crake! You didn't have to kill her!'

And Toby and Zeb were there. And Zeb said, 'Maybe she was already sick. Maybe he couldn't live without her.' And Snowman-the-Jimmy said, 'Oh Fuck, spare me the fucking clichés!'

And I said to Toby, 'What is *clichés*?' And Toby said that it was a word to help people get through a trouble when they couldn't think of anything else. And I hoped that Fuck was flying very quickly to help Snowman-the-Jimmy, because he was in very much trouble.

And I was in very much trouble too, because Snowman-the-Jimmy said these bone piles were Oryx and Crake. And I felt a very bad feeling, and I was frightened. And I said, 'Oh Toby, is this Oryx, and is this Crake? But they are a smelly bone, they are many smelly bones! Oryx and Crake must be beautiful! Like the stories! They cannot be a smelly bone!' And I cried, because they were dead ones, very dead ones, and all fallen apart.

But Toby said the bone piles were not the real Oryx and Crake any more, they were only husks, like an eggshell.

And the Egg wasn't the real Egg, the way it is in the stories. It was only an eggshell, like the shells that are broken and left behind when the birds hatch out of them. And we ourselves were like the birds, so we did not need the broken eggshell any more, did we?

And Oryx and Crake had different forms now, not dead ones, and they are good and kind. And beautiful. The way we know, from the stories.

So I felt better then.

Please do not sing yet.

And then after that we went all the way into the Egg. It was not bright there but it was not dark either, because the sun shone through the eggshell. But the feeling of darkness was all the way through the air. And then they were having a battle. A *battle* is when some wish to clear others away, and the others want to clear them away as well.

We do not have battles. We do not eat a fish. We do not eat a smelly bone. Crake made us that way. Yes, good, kind Crake.

But Crake made the two-skinned ones so they could have a battle. He made the Pig Ones that way too. They do a battle with their tusks, and the others do a battle with the sticks that punch holes and blood comes out. That is how they are made.

I don't know why Crake made them that way.

The Pig Ones chased the bad men. They chased them through the hallways, and they chased them into the centre of the Egg, where there were many dead trees. Not as when we were made there: then, there were trees with many leaves, and beautiful water, and it rained, and the stars were shining in the sky. But now there were no stars, only a ceiling.

The Pig Ones told me later of all the places where they chased the bad men. Toby would not let me go with them because she said I might get holes with blood, or else the bad ones might grab hold of me, and that would be worse. So I could not see everything that happened, but there was shouting, and the Pig Ones were screaming, and it hurt my ears. Pig One voices when screaming are very, very loud.

And there was the sound of galloping, and footsteps with

shoes on. And then it would be silent, and that was when thinking was happening: the thinking of the bad ones, and the thinking of the Pig Ones, and the thinking of Zeb, and Toby, and Rhino. They wanted the Pig Ones to chase the bad men past where they were so they could make holes in them with the sticks, but it did not happen. There were many, many hallways inside the Egg.

And one of the Pig Ones came and told me that there were only two bad men being chased through the hallways. But three had gone into the Egg. And the third one was above us: they could smell him. He was above us, but they did not know where.

And I told that to Zeb and Toby, and Zeb said, 'They've stashed Adam on the second floor somewhere. Where's the stairs?' And Snowman-the-Jimmy said there were fire stairs in four places. And Toby said, 'Can you take us there?' And Snowman-the-Jimmy said, 'So you go up one stairway and they come down another stairway and run away, and then what?' And Zeb said, 'Shit.'

Three of the Pig Ones became hurt when they were chasing the bad men in the hallways, and one of them fell down and did not get up again. It was the one who carried Snowman-the-Jimmy. And I saw that part of the battle, and I made the noises of a sick person. And I cried.

Then the two bad men ran up some of the stairs. *Stairs* are – I will tell you what stairs are later. But the Pig Ones cannot climb stairs. And when the bad ones reached the top, we could not see them.

And Zeb and Toby and the other two-skinned people told me to tell the Pig Ones to find the other stair places, and to scream if the bad ones tried to come down. Then they brought wood in from outside, and they made a fire, with smoke. And the smoke went up the stairs. And they put cloths over their faces and waited near the bottom of the stairs where the men had run up, and when there was much smoke – very much smoke, I saw it, I coughed! – two of the bad men came to the top of the stairs, and they were pushing the third man in front of them, and holding him by the arms, one on each side. And he had ropes on his hands. And he had only one shoe. On his foot. But that shoe did not have wings, and lights. Not like the shoes here, that were on my feet.

And Toby said, 'Adam!'

And that one began to say something, and a bad one hit him, the one with short feathers on his face. Then the bad one with the long feathers said, 'Let us past or he gets it.' And I did not know what he would get.

And Zeb said, 'Okay, free pass, hand him over.' And the other bad man said, 'Throw in the bitch, and we'll take the sprayguns too. And call off the fucking pigs!'

But the man Adam with the ropes on his hands shook his head, which meant no. And then he pulled away from them where they were holding him by the tops of the arms, and he jumped forward, and he fell, and he rolled down the stairs. And one of the bad men made a hole in him with his stick.

And Zeb ran forward to Adam, and Toby raised her gun thing and pointed it, and it made a sound, and the bad man that made the hole in Adam dropped the stick; and he fell down, holding on to his leg and screaming.

And Toby wanted to run to help Zeb with the man Adam, at the bottom of the stairs, and Snowman-the-Jimmy was trying to hold her back with one hand on her pink second skin. And Snowman-the-Jimmy pushed me behind him, but I could still see.

The other bad man was partway behind a wall, but his head

and arm came out, and he had the stick now, and he was pointing it at Toby. But Snowman-the-Jimmy saw it, and he went very fast in front of her, and he had the holes punched in him instead. And he fell down too, with blood coming out, and he did not get up.

And then Zeb used his stick thing, and the second bad man dropped his own stick thing and took hold of his own arm. And he screamed as well. And I put my hands over my ears because there was so much pain. It hurt me very much.

And Rhino and Shackleton and the other ones with two skins went up the stairs, and caught the two men, and tied them with ropes, and pulled them down the stairs. But Zeb and Toby were with Adam, and also with Snowman-the-Jimmy. And they were sad.

And we all went outside the Egg, which had smoke coming out, and then flames. And we walked very fast away from it. And there were some loud noises from inside.

And Zeb was carrying Adam, who was very thin and white-looking; and Adam was still breathing. And Zeb said, 'I've got you, best buddy. You're gonna be okay.' But his face was all wet.

And Adam said, 'I'll be fine. Pray for me.' And he smiled at Zeb and said, 'Don't worry. I wouldn't have lasted long. Plant a good tree.'

And I said to Toby, 'Oh Toby, who is *Bestbuddy*? This one is Adam, that is his name, you said so.'

And Toby said that Bestbuddy was another name for *brother*, because Adam was the brother of Zeb.

But after that, the man Adam stopped breathing.

*

And it was evening, and we walked slowly back, with the bad men being carried by the Pig Ones because of the holes in them, and the ropes. The Pig Ones were angry because of the deads, and they wanted to stick their tusks into those men, and roll on them, and trample on them, but Zeb said it was not the time.

And Snowman-the-Jimmy and Adam were carried too, and the dead Pig One. And in the night we reached the building where the children were, and the mothers, and the Mo'Hairs, and the Pig One mothers and babies, and the other two-skinned ones – Ren and Amanda and Swift Fox and Ivory Bill and Rebecca, and the others. And they came to meet us, and all of the people said very many things, such as 'I was so worried' and 'What happened?' and 'Oh God!'

And we, the Children of Crake, we sang together.

We slept there that night, and ate. And all who had been in the battle were very tired. They talked in low voices, and looked very carefully at the dead one Adam, and said he was not dead because of the chaos-clearing seed that Crake made but because of the holes with blood coming out. And they said anyway that it was a mercy that he was not dead of the Crake seed thing.

I will ask Toby later what a *mercy* is. She is tired now, she is sleeping.

And they wrapped the man Adam in a pink bedsheet, with a pink pillow under his head, and they were very quiet and sad. And some of the Pig Ones went swimming in the pool, which they liked very much.

And the next day we walked here, to the cobb house. And the Pig Ones carried Adam, on branches, with flowers, and the dead Pig One too, which was harder for them because she was big and heavy.

And they carried Snowman-the-Jimmy in the same way, though he was not dead, not when we began to walk. And Ren walked beside him, holding his hand and crying, because she was his friend; and Crozier walked on the other side of her, and he helped her.

But Snowman-the-Jimmy was travelling in his head, far, far away, as he had travelled before, when he was in the hammock and we purred. But this time he went so far away that he could not come back.

And Oryx was there with him, and she was helping him. I heard him talking to her, just before he went too far, out of sight, and stopped breathing. And now he is with Oryx. And with Crake too.

That is the Story of the Battle.

Now we can sing.

Moontime

Trial

The next morning they hold a trial.

They sit around the dining table – or the MaddAddamites and the God's Gardeners sit. The Pigoons sprawl on the grass and pebbles; the Crakers graze nearby, chewing their eternal mouthfuls of leaf, taking it all in.

The prisoners themselves are not present. They don't need to be there: what they've done isn't in question. The trial is about the verdict only.

'So, we're here to decide their fates,' says Zeb. 'Worse luck we didn't blow them away in the heat of the proceedings, but since we didn't, we have to make some decisions in cold blood. Vote now, or is there any discussion?'

Toby says, 'Are they common prisoners? Or prisoners of war? Because it's different, no?' She feels impelled to advocate for them in some way, but why? Is it simply because they don't have a lawyer?

'How about soul-dead neurotrash?' says Rebecca.

'Fellow human beings,' says White Sedge. 'Though I realize that this in itself is not a defence.'

'They killed our brother,' says Shackleton.

'Scumsucking fuckbuckets,' says Crozier.

'Rapists and murderers,' says Amanda.

'They shot Jimmy,' says Ren, starting to cry. Amanda puts an arm around her, gives her a hug. She herself is not crying: she looks flinty-eyed, like a wood carving of herself. She'd make a good executioner, thinks Toby.

'Who cares what we call them,' says Rhino. 'So long as it's not *people*.'

Hard to choose a label, thinks Toby: three sessions in the once notorious Painball Arena have scraped all modifying labels away from them, bleached them of language. Triple Painball survivors have long been known to be not quite human.

'I vote for all of the above,' says Zeb. 'Now let's get on with it.'

White Sedge enters a halfhearted clemency plea. 'We shouldn't judge,' she says. 'Surely their viciousness is a result of what was done to them earlier in their lives, by others. And considering the plasticity of the brain and how their behaviour was shaped by harsh experience, how are we to know that they had any control over what they did?'

'Are you fucking serious?' says Shackleton. 'They ate my little brother's fucking kidneys! They butchered him like a Mo'Hair! I want to rip out all their teeth! Through their assholes,' he adds, perhaps unnecessarily.

'Let's not get too fired up,' says Zeb. 'Hold the outrage. We all have cause. Though some more than others.' He looks older, thinks Toby. Older and grimmer. Finding Adam and then losing him again has dragged him down. We're all in mourning: even the Pigoons. Their tails are drooping, their ears are limp; they nuzzle one another in a consoling way.

'We shouldn't fight over what should be a purely philosophical and practical decision,' says Ivory Bill. 'The question is, do we have the facilities for correctional guardianship, or, on the other hand, the theoretical justification for . . .'

'It's not a time for hair-splitting,' says Zeb.

'Taking life under any circumstances is reprehensible,' says White Sedge. 'We shouldn't let our own moral standards slip, just because –'

'Just because most of the human race has been wiped out and the surviving remnant can hardly get enough solar going to run a light bulb?' says Shackleton. 'So you want to let these two cesspools bash your brains out?'

'I don't know why you're being so hostile,' says White Sedge. 'Adam One would have advocated clemency.'

'Maybe he'd have been wrong,' says Amanda. 'You weren't there, you don't know what they did to us. Me and Ren. You don't know what they're like.'

'Though, with so few true humans left,' says Ivory Bill, 'perhaps we shouldn't waste any increasingly rare human DNA. Even if the individuals in question must be eliminated, possibly their . . . their generative fluids should be, as it were, siphoned off, to provide genetic variety. An ingrown gene pool must be avoided.'

'Avoid it yourself,' says Swift Fox. 'Personally, the mere idea of having sex with those two festering bedsores just to capture their rancid DNA makes me nauseous.'

'You wouldn't need to have sex with them, as such,' says Ivory Bill. 'We could use a turkey baster.'

'Use it on your own self,' says Swift Fox rudely. 'Men are always telling women what to do with their uteruses. Excuse me, their uteri.'

'I'd rather slit my wrists than let any of their fucking generative fluids near me ever again,' says Amanda. 'It's bad enough as it is. How do I know my own kid won't be one of theirs?'

'Anyway, a child with such warped genes would be a monster,' says Ren. 'The mother couldn't love it. Oh, sorry,' she says to Amanda.

'It's okay,' says Amanda. 'If it's theirs, I'll hand it over to White

Sedge and she can love it. Or the Pigoons can eat the thing; they'd appreciate it.'

'We could try rehabilitation,' says White Sedge serenely. 'Incorporate them into the community, keep them in a safe place at night, let them help out. Sometimes, when people feel they can contribute, it makes for a genuine change in . . . '

'Look around,' Zeb says. 'See any social workers? See any jails?'

'Contribute to what?' says Amanda. 'You want to let them be in charge of the day care?'

'They'd put everyone else at risk,' says Katuro.

'There's no safe place to store them except a hole in the ground,' says Shackleton.

'The vote,' says Zeb.

They use pebbles: black for death, white for mercy. It has an archeological feel. The old symbol systems follow us around, thinks Toby, as she collects the pebbles in Jimmy's red hat. There's only one white pebble.

The Pigoons vote collectively, through their leader, with Blackbeard as their interpreter. 'They all say *dead,*' he tells Toby. 'But they will not eat those ones. They do not want those ones to be part of them.'

The rest of the Crakers are puzzled. They clearly do not understand what *vote* means, or *trial,* or why pebbles should be put into the hat of Snowman-the-Jimmy. Toby tells them it is a thing of Crake.

The Story of the Trial

The two bad men were put in a room at night, with ropes tying them. We could feel that the rope was hurting them, and making them sad and also angry. But we did not untie the rope the way we did before. Toby told us not to, because it would only cause more killing. And we told the children not to go too close, because the bad ones might bite them.

And then they were given soup, with a smelly bone.

In the morning there was a Trial. You all saw it. It was at the table. Many words were said. The Pig Ones were also at the Trial.

Perhaps we will understand it later, this Trial.

And after the Trial, all the Pig Ones went down to the seashore. And Toby went with them, and she had her gun thing that we should not touch. And Zeb went. And Amanda went, and Ren. And Crozier and Shackleton. But we did not go, we Children of Crake, because Toby said it would be hurtful to us.

And after a while they all came back, without the two bad ones. They looked tired. But they were more peaceful.

Toby said that now we would be safe from the bad ones. And the Pig Ones said their babies were now safe too. And they said also that even though the Battle was over now, they would keep the pact they made with Toby, and with Zeb, and they would not hunt and eat any of the two-skinned ones, and they would also not dig up their garden any more. Or eat the honey of the bees.

And Toby told me the words to say to them, which were: We agree to keep the pact. None of you, or your children, or your children's children, will ever be a smelly bone in a soup. Or a ham, she added. Or a bacon.

And Rebecca said, Worse luck.

And Crozier said, What're they saying, what the fuck is going on? And Toby said, Watch your language, it's confusing for him.

And I said that Crozier did not need to call Fuck right now because we were not in trouble and did not need his help. And Toby said, That's right, he doesn't like to be summoned on trivial matters. And Zeb coughed.

After the Pig Ones had gone away, Toby told us that the two bad men had been washed away in the sea. They had been poured away, as Crake poured away the chaos. So everything was much cleaner now.

Yes, good, kind Crake.

Please don't sing.

Because when you sing I can't hear the words that Crake is telling me to say, and also when we sing about him he can't tell me any words of the story, because he has to listen to the singing.

So that is the Story of the Trial. It is a thing from Crake. We do not have to have a Trial, among us. Only the two-skinned ones and the Pig Ones have to have a Trial.

And that is a good thing, because I did not like the Trial.

Thank you. Good night.

Rites

The Feast of Cnidaria, Toby writes. Waxing gibbous moon.

The Cnidaria phylum contains the jellyfish, the corals, the sea anemones, and the hydra. The Gardeners had been thorough – no phylum or genus was left out of their list of feasts and festivals, if they could help it – though some celebrations had been odder than others. The Festival of Intestinal Parasites, for instance, had been memorable, though not what you would call delightful.

The Feast of Cnidaria, however, had been an especially beautiful one. There had been paper lanterns in the shapes of jellyfish, and many decorations fashioned from objects found in dumpsters. A creative use was made of spent balloons and inflated rubber gloves with trailing filaments of string, sea anemones were created from modified round dish-scrubbing brushes, and hydras crafted from transparent plastic sandwich bags.

The children would do a little jellyfish dance, festooned with streamers and waving their arms slowly, and one year they'd composed and performed an interminable play on the subject of the life cycle of the jellyfish, which was uneventful. *First I was an egg, Then I grew and grew, Now I am a jellyfish, Green and pink and blue.* Though when the Portuguese Man O' War had made its entrance, drama had been possible: *I drifted here, I drifted there, My tentacles so fine to view, But don't get tangled up with me, Or I will put an end to you.*

Had Ren helped with that play? Toby wonders. Had Amanda? The song, the grabbing of a smaller child playing a fish, the stinging to death – they had the earmarks of Amanda; or of the streetwise pleebrat Amanda of those days, who, since the disposal of the two malignant Painballers, appears to have been reborn.

'After the disposal of the two malignant Painballers,' she writes. *Disposal* makes them sound like garbage, as in garbage disposal. She wonders if this kind of name-calling is worthy of her one-time position as Eve Six, decides it's not, leaves it anyway.

'After the disposal of the two malignant Painballers, Ren and Shackleton and Amanda and Crozier and I walked back along the AnooYoo forest path. We came to the tree where the Painballers had left poor Oates hanging with his throat slit. There wasn't much left of him – the crows had been assimilating him, and God knows what else – but Shackleton shinnied up the tree and cut the rope, and he and Crozier gathered together the bones of their younger brother and tied them up in a bedsheet.

'Then it was time for the composting. The Pigoons wished to carry Adam and Jimmy to the site for us, as a sign of friendship and interspecies co-operation. They collected more flowers and ferns, which they piled on top of the bodies. Then we walked to the site in procession. The Crakers sang all the way.'

She adds, ' . . . which was somewhat hard on the nerves.' But then, reflecting that Blackbeard is making so much progress in his writing that he might someday be able to read her entries, she scratches it out.

'Following a short discussion, the Pigoons understood that we did not wish to eat Adam and Jimmy, nor would we wish the Pigoons to do that. And they concurred. Their rules in such matters appear complex: dead farrow are eaten by pregnant mothers to provide more protein for growing infants, but adults, and especially adults of note, are contributed to the general ecosystem. All other species are, however, up for grabs.

Amanda added that she did not see a transition through pigshit as an acceptable phase in Jimmy's life cycle, but this remark was not translated by Blackbeard. There was not enough left of Oates for it to be an issue in his case.

'We buried all three of them near Pilar, and planted a tree on top of each. For Jimmy, Ren, Amanda, and Lotis Blue had made a trip to the Botanical Gardens, to the section called Fruits of the World – under the guidance of the Pigoons, who of course knew where it was, being fond of fruit – and had chosen a Kentucky coffeetree, which has heart-shaped leaves and produces berries that can be used as a coffee substitute. Many in our group will be pleased by that, as the roasted-root coffee is beginning to pall.

'For Oates, Crozier and Shackleton chose an oak tree, because it echoed his name. The Pigoons were delighted by that, as later on there would be acorns.

'For Adam One, Zeb as next of kin had the choice of tree. He selected a native crabapple, somewhat biblical – he said – and also fitting. Its apples would have the added virtue of making a good jelly, which would have pleased Adam: the Gardeners, though conscious of symbolism, were practical in such matters.

'The Pigoons had their own funeral rites. They did not bury the dead Pigoon, but set her down in a clearing near one of the park picnic tables. They heaped her with flowers and branches, and stood silently, tails drooping. Then the Crakers sang.'

*

'Oh Toby, what have you been writing?' says Blackbeard, who's come into her cobb-house cubicle – unannounced, as usual – and is now standing at her elbow. He's peering into her face with his large, green, luminous, uncanny eyes.

How had Crake devised those eyes? How do they light up from within like that? Or give the appearance of lighting up. It must be a luminosity feature, perhaps from a deep-sea bioform. She's often wondered.

'I am writing the story,' she says. 'The story of you, and me, and the Pigoons, and everyone. I am writing about how we put Snowman-the-Jimmy and Adam One into the ground, and Oates too, so that Oryx can change them into the form of a tree. And that is a happy thing, isn't it?'

'Yes. It is a happy thing. What is wrong with your eyes, Oh Toby? Are you crying?' says Blackbeard. He touches her eyebrow.

'I'm just a little tired,' says Toby. 'And my eyes are tired as well. Writing makes them tired.'

'I will purr on you,' says Blackbeard.

Among the Crakers, the small children do not purr. Blackbeard is growing quickly – they do grow faster, these children – but is he big enough to purr? Apparently so: already his hands are on her forehead, and the mini-motor sound of Craker purring is filling the air. She's never been purred on before: it's very soothing, she has to admit.

'There,' says Blackbeard. 'Telling the story is hard, and writing the story must be more hard. Oh Toby, when you are too tired to do it, next time I will write the story. I will be your helper.'

'Thank you,' says Toby. 'That is kind.'

Blackbeard smiles like daybreak.

Moontime

The Festival of Bryophyta-the-Moss. Waning crescent moon.

I am Blackbeard, and this is my voice that I am writing down to help Toby. If you look at this writing I have made, you can hear me (I am Blackbord) talking to you, inside your head. That is what writing is. But the Pig Ones can do that without writing. And sometimes we can do it, the Children of Crake. The two-skinned ones cannot do it.

Today Toby said Bryophyta is moss. I said if it is moss, then I must write *moss*. Toby says it has two names, like Snowman-the-Jimmy. So I am writing Bryophyta-the-Moss. Like this.

Today we made the pictures of Snowman-the-Jimmy, and of Adam as well. We did not know Adam, but we made the picture for Zeb and Toby, and for the other ones who did know him. For Snowman-the-Jimmy we used a mop, from the beach, and we used a jar lid and some pebbles, and more things. But not the red hat, because we need to keep it for the stories.

For Adam we used a cloth skin that we found, with two arms, and a white bag of plastic for the head, with feathers we took from a gull that did not need them any longer, and some blue glass from the beach, because his eyes were blue.

We made a picture of Snowman-the-Jimmy once before, to call him back, and it did call him back. These pictures will not call Snowman-the-Jimmy and Adam back this time, but it will make Zeb and Toby and Ren and Amanda feel better. That is why we made the pictures. They like pictures.

Thank you. Good night.

The Feast of Saint Maude Barlow, of Fresh Water. New moon.

Zeb has been recovering from the death of Adam. He and the others are working on an extension to the cobb house because they will soon need a nursery. The pregnancies are advancing much faster than is usual, and most of the women believe that all three of the babies will be Craker hybrids.

The garden is progressing well. The Mo'Hair flock is increasing – there have been three new additions to it, one blue-haired, one a red-head, and one blond – though one of the lambs was lost to a liobam. The liobams, too, appear to be on the increase.

'One of the Crakers reports seeing something that sounds like a bear,' Toby writes. 'It wouldn't be surprising. Perhaps we should set a guard for the beehives? There are two hives now, as another swarm was captured.

'Deer are proliferating: they are an acceptable source of animal protein. They are much leaner than pork, though not as tasty. Venison does not make top-quality bacon. But Rebecca says it is healthier.'

The Festival of Gymnosperms. Full moon.

Toby made the mistake of announcing to the others that this was the God's Gardener Festival of Gymnosperms. Several bad jokes about gymnasts and sperms and even male Crakers were made, one of them by Zeb, which is a good sign. Perhaps his time of mourning is coming to an end.

Three more functioning solar units have been installed. An existing one has gone out of commission. One of the violet biolets is malfunctioning. Shackleton and Crozier have experimented with making charcoal: the results have been mixed. Rhino, Katuro, and Manatee have gone fishing down by the shore. Ivory Bill is designing a coracle.

Two young Pigoons – barely more than piglets – dug under the garden fence and were discovered eating the root vegetables, the carrots and beets in particular. The MaddAddamites had slacked off their vigilance as regards the Pigoons, thinking that their agreement would hold. And it is holding, with the adults; but juveniles of all kinds push the rules.

A conference was called. The Pigoons sent a delegation of three adults, who seemed both embarrassed and cross, as adults put to shame by their young usually are. Blackbeard stood as interpreter.

It would not happen again, said the Pigoons. The young offenders had been threatened with a sudden transition to a state of bacon and soup bones, which seems to have made the desired impression.

The Festival of Saint Geyikli Baba of Deer. New moon.

The bees are productive: the first honey harvest has taken place. White Sedge has begun a Meditation to Music group, which many of the Crakers enjoy. Beluga is helping her. Tamaraw has been experimenting with sheep cheese, both hard and soft; also yogurt. The nursery has been finished, just in time. Very soon now, the three babies will be born, though Swift Fox claims she is having twins. Cradles are being discussed.

'Blackbeard has his own journal now,' Toby writes. 'I have given him his own pen, and a pencil. I would like to know what he is writing but I don't wish to pry. He's as tall as Crozier now. Already he is showing signs of blueness; very soon he will be grown up. Why does this make me sad?'

The Feast of Saint Fiacre of Gardens.

This is my voice, the voice of Blackbeard that you are hearing in your head. That is called *reading*. And this is my own book, a new one for my writing and not the writing of Toby.

Today Toby and Zeb did a strange thing. They jumped over a small fire and then Toby gave Zeb a green branch and Zeb gave Toby a green branch. And then they kissed each other. And all those with two skins watched, and then they cheered.

And I (Blackbeard) said, 'Oh Toby, why are you doing this?'

And Toby said, 'It is a custom we have. It shows that we love each other.'

And I (Blackberd) said, 'But you love each other anyway.'

And Toby said, 'It is hard to explain.' And Amanda said, 'Because it makes them happy.' Blackbeard (I am ~~Blackbard~~ Blackbeard) does not see why. But what makes them happy or not happy is strange.

Soon Blacbeard will be ready for his first mating. When the next woman turns blue, he will turn very blue also, and gather flowers; and maybe he will be chosen. He (I, Blackbeard) asked Toby if the green branches were like that, like the flowers that we give, to be chosen, and then we sing; and she said yes, it was something like that. So now I understand it better.

Thank you. Good night.

The Festival of Quercus. The Feast of Pigoons. Full moon.

'I have taken the liberty of adding the Pigoons to the regular calendar of Gardener feasts,' Toby writes. 'They deserve to have a day named in their honour. I've attached them to the Festival of Quercus, the oak tree day. I thought it was fitting, because of the acorns.'

The Feast of Artemis, Mistress of the Animals. Full moon.

Over the past two weeks, all three births have taken place. Or all four, because Swift Fox gave birth to twins, a boy and a girl. Each of the twins has the green eyes of the Crakers, which is a great relief to Toby; she'll have no tiny Zebs to contend with. She has made four small sunbonnets for them, out of a flowered bedsheet. The Craker women find these hilarious: what are such hats for? Their own babies do not sunburn.

Amanda's baby is fortunately of Craker descent, not Painballer: the large green eyes are unmistakable. The birth was difficult, and Toby and Rebecca had to perform an episiotomy. Toby did not want to give too much Poppy, for fear of damaging the newborn; so there was pain. Toby worried that Amanda might reject the baby, but she didn't. She appears to be quite fond of it.

Ren's baby is also a green-eyed Craker hybrid. What other

features might these children have inherited? Will they have built-in insect repellent, or the unique vocal structures that enable purring and Craker singing? Will they share the Craker sexual cycles? Such questions are much discussed around the MaddAddamite dinner table.

The three mothers and the four children are all doing well, and the Craker women are ever-present, purring, tending, and bringing gifts. The gifts are kudzu leaves and shiny pieces of glass from the beach, but they are well meant.

Lotis Blue is now pregnant herself, though she claims the father is not a Craker: Manatee was her choice. He is attentive to her, when not down at the beach fishing, or out deer hunting.

Crozier and Ren appear united in their desire to raise Ren's child together. Shackleton is supporting Amanda, and Ivory Bill has offered his services as soi-disant father to the Swift Fox twins. 'We all have to pitch in,' he said, 'because this is the future of the human race.'

'Good luck to it,' said Swift Fox, but she tolerates his help.

'Zeb and Rhino and I risked a trip to the drugstore,' Toby writes, 'and managed to scrounge several sackfuls of disposable diapers. But are they even necessary? The Craker babies are not cumbered with them.'

The Feast of Kannon-the-Oryx, and of Rhizomes-the-Roots. Full moon.

Toby says that Kannon is like Oryx. She says that Rhizomes is like roots. So I (Blackbeard) have written those things down.

Here are the names of the babies who have been born:

The baby of Ren is called Jimadam. Like Snowman-the-Jimmy, and like Adam too. Ren says she wanted the name of

Jimmy to still be spoken in the world, and alive; and she wanted the same for the name of Adam.

The baby of Amanda is called Pilaren. That is like Pilar, who lives in the elderberry bush, with the bees; and also like Ren, who is Amanda's very good friend and helper, through thick and thin, she said. I (Blackbeard) will ask Toby what *thick and thin* means.

The babies of Swift Fox are called Medulla and Oblongata. Medulla is a girl and Oblongata is a boy. Swift Fox says these names are for a reason that is hard to understand. It is about something inside a head.

All of the babies make us very happy.

I (Blackbeard) had his first mating, with SarahLacy, who chose his flower, so he is more happy than everyone. Soon there will be another baby, SarahLacy has told us, because he (Blackbeard) and the other three fourfathers did their dance of mating very well.

And their singing.

Thank you. Good night.

Book

Book

Now this is the Book that Toby made when she lived among us. See, I am showing you. She made these words on a *page,* and a page is made of *paper.* She made the words with *writing*, that she marked down with a stick called a *pen*, with black fluid called *ink,* and she made the *pages* join together at one side, and that is called a *book*. See, I am showing you. This is the Book, these are the Pages, here is the Writing.

And she showed me, Blackbeard, how to make such words, on a page, with a pen, when I was little. And she showed me how to turn the marks back into a voice, so that when I look at the page and read the words, it is Toby's voice that I hear. And when I speak these words out loud, you too are hearing Toby's voice.

Please don't sing.

And in the book she put the Words of Crake, and the Words of Oryx as well, and of how together they made us, and made also this safe and beautiful World for us to live in.

And in the Book too are the Words of Zeb, and of his brother, Adam; and the Words of Zeb Ate A Bear; and how he became our Defender against the bad men who did cruel and hurtful things; and the Words of Zeb's Helpers, Pilar and Rhino and Katrina WooWoo and March the Snake, and of all the MaddAddamites; and the Words of Snowman-the-Jimmy, who was there in the beginning, when Crake made us, and who led our people out of the Egg to this better place.

And the Words of Fuck, though these Words are not very long. See, there is only one page about Fuck.

Yes, I know he helps us when we are in trouble, and comes flying. He was sent by Crake, and we speak his name in Crake's honour. But there is not very much about him in this writing.

Please don't sing yet.

And Toby set down also the Words about Amanda and Ren and Swift Fox, our Beloved Three Oryx Mothers, who showed us that we and the two-skinned ones are all people and helpers, though we have different gifts, and some of us turn blue and some do not.

So Toby said we must be respectful, and always ask first, to see if a woman is really blue or is just smelling blue, when there is a question about blue things.

And Toby showed me what to do when there should be no more pens of plastic, and no more pencils either; for she could look into the future, and see that a time would come when no pens or pencils or paper could be found any more, among the buildings of the city of chaos, where they used to grow.

And she showed me how to use the quill feathers of birds to make the pens, though we also made some pens from the ribs of a broken umbrella.

An *umbrella* is a thing from the chaos. They used it for keeping the rain off their bodies.

I don't know why they did that.

And Toby showed me how to make the black marks with ink

that is made of walnut shells, mixed with vinegar and salt; and this ink is brown. And ink of different colours can be made from berries, and we made some purple ink from the elderberries with Pilar's Spirit in them, and we wrote the Words of Pilar in that ink. And Toby showed me how to make more paper out of plants.

And Toby gave warnings about this Book that we wrote. She said that the paper must not get wet, or the Words would melt away and would be heard no longer, and mildew would grow on it, and it would turn black and crumble to nothing. And that another Book should be made, with the same writing as the first one. And each time a person came into the knowledge of the writing, and the paper, and the pen, and the ink, and the reading, that one also was to make the same Book, with the same writing in it. So it would always be there for us to read.

And that at the end of the Book we should put some other pages, and attach them to the Book, and write down the things that might happen after Toby was gone, so that we might know all of the Words about Crake, and Oryx, and our Defender, Zeb, and his brother, Adam, and Toby, and Pilar, and the three Beloved Oryx Mothers. And about ourselves also, and about the Egg, where we came from in the beginning.

And I have taught all of these things about the Book and the paper and the writing to Jimadam, and to Pilaren, and to Medulla and Oblongata, who were born to Ren and Amanda and Swift Fox, our Beloved Three Oryx Mothers.

And they wanted to learn, although it is hard. But they learned these things, to help all of us together. And when I am no longer here among us but have gone where Toby and Zeb have gone, as Toby said I will go one day, then Jimadam and Pilaren and Medulla and Oblongata will teach these things to the younger ones.

Now I have added to the Words, and have set down those things that happened after Toby stopped making any of the Writing and putting it into the Book. And I have done this so we will all know of her, and of how we came to be.

And these new Words I have made are called the Story of Toby.

The Story of Toby

I am putting on the red hat of Snowman-the-Jimmy. See? It is on my head. And I have put the fish into my mouth, and taken it out again. Now it is time to listen, while I read to you from the Story of Toby that I have written down at the end of this Book.

One day Zeb went on a journey to the south. He went there because when he was out hunting for deer, he saw a tall smoke. And it was not smoke made by a forest on fire, but it was a thin smoke. And he watched it for some days, and it did not become any bigger or smaller, but stayed the same. But then one day it moved closer. And the day after that it moved closer still.

So Zeb told us that there might be others – more people from before the chaos, from before Crake cleared the chaos away. But would they be good people, or would they be bad and cruel men that would hurt us? There was no way to tell. But he did not want those people to get very close to us unless he could find out the answer to that question. If the answer was that they were good, then we would be their helpers, and they would be our helpers as well. But if they were not good, then he would not let them come near us, and hurt us, but would clear them away.

And Abraham Lincoln and Albert Einstein and Sojourner Truth and Napoleon wanted to go with him, to help; and I, Blackbeard, wanted to go as well, as I was not a child any more but had become a man, with blueness and strength. But Zeb said it might be too harsh, what would happen. And we were not sure what *harsh* meant. And Zeb said he hoped we would never have to find out. And Toby said we needed to stay behind, because it might be a Battle; and if we went, the others would be very sad if we did not come back. And Toby said she had asked Oryx and also the Spirit of Pilar, and they both said we should stay, and not go with Zeb. And so we did not go.

And Zeb took with him Black Rhino and Katuro. And Manatee and Zunzuncito and Shackleton and Crozier wanted to go too, but Zeb said they needed to stay, because there were young children to be protected. And Toby had to stay as well, with the gun thing we should not touch. So they did not go. And Zeb said that it was just a scouting trip, to see; and if it was bad news he would set a fire, another fire, and we would see the smoke, and then more could be sent to help him, and the Pig Ones could be told, though first we would have to find them, because they move from one place to another.

And we waited a long time, but Zeb did not return. And Shackleton took three of our blue men to see if the tall and thin smoke was still there. And they came back and told us it was not there any more. Which meant those making it had not been good, and Zeb our Defender must have done a sudden Battle, to make sure that those ones did not get any closer to us. But because he did not come back, he too must have died in the Battle, and Rhino, and Katuro as well.

And when she heard that, Toby cried.

Then we were all sad. But Toby was more sad than anyone, because Zeb was gone. And although we purred over her, she did not ever become happy again.

Then she became thinner and thinner, and shrunken; and after several months, she told us that she had a wasting sickness that was eating parts of her away, inside her body. And it could not be healed with purring, or with maggots, or with anything that she knew of; and the wasting sickness was increasing, and soon she would not be able to walk. And we said we could carry her wherever she wanted to go, and she smiled and said, Thank you.

Then she called each one of us to her, and said good night, a thing she herself taught us long ago. And it is a way of hoping that the other person will sleep well, and will not be troubled by bad dreams. And we said good night to her as well. And we sang for her.

Then Toby took her very old packsack, which was pink; and into it she put her jar of Poppy, and also a jar with mushrooms in it that we were told never to touch. And she walked away slowly into the forest, with a stick to help her, and asked us not to follow her.

Where she went I cannot write in this Book, because I do not know. Some say that she died by herself, and was eaten by vultures. The Pig Ones say that. Others say she was taken away by Oryx, and is now flying in the forest, at night, in the form of an Owl. Others said that she went to join Pilar, and that her Spirit is in the elderberry bush.

Yet others say that she went to find Zeb, and that he is in the form of a Bear, and that she too is in the form of a Bear, and is with him today. That is the best answer, because it is the happiest; and I have written it down. I have written down the other answers too. But I made them in smaller writing.

The three Beloved Oryx Mothers cried very much when Toby went away. We cried as well, and purred over them, and after a while they felt better. And Ren said, Tomorrow is another day, and we said we did not understand what that meant, and Amanda said, Never mind because it was not important. And Lotis Blue said it was a thing of hope.

Then Swift Fox told us that she was pregnant again and soon there would be another baby. And the fourfathers were Abraham Lincoln and Napoleon and Picasso and me, Blackbeard; and I am very happy to have been chosen for that mating. And Swift Fox said that if it was a girl baby it would be named Toby. And that is a thing of hope.

This is the end of the Story of Toby. I have written it in this Book. And I have put my name here – Blackbeard – the way Toby first showed me when I was a child. It says that I was the one who set down these words.

Thank you.

Now we will sing.

Acknowledgements

Although *MaddAddam* is a work of fiction, it does not include any technologies or biobeings that do not already exist, are not under construction, or are not possible in theory.

Most of the central characters in *MaddAddam* appear in the first two books in this series, *Oryx and Crake* and *The Year of the Flood*. Several of their names originated through donations in aid of various causes, including the Medical Foundation for the Care of Victims of Torture ('Amanda Payne') and *The Walrus* magazine ('Rebecca Eckler'). Joining them in *MaddAddam* are 'Allan Slaight,' courtesy of his daughter, Maria (his biography is called *Sleight of Hand*); 'Katrina Wu,' courtesy of Yung Wu; and 'March,' courtesy of a blind draw on Wattpad.com that was won by Lucas Fernandes. Saint Nikolai Vavilov came from Sona Grovenstein, and beekeeping tips from Carmen Brown of Honey Delight in Canberra, Australia.

My gratitude, as always, to my editors, Ellen Seligman of McClelland & Stewart (Canada), Nan Talese of Doubleday (U.S.A.), and Alexandra Pringle of Bloomsbury (U.K.).

Thanks also to my first readers: Jess Atwood Gibson; my

U.K. agents, Vivienne Schuster, Karolina Sutton, and Betsy Robbins of Curtis Brown; and Phoebe Larmore, my North American agent; and to Timothy O'Connell. Thanks also to Ron Bernstein. And special thanks to Heather Sangster of Strongfinish.ca for the marathon copy-editing session, after which she was faced with a blizzard and a car that wouldn't start.

And thanks to my office staff, Sarah Webster and Laura Stenberg; and to Penny Kavanaugh; and to VJ Bauer, vjbauer.com, VFX artist; and to Joel Rubinovich and Sheldon Shoib. And to Michael Bradley and Sarah Cooper, and to Coleen Quinn and Xiaolan Zhao. Also, to Louise Dennys, LuAnn Walther, and Lennie Goodings, and to my many agents and publishers around the world. I'd also like to thank Dr. Dave Mossop and Grace Mossop, and Barbara and Norman Barricello, all of Whitehorse, Yukon; and the many readers who have encouraged the writing of this book, including those on Twitter and Facebook.

Finally, my special thanks to Graeme Gibson, with whom I wander through the afternoon woods of life, foraging for nutritious bioforms, battling hostile ones wherever they appear, and eating them when possible.

Also by Margaret Atwood

Oryx and Crake

Pigs might not fly but they are strangely altered. So, for that
matter, are wolves and racoons. A man, once named Jimmy,
now calls himself Snowman and lives in a tree, wrapped in
old bed sheets. The voice of Oryx, the woman he loved,
teasingly haunts him. And the green-eyed Children of
Crake are, for some reason, his responsibility.

'In Jimmy, Atwood has created a great character: a tragic-comic
artist of the future, part buffoon, part Orpheus. An adman
who's a sad man; a jealous lover who's in perpetual mourning;
a fantasist who can only remember the past'
Lisa Appignanesi, *Independent*

'Superlatively gripping and remarkably imagined . . . the novel
is simultaneously alive with literary resonances'
Peter Kemp, *Sunday Times*

'A success and a breakthrough . . . a highly cinematic
adventure story of daring and survival'
Elaine Showalter, *London Review of Books*

The Year of the Flood

The sun brightens in the east, reddening the blue-grey haze that marks the distant ocean. The vultures roosting on the hydro poles fan out their wings to dry them. The air smells faintly of burning. The waterless flood – a manmade plague – has ended the world.

But two young women have survived: Ren, a young dancer trapped where she worked, in an upmarket sex club (the cleanest dirty girls in town); and Toby, who watches and waits from her rooftop garden. Is anyone else out there?

'Atwood knows how to show us ourselves, but the mirror she holds up to life does more than reflect ... *The Year of the Flood* isn't prophecy, but it is eerily possible' Jeanette Winterson

'A sharp observer of the female psyche ... Atwood's richly fertile imagination plays to exuberant and often comic effect' Caroline Moore, *Daily Telegraph*

'A gripping and visceral book that showcases her pure storytelling talents with energy, inventiveness and narrative panache' Michiko Kakutani, *New York Times*

In Other Worlds: SF and the Human Imagination

In Other Worlds is Margaret Atwood's account of her lifelong relationship with the literary form we have come to know as 'science fiction', from her days as a child reader, through her time at Harvard, where she studied the Victorian ancestors of the form, and later as a writer and reviewer. In this volume she brings together three Ellmann lectures, including 'Dire Cartographies' which investigates Utopias and Dystopias, and touches on Atwood's own ventures into those constructions. In further essays Atwood explores and elucidates the differences – as she sees them – between 'science fiction' proper, and 'speculative fiction'. For readers who loved the MaddAddam trilogy, *In Other Worlds* is a must.

'Margaret Atwood is a writer of metaphysical wit, who can always twist our preconceptions . . . She is genuinely inventive, and her quirky and satirical wit does not limit or define her' *Sunday Telegraph*

'Eminently readable and accessible . . . The lectures are insightful and cogently argued with a neat comic turn of phrase . . . Her enthusiasm and level of intellectual engagement are second to none' James Lovegrove, *Financial Times*

Alias Grace

'Sometimes I whisper it over to myself: Murderess.
Murderess. It rustles, like a taffeta skirt along the floor.'

Grace Marks. Female fiend? Femme fatale? Or weak and
unwilling victim? Around the true story of one of the most
enigmatic and notorious women of the 1840s, Margaret Atwood
has created an extraordinarily potent tale of sexuality, cruelty
and mystery.

'A sensuous, perplexing book, at once sinister and dignified,
grubby and gorgeous, panoramic yet specific . . . I don't think
I have ever been so thrilled . . . This, surely is as far as
a novel can go' Julie Myerson, *Independent on Sunday*

'Brilliant . . . Atwood's prose is searching. So intimate it
seems to be written on the skin' Hilary Mantel

virago

To buy any of our books and to find out more
about Virago Press and Virago Modern Classics,
our authors and titles, as well as events and
book club forum, visit our websites

www.virago.co.uk
www.littlebrown.co.uk

and follow us on Twitter

@ViragoBooks

To order any Virago titles p & p free in the UK,
please contact our mail order supplier on:

+ 44 (0)1832 737525

Customers not based in the UK should contact
the same number for appropriate postage
and packing costs.